W9-CEP-984

WATER OF DEATH

WATER OF DEATH

Paul Johnston

ST. MARTIN'S MINOTAUR ✠ NEW YORK

www.minotaurbooks.com

ISBN 0-312-27311-8

First published in Great Britain by Hodder and Stoughton, a division of Hodder Headline PLC

First St. Martin's Minotaur Edition: March 2001

10 9 8 7 6 5 4 3 2 1

WATER OF DEATH

Edinburgh, July 2025. Sweat City.

When I was a kid before independence, summer was a joke that got about as many laughs as a hospital waiting list. There was the occasional sunny day, but you spent most of the time running from showers of acid rain and the lash of rabid winds. To make things worse, for three weeks the place was overrun by armies of culture victims chasing the hot festival ticket. Now the festival is a year-round event — though a lot of the tourists are only interested in the officially sanctioned marijuana clubs — and "hot" doesn't even begin to describe the state of the weather. Over the last couple of years temperatures have risen by three to four degrees, causing tropical diseases to migrate northwards and bacteria to embark on a major expansion programme. Scientists in the late twentieth century would have got closer to the full horror of the phenomenon if they'd called it "global stewing" — except we haven't got enough fresh water to stew anything properly.

What we do have is a cracker of a name for the season between spring and autumn. To everyone's surprise the new-look, user-friendly Council of City Guardians didn't saddle us with an updated designation for the period (think French Revolution, think Thermidor). Our masters were probably too busy discussing initiatives to relieve the tourists of even more cash. As the blazing days and stifling nights dragged by, ordinary citizens gave up distinguishing between the months of June, July and August. And even though the classic *noir* movie hasn't been seen in Edinburgh since the cinemas were closed and television banned by the original Council, people have taken to calling this season the Big Heat. That kills me.

Still, in Sweat City we're really civilised. Unlike most states, we've done away with capital punishment and the nuclear switch has been flicked off permanently – the reactors at Torness were recently buried in enough concrete to give a 1990s town planner the ultimate hard on. On the other hand, the Council set up a compulsory lottery last year, turning greed into a virtue and most citizens into deluded fortune-hunters. Deluded, very thirsty fortune-hunters given the water restrictions.

Then some Grade A headbangers came along and raised the temperature even higher than it had been during Big Heat 2024. Giving me a pretty near terminal case of the "Summertime Blues".

Chapter One

⸺◦◦◦◦⸺

I was lying in the Meadows with a book and a heat-induced headache, making the most of the shade provided by one of the few trees with any leaves left on it. It was five in the afternoon but the sun still had plenty of fire in its belly. The rays glinted off a big hoarding in the middle of the park. It was advertising the lottery. Some poor sod who'd won it was dressed up like John Knox, a bottle of malt whisky poking out of his false beard. "Play Edlott, the Ultimate Lottery, and Anything Goes", the legend said. If you ask me, what goes, what's already gone, is the last of the Council's credibility. There's an elaborate system of prizes ranging from half-decent clothes, to bottles of better-than-average whisky like the one Johnnie the Fox had secreted, to labour exemptions and pensions for life — but only for a few lucky sods. Edinburgh citizens were so starved of material possessions in the first twenty years of the Council that they now reckon Edlott is the knees of a very large Queen Bee. They even willingly accept the value of a ticket being docked from their wage vouchers every week. I think the whole thing sucks but I'm biased. I've never won so much as a tube of extra-strength sun-protection cream.

All round me Edinburgh citizens were lying motionless, their cheeks resting against parched soil that hadn't produced much grass since the Big Heat arrived. I was one of the lucky ones. At

3

least I was wearing a pair of Supply Directorate shades that hadn't fallen to pieces. Yet.

I rolled over and peered at Arthur's Seat through the haze. People say the hill looks like a lion at rest. These days it's certainly the right shade of sandy brown, though the desiccated vegetation on its flanks gives the impression of an erstwhile king of the beasts who's been mauled by a pride of rabid republicans. As it happens, that isn't a bad description of the Enlightenment Party that led Edinburgh into independence in 2004. But things have changed a hell of a lot since then. For a start, like the nerve gas used by demented dictators in the Balkans twenty-plus years ago, you can smell Edinburgh people coming long before you can see or hear them. Water's almost as precious as the revenue from tourists here.

I glanced round at my fellow citizens. If Arthur's Seat is a lion, we must be the pack of ragged hyenas that hangs around it. Everyone was in standard-issue maroon shorts (standard-issue meaning too wide, too long and not anything like cool enough) and off-white T-shirts. Those whose sunglasses have self-destructed wear faded sunhats with a Heart of Midlothian badge on the front. Up until the time of the "iron boyscouts" – the hardline lunatics who ran the Council of City Guardians between 2020 and 2022 – only the rank of auxiliaries was entitled to wear the heart insignia, which has nothing to do with the pre-Enlightenment football team. The present Council's doing its best to make citizens feel they have the same rights as the uniformed class who carry out the guardians' orders. Except the auxiliaries don't have to wear clowns' outfits.

The hard ground was making my arms stiff. I stretched and made the mistake of breathing in through my nose. It wasn't just that the herd of humanity needed more than the single shower lasting exactly sixty seconds which it gets each week. (One of the lottery prizes is a five-minute shower every week for a month.) The still air over the expanse of flat parkland was infused with the reek from the public shithouses that have been set up at the end of every residential street. Since the onset of the Big Heat, citizens have had no running water in their flats. People get by one way or another and the black marketeers do good business in bottles, jars, chamberpots — anything that will hold liquid. But the City Guard has to patrol the queues outside the communal bogs first thing in the morning. It doesn't take long for dozens of desperate citizens to lose their grip and turn on each other.

It was too hot to read. I lay back and let an old blues number run through my mind. No surprises what it was — "Dry Spell Blues". Before I could work out if Son House or Spider Carter was singing, the vocal was blown away by a sudden mechanical roar.

"Turn that rustbucket off, ya shite!" A red-haired kid of about seventeen jumped to his feet and started waving his arms at the driver of a tractor towing a battered water trailer. They come daily to refill the drinking-water tanks at every street corner. It stopped about fifty yards away from us.

"Aye, give us a break or I'll give you one," shouted another young guy who obviously fancied himself as a hard man. The pair of them had done everything they could to make their clothes distinctive. They had their T-shirt sleeves folded double and their shorts stained with bleach, pieces of thick rope holding them up. Sweat City chic.

The driver had switched off his engine. Now that he could hear what was being broadcast to him, he didn't look happy. He was pretty musclebound for someone on the diet we get, and the set of his unshaven face suggested he didn't think much of the Council's recent easy-going policies and their effect on the young.

"You wee bastards," he yelled, waddling towards the kids as quickly as his heavy thighs allowed. "Your heads are going down the pan."

There was a collective intake of breath as the citizens around me sat up and paid attention, grateful for anything that took their minds off the stifling heat. I watched as a woman sitting with a small child near the loudmouthed guys started gathering up her towels and waterbottles nervously.

Our heroes took one look at the big man coming their way, glanced at each other and turned to run. Then the tough guy spotted the woman's handbag. She'd left it lying open on the ground as she leaned over her child.

"Tae fuck wi' the lot o' ye," the kid shouted in the local dialect that the Council outlawed years ago. He bent down to scoop up the bag and sprinted after his pal towards the streets on the far side of the park. "Southside Strollers rule!" he yelled over his shoulder.

The woman shrieked. Her kid joined in. The citizens nearest to them crowded round to help but nobody else moved a muscle. Even the tractor driver had turned to marble. It wouldn't have been the first time they'd seen a bag snatched by the city's new generation of arseholes. It wasn't the first time I'd seen it either. Maybe because I'd once been in the Public Order Directorate, maybe because I was theoretically still a member of the Enlightenment, maybe just because I fancied a run — whatever, I got to my feet and gave what in the City Guard we used to call "chase".

Bad idea.

After fifty yards they were still going away from me, dust rising from their feet and hanging in the air to coat my tongue and eyes. But after a hundred yards, when my lungs were clogging and my legs had decided enough was enough, the little sods had slowed to not much more than a stride: evidence of loading up on illicit ale and black-market grass, I reckoned. Then I cut my speed even more. People who get into those commodities at an early age usually learn how to look after themselves.

They turned to face me and started to laugh in between gasping for breath.

"Hey, look, Tommy, it's the Good fucking Samaritan," the redhead said. Obviously he'd learned something in school,

though the Education Directorate would have preferred something more in line with the Council's atheist principles to have
stuck.

Tommy was rifling through the woman's bag, tossing away
paper hankies and the Supply Directorate's version of cosmetics
and stuffing food and clothing vouchers into his pocket. When
he'd finished, he looked up at me and smiled threateningly. The
teeth he revealed were uneven and discoloured.

"Get away, ya wanker," he hissed, raising his left fist. It had
the letters D-E-A-D tattooed amateurishly on the lower finger
joints. I was betting the right one had the word "YOU'RE" on
it, spelled wrong. "Come on, Col. We're gone."

He'd got that right. I took my mobile phone from the back
pocket of my shorts and called the guard command centre in the
castle. As soon as I started to speak, the two of them turned back
towards me, their eyes empty and their fists drawn right back.

Like I said — bad idea.

"Are you all right, Quint?"

"What does it look like, Davie?" I took a break from flexing
my right wrist and stood up to face the heavily built guard
commander who'd just arrived in a Land-Rover and a dust
storm.

"Bloody hell, what did you do to those guys?"

I walked over to the bagsnatchers. The carrot-head was
leaning forward on both hands, carrying out a detailed examination of what had been his lunch. Tommy the hard man was
still on his arse. Unfortunately he'd turned out to have a jaw that
really was hard. I had a handkerchief wrapped round my seeping
knuckles.

"Where did you learn to fight like that, ya bastard?" he
demanded, trying to get to his feet. Then he ran his eye over
Davie's uniform. "I might have fuckin' known. You're an
Alsatian like him." The city's lowlife refer to the guard as dogs
when they're feeling brave.

Davie grabbed the kid's arm and pulled him upright. "What was that, sonny?"

Tommy decided bravery was surplus to requirements. "Nothing," he muttered.

"Nothing what?" Davie shouted into his ear.

"Nothing, Hume 253." Tommy pronounced Davie's barracks number with exaggerated respect, his eyes to the ground.

"That's better, wee man. And for your information, this citizen is not a member of the City Guard."

"He fuckin' puts himself about like one," Tommy said under his breath.

Davie grinned at me. "And there was me thinking you'd forgotten your auxiliary training, Quint."

"Quint?" the boy said with a groan. "Aw, no. You're no' that investigator guy, are you? The one wi' the stupid name?"

Davie found all this highly amusing. "Quintilian Dalrymple?" he asked.

"Aye, the one who's in the paper every time you bitches cannae do your job."

Too much adulation isn't good for you. "So what are you going to do with this pair of scumbags, Hume 253?" I asked.

Colin the carrot finally managed to get to his feet.

"Cramond Island, I reckon," Davie replied. "The old prison'll be a great place to give them a hiding."

The carrot hit the dust again.

"You cannae do that," Tommy whined. "We've got rights. The Council's set up special centres for kids like us."

He was right. In their desperation to be seen as having citizens' best interests at heart, the latest guardians, or at least a majority of them, haven't only given citizens more personal freedom — apart from anything involving the use of water — and a lottery, but they've organised a social welfare system that treats anyone who steps out of line as an honoured guest. To no one in the guard's surprise, petty crime has risen even faster than the temperature.

"Who are the Southside Strollers?" I asked.

"What's it to you?" Tommy said, giving me the eye.

Davie grabbed his arm and stuck his face up close to the boy's. "Answer the man, sonny."

"Awright, awright." Tommy had gone floppy again. "It's our gang. We all come from the south side of the city."

"And you spend your time strolling around nicking whatever you can?" I said.

Tommy shrugged nonchalantly, his eyes lowered.

A couple of auxiliaries from the Welfare Directorate looking desperately eager to please turned up to collect the boys. Colin the carrot was busy holding on to his gut but Tommy flashed a triumphant look at us.

"Just a minute, you," I said, moving over to him. I stuck my hand into his pocket and relieved him of the vouchers he'd taken, leaving a streak of blood from my knuckles on his shorts as a souvenir. "Oh, aye, what's this then?"

The pair of them suddenly started examining the ground.

"What do you think, Davie?" I said, opening the scrap of crumpled paper and sniffing the small quantity of dried and shredded leaves.

Davie shook his head. "If it was up to me . . ."

"But it isn't," the female auxiliary from the Welfare Directorate's Youth Development Department said, stepping forward and looking at the twist of grass. "Underage citizens are our responsibility, not the City Guard's. We'll see they're rehabilitated."

Davie looked at her disbelievingly. Like most of his colleagues, he had serious difficulty in accepting the Council's recent caring policies. Not that he had any choice.

Tommy smirked then bared his teeth at me again. "You're dead, pal."

"Oh, aye, Tommy?" I said. "And what does that make you?"

I handed the grass to Davie. We watched the miscreants get

into the Youth Development Department van then I turned back to get my gear.

"The future of the city," Davie said morosely as he caught up with me. "Giving these headbangers special treatment is only going to make them harder to control later. Anyone caught with black-market drugs should be nailed to the floor like in the old days."

"Hand that stuff over for analysis, will you?" We both knew that wouldn't make any difference. The guard's no longer permitted to give underage citizens the third degree so they probably wouldn't find out where the grass came from. I shrugged. "Stupid bastards. I told them to keep their distance but they had to have a go."

Davie laughed. "They weren't the only ones. You sorted them out pretty effectively, Quint."

"I'll probably end up on a charge. Unwarranted force."

"I don't think so. I'll be writing the report, remember."

The citizens under the trees were pretending they'd gone back to sleep. Davie's presence was making them shy. Even in the recently approved informal shirtsleeve order, the grey City Guard uniform isn't the most popular apparel in Edinburgh. The woman came to reclaim her vouchers, flashing me a brief smile of thanks. She probably thought I was an undercover guard operative.

"I'll give you a lift home," Davie said as we headed for his vehicle. "What were you doing here anyway?"

"Trying unsuccessfully to find somewhere cool in this sweat pit to read my book."

"What have you got?" Davie took the volume from under my arm and laughed. "*Black and Blue*? Just like the state of your knuckles tomorrow morning."

"Very funny, guardsman."

"Isn't it that book on the proscribed list?" he asked dubiously.

"The Council lifted the ban on pre-Enlightenment Scottish crime fiction at the end of last year. Don't you remember?"

"I just put a stop to crime," he said pointedly. "I don't read stories about it."

"That'll be right. You said something about taking me to my place?"

Davie wrenched open the passenger door of one of the guard's few surviving Land-Rovers. "At your service, sir," he said with fake deference. "Number 13 Gilmore Place it is, sir."

But as things turned out, we didn't make it.

Tollcross is as busy a junction as you get in Edinburgh. A guard vehicle on watch, a couple of Supply Directorate delivery vans, the ubiquitous Water Department tractor and a flurry of citizens on bicycles constitute traffic congestion these days. There was even a Japanese tourist in one of the hire cars provided by an American multinational that the Council did a deal with. He was scratching his head. The lack of other private cars in the streets was obviously worrying him.

"Why were you frying yourself in the Meadows, Quint?" Davie asked. "There are bits of grass around the castle that actually get watered. It's quieter there too."

I looked at the burly figure next to me. He was still wearing the beard that used to be required of male auxiliaries even though the current Council's made it optional. God knows what the temperature was beneath the matted growth.

"Quiet if you don't mind being stared at by sentries," I replied. "Since they moved the auxiliary training camp away from the Meadows, it's become a much more relaxing place."

"Arsehole." Davie was shaking his head. "Anyone would think you hadn't spent ten years as one of us." He laughed. "Till they saw how handy you are with your fists."

My mobile rang before I could tell him how proud I was to have been demoted from the rank of auxiliary.

"Is that you, Dalrymple?"

I let out a groan. I might have known the public order

guardian would get his claws into me late on a Friday afternoon. Not that his rank take weekends off.

"Lewis Hamilton," I said. "What a surprise."

"Where are you, man?" he demanded. "And don't address me by name." Lewis was one of the old school, a guardian for twenty years. He didn't go along with the new Council's decision allowing citizens to use guardians' names instead of their official titles.

"I'm at Tollcross with Hume 253."

"Distracting my watch commander from his duties again?" Davie had been promoted a few months ago, though that didn't stop him helping me out whenever something interesting came up.

"And the reason for your call is . . . ?" I asked.

"The reason for my call is that the people who run the lottery need your services."

I pointed to Davie to pull in to the kerbside. "Don't tell me. They've lost one of their winners again."

"I know, I know, he'll probably turn up drunk in a gutter after a couple of days . . ."

"With his prizes missing and his new clothes covered in other people's vomit. Jesus, Lewis, can't you find someone else to look for the moron? Like, for instance, a guardsman who started his first tour of duty this morning?"

Hamilton gave what passes for a laugh in his book. "No, Dalrymple. As you know very well, this is a high-priority job. One for the city's freelance chief investigator. After tourists my fellow guardians' favourite human beings are lottery-winners." I knew he had other ideas about that himself. As far as he was concerned, Edlott was yet another disaster perpetrated by the reforming guardians who made up the majority of the current Council. Hamilton particularly despised the culture guardian whose directorate runs the lottery for what he called his "lack of Platonic principles", whatever that means. I don't think he was too keen on his colleague's eye for a quick buck either. The underlying idea of Edlott was to reduce every citizen's voucher entitlement for the price of a few relatively cheap prizes. Still, the public order guardian's aversion to the lottery was nothing compared with the contempt he reserved for the Council members who forced through the measure permitting the supply of marijuana and other soft drugs to tourists. As I saw in the park, foreign visitors weren't the only grass consumers in the city.

"Any chance of you telling Edlott I'm tied up on some major investigation, Lewis? I mean, it's Friday night and the bars are—"

There was a monotonous buzzing in my ear.

"Bollocks!" I shouted into the mouthpiece.

Davie looked at me quizzically. "Bit early to hit a sex show, isn't it?"

I got the missing man's name and address from a new generation auxiliary in the Culture Directorate who oozed bonhomie like a private pension salesman in pre-Enlightenment times.

"Guess what, Davie? We're off to Morningside."

"What?" Davie turned on me with his brow furrowed. "*You're* off to Morningside, you mean."

"Your boss just told me this is a high-priority job. The least you can do is ferry me out."

Davie looked at his watch and gave me a reluctant nod. "Okay, but I'm on duty tonight and I want to eat before that."

"You pamper that belly of yours, Davie."

He gave me a friendly scowl.

We came down to what was called Holy Corner before the Enlightenment. The four churches were turned into auxiliary accommodation blocks soon afterwards. They form part of Napier Barracks, the guard base controlling the city's central southern zone. The checkpoint barrier was quickly raised for us.

"Where to then?" Davie asked.

I looked at the note I'd scribbled. "Millar Crescent. Number 14."

He headed down the main road, the Land-Rover's bodywork

juddering as he accelerated. Ahead of us, a thick layer of haze and dust obscured the Pentland Hills and the ravaged areas between us and them. What were once pretty respectable suburbs became the home of streetfighting man in the time leading up to independence. They had only been used again in the last couple of years and the part beyond the heavily fortified city line a few hundred yards further south was still an urban wasteland. It was haunted by black marketeers and the dissidents who've been trying and failing to overturn the Council since it came to power. On this side of the line, the Housing Directorate has settled a lot of the city's problem families into flats that used to be occupied by Edinburgh's blue-rinse and pearl-necklace brigade. The Southside Strollers were the tip of a very large iceberg.

"Ten minutes, Quint," Davie said as he manoeuvred round the water tank and the citizens' bicycle shed at the end of Millar Crescent. "That's all I'm giving you." Then his jaw dropped.

I followed the direction of his gaze. A young woman was on her way into the street entrance of number 14. She was wearing a citizen-issue T-shirt and work trousers that were unusually well pressed despite the spatters of paint on them. She also had a mauve chiffon scarf round her neck which had never seen the inside of a Supply Directorate store. She had light brown hair bound up in a tight plait and a self-contained look on her face. Oh, and she was built like the Venus de Milo with a full complement of limbs.

Davie already had his door open. "Well," he said, "make it half an hour."

We climbed the unlit, airless stairs to the third floor. The name Kennedy had been carved very skilfully in three-inch-high letters on the surface of a blue door on the right side of the landing. The incisions in the wood looked recent.

"This is the place," I said, raising my hand to knock.

"Where did she go?" Davie asked, looking up and down the stairwell.

14

"Will you get a grip?" I thumped on the door. "Exert some auxiliary self-control."

"Ah, but we're supposed to come over like human beings these days," he said with a grin.

"Exactly. Like human beings, guardsman. Not like dogs after a . . ."

Then the door opened very quickly. The woman we'd seen stood looking at us with her eyes wide open and a faint smile on her lips.

"Dogs after a . . . ?" she asked in a deep voice, her dark brown eyes darting between us. A lot of citizens would have made the most of that canine reference in the presence of a guardsman, but there didn't seem to be any irony in her tone.

There was a silence that Davie and I found a lot more awkward than she did.

"Em . . . I'm looking for Citizen Kennedy," I said, pulling out my notebook and trying to make out my scribble in the dim light. "Citizen Fordyce Kennedy."

"My father," she said simply.

"And you are . . . ?"

She looked at me blankly for a couple of seconds then smiled, this time with a hint of mockery. "I'm his daughter." She hesitated then shrugged. "Agnes is my name."

"Right," I said. "So is he in?"

"Of course he isn't in," she said, her voice hardening. "That's why we called you." She leaned forward on the balls of her feet and examined my clothes. I breathed in a chemical smell from her. "You are from the guard, aren't you?" Then she turned her eyes on to Davie's uniform. "I can see the big man is."

Something about the way she spoke the last words made Davie, who's never been reticent with women, look away uncomfortably.

"I'm Dalrymple, special investigator," I said. "Call me Quint." I registered the reserve in her eyes. "If you want."

She didn't reply, just looked at me intensely like an artist eyeing up a new model. I resisted the urge to check if my clothes had suddenly become transparent.

"Who's that?" The voice that came from the depths of the flat was faint and uncertain, the accent stronger than the young woman's. "Who's that out there?"

"Is that your mother?" I asked.

"My mother," Agnes Kennedy agreed, nodding slowly. "Her name's Hilda. She's a bit upset. And . . . and her mind wanders." She looked at me and succeeded in imparting a curious hybrid of appeal and threat. "Be sure you don't upset her." She held her eyes on me for a few moments then turned abruptly and led us down the dimly lit corridor.

"It's the men from the guard, Mother," she said to the thin figure that was leaning against the wall. Then she took her arm and pushed open the door at the far end of the passage. I heard her continue talking in a smooth, low voice, as if she were the parent having to comfort a frightened child. "They're going to find Dad for us . . ."

Before I got to the door, I heard the sound of curtains being drawn rapidly. I came into the room and blinked in the subdued light, trying to make out the bent woman who stood moving her head from side to side like a lost sheep. She relaxed a bit when Agnes came back from the windows and took her arm.

"You don't like strong sunlight, do you, Mother?" the young woman said. "It's all right. Agnes has fixed it for you."

My eyes accustomed themselves to the crepuscular gloom. The women sat down on the sofa, the senior of them looking at her daughter with a confused expression that only gradually faded from her features. Like many Edinburgh citizens, she'd been adversely affected by twenty years of what the Medical Directorate regards as a satisfactory diet. At least there's been a massive reduction in the heart disease resulting from the garbage we used to eat before the Enlightenment. These days people are more likely to die of respiratory failure or skin cancer brought about by the climate change. But this woman looked like she'd been gnawed by mental as well as physical demons.

"How long's your husband been missing, citizen?" Davie asked with customary City Guard forthrightness.

Agnes glared at him angrily then glanced back at her mother, who showed no sign of having heard the question. "Since yesterday morning," Agnes answered.

"Under thirty-six hours?" Davie was unimpressed. "That's not long."

Hilda Kennedy suddenly came to life. She stood up with surprising speed and moved in front of Davie. She stooped and the top of the ragged scarf covering her long grey hair reached not much more than halfway up his chest. "It's maybe not long to you, laddie, but my man's never late for his tea." Then she stepped back, the surge of energy already gone.

I nudged Davie with my elbow. Although the guard usually don't check out missing persons for at least three days, lottery-winners are special cases.

"When did he leave the house, Hilda?" I asked.

She inspected me before answering, trying to work out whether to treat me as an auxiliary or an ordinary citizen. My use of her first name seemed to get me off the hook. "First thing in the morning," she said.

Agnes was standing next to her mother now. She took her arm again and tried to make her sit down, but the older woman wasn't having it.

"He went to work?" I continued.

Hilda looked at me like I was a backward child. "What work? He won the top prize in the lottery, son."

"It was six weeks ago," Agnes put in. "He was exempted from work for life. Apart from two afternoons and two evenings a week publicity for Edlott."

So the Culture Directorate had chosen Fordyce Kennedy to advertise the lottery like the citizen dressed up as John Knox on the poster I'd seen earlier.

"Which character did he get assigned?" I asked.

"That writer fella," Hilda said. "The one who did *Treasure Island*."

"Robert Louis Stevenson."

"Aye." She shook her head. "He looked like a right idiot with his false moustache and bloodstained hankie."

I looked round the room in the light that was coming in at the sides of the curtains. The furniture was dark-stained wood, the sideboard, dresser and table beautifully carved. They were about as far from the standard citizen-issue sticks as you can get.

"Did your husband make all this?" I asked.

Hilda nodded, smiling unevenly. "Aye, he's a cabinet-maker. Used to make stuff for the tourist hotels till he won the lottery. He did all this in his spare time."

I went over to the dresser and looked at the photographs arrayed on it. There were individual shots of a washed-out man in his fifties, of Agnes and of a sullen young man with hair at what used to be the regulation citizen length of under an inch. There was also a family group. Hilda must have moved when the flash went off, blurring the shot and giving her the look of a corpse that had just jerked up on the sofa. Her daughter had the same faint smile that she'd greeted us with when she opened the door, while the son was frowning. Fordyce Kennedy just looked exhausted. Like many citizens, the family had taken advantage of the Council's loosening of the ruling that banned photos. The original guardians regarded them as socially divisive – they reckoned one of the main reasons for the disorder leading to the break-up of the United Kingdom had been the cult of the individual. Apparently we can be trusted with a few snapshots now.

"How old's your son?" I asked.

"Allie? He's . . ." Hilda broke off. She gave an almost imperceptible shake of her head but didn't say anything else.

"Twenty-six," Agnes said, completing the sentence. "A year older than me."

"At work, is he?" Davie asked.

"Him? At work?" Agnes laughed humourlessly. "He spends most of his time with his lunatic friends. Too keen on drinking and messing about."

He wasn't the only young man like that in the city.

"How about you?" I asked Agnes. "What do you do?"

She looked at me coolly like she was wondering whether I was entitled to ask that question. "I'm an interior decorator," she said. That explained the paint on her clothing and the smell of a chemical like turpentine. "I spend most of my free time looking after Mother." She glanced at the woman beside her, who didn't seem to be following the conversation. "She began to lose it last year," Agnes added in a low voice.

"And your father?"

Her eyes flashed at me aggressively. "What about my father?"

I smiled nervously. "Did he have any lunatic friends like your brother?"

"My father doesn't go out much," Agnes said, her eyes fierce. "He's a missing person. He hasn't committed any crime."

"All right," I said quietly. "I wasn't implying anything."

I pulled out my notebook and sat down. You usually run the risk of getting a broken spring up your arse from a Supply Directorate sofa but the lottery-winner must have fixed his.

Hilda Kennedy suddenly twitched her head and looked at me. Maybe she had been following the talk after all. "Fordyce was never the pally sort. He liked to stay in and work wi' the wood." She let out a sudden sob and dropped her chin to her flat chest.

"My father loved his work," Agnes said, stroking her mother's arm.

"So how's he been spending his days since he won the lottery?" I asked.

Hilda looked up again, her eyes taking time to focus on me. "I wish I knew, son. Like I say, he's always back for his tea. But during the day he just disappears. I've asked him what he does but he wouldn't answer. Said something about walking the streets once." She stared at me. "He wasn't happy. They shouldn't have taken his work away." She sobbed again and bent her head.

Agnes looked at Davie and me angrily, her face flushed. "Isn't that enough?" she demanded in a low voice.

"They shouldn't have taken his work away," her mother repeated dolefully.

"Don't worry," I said with as much encouragement as I could muster. "He'll turn up."

"Will he?" Hilda said, suddenly turning her eyes on me, her dry lips quivering. "Are you sure, son?"

I avoided her gaze as I made for the door.

"Pretty strange pair," Davie said as we drove back towards the city centre. The sun was blinding where it shone through the gaps between buildings.

"You didn't have to come in with me," I said. "That'll teach you to chase female citizens."

"What do you mean chase?" he said, laughing. "You saw the way she was looking at me."

"Correct me if I'm wrong, guardsman, but don't the City Regulations forbid fraternisation between auxiliaries and citizens under thirty?" Until a few months ago auxiliaries weren't allowed to fraternise with citizens of any age. Another one of the Council's attempts to break down the barriers.

"Aye, I suppose you're right." Davie shot me a suspicious glance. "What are you up to, Quint? Oh, I get it. You reckon that you can have a go at the delectable Agnes on the grounds that you're a demoted rather than a serving auxiliary."

I held my breath as we passed through the cloud of exhaust fumes a guard vehicle had belched out. "Me? Certainly not. I'm already spoken for."

Davie laughed, this time raucously. "Like hell you are."

I let him go on thinking that.

Five minutes later he dropped me at my flat in Gilmore Place.

I pulled the street door open impatiently, wondering if any traces of the perfume I'd got used to over the last couple of weeks would be lingering in the hot air.

They were. I raced up the stairs, opened my door and got an eyeful of the woman I'd been hoping would be there.

That didn't do anything to cool me down at all.

Chapter Two

"Hello, guardian."

The Ice Queen turned and gave me one of the Antarctic glares that led to her nickname. Her short, silver-blonde hair also had something to do with that, as did the high cheekbones and tight lips that were unadorned by make-up. "Where have you been, Quint?" She sounded more like an exasperated schoolmistress than the city's highest-ranking medical officer. "I've been waiting for half an hour."

"Did we have a rendezvous then?" I have a thing about being scolded. Besides, I was parched and I had a nasty feeling I'd forgotten to refill my waterbottles. A quick glance at the collection of empties in the corner of my living room that passes for a kitchen confirmed my fear. I looked at my watch. "Shit."

The medical guardian read my mind. "Missed the street tank?"

I nodded. The Water Department locks up drinking supplies at six in the evening to restrict consumption.

"Don't worry," she said, opening her briefcase. "I've got a couple of pints."

I crossed to my sideboard. It was a lot grottier than the one the missing lottery-winner had made for himself but there was something in it I fancied.

"I'm not worried," I said, taking out a bottle of citizen-issue whisky.

The Ice Queen twitched her lips in disapproval as I downed a slug.

"Relax. I'm not planning on offering you any." I breathed in hard as the rough spirit cauterised the inside of my throat. "Jesus, what do they put in this stuff?" I raised my hand. "No, don't tell me." If I'd let her, she'd have provided me with a full chemical analysis. You don't want to give scientists any encouragement. "How about some music?"

"That's not exactly what I came for." The guardian was looking out of the window into the street, her arms stretched out against the frame. The white blouse and grey skirt that female Council members wear during the Big Heat made her look like the strait-laced schoolteacher her voice had suggested. She was of medium height, slim, her body carrying no more weight than the average female citizen's. Then again, her chest was a lot more eye-catching than the average female citizen's so maybe years of a senior auxiliary's diet had some effect. The guardians have always claimed their lifestyle is ascetic but you don't see many signs of malnutrition in their residences in Moray Place.

I was rooting around in my tape collection trying to find something that wasn't the blues — despite the relaxation of regulations, they're still seen as subversive. The trouble is, I don't have much apart from the blues. Eventually I put on a Rolling Stones recording from 2001. No one could call that subversive.

"I said that wasn't what I came for," the guardian repeated, moving towards where I was kneeling by my ancient cassette deck.

I turned my head and got a look that didn't originate in the polar regions. In fact, it was positively provocative. Despite the heat, I shivered. A few months ago the Council decided to loosen the rules governing guardians' personal lives. For years they were expected to live on their own in total celibacy. Now they're supposed to show they're ordinary people like the rest of us by getting laid. I still haven't got used to guardians showing their feelings, let alone guardians having sex. Especially not with me.

"Take your hand away, Quint." .

That sounded more like what you'd expect a female Council member to say. Then again, it was after midnight, my bedroom was as steamy as the innermost room of a Turkish bath and we'd already made it twice.

I moved my hand from her thigh. "Sorry, Sophia," I said, keeping my eyes on her. It wasn't till we'd spent three nights together that she allowed me to use her name, and she didn't like me using it anywhere other than in bed. Although she was still in her thirties, the medical guardian was on the reactionary wing of the Council, like Lewis Hamilton. The idea of ordinary citizens being allowed to address their rulers by first name was about as popular with her as compulsory duty in the coal mines used to be with ordinary citizens until the regulations were changed. Sophia had been one of the disciplinarian "iron boyscouts" who ran the Council before they were discredited. She kept her job because she was so bloody good at it.

"Anyway, you must have had enough of me by now." She was lying on her back, her arms behind her head and her knees apart, trying to cool down. There was a sheen of sweat on her skin. Her small rose-coloured nipples were soft now. She saw the direction of my gaze and covered her breasts with an arm. Being celibate for years had made her modest. Well, most of the time. In bed she combined that modesty with a degree of lasciviousness that wouldn't have been out of place in a nunnery in the days before organised religion went out of fashion.

"It isn't just about sex, you know," I said.

Sophia returned my gaze. "Isn't it?" she asked, her face blank. Then the hint of a smile creased the corners of her mouth. "Men are such romantics."

"Is that right?" I said sharply, rolling over on to my right side and confronting the heap of dirty clothing that had built up in the corner of my bedroom. I'd managed to miss my session at the wash house last month.

"Don't be childish, Quint," she said, slapping my shoulder lightly. "What are you working on at the moment?"

"The usual. Trying to find the shithead who's running that gang of pickpockets on Princes Street, chasing a Swedish porn dealer who's operating out of Leith. Where are the master criminals, for Christ's sake? Today they got me on to a lottery-winner who's done a bunk. Can't say I blame him."

The Ice Queen let out an impatient sigh. "What are you saying, Quint? Would you prefer us to have trysts at murder scenes and in the mortuary like we used to? I don't approve of all the changes my colleagues in the Council have made but at least we've kept a grip on crime." She shook her head. "Though setting up marijuana clubs for the tourists is asking for trouble."

I knew she and Hamilton had argued hard against that policy. No one bothered to ask me what I thought. I'm a big fan of irony and since the Enlightenment came to power with a mission to root out drugs from the city, the irony quotient in this volte-face is pretty high. But despite an increase in drugs-related petty crime like the one I witnessed in the Meadows, there hasn't been much sign of Edinburgh people wandering around in a grass-induced haze. The fact that citizens have bugger all to trade for dope seemed to regulate demand pretty effectively – there's no cash in the city apart from foreign currency, and the distribution of food and clothing vouchers is closely monitored.

There was a sibilant snore from the far side of the bed. Sophia had fallen asleep as rapidly as usual. Despite, or perhaps because of, the move towards accessibility and openness, the guardians still work ridiculously long hours. At least the daily Council meetings take place at midday now rather than in the evenings, but the medical guardian continues to put in a fifteen-hour day. My experience in the short time she'd been coming to me was that she'd be away to her office in the infirmary by five in the morning.

I got up carefully so as not to wake her and went into the living room. My throat was dry but my skin was drenched in sweat. I gulped water from one of Sophia's bottles and sat down gingerly on my sphincter-endangering sofa. Outside, the street was so quiet you could almost hear the tar bubbles popping in the heat. The curfew for citizens has been moved from ten to twelve p.m. but the guard still enforce it rigidly. As usual, sleep was as far from me as a cool breeze was from the city.

During the Big Heat my mind likes to pretend it's a nocturnal organism. Just as well. I had a lot to think about. Having sexual relations with Sophia was great, especially as I gave up sex sessions when they became non-compulsory a year back and my body was beginning to suffer serious deprivation. I still dreamed about my ex-lover Katharine Kirkwood and I used to kid myself that we still had some kind of tie, even though she walked away from me in January 2022 and I hadn't seen her since. But I couldn't figure out exactly what Sophia wanted from me. When she first showed up at my door and grabbed the contents of my underpants, I was more surprised than I'd been when the Council opened up its meetings to ordinary citizens. Like I say, the idea of the medical guardian having sex with anyone was pretty weird. Still, I suppose she had urges like everyone else. But why had she chosen me rather than a superfit young guardsman or a high-flying auxiliary? Something told me it was more than just the use of my genitalia she wanted. When we were together Sophia often asked me what I was working on, as she'd done tonight. Was that simply idle curiosity or was she after something else? Like information she could use against Council members who were more progressive than her?

I took the bottle of whisky into the bedroom and gulped from it as I sat on the bed. A stirring came from the other side.

"You should cut down on the spirits, Quint," the Ice Queen said blearily, one eye half open. "They'll poison your system."

I raised the bottle to her and drank again. I've made it a strict rule never to take advice from guardians.

I eventually passed out. I didn't register Sophia leaving and it was eight in the morning before I came round to the racket of clapped-out buses and kids complaining on their way to school. Saturday's a working day in Enlightenment Edinburgh for most citizens, schoolchildren included. They shouldn't complain too much – at least they only have half a day of lessons on Saturdays during the Big Heat. Maybe they were looking forward without enthusiasm to the summer holidays. They last all of two weeks, one of which is spent picking litter from the beaches. At least we still have beaches – unlike the west of Scotland which has been subject to catastrophic flooding because of rising sea levels. Some of the countries that used to send plenty of tourists such as China have gone into subaquatic pursuits in a big way too. We don't find out much about the rest of the world in our little wire-fenced paradise but news sometimes filters through from tourists and traders. The last I heard, the democratic system in Glasgow was hanging on but had come under heavy pressure from food shortages and organised crime. Most of the other states in Scotland have reverted to anarchy, while what used to be England is going through a modern version of the Dark Ages despite fifteen hours of skull-splitting sunshine every day.

I stumbled through to the living room and discovered that Sophia had left one of her bottles with enough water for me to make a mug of coffee. That commodity used to be harder to find in Edinburgh than silk knickers but the Council recently got into bed with a Swiss food and drink multinational – not that ordinary citizens get anything other than the scrapings from the factory floor. I chewed the end of a three-day-old loaf of bread and had a go at planning the day. What I should have done was try to find a new chain for my wreck of a bicycle, except I didn't fancy queuing for hours at the local Supply Directorate depot. Besides, I told myself, walking is good for you. And the city archive where I needed to go to find the missing lottery-winner's records isn't that far from my flat.

Dragging myself up what is a deceptive gradient on Lauriston Place in the morning sweatbath made me change my mind. It would have been worse on my bike but at least it would have been over quickly. The air was heavy and the stink from the breweries was cut with the acrid tang of sewage coming to the boil in the undermaintained pipes beneath the streets. These days Japanese tourists are told to bring along the little masks they wear in the busy streets back home. Edinburgh citizens haven't been allowed cars for years so there isn't much of a problem with exhaust fumes here. Unfortunately the Council hasn't yet found a way to stop people shitting during the Big Heat. No doubt Sophia's got the Medical Directorate working on that.

Things got a bit better when I reached George IVth Bridge. It's in the central tourist zone, so the pavements are washed down overnight and maroon awnings are hung to keep the sun off the city's honoured paying guests. Further on at the next checkpoint, guard personnel were looking out for ordinary citizens. For all the Council's attempts at openness, the High Street is still off limits unless you have work there. I had a Public Order Directorate authorisation but I wasn't going as far as the barrier. I turned into the archive and felt my body temperature begin to drop immediately in the polished-stone entrance hall. Before the Enlightenment the building was the city's central library, but the original Council's policy was to bring books – meaning the ones they approved of – closer to citizens, so they increased the number of smaller libraries in residential areas. Which gave them the chance to convert the main library into something they were even keener on – a centralised store containing everything they wanted to know about every citizen, without the citizens being allowed access. It's all on paper, of course. The guardians have always been suspicious of computers, forbidding citizens to possess them and under-using the few they kept for themselves.

"Morning, Citizen Dalrymple."

"Morning, Ray. What's the problem?"

The one-armed auxiliary looked pointedly at the sentry who'd just checked my pass then beckoned me into his office.

"Jackass," he said in a low voice. "You know you should call me Nasmyth 67 in public, Quint." Although the guardians have been encouraging citizens to use their names, auxiliaries are still to be addressed by barracks number – after all, they're the ones who keep control.

"Bugger that," I said. "We served together for years."

"Till you got demoted and I got crippled." Ray looked down at the stump that was protruding from his auxiliary-issue grey shirt. He always rolled the sleeve up as high as he could to make sure everyone got an eyeful.

I held up my right hand with the missing forefinger to remind him we were brothers in arms.

"So what are you after in my house of files this sweaty morning?" He filled a glass of water and handed it to me. During the Big Heat people do that without asking. It suddenly struck me that Agnes Kennedy hadn't given Davie and me a drink yesterday. Maybe she was more wound up about her missing father than I realised.

"There's a lottery-winner who's made a break for freedom," I replied. "Or drunk himself into a stupor somewhere."

"Well, you know your way around." Ray sat down and wrapped his good arm round a heap of folders on his desk.

"Unfortunately. I seem to have spent half my life in here."

Ray looked up and laughed derisively. "You only come for the bogs."

"You noticed? Auxiliary-issue paper, no queues. In fact, now you mention it . . ."

"Goodbye," he said rapidly.

"I'll see you later. I've got something for you."

"Don't forget to wash your hands."

I raised my fist, this time giving him only the middle finger.

Ahead of me lay what had been the pilastered reference room. Its domed ceiling is still visible, but there isn't much else to see apart from stacks and shelves full of grey cardboard folders. Bureaucrat heaven. The people who work in the archive are all auxiliaries. They tend to be specimens whose devotion to the Enlightenment is a lot greater than their physical capabilities. Short-sighted women and puny guys were poring avidly at mounds of files like gold prospectors who'd struck pay dirt.

"Can I help you?" asked a middle-aged man with pepper-and-salt stubble. It was probably as close as he could get to what used to be the regulation male auxiliary beard.

I declined his offer. The archivists always take a note of the files they bring you, so I collect my own. There's enough surveillance going on in this city without my activities being added to the list. I found Fordyce Bulloch Kennedy's file after a lot of scrabbling and heaving. In the process I inhaled enough dust to clog my bronchial tubes as effectively as a twenty-a-day coffin stick habit − so much for any improvement in my health brought about by the Council's long-standing ban on smoking. I took the thick file to a booth in a corner away from prying eyes and got stuck in.

As usual, most of the documentation was a waste of time − annual evaluations of worker competence, personal development statements, lifelong education credits, Platonic philosophy debates attended etc., etc. The original Council was genuinely committed to improving citizens' lives and, more important, citizens' abilities to make more of themselves. Whence the stress on education, the availability of better jobs for those who gained higher qualifications, the chance of roomier accommodation and so on. Even after twenty years no one has much of a problem with those ideals, although these days it's the lottery prizes that provide most of the concrete benefits and very few people win those. You get the impression that the Council, desperate as it is to please the tourists, only goes through the motions with its own citizens. It's the bureaucracy that's taken charge, a vast, paper-consuming machine that piles up more and more data and requires a huge staff to satisfy its demands. But I wonder if anyone's life is actually improved by the machine. Most of the files I see are only opened when new pages are inserted. No one has the time or inclination to read the contents.

Except in the case of Fordyce Bulloch Kennedy. The consultation sheet stapled to the inside front cover showed that an auxiliary from the Edlott Department of the Culture Directorate had examined the file on 8 June. I checked inside and found that was the day after Fordyce's ticket did the business. Obviously Edlott wanted background information on their latest winner. They'd even taken copies of particular pages, which was interesting because there are hardly any operational photocopiers in the city and auxiliaries are encouraged to make handwritten notes – thus adding to the bureaucracy. Paper in Edinburgh breeds faster than the nuclear reactors that put pockmarks all over the former Soviet Union in the early years of the century. I wrote down the barracks number of the auxiliary who'd been there before me – it was Nasmyth 05.

As for the missing man, he seemed like a pretty average guy – early fifties, highly commended cabinet-maker, no violations of the City Regulations, no contacts with known dissidents or deserters, plenty of Mentioned in Annual Reports for giving voluntary lessons in furniture-making in his spare time. The only black mark was that he was a bit too devoted to his kids – the Council has always discouraged excessive emotional attachment to offspring because they want the city's children to grow up strong and self-reliant. He was also very close to Hilda and had taken what was the risky step back in the early years of the Enlightenment of insisting they continue to live together. The Council then was keen on breaking up what it regarded as the constricting bonds of marriage and encouraging "personal growth". The guardians eventually realised that it was easier to let couples stay together if they wanted to. In general Fordyce Kennedy seemed to be an all-round good citizen. In my experience that's not necessarily a good sign.

I went back to the stacks and pulled the files on his wife and children. As regards the female members of the family, there was nothing out of the ordinary. Hilda had been a cleaner in various tourist hotels until her mental state had begun to deteriorate, while Agnes had trained as a painter and decorator at the Crafts College. Her school records showed that she'd been an average student, one who'd shown no interest in becoming an auxiliary. For the last three months she'd been working in a former school that was being converted into a tourist hostel.

The son Alexander – known as Allie – was a bit more interesting. He'd been a rebel when he was a teenager and had served several spells in the Gulag-like youth detention centres the Council used in the past to sort out nonconformists. He was a postman after that but his recent work records were pretty random. Under previous Councils he'd have been nailed as soon as he missed a day, but things are less strict now and the bureaucracy sometimes doesn't function as effectively as it thinks. I began to wonder what Agnes's older brother was up to. He looked like he might be worth a question or two.

The only other thing that struck me about the family was that the two children were still registered as living with their parents. The Council always encouraged children to move into their own accommodation as soon as they were eighteen in order to break what it regarded as the divisive effects of the family on broader society. Of course, there was never enough decent housing to enable the guardians to insist on the policy for all citizens, but it was still a bit unusual for offspring in their mid-twenties to stay at home. Agnes's excuse was that she was looking after her mother. What was her brother's?

I called the guard command centre in the castle on my mobile and asked the duty watch commander if she'd been informed about the missing lottery-winner. She answered in the affirmative without taking more than a second to think. Lewis Hamilton himself had told her to circulate a description to all barracks. They'd been on the lookout for Fordyce all over the city since last night but there had been no sign of him. I asked her to keep me advised and signed off. Then I finished taking notes from the folders and replaced them, following my normal practice of omitting my name from the consultation sheets. It keeps people guessing.

On my way out I stopped off at Ray's office. He was deep in his mass of paperwork. I dug into my shoulderbag and tossed over his book.

"Ah, *Black and Blue*," he said, giving it a quick glance. "What did you think?"

"Good, my friend. It was the only one of Ian Rankin's that I hadn't read. A state-of-the-nation novel, no less. I'd almost forgotten that Scotland actually used to be a country."

"Before the robber barons in the Scottish parliament tore each others' throats out and the drugs gangs divided up the territory," Ray said, shaking his head. He sat back in his rickety chair and smoothed the folds of skin on his neck. In the guard he'd been a unit leader renowned for his upper body strength, but since he lost his arm nearly ten years ago he'd turned into a wraith-like figure. His black hair went pure white in the space of a few weeks and the eyes above his grey beard were lustreless. He put his hand on the tattered paperback I'd returned. "There was still oil in the North Sea then," he said emptily.

"Not for long there wasn't," I said, catching sight of his fingernails. They were ingrained with dirt that looked a lot more heavy duty than the usual archive dust. "How's the book trade?"

Ray looked up at me sharply and bit his lip. If I didn't know him better, I'd have said he was trafficking more than the odd crime novel. "Not so loud, Quint," he said. "That American dealer's still around, I think. Any special requests?"

"Whatever early editions of Chandler he's got. Especially *The*

Lady in the Lake. It's my favourite." I smiled. "Cheap early editions, of course."

He nodded. "Aye, of course. What have you got to trade?"

"I still have a couple of E.C. Bentleys I can live without." I gave him a wave. "See you, pal."

"Don't let them grind you down, Quint."

"You know that's not in my nature, Ray." As I turned to go, I accidentally kicked a book across the ragged carpet on his office floor.

"It doesn't matter," he said quickly. "I'll pick it up later."

"No worries," I said, bending down. I put the copy of Wilfred Owen's collected poems on top of *Black and Blue.* "Ian Rankin and Wilfred Owen. What you might call a strange meeting."

Ray's mouth opened as if he were about to speak then shook his head slowly and went back to his files.

I hit the street and sheltered from the sun under the awning. Opposite stands what used to be the National Library of Scotland and is now the Edinburgh Heritage Centre. For tourists, mind — no locals allowed. A group of Middle Eastern women in long robes and veils had gathered on the pavement. Their guide, an Arabic-speaking female auxiliary dressed up as a society hostess from the time of Sir Walter Scott, was trying hard to whip up interest. No doubt the visitors would just love the exhibition halls stuffed with Council propaganda. The photographs of the riots in 2002, the year before the last election, are apparently a big draw — drug dealers handing out free scores on street corners, policemen being stoned, pub cellars under siege by the mob. No wonder the Enlightenment Party got the biggest majority in British history, then promptly declared independence and left the rest of the UK to mayhem and pillage.

So, I wondered, what to do about Fordyce Bulloch Kennedy? There were several things I wanted to look into. The most obvious was Edlott. He would have a handler in the Culture

Directorate, perhaps the one who'd consulted his file, to arrange his appearances as Robert Louis Stevenson and make sure he didn't do anything embarrassing. That auxiliary was probably waiting to be packed off to the border on fatigue duty for not keeping a closer eye on him. The Labour Directorate was another possibility. They're forever drafting citizens into emergency squads when pitprops collapse in the mines or workers desert from the city farms. The missing man may have been picked up by mistake, in which case his name should be on a list. Then there was Fordyce's family. When she was lucid, his wife gave the impression of being worried that he'd disappeared for good but you never know. Most violence is committed by the people closest to the victim, even in this supposedly crime-free state, and it looked like the son might have been moving in dodgy circles. But there was one possibility I had to rule out before any of those. I turned left and headed towards the checkpoint.

The guardswoman on duty was middle-aged, her fading red hair pulled back in a tight ponytail despite the recent ruling that female auxiliaries don't have to tie their hair down any more. She raised the barrier before I got to it and waved me through, giving me a tight smile. She must have known who I was. Christ, she may have served with me in the guard years ago. Or perhaps it was just that she'd seen my photo in the *Edinburgh Guardian* after one of the big cases.

I walked up to the Lawnmarket and turned left at the gallows where they still put on a weekly mock hanging for the tourists. A hot wind from the east gusted up the High Street, filling my eyes with dust. Across the road tourists were panting up the hill but I didn't feel too sorry for them – unlike the locals, they could look forward to air-conditioning in their hotels. A couple of them turned into Deacon Brodie's Marijuana Club. I stood for a moment and watched. Guard personnel dressed in eighteenth-century costume were checking passports, making sure no Edinburgh citizens who'd managed to slip past the checkpoint got into the premises. One of them looked across suspiciously at my faded shorts and crumpled T-shirt. I stared back then took in the garishly painted building. Like I said, there's a lot of irony about the way the Council's gone back on its anti-drugs policy. There's also plenty of cynicism. The city's a strictly no smoking zone for the natives on grounds of health but if foreigners want to fill their lungs with the smoke from cigarettes and joints supplied with the guardians' approval, who gives a shit? As long as they pay upfront.

I walked across the suntrap of the esplanade towards the castle gatehouse, ranks of guard vehicles drawn up on both sides. The guard command centre in the old fortifications is about as imposing a place as you can find, even in this spectacular city. It's just a pity that the battered Land-Rovers and rusting pick-ups make the place look like a scrap merchant's yard. The only vehicle with any class is a ten-year-old Jeep donated to the Council by a grateful American tourist agency. Somehow it's ended up as Lewis Hamilton's personal transport.

I found the guardian in his quarters in what was once the Governor's House.

"Ah, there you are, Dalrymple," he said, looking up from the neat array of papers on his desk. "I was wondering when you'd show up. I suppose you want to find out if the missing lottery-winner is in my records."

"Well spotted, Lewis." I went over to the leaded windows and ran my eye over the northern suburbs. Across the firth I could just make out the hills of what was Fife in the old days and is now a Scottish version of the Wild West, complete with gunmen on horseback, massacres of the locals and abandoned mining towns – badlands in spades, pardner.

Hamilton joined me. "As much as another month of this bloody heat to go," he said, wiping the sweat from his wrinkled forehead. Although he was in his seventies, the public order guardian still had a firm grip on the City Guard. His beard and hair were almost completely white but his bearing was as military as ever. "Well, I've checked all my Restricted Files. There's no reference to Kennedy . . ." He broke off and went back to the papers on his desktop. "What the hell was his first name?"

"Fordyce," I said. "Fordyce Bulloch Kennedy."

"Thank you." Hamilton's acknowledgement was curt. He didn't like being helped out, especially by an auxiliary who'd been demoted from his own directorate.

I can never resist having a go at guardians, especially one as thin-skinned as my former boss. "You would tell me if he was one of your undercover operatives, of course."

The guardian's eyes bulged as he glared at me. Finally he managed to spit something out. "I tell you he's not."

"But how do I know you're telling the truth, Lewis?" I asked, prolonging the fun.

"How do you know . . . ?" Hamilton took a couple of deep breaths. Even in these more open times guardians don't like having their veracity impugned, as Councilspeak would have it. Auxiliaries are taught tension control techniques but Lewis was appointed by the first Council and never went through the training programme – unlike me. "You're doing it deliberately, aren't you? Grow up, man."

"Grow up, man," I repeated dubiously. "Bit of an oxymoron, wouldn't you say?"

The desk telephone buzzed, saving me from the guardian's tongue. I watched his expression change as he answered.

"What?" Hamilton bellowed. "Where?" He listened for a couple of seconds. "When?" He listened again. "Any ID?"

Shit. I'd been calculating the odds of him running through the full set of interrogatives beginning with "wh".

"Very well. Tell the barracks commander to keep me informed." He slammed the phone down.

"What's going on?" I asked, trying to give the impression of idle curiosity.

"Nothing for you to worry about, Dalrymple," Hamilton said, shuffling files.

Nothing makes me suspicious quicker than a guardian telling me not to worry. "What is it, Lewis?" I said insistently.

He caught my tone and looked up. "Oh, very well. Body found by the Water of Leith. Sounds like heatstroke or the like."

"Tell me more," I said, leaning over him.

"Middle-aged male. No identification on the body." The guardian glanced at me then reached over for a buff folder. "Ah, I see what you mean. What age is that missing lottery-winner?"

"Fifty-two."

"You don't think it's him, do you?"

"Only one way to find out, Lewis," I replied, heading for the door. "Call your people and tell them to keep their sticky fingers off the body till we get there."

Chapter Three

We piled into Hamilton's Jeep and headed off the esplanade. His driver, a middle-aged guardswoman with a heavily freckled face, seemed to be enjoying herself as she turned down Ramsay Lane at speed.

"What do you reckon?" I said to the guardian as we roared past the Assembly Hall where the Council used to hold its daily meetings. "Murder, suicide, accident or natural causes?"

"My driver has a perfect safety record."

I almost fell off my seat. There had never been much evidence that Lewis Hamilton possessed a sense of humour, let alone that he was prepared to show it off in front of his staff.

"Surely we shouldn't be prejudging, Dalrymple," he went on. "But if you insist on playing games, our statistics clearly show that death from natural causes is the most likely, especially at this time of year. Accidental death comes next. Apart from dissident-related killings around the city line, there have been hardly any murders in Edinburgh since 2022. And, I'm glad to say, suicide is still illegal."

I put my hands out as we swung on to the Mound and down towards Princes Street. The guardian was having a veiled go at the members of the Council who had tried to repeal the regulation banning suicide. There had been an idea that citizens would feel they had greater control over their lives, or rather deaths. The conservative wing had won that particular battle.

I took in the panorama from our elevated position. To the right protruded the stump of the Enlightenment Monument, as the original Council had renamed the Scott Monument. Its upper sections have been dropping off regularly in recent years and there's now a rectangular structure of scaffolding covered with tarpaulin around the top. There are vast maroon hearts painted on each side, along with the names of the foreign companies that have done sponsorship deals with the Council.

To my left a dustcloud was rising from the racetrack in the gardens. During the Big Heat spectators watch the horses from air-conditioned stands that look like a giant's greenhouses. What used to be lawns and flowerbeds are mostly rock gardens filled with cacti these days, though the floral clock has been kept in operation. It was being watered by a morose Parks Department labourer who had his hose at arm's length like he'd been asked to hold someone else's dick. Splatters of the city's precious water raked our windows as we reached the main thoroughfare. Before we crossed to Hanover Street I caught an eyeful of awnings and flags. Edinburgh has turned into an open-air café society, at least in the centre where the tourists go. They were easy enough to spot, their well-cut clothes in stark contrast to the faded Supply Directorate waiters' uniforms and overalls worn by the citizens who work in the tourist zone. Some young Chinese were watching satellite television from micro-receivers on their wrists. No doubt they were keeping up with the Beijing Stock Market – pandaflation had been rampant.

"I still don't see why you're coming with me," the guardian said testily. "The chances that this is your missing Edlott winner can't be very great."

I shrugged. "So we rule out this guy and I get back to the search."

Hamilton glanced at me. "You can't resist a body, can you, Dalrymple?"

"And you can, can you, Lewis?" I asked with an ironic grin.

"You were out of your office like a vulture in the mating season."

I heard the guardswoman stifle a laugh and the conversation rapidly terminated.

In a few minutes we reached the guard checkpoint at the bottom of Dundas Street and moved into the citizen residential area of Stockbridge. The surroundings were immediately less salubrious, the road surface uneven and buildings stained black by the coal we've been burning in winter since the electricity restrictions bit years ago. Citizens working here don't have to bother with the uniforms they wear in the centre, so the streets were filled with people in dirty T-shirts and faded shorts. I felt at home again.

Just before the bridge there was a maroon and white striped Edlott booth with a queue of citizens snaking away from it. A character wearing an eighteenth-century coat and what was probably a false paunch was giving them a speech. The billiard cue he was carrying told me who he was meant to be – David Hume, Edinburgh philosopher and bon viveur. Christ knows what the old sceptic would think of his home town's condition in the twenty-first century. Maybe he'd be amused that a lottery-winner was impersonating him. He might even be impressed that a fair number of the populace was well read enough to recognise him.

"I sincerely hope it isn't the lottery-winner who's dead, Dalrymple," Hamilton said, staring past me at the booth. "The Culture Directorate will make my life hell."

He was probably right. Since the success of Edlott, the directorate handling it had become one of the most influential in the Council. Even the once all-powerful Finance Directorate had to listen to the culture guardian and his gang of smartarse senior auxiliaries – especially since they'd started developing initiatives with the Tourism Directorate, the city's other hotbed of money-grabbing schemers.

I smiled. The guardian was quite capable of looking after himself in Council meetings. "What's your problem, Lewis?" I asked. "You don't even approve of Edlott. You once told me it was run by fools for fools."

He stared at me with hostile intentions. I shouldn't have wound him up by talking down the lottery in front of the guardswoman. Not that she gave any sign of having noticed – personnel who work in the proximity of the public order guardian learn to turn off their hearing regularly.

"I don't know what you mean, man," Hamilton said unconvincingly. "Citizens deserve to have the chance to change their lives. They need to know that their dreams might come true. Anyway, the Council approved the setting up of Edlott unanimously."

The Council always approves measures unanimously, or says it does. And the reason the guardians went for Edlott was because they were desperate to calm citizens down when food and power shortages threatened to cause major disorder.

"Here we are." The guardian pointed ahead. A roadblock had been set up at the junction of St Bernard's Street and the main road. A couple of glowering guardsmen were holding some disaffected locals at bay. We were waved through, my citizen-issue clothes getting a dubious look from one of the auxiliaries.

"Where exactly are we headed?" I asked.

"The Colonies," the guardian replied. "The barracks commander's waiting for us in Bell Place."

We drove past the local citizens' bathhouse in what was once a swimming-pool and reached the Colonies, a housing scheme started in the 1860s by a group of stonemasons. As many as 10,000 people lived in the closely built streets at first, but the houses went upmarket in the second half of the twentieth century and the number of residents dropped. We took a left turn and found the road full of guard vehicles.

A careworn auxiliary appeared at the Jeep door. "Good morning, guardian."

"Raeburn 01." Hamilton acknowledged the commander of the local guard barracks and nudged me impatiently. "Come on then, Dalrymple. No time to lose."

I stepped reluctantly into the heat then took in the neat lines of houses to our right and left. By Housing Directorate standards they were in unusually good condition. The railings running up to the first-floor entrances had been repainted recently. There was even the occasional flowerbox, water for them presumably taken illicitly from the river at the road end.

"Where's the body?" I asked.

"Follow me." Raeburn 01 led us down the street. A guard had been placed outside each front door. Through the windows I could see anxious citizens looking out at us, in one house a mother standing with her arm round her daughter's back. The little girl gave me a cautious smile. I winked back and her eyes opened wide in surprise. She probably thought from my appearance that I was a clown the guard had brought along to cheer themselves up.

"Down here." The commander took us through a small garden and down to the river bank. Then he raised his arm and pointed.

There were a few moments of silence as we focused on the Water of Leith. In the nineteenth century the river had been the sewer of the New Town and it didn't smell too healthy now. Water was running sluggishly through a narrow central channel, the rest of the river bed made up of bone-hard dried mud and stones that hadn't been submerged since last winter. By the end of the Big Heat there wouldn't be much more than a trickle in the channel.

Not that the guy lying on his front with his head in the flow cared about that any more. The hot wind gusted from the east down the river bed and billowed his shirt up from his back, baring pale, unwashed skin. The legs in frayed dark blue work trousers were spread wide open at a disturbing angle. There was a shoe missing from the man's right foot and the skin on the underside was covered in dried blood.

Then the silence was broken by a sound that's become common at this time of year in the few parts of the city where there's even a dribble of water. Our very own version of the "Bullfrog Blues".

"Have your people touched anything?" I asked the barracks commander after I'd had a quick look around the site.

"Certainly not," he replied with an affronted look. "We know the procedures."

I got a glare from Hamilton for my trouble as well. "Okay, okay. Who found the body?"

An eager guardsman who couldn't have been long out of the auxiliary training programme stepped up. "I did, citizen. I was on foot patrol on the other side of the water. I called in immediately."

"Right." I took the pair of protective gloves offered by a scene-of-crime squad auxiliary, pulled them on and kneeled down by the body. Flies rose up angrily and cannoned off me. The shallow river was washing over the dead man's face and forehead, sluicing past the head with a gentle gurgling noise.

I twisted round towards the guardsman. "Are you sure you didn't touch anything?"

He shifted his weight uneasily.

"Only I'd have expected you to check whether this citizen was alive and getting his mouth and nose out of the water would have been a perfectly natural reaction."

The guardsman looked at his commander, keeping his eyes off the guardian, then nodded. "I . . . I did lift his head out for a short time. But I put it back again as soon as I ascertained he wasn't breathing."

I nodded at him, giving his superiors a tight smile. "Just so we're clear on that. Anyone else touch anything? Check in his pockets?"

There was a collective shaking of heads. I didn't believe them – the guardian had asked if there was any ID when he was contacted on the phone – but I'd made my point. It's always a good idea to impose yourself on auxiliaries.

"Can we get on, Dalrymple?" Hamilton demanded.

I lifted the dead man's head and looked at his face. The unshaven skin was only slightly wrinkled, suggesting he hadn't been in the water for long. Initially it was difficult to be sure from the photographs I'd seen of the missing lottery-winner. He was around the same age. But I soon realised the build and weight were different. The man at the riverside was pretty short and his face looked markedly thinner than Fordyce Kennedy's.

"I reckon you're in the clear with the Culture Directorate, Lewis," I said. "The question is, who's this guy?"

I checked the dead man's pockets: a heavily stained handkerchief and a lottery ticket stub, but no sign of the identity card citizens have to carry at all times. There were no obvious injuries so murder didn't look like a banker. Suicide wasn't too likely either — he'd have had a hell of a job drowning himself in the Water of Leith's less-than-raging torrent. Natural causes was still the best bet. He might have suffered a heart attack while he was walking by the river, or maybe succumbed to heatstroke. But the angle of his legs and the missing shoe made me wonder. Walking with only one shoe? Hit by a spasm that jerked the legs out at such an extreme angle? I twitched my head and tried to restrain my imagination.

I stepped back and let the Public Order Directorate photographers get stuck in. While they were busy, I took a walk around. Auxiliaries in protective suits had already sectioned off the stretch of ground from the road end to the river. Three of them were crawling around looking for prints or traces. A small group of local residents, those who obviously worked earlier or later shifts, had gathered behind the tape that had been run between the flaky trunks of two trees. I went over to them.

"We'll need one of you to have a go at identifying the dead man," I said.

They looked at me doubtfully, trying to work out what one of their rank was doing in the middle of a guard operation. Eventually a tall, gangly guy in his fifties with a badly set broken nose and thick grey hair nodded.

"All right, son. I'll help you out."

I lifted the tape and led him down, skirting the area the scene-of-crime squad were scrutinising.

"Here," the man said in a low voice, "what's in it for me?"

I looked round at him. He was wearing brown overalls bearing the badge of a Supply Directorate storeman. His kind was on the take years before the Council relaxed the penalties for involvement in the black market. Now they only get six months in the mines.

I gave him an encouraging smile. "What's your name?" I asked.

"Angus Drem." He returned my smile, sensing a payoff.

"Well, Angus, here's the deal. See the old fellow with the beard over there?"

His smile faded. "That's the public order guardian, isn't it?"

"That's right. He's the one who negotiates payments to citizens." I headed towards Lewis Hamilton. "I'll just let him know you're in the market, shall I?"

"No!"

The citizen's shout made everyone turn towards us.

"No, son, I was just kidding," he said hastily. "After all, this is a public duty. You must've misunderstood me."

"Uh-huh." I kneeled down by the dead man again and lifted his head out of the water. "So do you know him, Angus?"

The man's face had gone white. "Oh fuck, aye," he said in a whisper. "It's Frankie Thomson, the poor bugger. He lives in number 19."

I beckoned to the commander. "Get one of your people to take a statement from Citizen Drem here. Everything he knows about the dead man, when he last saw him, any visitors to his . . ."

"I know the procedure, citizen," the auxiliary interrupted, leading the citizen away.

"What have we got then?" asked a cool voice from behind me.

I turned to find the medical guardian kneeling on the other side of the body.

"Sophia," I said, unable to keep the surprise from my voice. "I didn't expect to see you down here."

If she was unimpressed by my use of her name in front of auxiliaries, she didn't show it. "You know how it is. There are so few sudden deaths in the city . . ."

Not so few during the Big Heat that the medical guardian checks each one out personally, I thought.

"Also," she said, head bent over the corpse, "I was informed that both the public order guardian and you were attending. That piqued my curiosity."

I still wasn't convinced. Maybe she'd just wanted some fresh air – in which case she was in the wrong place. Frankie Thomson was in need of cold storage.

"Have the scene-of-crime people finished with the body?" she asked.

I looked round at the auxiliary in white plastic who was hovering behind us. He nodded.

"So it seems. What do you think then?"

Sophia lifted the dead man's head and examined the mouth and nostrils. "No sign of the foam that drowning would produce, but then the flow of water would have washed that away. Flesh beginning to whiten. The goose bumps on his cheeks show the onset of cutis anserina." She felt the limbs. "Rigor mortis is under way in the arms and legs but he hasn't been here for too long. Twelve hours maximum, I'd say provisionally, though the high ambient temperature complicates things." Now she was at the lower half of the body. "Curious angle of the legs, don't you think?"

I nodded.

She leaned closer and sniffed. "I can smell faecal matter. He lost control of his bowels."

I looked closer. The dead man's trousers had a stain on the backside which the sun had dried. "Significant?" I asked.

"Maybe. Don't get your hopes up though. He may just have eaten something bad."

"Never. Your directorate's dietary planning doesn't allow for that."

Sophia ignored my sarcasm. "Abrasions on the sole of the foot but not elsewhere. So he walked here, he wasn't dragged."

"Can we get his head out of the water now?" I asked.

"Why not?" Sophia stood up and wiped sweat from her brow. Even the Ice Queen must have been boiling in the protective suit she was wearing over her clothes.

Scene-of-crime personnel lifted the body away from the water. Sophia signalled to them to turn it over on its back. Then she kneeled down by the upper abdomen and undid the buttons of the citizen-issue shirt.

"No signs of any bruising or abrasions here." She looked at the fabric of the shirt.

"What is it?" I asked.

"Look at these patches." She put her nose up to them and inhaled. "Vomit. He definitely had something that didn't agree with him."

"For example?"

She shrugged. "There are plenty of possibilities."

"But you'll narrow them down in the post-mortem?"

She gave me the hint of a smile. "We'll narrow them down all right, citizen," she replied in a cold voice, glancing up at Lewis Hamilton who'd just joined us.

I swallowed a bitter laugh. I'd been in bed with her a few hours ago, but as far as she was concerned I was nothing more than a demoted auxiliary on special investigation duties.

"What next?" the public order guardian asked.

"The medical guardian takes the body to the morgue," I said. "And we stick our noses into Frankie Thomson's flat."

I was standing outside number 19 Bell Place gulping water from a bottle I'd got from Hamilton's driver. The sun was at its zenith and the heat was as big as it gets. A guard Land-Rover came round the corner at speed and screeched to a halt six inches from the guardian's Jeep.

"Well parked, Davie," I called.

"What are you doing here, Hume 253?" Hamilton asked, peering at the gap between the bumpers.

"Good morning, guardian," Davie said, trying to pretend that his driving was beyond criticism. "I heard from the command centre that a body had been discovered." He looked at me hopefully. "I thought you and citizen Dalrymple might need some help."

"Oh, you did, did you? So you drove down here like a madman and . . ." The guardian finally took his gaze from the back end of his Jeep. "Anyway, what makes you think Citizen Dalrymple has any involvement in this case?" He glared at me. "You wanted to know if this body was that of the missing Edlott winner. It isn't. Why are you still here?"

Typical Hamilton. For him, things were either black or white. I've always tended to operate in grey areas.

"Look," I said, "the missing guy will probably turn up with a hangover any time now. That poor sod over there's had his last hair of the dog and I'm not convinced he just dropped dead on the river bank. I'm your special investigator, for God's sake. Let me confirm this isn't a suspicious death."

For a few moments it seemed Hamilton wasn't going to buy it, then he nodded reluctantly. "Oh, very well. But I want you back on the Edlott case as soon as possible." Before I could celebrate my minor victory his lower jaw jutted forward aggressively. "Don't think you can use any guard personnel you want, Dalrymple. In case it's escaped your attention, Hume 253 is a guard commander and as such is subject to my orders."

"I know," I said, playing it cool. "That's why I'm asking you to let him assist me here. It'll mean I get things finished quicker."

The guardian couldn't really argue with that. "Now I suppose

I'm going to have to rearrange the watch commanders' rota," he grumbled, looking round for a minion to bawl out.

I led Davie up the steps to the dead man's front door. "Next time pull up further away from his precious Jeep," I suggested.

"Did I hit it?" Davie demanded. "Did I?"

"Calm down." I handed him a pair of rubber gloves and led him inside. Scene-of-crime people were already at work finger-printing and taking photographs.

"Not bad," Davie said, taking in the living room and separate kitchen from the hall. "You could have a whole family in here."

"Yes, you could." I put in a call to the Housing Directorate and discovered that Thomson, Francis Dee, had lived here on his own for fourteen months. They weren't able to tell me why he hadn't been allocated single-citizen accommodation. It may simply have been that the bureaucracy had fouled up.

"Right, where do we start?" Davie said, going into the living room.

"You know the drill by now, guardsman."

"Confirm ID, collate forensic evidence, list personal belongings . . ."

"All right, smartarse. I'll take the table, you take the rest."

"Done."

Although there was the usual range of Supply Directorate furniture in the room, I'd actually given Davie the easy bit. It looked like almost all of Frankie Thomson's worldly possessions were on the table that stood under the front window — papers, dirty cups, old copies of the *Edinburgh Guardian*, a pair of socks with holes in the toes and a darning needle stuck through them, a couple of well-thumbed Ngaio Marsh novels. And, on the top, his ID card. That saved us some time. It also gave me a medium-voltage shock.

"Well, well," I said.

"What have you got?" Davie came over.

I fended him off. "Thomson, Francis Dee," I read. "Status — citizen. Born 24.4.1972, height five feet five inches, weight eight stone six pounds, hair grey, teeth incomplete (upper rear denture plate), distinguishing mark none, employment Cleansing Department, Tourism Directorate, address 19 Bell Place, Colonies, next of kin none." The face staring out was the one I'd seen by the river. In life the eyes looked as vacant as they did now.

"Is that it?" Davie sounded disappointed.

"No, it's not," I said, turning the laminated card round and holding it in front of his face.

"Ah," he said, registering the letters "DM" in bold maroon type at the bottom. "The dead man was a demoted auxiliary."

"Kind of changes things, doesn't it?" I said, putting the card into my pocket. Although the Council carefully avoids doing DM-class citizens like me any favours when we're alive, they find us much more interesting when we're dead. Because demoted auxiliaries are by definition untrustworthy characters who've sold the Enlightenment out one way or another, their deaths are automatically treated as suspicious until proved otherwise.

"I'd better notify the guardian," Davie said, turning away.

I reached out an arm and grabbed his shoulder. "Hold on. He'll be off to the Council meeting soon. Let's sit on this for a bit till we dig up some more about the guy."

"Are you out of your mind?" Davie said, his eyes wide open. "The guardian'll have my balls for breakfast if he finds out I've colluded in suppressing significant information."

"Who's going to tell him?" I asked. "Anyway, you don't have to work with me on this if you don't want to." I gave him a tight smile. "Or if I don't want you to."

"Why are you doing this?" he asked desperately. "It's just a waster who passed out in the sun, for Christ's sake."

I ran my fingers across my unshaven cheek slowly. I wasn't too sure what I was doing myself. Maybe I felt some irrational sympathy for a fellow former auxiliary. But more than that, something I couldn't put my finger on felt strange about the whole set-up.

"Don't worry," I said. "I'll give your boss a full report later on. Anything else interesting?"

Davie shook his head in extreme frustration then continued his search. He'd taken the few books off the shelves and checked them for inserts. It's amazing how many citizens put letters and other bits of paper they want to keep inside books. Maybe it's a side effect of the Council's drive to increase reading. He shook his head. "Nothing, Quint."

I went over to the rear wall and looked behind the Supply Directorate print of the castle. No interesting stash there. Then I looked round the room, wondering again about the accommodation Frankie Thomson had been allocated. Demoted citizens are supposed to get standard citizen-issue everything – housing, clothes, jobs, whatever – so how had he ended up with more rooms and space than single citizens are entitled to? I made a note about that for when I checked his file. Then I pulled out my mobile and rang the Tourism Directorate. It took some shouting and a three-minute wait but I got what I wanted.

"What do you think of this, Davie?" I said as I cut the connection. "The dead man was a cleaner at the Smoke on the Water marijuana club in the Dean Village."

"Smoke on the Water? Isn't that a piece of music?"

"Depends how you define music, my friend."

A female scene-of-crime auxiliary appeared at the door. "Citizen? There's something you should see in the kitchen."

We followed the white-suited figure into the back room. She pointed to the kitchen table. Three bottles of whisky stood in the centre of it, the caps screwed on and the labels facing the door.

"The Ultimate Usquebaugh," Davie read. "I've never heard of that brand."

"That's what I mean," the auxiliary said. "I contacted the Alcohol Department in the Supply Directorate and they said the same thing."

I stepped closer and examined the bottles without touching

them. "Be very careful when you dust for prints," I said. "If this is contraband, we'll need to trace it."

"The dead man worked in a club," said Davie. "He probably got it there."

I nodded, still looking at the whisky. It was a dark brown colour. A small amount had been taken from the front bottle. The other two were full. The label looked to have been professionally printed but there wasn't much else to go on. The Ultimate Usquebaugh were the only words, in maroon on a grey background with no other design features. "Usquebaugh" means "water of life" in Gaelic. For some reason that didn't make me feel good.

"Any glasses?" I asked the auxiliary.

She shook her head. "No dirty ones anywhere. There are a couple of clean ones in the cupboard." She pointed to the floor under the table. "There's also this."

I bent down and saw a citizen-issue brown shoe that matched the one on Frankie Thomson's left foot. I picked it up carefully – the scene-of-crime staff had traced round it with chalk – and looked in it. There were no bloodstains. As the dead man had no sock on either foot it was reasonable to suppose that, like a lot of Edinburgh people during the Big Heat, he didn't bother with them. But would he have walked voluntarily to the rough terrain by the riverside with only one shoe on?

"Our man liked a drink," Davie said. He had his foot on the bin pedal. Inside were two empty bottles, this time standard Supply Directorate stuff: Cream of Auld Reekie. There was also a half-empty bottle of the same brand on the windowledge.

"Dust all these then send them to toxicology – along with the Ultimate Usquebaugh," I said to the female auxiliary.

"He definitely had his ultimate drink, eh?" Davie said with a grin.

I wasn't on for grinning back at him. I was getting a bad

feeling about what had gone on in number 19 Bell Place and at the side of the Water of Leith.

The barracks commander Raeburn 01 came up from the street. "We've located all the residents," he said, trying and failing to give the impression that he enjoyed reporting to an ordinary citizen like me.

"And?" I wasn't going to let him off the hook.

"And only two of them admit to ever having spoken to the dead man."

I wasn't too surprised. After twenty years of the guard's sledgehammer public order tactics, ordinary Edinburgh folk don't do them any favours.

"So what you're saying is that the rest of them didn't know Frankie Thomson except to ignore on the street and didn't see or hear what he was up to last night?"

"Correct." The commander bit the end of his pencil.

"Who are the two you've managed to strongarm into talking?"

Davie nudged me hard in the back as the guardian loomed in the hallway.

Raeburn 01 stared at me then looked at his notebook. "There's a female citizen called Mary McMurray who heard some noise here late last night."

"I'll talk to her," I said. "Who else?"

"Citizen Drem."

"Angus with the broken nose?" I didn't fancy listening to that scumbag again. "What did he tell you?"

"Oh, he was very obliging."

"I'll bet," I said. He was no doubt the type who likes to make contacts in the guard. That's how the black market prospers.

"But he didn't have much to tell. Apparently Citizen Thomson often drank to excess." The commander wrinkled his nose. Senior auxiliaries usually have no time for human weaknesses like heavy drinking, despite the provision of alcohol in barracks messes. "Drem said he often saw him slumped over the table in his window."

I took Davie aside. "I want you to put the shits up Angus
Drem. Threaten him with the third degree, a cell in the castle,
whatever it takes. I want to know if he's ever been involved in
handling contraband whisky. Don't mention the name of that
stuff we found though. And Davie?" I lowered my voice. "Find
out if he knew Frankie Thomson was DM."

Davie gave me a grim smile and headed out. I reckoned the
Supply Directorate storeman would soon be regretting that he'd
identified the body.

"Where does the female citizen live?" I asked Raeburn 01.

"Next door to the right. Number 21."

I went outside and looked down the street. Lewis Hamilton
was speaking on the phone in his Jeep – probably still playing with his rosters. I knocked on the neighbouring front
door.

Mary McMurray was the woman I'd seen on my way to the
body. She was painfully thin and had mousy hair, her face
sunburnt and dotted with what I hoped were benign melanomas.
Her daughter was right behind her, clutching her hand.

"Don't worry," I said, kneeling down and smiling at the little
girl. She was about five, her fair hair done up in plaits. "I'm not
one of those nasty people in uniforms. I don't like them."

The girl stared at me seriously then shook her head. "Neither
do I. They stamp their feet and shout all the time."

I laughed. "My name's Quint. What's yours?"

She was still looking at me with a grave expression. "Quint's a
silly name. I'm called Morag."

"You're right, Morag. Quint is a silly name." I decided against
telling her it was short for Quintilian. "Will you go and play
while your mum and I have a wee chat?"

Mary McMurray shook her head. "Forget it, citizen. When
I'm home, she never lets me out of her sight." She led me into the
front room. It was clean and tidy, the curtains partially drawn
against the sun. Above the fireplace was a photograph of a
handsome smiling guy.

"That's my daddy," the little girl said, catching me looking at it. "He's gone to heaven."

I looked at her mother. After a moment she shrugged.

"What could I tell her, citizen? I know we're supposed to be atheists but she won't have it any other way."

"Border duty?" I said in a low voice.

She nodded. "Cattle raid two years ago."

After a bit Morag went to the corner and started playing with a doll.

"So tell me about Frankie Thomson, Mary."

She hesitated. "You're the investigator they sometimes write about in the *Guardian*, aren't you?"

I nodded.

"But you do things for ordinary citizens as well as work for the Council?"

"I'm a free agent, Mary. That's why I'm dressed in rags."

She smiled reluctantly. "All right. But I haven't much to tell you, citizen."

"Call me Quint."

"I still haven't much to tell you, Quint." The smile had stayed on her lips but her eyes were as sad as any I've seen in the city. "Frankie, och, he was okay as a neighbour. Apart from the drink. He got steaming a couple of nights every week. I suppose he had the booze from the club where he worked." She looked out of the gap between the curtains for a moment. "Like I say, he was all right. At least he was quiet." She turned back to face me. "Apart from last night."

That sounded interesting. I moved closer to her. "You heard something?"

"Aye. It was the singing. It woke Morag up."

"What time?"

"Just after three. They were really belting it out — something about the moon in Alabama, I don't know."

"They?" Now I was really hooked.

"Yeah, there was someone else in his place. Another guy. I pounded on the wall and they shut up. Eventually."

"Then what?"

"Then I heard his front door open and close, and their voices move down the street towards the river. I couldn't see much, of course, with the streetlights not being on but . . ." She broke off. The way she was biting her lip kept my interest.

"Did you see something, Mary? Anything at all?"

She shrugged. "I did look out the window. It was pretty dark, but I caught a glimpse of the man who was with Frankie."

"What did he look like?" I asked, my throat suddenly dry.

"Och, I don't know." Mary's shoulders slumped. "I couldn't really see. He was a bit taller than Frankie and he had dark clothes on. Maybe that's why it stuck out."

"It? What was it?" I'd raised my voice involuntarily. Morag gave a frightened moan from the other side of the room. "Sorry," I said more quietly. "What was it that stuck out, Mary?"

"His head," she said, frowning at me. "His head. The hair was cut right down to the scalp."

Great. In a city where water's rationed and decent shampoo's scarcer than self-effacing guardsmen, there's no shortage of men who shave their heads. Christ, some of the women do it too. "Anything else?" I asked. "Did he have any hair on his face?"

She thought for a few seconds. "No, he was clean-shaven."

"What age do you think he was?"

She shook her head. "I don't know. He put what looked like a sunhat on as soon as he got to the pavement. The only other thing I saw was that he had a bottle in one hand."

I wondered if that had been the Ultimate Usquebaugh. "What build was he?" I asked.

"Slim," she said after a few seconds' thought. "Definitely slim."

"Are you sure you don't remember anything else?"

"Nothing. Except . . . except I was just dropping off again when I heard this shout. From the river. Well, it was more like a scream now I think about it." She shook her head and looked guilty. "Now I know what's happened."

I glanced over at the corner. Morag was facing us but she was more interested in the conversation she was having with her doll.

"Did you hear anything else?"

"No. I was knackered after my shift on the bus."

"The other voice, can you tell me anything more about it? Was it a tenor or a bass?"

She looked at me uncomprehendingly. "I don't know. The two of them were singing. That's all I remember."

I waited. It's surprising what people remember if you don't hassle them too much.

"The other guy's voice wasn't particularly deep, if that's what you mean. Kind of in the middle." She stared at me, the flawed skin on her face taut. "What happened to Frankie? Was he . . . was he murdered?"

"Of course not. He probably just had too much whisky." I could tell she wasn't convinced. "Listen, Mary. Did you know he was a demoted auxiliary?"

She held her eyes on me then shook her head slowly. "Does that matter now?"

I met her gaze. "Not to him it doesn't," I said, turning to the door. "But it might do to me."

Chapter Four

I came out on to the street, saw that Hamilton's Jeep had gone and breathed a sigh of relief. He'd be tied up in the Council meeting for a couple of hours. By the time he was back at his desk in the castle I'd have checked the dead man's DM file in peace.

I cadged a bottle of water from a guardsman and crossed the street. Through the window I could see the storeman Angus Drem in a chair, his shoulders in a state of collapse and his face drenched in sweat. I tapped on the pane and signalled to Davie to suspend operations.

"What's the story then?" I asked when he joined me.

"Standard bottom-feeding Supply Directorate lowlife." Davie grinned. "I'm ninety-nine per cent sure he's coming clean with me."

"So what have you got?" I emptied the waterbottle. "Did he knock around with the dead man?"

Davie shook his head. "Says not. He shared the odd bottle with him but nothing more than that. He says Frankie Thomson was a tight bugger. He didn't say much even when he was pissed. Drem reckoned there was more to Frankie Thomson than he was letting on, but he could never get him to talk about himself."

"So he knew Frankie was a demoted auxiliary?"

"Aye. He saw his ID card not long after he was billeted here."

"The bottles they shared – who provided them?"

"They both used their weekly vouchers. Drem's never worked in the Alcohol Department."

"We can check that easily enough. Not that where you work in the Supply Directorate makes any difference. The guys in the black market can provide anyone with anything."

Davie nodded. "Still, I reckon he's telling the truth about the booze. He's been very co-operative."

"I'll bet. You didn't leave any marks on him, did you, guardsman?"

He gave me a disapproving look. "Certainly not. That would be contrary to the *Public Order in Practice* manual."

"Very amusing." I'd written that when I was in the directorate.

"How about you? What did you find out from the woman?"

I told him Mary's story.

"There was another man drinking with him last night?"

I nodded. "It couldn't have been Drem though. He's the wrong build and Mary would have recognised him."

"What shall we do with that streak of piss?"

"Hand him over to Raeburn 01 and get him put in a cell. Not too uncomfortable, mind. We might need his co-operation again."

Davie smiled grimly. "You're too soft, Quint."

Sometimes I worry about my assistant. Like most of the guard, he's become more hardline since the Council loosened the City Regulations. Then again, he definitely has his uses. But what kind of two-faced bastard do I make myself by encouraging him?

The scene-of-crime squad was still hard at work in the dead man's house and the Raeburn auxiliaries were taking statements from the residents of Bell Place. Time for us to move on.

The barracks commander came over as Davie and I were getting into the Land-Rover. "I want to redeploy my personnel," he said, glancing around. There were a lot of sweat-stained and short-tempered auxiliaries in the vicinity. "They've got other duties and this isn't exactly a high-priority operation."

"I'll pass your views on to the public order guardian," I said sharply. Raeburn 01's jaw dropped. I liked that. I wasn't going to feed the gossip mill by telling him Frankie Thomson was a DM so I had to tighten the screw. "You're probably right, commander. It's probably natural causes." I held my eyes on his. "But just imagine what'll happen to your career if you take people off the case and it turns out to be a suspicious death." I gave him an acid smile. "Do you like picking potatoes?"

Raeburn 01 pursed his lips and decided against answering that question.

"We're done here," I said. "Send copies of all the statements to the castle and post a couple of sentries at the area the scene-of-crime squad has sectioned off."

"Could it be a murder case?" the commander asked in a low voice.

I shrugged. "I won't be able to decide that if your auxiliaries don't stay on the job."

He gave me a snotty look and turned away.

"Raeburn 01?" I called.

He stopped and glanced back.

"Thanks for your help."

He almost fainted. Politeness doesn't feature much in contemporary Edinburgh, especially during the Big Heat. I like to maintain standards.

"Don't take the piss, Quint," Davie said in a loud whisper.

My mobile rang as we were heading for the central zone.

"Where are you?"

"Great goddess of wisdom, your voice is—"

"Be quiet, Quint. I'm standing in the mortuary waiting to begin the post-mortem. I have a special dispensation to miss the Council meeting. Are you coming or not?"

Shit. I'd forgotten about the p-m. Frankie Thomson's file

would have to wait for a while. "On my way, Sophia. Out," I said, wondering again why she was so interested in this particular dead citizen.

"Sophia?" Davie asked, a smile blossoming beneath his beard. "Sophia? Tell me it isn't true."

I became aware of a burning sensation on my cheeks. "What do you mean?"

"Not the Ice Queen? You're not . . . ?"

"The infirmary, guardsman. At speed." I glanced at him. "And if you want to stay part of this investigation, I advise you to keep your mind on the job."

"Okay, boss." He grinned and turned right on to Queen Street. "As long as you promise to do the same."

"At last." The medical guardian, in green robes from head to toe, looked up from the naked corpse on the table. "I could have finished this by now. I don't know why the regulations require investigating officers to be present."

I shrugged as I pulled on surgical overalls. "Blame the moron who wrote them."

She gave me a piercing look. "I do, citizen."

"Very good, guardian." I joined her by the slab. "My experience shows that senior medical staff sometimes need to be carefully watched." The medical auxiliary who was assisting took such a sharp breath that his mask almost disappeared into his mouth. I smiled at Sophia and pulled up my own mask.

"As you can see," she said, "we've stripped the body and started the preliminary investigation. Samples of the faecal matter on the dead man's underwear and trousers have been taken for analysis, as have scrapings from his fingernails. Hairs from head and pubis plucked, fingerprints taken, dried blood swabbed from his right foot—"

"As per routine," I interrupted. "Anything unusual strike you?"

She shook her head, as much to let me know that she wasn't going to be rushed into a premature opinion as to answer the question. She'd swallowed a lot more manuals than I'd written and she was never one to let her imagination roam free.

"Photographs taken, clothing removed, stains sampled," she continued. "Fibres removed, individual garments bagged."

I looked over at Davie and raised my eyes to the ceiling. He didn't respond. Like Hamilton, he's never been fond of autopsies, but unlike his superior he's tried to pay attention to mortuary procedures. Even if they put his breakfast at risk.

"Right, let's get on to the important part." Sophia's voice was still dispassionate.

I joined her by the upper part of the body. Frankie Thomson's mouth was open, the tongue partially protruding. The arms were by his sides and his legs were about six inches apart. In the warmth outdoors rigor mortis had been relatively slow to develop, allowing the morgue staff to reduce the wide angle between the legs that we'd seen on the river bank. Lividity brought about by the body's position face down on the ground was visible on the front parts of the trunk and limbs.

Sophia was talking into a microphone suspended from the ceiling – a technological advance on the old Medical Directorate style of nurses taking dictation that she was very proud of. The fact that it had been standard equipment for decades in pre-Enlightenment Edinburgh didn't bother her. She walked round the table slowly, stopping from time to time. Apart from the body's undernourished look, probably a combination of bad food and excessive alcohol, it was in reasonable condition. I thought back to the horrors I'd seen in this room – torsos without heads, mutilated bodies with organs missing, cadavers with items stuffed into their innermost recesses. Frankie Thomson was a picture compared with them, at least for the time being. Even Davie looked in command of himself.

Then Sophia picked up her dissecting knife. She opened the neck and her assistant took a sample of blood from the jugular vein.

"He seems to have been a heavy drinker," I said.

She nodded. Then she started to make the long Y-incision from inside the shoulders to the groin, describing a semi-circle round the tough tissue of the navel.

Like Davie, I took my eyes off the body as the dissection proceeded. There was a time when I followed the pathologist's every move. Not because I didn't trust Sophia's predecessors — though there had been at least one who misbehaved — and not because of some dubious macho desire for blood and guts and gore. No, the post-mortem used to be the royal road to understanding the deaths I was investigating. It was in the mortuary that you found out how the killers' minds worked and how their victims were tied to the crimes they committed. The problem was, you also found out how low human beings can sink. That kind of knowledge pollutes your soul, so now I let the experts get on with it and try to keep my eyes off the worst.

"Stomach now," the guardian said to her assistant. She drew it away from the abdomen and put it carefully into the large stainless-steel receptacle he held out.

"Shall I open the wall?" the auxiliary asked.

"No," Sophia replied firmly. "I'll examine it afterwards."

I remembered what she'd said about the dead man having consumed something that didn't agree with him. "Anything particular in mind?"

"I don't make presuppositions," she replied, glancing across at me. "Neither do I rule anything out."

I should have known better than to try and force her hand.

"I'll examine the liver later too." Sophia held up the dark red organ and scrutinised it briefly. She put it in the scales and read off the weight. Then she moved back up the abdomen and waited as her assistant opened the thoracic cavity.

Davie stepped back as the bones were cracked, looking like he wished he was back on the border in the middle of a dissident raid.

Sophia took the lungs out and applied her blade. Then she

stood up straight. "He didn't drown, Quint. There's no sign of any froth inside."

"Right, that's one possibility ruled out. What else can we say?"

"Very little as yet, citizen." She was back in Ice Queen mode. "As I said, I'll be running tests on the stomach and its contents and the liver. Also the heart, blood, vitreous humour and so on."

"And you'll let me know." I stepped back, beckoning to Davie.

She gave me what might have been the slightest hint of an amused look. "And I'll let you know."

"No chance of any prognosis about time or cause of death, I don't suppose?" I said from the door.

"You don't suppose correctly."

Squad dismissed.

I wanted to get across to the archive but I badly needed to take on more liquid. The infirmary had been fitted with air-conditioning in the early years of the century, but it hadn't been turned on for a long time and the Black Hole of Calcutta would have been cooler. We went to the canteen, where Davie rapidly got over the post-mortem and put away what he regards as a normal lunch. I had just the one filled roll with my jug of water. There's a limit to how much grit-ridden luncheon meat and grey mayonnaise I can eat. Nursing auxiliaries and citizen workers sat slumped over the Formica-topped tables in the heat, their eyes anywhere except on their plates.

"So what do you reckon, Quint?" Davie asked, his mouth full. He once told me that after the rations he'd had on the auxiliary training programme, he could eat anything. I thought he was joking.

I poured the last of the jug's contents into my chipped glass. "I reckon we're going to the castle, my friend. You can keep Hamilton off my back while I hit the DM archive."

"Keep the public order guardian off your back?" Davie asked. "How do you expect me to manage that?"

I got up from the table. "You'll think of something, my friend."

"Oh, aye." He followed me to the door. "I tell you what. I'll distract him with a heap of barracks surveillance reports if you answer me one question."

I fell for it. "Okay, what do you want to know?"

He caught up with me and grabbed my arm. "Are you really messing about with the medical guardian, Quint?"

I glared at him. "No comment, guardsman."

He laughed at length. "Just watch out for chilblains on your . . ." He broke off as a pair of winsome young nursing auxiliaries passed into the canteen.

Saved by the belles.

The archive containing all the files on the city's demoted auxiliaries is maintained by the Public Order Directorate and housed in the castle for maximum security. Imagine the embarrassment to the Council if the crimes committed by its trusted servants became common knowledge. Some of the reasons for demotion are seriously pathetic: repeated refusal to accept a partner in the weekly sex session, illicit meetings with the family members auxiliaries are supposed to cut themselves off from, even persistent failure to report for duty on time. On the other hand, some offences are potentially scandalous: bribery, corruption, summary execution of deserters. Most demoted auxiliaries fall between the two poles, disobedience being the most frequent violation of regulations. That's what did for me back in 2015. I lost my lover Caro and my faith in the Enlightenment at the same time, and it was easier to drop out than to take any more orders in the directorate. One thing about being a DM is that you understand what it's like to reach the end of the road, meaning that you regard fellow ex-auxiliaries in a different light from other ranks in the city – which was partly why I wanted to find out about Frankie Thomson before anyone else did. But that wasn't all. I was still puzzled about the way he was sprawled on the river bank wearing only one shoe. And about the presence in his kitchen of three bottles of a previously unknown brand of whisky with little more than a sip taken from one of them.

The DM archive is in what were originally cart sheds at the western end of the castle rock. They were turned into tearooms in the last century but the Public Order Directorate has no time for such frivolities, especially since no tourists have been allowed through the gatehouse since the Council took charge.

I flashed my authorisation at the senior of the two guardsmen at the entrance. I could tell he knew me, but he still went carefully through the procedure of confirming my credentials with the command centre and entering my details in a logbook. Eventually I was allowed in to the building. An elderly female auxiliary with a sour face met me and led me to the requisition desk. There was absolutely no chance of me getting away with omitting my name from the records like I'd done in the citizen archive. I filled in the form for Thomson, Francis Dee, and waited in the stifling heat for the file to be located.

"Here you are, Citizen Dalrymple," the clerk said drily. "I'll be checking that all the pages are intact before you're allowed to leave."

I resisted the temptation to make a comment involving the Latin word "intacta" and took the weighty grey folder to a desk in the far corner of the poorly lit room. All the windows were shuttered to keep the sun and curious eyes out.

I got stuck into the dead man's tale – and a rather curious one it was. Frankie Thomson had been an Enlightenment member for two years when the party won the last election. He'd worked for the only Scottish bank to survive the chaos of the financial crash of 2001 and, reading between the lines, I got the idea that he'd handled some deals that benefited the party. After independence, even though he was in his thirties, he went through the newly instituted auxiliary training programme – tours of duty fighting on the border and against the drugs gangs included – then had been posted to Napier Barracks in the south of the city. His barracks number was Napier 25 and he'd spent ten years doing general administrative work, interspersed with periods of active duty on the streets – even senior auxiliaries had to do that at the height of the drugs wars.

Then things went murky. The old harpy at the desk might be keeping a close eye on what I did with the file but that hadn't always been the case. From 2013 until he was demoted in April 2024, Frankie Thomson's documentation was much less complete. There were the usual barracks evaluations, sex session reports (he was hetero), medical records (which referred to his fondness for the bottle) and lists of close colleagues – the last with very few numbers on them, suggesting the dead man wasn't exactly the sociable type. But, contrary to standard practice, there was hardly anything about what he actually spent his days doing. There were none of the pro formas detailing work rosters and no progress reports by senior auxiliaries. Someone had weeded this file, probably before it arrived in this archive. It was only by chance that I came across a reference to his place of work in a physical fitness programme he'd been ordered to attend in 2018. It made me think though. Apparently Napier 25 worked in the Finance Directorate – and not just in any old department. He'd been a member of the elite Strategic Planning Department.

I leaned back and the poor-quality chair beneath me creaked alarmingly. Frankie Thomson might have ended up as a bog cleaner but he was massively overqualified for that job. I turned pages and found his Demotion Charge Sheet. At least no one had pilfered that. He'd been done not for ripping off the city, like certain people I could think of in the Finance Directorate, but for sticking his hand down a female tourist's blouse in the Three Graces night club – she'd been a member of a group of potential investors Frankie was entertaining. Molesting the city's visitors is as heinous a crime as you can commit in the Council's eyes, especially in a joint like the Three Graces where the biggest spenders go, but something bothered me about the charge. I turned back to the front of the file. The dead man stared out at me from his auxiliary-entry photograph, his face twenty years younger and partially obscured by the beard required of his rank until recently. He had been thin then as well, his features weaselly, and his eyes seemed to look at the lens reluctantly. I went back to the sex sessions reports I'd scanned earlier and confirmed what I thought I'd registered – that he was so lukewarm in his relations with female auxiliaries that several of them had filed complaints about his "lack of zeal", as the barracks phrase goes. So what the hell was he suddenly doing grabbing the fifty-nine-year-old breasts of a Lebanese casino owner's wife?

Before I got any further, my mobile rang.

"Dalrymple? Where are you?" The public order guardian sounded unusually mellow. Perhaps the Council had voted to reinstate flogging.

"Checking some records." Never be any more specific than you have to when reporting to guardians.

"Are you any further on with the dead man?"

"Getting there. I need a bit more time."

There was a pause and I thought I was about to be blasted. "I hope it's worth it," Hamilton said threateningly.

"Catch you later, Lewis. Out."

I looked down at the photograph of Frankie Thomson – Napier 25 as was – and rubbed my cheek. Time was beginning to press and I knew where I wanted to go next. I punched Davie's number.

"I thought you were meant to be distracting you know who."

"I tried, Quint. I thought he'd got sidelined laying into a guardsman who was caught listening to Radio Free Glasgow."

"That explains why he sounded cheerful."

"Yeah, well, the guardsman answered him back and that reminded the guardian of you."

"Brilliant." I headed for the desk to return the file. "Fancy spending some time in a smoke-filled room?"

The elderly auxiliary took the file and gave me the eye.

"Frankie Thomson's place of work?"

"Well spotted, guardsman. Can you find something appropriate to wear? Your uniform won't go down too well with the tourists."

"And your festering T-shirt and stained shorts will?" Davie said sarcastically. "And stop calling me guardsman. You're the only person who still does."

"I haven't got used to you being a commander," I said. "We can go via my place so I can change, guardsman."

"What difference will that make?" he asked, laughing and then breaking the connection.

We left the Land-Rover round the corner in Belford Road and hoofed it to the club in Bell's Brae. It was on the ground floor of what had been a nineteenth-century coachhouse before the trendy modernisers got to it fifteen years before the Enlightenment. Dean Village was a classic example of a former working area that changed beyond all recognition because of the demand for accommodation near the city centre. The old tanneries and flour mills ended up as luxury hotels and flats – till the economy went down the toilet and what used to be the UK became several dozen versions of the field of Armageddon. Below us the Water of Leith skirted frog-haunted reeds, trickling its meagre stream around the moss-covered stones.

The marijuana club advertised its presence by means of a purple and green façade. Above the door there hung a large sign with writing that was supposed to look spaced out, man. The word "smoke" was enclosed in a white cloud drifting over an expanse of water that was much deeper and much bluer than the neighbouring river. And just in case customers got the idea that designers in Edinburgh were completely lacking in imagination, the guardsman on the door was wearing a long black wig, tight satin trousers with gold fly buttons, and a yellow shirt open to display his massive pectorals. No doubt he also played air guitar solos when he got bored.

Not that he was bored now. One look at Davie's beard and off-duty guard personnel khaki trousers was enough for him to identify his rank. He needed a few more looks at me though. It must have been the tight-legged black trousers and the T-shirt with the "Heavy, Oh So Very Heavy" logo I'd dredged up from the suitcase of antediluvian rags I keep under my bed. Eventually I put him out of his misery by flashing my directorate authorisation.

"What's the problem?" he asked, now even more worried.

"Don't worry, we're not doing an inspection." He'd probably heard that one before. All the city's tourist premises are subject to spot checks for black-market activities and inspectors often go in disguise. They've also been known to pretend they're on other business to gain the confidence of staff — just one of the many ways the Council keeps a grip.

"Do you know Frankie Thomson?" I asked.

"Frankie who?" he asked, squinting into the sun.

"Frankie Thomson. He's a cleaner here."

"Oh, him." The auxiliary looked unimpressed. "The piss artist. Makes more mess than he cleans up, I reckon. I haven't seen him today." Then he got a bit more excited. "Why? What's he done?" Typical guardsman's suspicious mind.

I ignored the question. "Who does he knock around with? Have you seen him sneak his pals in?" Citizen staff have been known to do that after doing a deal with bent auxiliaries.

He shook his wig emphatically. "No way. They don't get away with that here. We run a tight ship."

I looked up at the sign above his head. "Looks like your funnel could do with a clean."

He stared at me uncomprehendingly as I walked inside.

"Don't mind him," I heard Davie saying. "Heat's fried his brains."

"Such loyalty," I muttered, then pushed open the inner door. We were immediately enveloped in a fug of bittersweet smoke. The lights were low and it was hard to make things out. The same couldn't be said for the music. It wasn't loud enough to bring the walls of Jericho down but it would have made a fair start. The pounding of the bass and drums came up your legs from the floor like unfriendly boa constrictors and set your inner organs in violent disarray. I was all shook up, and not just because they were playing "Paranoid".

A female auxiliary loomed out of the murk wearing a torn vest that made a major exhibition of her breasts and leather shorts that must have hurt like hell – what the Tourism Directorate imagined a rock chick looked like. She clocked us immediately and the false smile died on her purple-painted lips.

"Who's in charge?" I shouted.

She pointed to the bar and went back to her customer. There was an old-fashioned propeller fan doing not much to clear the air in the middle of the cavernous room. As it was early afternoon, only a few of the tables were occupied – mainly lone tourist guys with beer bellies, joints between their fingers and Prostitution Services Department women leading them on. The one who met us was already grinding her backside into an oriental's groin. His hands were on her breasts through the rents in her top, his eyes rolling back in a half-stupor. He had his lower lip between his teeth like he was trying to get his priorities straight. Meanwhile the woman was going for world championship lap-dancing gold.

Another female auxiliary appeared in front of us. This one was middle-aged, with short grey hair, a matching grey skirt and a hard set to her jaw. The boss. I pointed to the door at the back marked "Strictly Private" and followed her over. Davie went to check out the bar.

"And you are?" she asked, closing the sound-proofed door.

I shook my ears back into action. "Dalrymple."

The auxiliary's eyes opened wide.

"Don't worry, it's only a routine enquiry."

"Since when did you handle routine enquiries, citizen?" She reached into a drawer and took out her barracks badge.

"Have we met before?" I leaned forward. "Knox 42?"

She shook her head. "I know you though. You catch the bad

people." Her eyes were more playful than the rest of her face, which wasn't a hard trick for them to pull off.

"The bad people. Yes, well, I don't know if the person I'm going to ask you about was necessarily one of those."

Knox 42's lips twitched for a second or two. She probably thought that constituted a smile. Still, some of her rank don't even make that much of an effort to be human.

"You never know, citizen. It's often the most unlikely people who turn out to be the worst ones of all." Her voice was flat and empty. She was old enough to have been in the Enlightenment from the beginning like I had. Like Frankie Thomson had. We were the ones who had the most to be disappointed about, who'd been let down most by jokers who should never have been allowed on to the Council. If I'd been put in charge of a licensed dope and wanking parlour, I wouldn't have been too happy either.

"True enough," I said. I'd have liked to talk to her about the old days and what we used to believe in but it was far too late for that. "Frankie Thomson. What can you tell me about him?"

"What can *you* tell *me* about the old sot, citizen?" No twitch of the lips this time. "He didn't turn up for work this morning. I had to get a couple of the girls to clean out the bogs."

"I hope they washed their hands before you set them loose on clients."

That went down like compulsory overtime at harvest time on the city farms. Eventually Knox 42 went to the filing cabinet on the rear wall of the windowless room.

"What do you want to know, citizen?" she asked wearily.

"Why don't you just give me the file?" I took a chance and smiled at her. Amazingly that worked. She handed it over.

I flicked through the pages. They were mainly time sheets and appraisals. Frankie T. didn't seem to have been a favourite of his boss.

"You knew he was a DM."

"As you see." Knox 42's gaze was unwavering.

"Did that cause you any problems?"

"Why should it? City Regulations state that demoted auxiliaries are to be treated in exactly the same way as other ordinary
citizens."

I smiled. "That's a nice fairy-tale. You and I both know that
auxiliaries often give their former colleagues a bad time."

Knox 42 shrugged. "I don't work that way. DMs aren't my
favourite people but I don't come down hard on them."

"That's a relief," I said. "What about the things you don't put
in here?"

The auxiliary poured herself a glass of water from a bottle she
took from her drawer and drank deeply. She didn't offer me one.
"Like what, citizen?"

"Like did you let him take the remains of the joints from the
ashtrays? Did you let him bring his friends in for a peek at the
girls? Did you feed him booze to keep him quiet when things in
here got out of hand?"

The edge I'd slipped into my voice didn't seem to get to her.

"No, citizen," she said, looking at me stolidly. "None of
those."

"Come on," I scoffed. "Everyone knows that cleaners in the
clubs are a source of black-market grass and tobacco."

Knox 42 shook her head. "Not from here they aren't. I check
the grass and hash stocks every day personally and I distribute
them to the girls myself. All personnel are body-searched every
time they leave the premises. And the ashtrays are emptied into a
sack that's sealed and sent back to the Drugs Department daily
for reconstitution." She gave me a stern glare that Hamilton
would have applauded wildly. "As for citizens other than
accredited staff even reaching the front door, forget it."

Impressive. I almost believed her and, anyway, the scene-of-
crime squad would report any traces of grass or tobacco found in
the dead man's flat. But it was all a bit mechanical.

"How about whisky? Frankie was a big fan of that."

She blinked involuntarily. "Whisky? We don't keep any."

Marijuana clubs exist to supply soft drugs to the tourists. Even on these premises clients are restricted to three joints per person per day. The only alcohol they're meant to sell is low-strength beer — known throughout the city as "Golden Drizzle" — so that the customers don't get too wrecked. But it's common knowledge in the guard that tourists with a big wallet can get anything they want.

I decided to play with a concrete ball. "All right, Knox 42, here's the story. Frankie Thomson's dead." I watched her closely but she was being a good auxiliary and impersonating a block of granite when tension mounts. "There's a chance that he drank himself to death and I want to know where he got the whisky."

"Citizens earn vouchers for Supply Directorate spirits," she said in a monotone. "Why do you think he got his whisky here?"

I wasn't planning on telling her about the bottles of the Ultimate Usquebaugh we'd found. "Look, Knox 42, we both know you get supplies of top-quality whisky for seriously loaded customers. Give me the paperwork, please."

She did. I made sure she stayed where she was while I went through it. It didn't take long. She had only twenty-three bottles in stock, none of them with the same name as those in the dead man's flat.

"Are you sure there's nothing more you can tell me about Frankie Thomson?" I said as I got up to go.

Knox 42 shook her head slowly. "He was just a cleaner. He came in the morning, cleaned the bogs — not very well — and the tables and floors. He didn't pilfer drink, he didn't get his hands on reefer butts and he didn't bring his friends in. I very much doubt that he had any friends, citizen." She may well have been right; that squared with what Drem had told Davie.

I went back out into the smoke and aural thunder zone. My side-kick was behind the bar writing in his notebook, a barman in a frizzy blond wig staring at him moodily.

"Are you done?" I asked in as loud a voice as I could manage.

He nodded. "Just about. I've checked the cellar and the rest of the rooms. They've got twenty-three bottles of the hard stuff, none called . . ."

I raised a finger to stop him just in case the barman could lip-read.

A few minutes later we shouldered our way out past a group of excited Russian tourists with clippered hair and tattoos on their forearms. I was willing to bet that the stock of whisky was about to take a big hit. And that the rock chicks were in for a lot of sedentary bump and grind.

The music had changed but not for the better. Now they were playing "Mistreated".

"What next?" Davie asked as we got back to the guard vehicle.

"You tell me." My throat was dry and the walk had made me short of breath. Or perhaps my lungs had contracted something virulent from the atmosphere in the club.

"The archives again?"

"Who's a clever boy then? I want to see Frankie Thomson's ordinary citizen file. Maybe we'll strike lucky and find someone he used to get pissed with."

"And more likely we won't."

"Don't be so pessimistic." I climbed in and beat him to the bottle under the driver's seat.

"Bastard," he said. "That's my water."

I sluiced down my throat. "Now, now. Citizens and auxiliaries have equal rights in Edinburgh nowadays." I handed him the bottle and watched as he tried to laugh and drink at the same time. Not many guard personnel took that line seriously.

"Right?" Davie said, starting the engine. "You have the right to spend the rest of the day sweating in file graveyard and I have the right to leave you to it." He ground up the hill towards Queensferry Street. The sun was to our left, making me blink and then curse. I'd left my shades at home.

"You might as well go up to the castle while I'm checking out

78

Frankie Thomson," I conceded. "Maybe have a go at pretending to Hamilton that you're a real guard commander."

"Rather than your chauffeur, you mean?"

We passed an Edlott booth. Customers at this one were being harangued by a former winner dressed as King James VI, complete with catamite. Some tourists were examining the small boy with confused looks on their faces. The tableau reminded me of Fordyce Kennedy. I'd been ignoring that case completely.

"Davie, when you're in the castle check with the command centre if the missing Edlott winner's turned up."

"Okay." He turned and gave me a dirty grin. "If you like, I'll even go and visit his delectable daughter."

A vision of the sultry Agnes floated up before me. It struck me that maybe I was spending far too much time on the DM who'd been found by the Water of Leith.

Chapter Five

I hit the central archive on George IVth Bridge for the second time that day and got my body temperature down to a reasonable level in the marble halls. I could have gone to Napier Barracks and tried to track down anyone who knew the dead man – I was still intrigued by the fact that his file in the demoted auxiliary archive had been weeded – but it was less hassle to follow up this angle first. Sitting at a desk in the double-height room, I worked through Frankie Thomson's ordinary citizen file, the one covering his life after he'd been demoted. You'd think the Public Order Directorate would want to keep such records with the DM files in the castle, but the rationale seems to be that people reduced to the ranks are no longer entitled even to archive space in such hallowed ground. I smelled some kind of half-baked symbolism.

All I got was confirmation of what I'd already learned – that Frankie Thomson kept himself to himself and liked the booze. Ordinary citizens are not subject to quite as much supervision as auxiliaries but they still have to list their friends and workmates. The only name given by the dead man was Angus Drem and Davie had already established how limited that relationship was – though it might be worth putting the shits up the storeman again in case he'd been lying. Frankie T. apparently didn't have anything going with members of the other gender either. After the Council made the weekly sex session voluntary, he'd left the sexual relations section of his personal evaluation form blank. I began to feel even sorrier for him as I read his work records. He'd been a cleaner at several other marijuana clubs before Smoke on the Water and his work reports were mostly unfavourable. His latest medical had turned up signs of cirrhosis and he'd been told to stop drinking. The bottles in his kitchen showed how much attention he'd paid to that instruction. Frankie's handwriting had become a random scrawl and the little he said about himself struck me as a coded call for help that no one had picked up.

" 'The drink doesn't work'," read a voice from behind my shoulder. "It looks like it worked plenty of damage on his handwriting though."

"What are you doing sneaking around behind people, Ray?"

The archivist put his hand on the back of my neck and squeezed hard. "I work here, remember? In fact, I'm in charge here." He leaned closer. "Thomson, Francis Dee. Who he?"

I put down the form and turned towards him. "Thomson, Francis Dee, deceased, he."

Ray sat on the desk and scratched the stump of his arm. He seemed to have been doing a lot of that recently. Maybe the heat was getting to him. "What happened to him? Why are you so interested?"

"I'm not so interested. I'm just checking his background. We found him on the bank of the Water of Leith with his face in the stream."

"Really?" Ray looked surprised. "Heatstroke?"

"Could be. We'll soon find out from the post-mortem." I started putting the papers back in some sort of order then looked round at him. "I don't suppose you knew the guy? He was a DM. Napier 25 was his barracks number."

Ray thought for a moment then shook his head. "Nope. I've never known many people in Napier." He glanced down at the papers on the desk, the expression of surprise still on his face.

"I'll look after that," he said. "The file will have to be taken off the open shelves now the subject is dead. You've saved me the trouble of finding it when the death notification comes in."

"On the house, my friend."

"Speaking of which, do you fancy a dram?" He picked up the grey folder and moved away, not bothering to wait for an answer.

Up in his office, Ray scrabbled around in a drawer for a couple of glasses then pulled out a bottle of barracks malt.

"Highland Breeze," I read. "Never heard of that one."

"New shipment," he said, stripping the seal and pulling the cork with his teeth — which impressed me a lot — before pouring a couple of heavy slugs. "Apparently there's been a shake-up of the suppliers the Council has started using across the firth."

"You mean the gangs have been playing bury the claymore again?"

"Bury the claymore," he repeated, laughing quietly. "I like it." He pushed one of the glasses across his desk.

"Still reading Wilfred Owen?" I asked.

"What?" For a couple of seconds he looked like he'd seen an unfriendly ghost.

I inclined my head towards the book that was lodged behind a file at the front of his desk.

Ray leaned forward and took it clumsily. "Wilfred Owen." He repeated the name slowly. "He really was a great poet, you know." He didn't sound all that convinced.

I had the glass halfway to my lips when my mobile rang. I put the glass down and eventually got the contraption out of my bag.

"Dalrymple."

"Quint, listen to this." Sophia's voice was at a higher pitch than normal. I even thought I heard it waver, which was definitely a first. "What the dead man drank . . . it wasn't straight whisky."

"What do you mean? It's not illegal to add water."

"This is serious," Sophia said, with what almost amounted to a scream. "The whisky he drank was lethal."

"Lethal? How?"

"I can't talk now. This connection may not be secure." There had been a few cases of dissidents listening in to guard communications but I wasn't worrying about them at this point. I'd just got the message. "There's an emergency Council meeting in a quarter of an hour. Be there. Out."

"Put it down, Ray!" I yelled.

He froze, the measure of whisky he'd just poured himself an inch from his lips.

"The glass! Put it down!"

This time he did what I said.

"What the fuck . . . ?"

I plugged the cork back in the bottle and stuck it in my bag.

"Here, that's mine," Ray said weakly.

"Trust me," I said. "Don't drink any unfamiliar brands of whisky till you hear from me again. And don't talk to anyone about the dead man, Ray." I leaned over and relieved him of Frankie Thomson's file.

As I reached the door, I glanced back. Ray was standing with his mouth open, his single arm clutching the book of Great War poetry to his chest.

My mobile went three more times when I was on the street. I told Davie and Hamilton to meet me on the Lawnmarket and the chief toxicologist to get himself down to the Council chamber at maximum speed. It turned out he was already there.

"This is a nightmare, Dalrymple," Hamilton said as Davie floored the Jeep's accelerator. Tourists on the High Street suddenly got very close to the shopfronts.

"Not yet it isn't but it may well turn into one. I presume you're arranging searches of all stocks of spirits for the Ultimate Usquebaugh?"

He nodded. "The command centre's on that, pending Council approval. Guard personnel are going to contact every bar in the tourist zone."

"I suppose they'll get round to the citizen outlets eventually,"

I said ironically. It was typical of a guardian to safeguard the city's customers before its local population.

"The Supply Directorate's going to do that, Quint," Davie said, giving me an angry glance.

"Okay." I nodded at the guardian. "Sorry."

He ignored that. "The bonded warehouses are also being advised," he said. "And the Transport Directorate is vetting all deliveries."

"What else?" I grabbed the bottom of my seat as Davie skidded round the corner at the bottom of the Canongate and roared into the yard outside the Council chamber. I had a sudden vision of my father. "Jesus, the retirement homes." The city's pensioners get a dram every day to keep them sweet.

"Done," Davie said. "I told the supervisor at Hector's place to keep the whisky supply locked up."

I smiled at him lamely, embarrassed that he'd remembered the old man before I had.

We juddered to a halt.

"Come on, Dalrymple. We'll be late."

"All right, Lewis." I looked back at Davie. "Keep on top of all this while we're tied up here."

He nodded. "I'll be in the command centre till you're finished."

I followed the public order guardian up the steps and into the meeting place. The building was in the shape of an upturned boat. It was the only one of a cluster of similar structures that had survived the wave of destruction before the last election. Behind us a convoy of Land-Rovers and stationwagons carrying guardians had blocked the entrance to the car park. You don't get many traffic jams in Enlightenment Edinburgh. Then again, it isn't every day that someone puts something lethal in a bottle of whisky. The Ultimate Usquebaugh my arse.

We were admitted to the Council chamber. In the old days, when the guardians weren't interested in openness, they were happy to use the Assembly Hall on the Mound – it's nearer the castle and most of the guardians' directorate headquarters. But they were forced to make an effort at public accountability in the wake of the "iron boyscouts" and the unrest caused by their harsh regime a couple of years ago. So some bright spark came up with the idea of moving the location of the Council's daily meeting to what used to be the Scottish Parliament – as if that ever had much to do with open government, with its carefully selected party lists and craven protection of vested interests.

I walked into the main hall and looked around the rows of leather seats and pine desks. No expense had been spared when the place was built on a site previously occupied by a brewery. Fluids of various kinds were apparently a major interest of the architect – it did rain a lot more then, I suppose. In addition to the boat design, there were pools of water placed inside and outside the structures to reflect the walls and sky. They don't do much of that these days as water's so precious that even the Council chamber has to do without it. The pools have been filled in with earth and layers of maroon and white pebbles laid over. During the civil disorder in 2003 some bent former policemen started stealing the furnishings and fittings, including the hundreds of computers and other electronic equipment. Unfortunately for them, the Enlightenment won power and declared that looting was punishable by death. The walls round the back which were pockmarked by the firing squad's bullets are a tourist attraction now.

The parliament chamber itself was decorated with as many native Scottish materials as the designers could think of – granite slabs, red sandstone facings, tapestries spun in the Outer Hebrides, chandeliers of Cairngorm quartz and the like. It was a pity the original occupants hadn't been worth as much. They spent their time abusing each other, extolling the supposed virtues of their socially divided land and claiming gigantic expenses. Unlike the building, they did not escape the wrath of the indigenous population.

"Take your seats, please." The senior guardian was the chief

of the Tourism Directorate. That explained why he looked like
he'd recently had several heart attacks. If a tourist went the way
of Frankie Thomson, the city's finances would be on a one-way
trip to the centre of the earth. He looked around nervously then
nodded to the sentry to pull shut the shining steel door that bore
the Council arms superimposed over the St Andrew's cross.
"This session will be in camera," he announced, his voice
unsteady. "Ordinary citizens are not attending."

I'd been wondering where the citizen observers were. Ten of
them are chosen by lot to oversee every Council meeting and one
of them even gets the privilege of being elected honorary
guardian for a day. The Council got the idea from the ancient
Athenian constitution. Not that it stops them running the city
how they see fit. They're just more careful about covering their
traces now.

"Before we move to the main business of this emergency
session, I am required to step down from the position of acting
senior guardian. My tenure of thirty meetings is concluded."

I swore under my breath. Typical bloody Council. If they'd
been on the *Titanic*, they'd have spent the minutes before the ship
went rudder-up discussing the details of the next three-year plan.
The idea behind the rotation of the senior guardian was
reasonable enough – to stop individual guardians gathering
too much personal power. I just wished the expiry of his term
had fallen on a different day.

The worst was yet to come.

"The rota shows that the medical guardian will take over." He
beckoned to Sophia to come to the rostrum and receive the
official gold badge adorned with the city's maroon heart emblem.
She didn't look too keen. Neither was I. Her workload had just
gone up by the power of ten and overnight sessions in my bed
would be very difficult for her to fit in.

Sophia pinned the insignia on her blouse and accepted the
thick file that her predecessor passed to her. Then she pulled out
a handkerchief and wiped her forehead. Like her colleagues she'd

turned up in formal dress for the meeting, as if the Big Heat didn't exist. They were all sweltering, the men in tweed jackets and corduroy trousers and the women in starched blouses and thick skirts. It wasn't long before they began to discard outer garments.

The new senior guardian took a deep breath and got going. "I must report to colleagues that we are facing a potentially dangerous situation. As you will have heard, a citizen was found dead on the bank of the Water of Leith this morning. Normal procedures were followed." She broke off her address that was in the stilted diction still favoured by the Council and glanced at me. "Citizen Dalrymple, the Council's special investigator, was involved from the outset."

I felt fifteen pairs of eyes on me. Fourteen of them belonged to guardians — there are fifteen members of their rank but Sophia was no longer on for eye contact. The other pair were the chief toxicologist's. Lister 25 pressed his lips together and nodded at me. His skin was wrinkled like a pachyderm's and he had a worrying habit of pouting at members of his own sex, but he was a secret blues freak who regarded Robert Johnson as a genius so I had no problem with him.

"Citizen?" Sophia's voice was sharp.

I smiled at her. "Senior guardian?" The title flowed from my tongue like peat.

"Kindly favour us with your report."

"Right," I said, pulling my thoughts together. It would have helped if Sophia gave the post-mortem results first but she had even more on her mind than I did. "The dead man Frankie — Francis Dee Thomson — was a demoted auxiliary."

A series of deep breaths was taken around the chamber. The guardians sat motionless. Lewis Hamilton was glaring at me, his cheeks darkening. I should have let him know about that on the way down. "His barracks number was Napier 25." I looked at the guardians. "Did any of you know him?"

They all shook their heads, some quicker than others. I wasn't too convinced. Then again, they were hardly likely to own up in front of their colleagues. The finance guardian looked blank – he'd taken over the directorate after Frankie Thomson's demotion.

I filled the guardians in about the dead man's background then turned to the physical evidence. "He seems to have had a pretty heavy alcohol problem. Three bottles of whisky with a label that hasn't previously been seen in the city were found in his flat. A small amount had been taken from one of them." I looked over at Sophia but she kept silent, wanting me to finish before we got into the technicalities. "Although the dead man seems to have been a solitary type, there's evidence from a witness that he had company last night. Apparently a thin man of average height with close-cropped hair. I've tried to identify potential contacts in the archives, without success as yet. Frankie Thomson was a cleaner at the Smoke on the Water marijuana club but the auxiliary in charge knows nothing about his private life."

"If I might come in here." Hamilton was eager to muscle in on my patch. "This afternoon I reviewed the statements taken by Raeburn Barracks personnel. I can confirm that the dead man's neighbours are unable or unwilling to supply any information about his activities or contacts. It may be necessary to press them harder."

"Did the scene-of-crime personnel turn anything up?" I asked.

Hamilton shook his head. "Not yet. No decent prints from the flat. No traces or prints around the body. We may still be lucky but . . ." His voice trailed off.

When the public order guardian starts talking about luck you know you're in big trouble.

I looked back at Sophia. So did everyone else.

"Your turn," I said encouragingly.

She wasn't impressed. "Thank you, citizen," she said icily, opening a large spiral notebook and running her finger down a page. "Very well. The post-mortem results are as yet incomplete but events are in danger of getting ahead of us. What I know so far is that death occurred between three and five o'clock this morning. I will be able to narrow that down further when my technicians complete other tests."

I was getting impatient. Judging by the rustling of papers and the shifting of backsides, I wasn't the only one. "The cause of death, guardian?" I asked. "Please."

She caught the desperation in my voice and blushed enough for me to notice. Maybe it reminded her of another place — one where she was wearing a lot less clothing than now. "I'm coming to that," she said hurriedly. "Anoxic anoxia." She glanced around at the mainly blank faces. "Asphyxia due to paralysis of the respiratory system."

I had to ask a leading question. Like most scientists, she was reluctant to report until she'd finished all her tests. "And the paralysis was caused by?"

Sophia looked over at the chief toxicologist. "The indications are that it was caused by nicotine poisoning."

There was a brief silence while the guardians took this in. It wasn't long before puzzled expressions began to develop. I was probably exhibiting one myself.

"Nicotine poisoning?" repeated the information guardian, the only other one apart from Hamilton who'd survived since before the "iron boyscouts". She tugged nervously at the plait she always made of her red hair. "Nicotine as in cigarettes?"

Sophia managed to nod and shake her head at the same time. "The same alkaloid substance, yes. But it is present in minuscule quantities in smoking tobacco."

"Is there any doubt about this?" Hamilton asked.

Sophia shook her head. "We were fortunate to locate the poison so quickly. Chief toxicologist?"

Lister 25 got to his feet with difficulty, the folds of flesh on his face vibrating. "Thank you, acting senior guardian. As you say, we were lucky. As soon as I received the bottles of the Ultimate Usquebaugh . . ."

"The Ultimate Usquebaugh?" The culture guardian gave an uncertain laugh. He was tall and thin, an expert in late-twentieth-century sensationalist art. No doubt that helped him in the running of Edlott. "Is that some kind of joke?"

"If so, it's not a particularly funny one," the toxicologist said, nettled by the interruption. "Something about the colour of the liquid immediately made me think of nicotine. In its pure form, it's a pale yellow oil but light makes it turn dark brown. Of course, it was entirely fortuitous that I formed the connection. The quantity of nicotine in the whisky is lethal but it has no effect on the whisky's overall colouring. All three bottles are contaminated."

"And you informed the medical guardian?" I asked.

"Correct," Sophia said, cutting in. "And when we looked for it, we found traces of nicotine in the oesophagus, stomach and other tissue."

"If you hadn't known what you were looking for you wouldn't have come across the nicotine so quickly."

She nodded. "Correct, citizen. There are no specific post-mortem pointers. After drinking the poisoned whisky the victim would have experienced painful burning in the mouth and oesophagus, then vomiting and diarrhoea. Death would have been preceded by violent spasms—"

"Whence the odd angle of the legs," I put in. "How long would it have taken for him to die?"

"As little as a minute or two."

I leaned back in my chair and looked up at the blue and white inlaid ceiling. The fact that the opened bottle of poisoned whisky was in Frankie Thomson's flat while the body was over fifty yards away bothered me.

"Are we dealing with a case of accidental death here?" The question came from the labour guardian, a middle-aged woman with an unusually fat face for a member of her ascetic rank. "Or of murder?"

Hamilton snorted to show what he thought of that, but his colleague had a point.

"Theoretically it could have been accident, suicide or murder," Sophia said. "But that doesn't change much regarding the measures that will need to be taken to prevent other deaths."

"What about the man who was with the victim?" Hamilton demanded, looking at me.

I shrugged. "He might have panicked and done a bunk." I shook my head. "I'm not convinced. I reckon suicide's a nonstarter. How would Frankie Thomson have known there was poison in the whisky? And how many people commit suicide when they've got company? He was an alcoholic. He'd have drunk anything for a hit. No, the whole set-up is strange – no fingerprints, the bottles sitting dead centre on the table with the labels facing the door, a slug taken from only one. My money's on murder."

"Pretty elaborate way to kill someone," the culture guardian muttered.

"That's what worries me," I said. "We've got to track down the source of the bottles as well as the guy who was with the victim."

Sophia cleared her throat. "Assuming it was murder, how would the killer obtain pure nicotine? Chief toxicologist?"

"He'd need a lab or a contact who had access to a lab. You can extract nicotine from chemical compounds. It's used in insecticides, for example. I can check how many such compounds are in the city."

I nodded slowly. This was getting worse by the minute. "But there's no public access to labs in Edinburgh. So we're either up against a corrupt auxiliary . . ." I glanced round at their faces, which were suitably shocked and horrified ". . . or someone from outside the border."

No one spoke for a while.

"Dissidents."

I was glad Hamilton had supplied the word. It's not one that guardians appreciate hearing from the likes of me. Dissidents officially don't exist but everyone knows someone who deserted and is trying to get back in. Some of them want to destabilise the

Council, but a lot of them are just headbangers who've discovered how unpleasant life is in the so-called free states outside the border. They're usually after easy pickings from the tourists. The City Guard catches the overwhelming majority of them.

"That will be for Citizen Dalrymple to ascertain," Sophia said, breaking the silence. It looked like I was officially off the search for the missing Edlott winner. "We must now discuss how we handle the wider implications of this death."

The tourism and culture guardians got to their feet simultaneously and started to speak. It was difficult to separate their words but the ones that featured most were "tourist revenue", "new Edlott initiative" and "overreaction".

Sophia's expression hardened during this joint tirade. When it eventually finished, she motioned imperiously to the guardians to sit down. "Do I understand you correctly, guardians?" she asked in an incredulous voice. "Are you seriously recommending nothing more than a cursory check of whisky supplies?"

The two guardians looked in surprise at their new leader. She was at least ten years younger than them.

"Well, yes," the tourism guardian said uncertainly. "Any disruption to the supply of whisky will immediately cause complaints from the city's visitors."

Sophia was shaking her head. "That is completely unacceptable. Imagine how much worse the consequences will be if a tourist dies from drinking poisoned whisky."

The culture guardian's normally suave appearance had gone walkabout. "But this Ultimate Usquebaugh is an unknown brand," he said, wiping his forehead with a bright green silk handkerchief that definitely didn't come from the Supply Directorate. "There are no grounds to presume that any of the normal brands are affected."

"It is impossible to be sure of that," Sophia said firmly. "Whoever was responsible for the bottles in the Colonies could have adulterated standard-issue supplies. As medical guardian I cannot allow any whisky to be supplied either to tourists or to citizens until it has been tested." She ran her eyes slowly around her colleagues. "As acting senior guardian I insist that the Council accepts this recommendation."

I was impressed. Sophia seemed to be completely committed to the health of everyone in the city whatever the danger of pissing off the drinking population. The senior guardian's powers only run as far as a casting vote in normal circumstances but in emergencies he or she can force rulings through. No one in the Council had the nerve to argue that this wasn't an emergency. On the other hand, Sophia was maybe overreacting by insisting that all whisky be tested.

There was then a discussion of the practicalities. These were to be overseen by Hamilton, reporting to Sophia, with the chief toxicologist in charge of the tests. Sophia also told Lewis that he was to give me everything I needed to find who was behind the nicotine poisoning.

As the talk continued, I drifted off into a reverie about the Ultimate Usquebaugh. What was the point of the name? I was bloody sure it had been chosen deliberately since the labels had been specially printed. I didn't get the chance to reach any conclusion about that.

"Citizen?" Sophia's voice was like a chainsaw hitting a steel cable. "Do you agree that no news of the poison should be publicised in any medium?"

"On the grounds that tourism will vanish overnight and the locals will take to the streets?" I asked ironically. I nodded reluctantly. "I suppose so. Of course, the auxiliary and citizen rumour factories will be working triple time, especially when people find out that their whisky vouchers are unredeemable."

"Let them drink beer," the culture guardian said with a high-pitched laugh.

Sophia gave him a dismissive look. "To recap. Chief toxicologist, you will oversee the testing of the stocks of whisky in the bonded warehouses, bars, the two city distilleries and citizen outlets. Public order guardian, you are to provide guard personnel to assist. Citizen Dalrymple, you are to track down the per-petrators of this lunacy."

No problem, I thought. We'll be done by tea-time.

The city's new chief executive looked across pointedly to the tourism and culture guardians. "All other colleagues will attempt to minimise the effects of this disruption to routine activities."

The meeting was adjourned. I walked out of the chamber. There were gaps in the members' desks where state-of-the-art computer equipment used to be before the guardians had it removed. For some reason the holes made me think of icons with the eyes poked out. That wasn't the only potent image around here. It struck me that discussing poisonous whisky in the former national parliament building that was located on the site of a brewery produced a vicious cocktail of signs and metaphors. I banished them from my mind and walked out humming Will Shade's "Better Leave That Stuff Alone".

I used to be dubious about that advice. Not any more.

Hamilton let Davie know we were finished and the Jeep appeared in a few minutes. As we accelerated out of the Council yard, he stood on the brakes. I almost went through the windscreen.

"Jesus, Davie." I retracted my face from the glass.

"Are you all right, Dalrymple?" the guardian asked, showing unusual concern.

"Just."

"Sorry, Quint." Davie had his head out the window. "Are you blind, citizen?" he shouted. "I'll have your licence."

"There's no time," I said, checking that my nose was unscathed and looking over at the Water Department tractor that had shot out in front of us. There was no tank on tow, so the driver had probably been playing "Give the Tourists Heart Failure". It's a game that's becoming more and more popular with citizen drivers.

"Stupid bastard," Davie said, mouthing the word again at the tractorman as we pulled past him.

Hamilton ignored that lapse from auxiliary standards of vocabulary. He had other things to worry about. "How are we going to handle this, Dalrymple?"

"You can put all your people on double shifts for a start. As well as the toxicology tests, we're going to have to check where every bottle of whisky in the city came from."

He nodded. "Hume 253's been working on the framework for that."

"We're getting there," Davie said. "I've got a team in the command centre allocating personnel to locations."

Hamilton was staring out at the garish shopfronts on the Royal Mile. "We haven't exactly got much to go on, have we?"

"You can say that again," I said.

We split up when we got to the castle. I set up camp in the guardian's office and tried to track down Napier Barracks personnel who knew the dead man. It wasn't long before I realised I was wasting my time. Everyone not on normal duties was involved in the whisky checks.

Then Davie called me from the command centre. "A case of undocumented whisky's been found in Bond No. 2 in Leith." His voice was unemotional but I could tell he was excited. "It's an unknown brand."

"Right." I headed for the door. "I'll get down there."

"I'm coming too."

"No, you're not. The guardian needs you more than I do." I glanced over at Hamilton, who nodded his agreement. "I'll let you know if it's what we're after. Out."

I jumped into the first guard vehicle I came to on the esplanade and flashed my authorisation. The driver was so big that his head touched the Land-Rover's ceiling and his knees were crushed against the steering wheel. I told him where to go and how fast to do it. A grin spread across his face and he hit the gas. As we reached the narrow passage of Castlehill a small Japanese boy wearing only a pair of shorts ran across the cobbles. His parents, one on each side of the road, looked suitably aghast. I gave them a gracious smile – my contribution to the city's soon-to-be-strained foreign relations.

We made it to the main spirits bond in one piece and I sent the gorilla back to the castle. I didn't fancy another trip with him and I had no idea when I'd be finished. The warehouse is a long Georgian building on Great Junction Street with surprisingly delicate overarched windows – till you notice the heavy steel wire over the glass and the sentry post with gun slits at the main entrance. The place was under siege more often than I went up against the drugs gangs during the early years of the Enlightenment. Nowadays Leith's a fairly well-behaved citizen residential area, but Baltic Barracks personnel still pound the streets around the clock – especially the streets near the bond.

A female senior auxiliary with a suntanned face emerged from the heavy door as I was being surrounded by a scrum of suspicious guardsmen.

"Citizen Dalrymple? Baltic 04." The woman sounded efficient beyond even the Council's demanding standards. "I'm afraid we may have got you down here for nothing," she said apologetically as she led me down to the cavernous cellars. There were mock-ups of the Ultimate Usquebaugh label on the walls and a horde of auxiliaries was checking stock. "The chemists have just advised me that the whisky we found is unadulterated." She stopped at a table where a pair of white-coated auxiliaries from Lister 25's department had set up a mini-lab.

I looked at the bottles and the unmarked cardboard box they'd come from. The labels bore the name Braes of Oblivion and the liquid in the bottles was a deep brown colour. "There was no documentation?"

Baltic 04 shook her head. Her cheeks had taken on a faint reddish hue. "One of my people must have slipped up," she said, shaking her head. I had a feeling that particular individual's career was about to end. "We receive previously unknown brands from time to time. Contraband the guard picks up, stuff the cruise ship crews try to smuggle in . . ."

"And there's definitely no trace of nicotine?" I said to the senior of the chemists.

He shook his head, already busy with another brand.

I walked down the cellar and watched the search squads in action for a bit. It was going to be a long job. The chief toxicologist rang and told me that the main stills in the city distilleries had been passed clean. So far all the whiskies imported officially from the Highland states had come up clear too. Then Davie called to report that none of the Supply Directorate stores and shops had produced anything lethal. Five minutes later I had Hamilton on the line complaining that the Tourism Directorate was after him to release stocks of booze that had been approved. Apparently there had been what he called "serious disturbances" in several hotel bars. The poor wee foreigners were suffering. I referred him to the chief toxicologist and the medical guardian.

I was sharing a bottle of water with Baltic 04 when a thought struck me. I called Davie. "Still no joy?" I asked.

"No. Maybe that bottle was a one-off, Quint. Maybe this is all somebody's idea of a piss-take."

"I bet Frankie Thomson's laughing. Listen, Davie, I've had an idea."

"You've had an idea," he repeated slowly. "Oh, shit."

"Oh, shit is right," I said, laughing. I don't know why I was laughing. My idea was more worrying than a pre-Enlightenment party political broadcast. "Get down to the bond. And bring your guard helmet as well as your party frock. Out."

I smiled at the senior auxiliary. She was staring at me, her expression suggesting I was a very sad case indeed. She was probably right.

I went into the street. It was quiet even though it wasn't curfew time yet. Without any whisky in the bars, the locals were

probably having an early, discontented night. I thought of
Sophia and wondered when I'd next have an early night with her.

"You're joking," Davie said, shaking his head.

"No I'm not."

"Don't you remember what those guys are like, Quint? If
they're not on patrol, they'll be fighting drunk. And you know
what they think of ordinary citizens like you."

I kept quiet. For a long time.

"All right," Davie said, starting the Land-Rover. Hamilton
obviously hadn't let him take his Jeep this time. "But don't blame
me if you get a broken head. Or worse."

"I checked with the port commander. They're not going out
tonight."

He grunted. "Prepare to meet your doom then."

There was no reply to that. I was about to put the squeeze on
one of the city's most dangerous men, one who had plenty of
opportunities to lay his hands on illicit whisky. He also
happened to have very little hair on his head.

Chapter Six

The sentry inside the dock gate stared out at us belligerently when our headlights illuminated his box. Eventually he came over and registered Davie's uniform. I held up my authorisation but he still wanted to check with his superior.

"Wait here," he shouted after he put down the phone.

Davie edged forward till the Land-Rover's bumper was touching the gate then smiled humourlessly at his fellow guardsman. "Arsehole," he said, turning to me.

"Thanks a lot."

"Not you." He scowled at me. "Though this is all your fault."

Soon a pair of lights appeared deep inside the port area and came towards us.

"Looks like we're getting a welcoming committee," I said. "Are they usually this touchy?"

"This is the Fisheries Guard base, Quint. You know how crazy those guys are."

I nodded, remembering the time we'd taken a trip on a seriously rust-eaten hulk. Davie was right. The auxiliaries who get drafted into the Fisheries Guard are headbangers who are too fierce even for border duty. They're all male, of course. They man the small fleet of ex-trawlers that patrols the city's waters and intercepts hostile vessels, a Council euphemism for beating the crap out of smugglers and raiders from across the firth.

The lights inside the fenced compound came towards us at a hell of a rate.

"Jesus," I said, getting ready to jump for it.

"I wonder if that's who I think it is," Davie said.

I shaded my eyes from the dazzling white light and, after an excruciating delay, heard the screech of brakes.

A door opened and the lights were doused.

"Kill yours too," shouted the driver. I recognised the heavy tones immediately.

Davie did as he was told then got out. I reckoned I was better off staying put.

"What the fuck do you want?"

"Hiya, Harry," Davie said. "I thought you'd be out killing raiders."

My eyes got used to the dark and I watched as the bulky figure on the inside unchained the gate and pulled it open. It was Jamieson 369 all right.

"Davie, you mad bastard." Harry punched him hard on the shoulder but kept on glaring at him. They'd been through the auxiliary training programme and had served together on the border but Harry didn't exactly look overjoyed to see him. He was even less pleased to see me.

"Fucking brilliant," he groaned, coming over to my door. He was wearing a tattered cap, the peak half torn off. "Citizen Six Brains Dalrymple." He bellowed a laugh that would have scared off a rutting stag. "Just the man I wanted to see." He turned away. "Going into the dock lashed to an anchor."

"I'm really pleased to see you too, Harry," I called after him.

He looked back and gave me a malevolent grin. "Not for long you won't be." He turned to Davie. "Since you've decided to honour us with a visit, I suppose you'd better come to the mess hall."

I breathed a sigh of relief. At least we weren't going to the leaky wreck he commanded. As Harry's maroon pick-up pulled away in our lights, I made out the shafts of what looked like pick-axes and spades standing up in the back. The crossgrips at the top gave them the look of stunted, minimalist grave markers. Considering what had happened to Frankie Thomson, I felt they were very appropriate.

The crew mess wasn't much better than Fisheries Guard seagoing accommodation. It was at the end of a dilapidated dock building, the windows that still had panes in them flung open in the forlorn hope of attracting a cooling breeze. A sign bearing the unit's fish and heart emblem was hanging down over the entrance at one end. It quivered when Harry hit the door. Someone had drawn a harpoon through the heart, an act of unruliness that would have made Hamilton apoplectic. But, like all the guardians, he gave the Fisheries Guard a very wide berth.

Davie and I followed the big man inside. The mess was a three-dimensional pun vivant, sailors with legs in oil-stained overalls draped over the arms of armchairs that had spewed stuffing out of torn fabric. Everyone went quiet when we appeared.

Harry, his clothes even filthier than his men's, went straight to what passed for a bar — a table laden with beer and whisky bottles. "We've got company," he shouted, pulling off his cap. "My good friend Davie from the castle — formerly of training squad J and border posts 12 and 16." He tossed an unopened half-bottle of barracks malt in Davie's general direction. The crewmen roared in approval as he caught it. Then Harry looked at me. Since I'd last seen him he'd either lost his hair or started shaving his head. That made the large dent in his skull even more obvious. "And this is Quintilian Dalrymple. A Council investigator." He spoke the words like they made his tongue smart. The room went quiet again. "Andy, see if we've got a sweet sherry for the citizen."

There was a barrage of raucous laughter as the auxiliary minced out of the room. I let it die down before I went across to the table.

"I prefer the hard stuff," I said, picking up the nearest bottle of whisky and raising it to my lips. The cheering started again and it was only after the fifth gulp that I realised what I'd done. Or rather, what I hadn't done. In my desperation to show I really was one of the boys, I'd completely forgotten to check the label.

After five minutes I began to calm down. Even though the whisky was called Salamander Pride and was a product of the Council distillery in Fountainbridge, it could still have been got at. But apart from the usual burning sensation that city whisky produces in your throat, I seemed to have survived. So I had another slug.

"Are you going to tell us what the fuck you're doing down here?" Dirty Harry demanded. He was still looking at me like I'd just crawled out of a septic tank.

I pointed at the table of bottles. "There's been a case of nicotine poisoning. A whisky called the Ultimate Usquebaugh. Were you not advised by the guard command centre?"

"I don't pay much attention to what those wankers say." He grinned at Davie. A dark blue vein was pounding away on his misshapen skull. He'd taken a blow from a raider's crowbar years back. "Nicotine poisoning," he repeated with a guffaw. "Pretty fucking good in a city where smoking's been banned for twenty years." He glanced at me. "Someone dead?" His voice was suddenly more sombre.

I nodded. "A male citizen."

The serious tone vanished. "So it was definitely his ultimate—"

"That's getting to be a bit of an old joke, Harry," I interrupted, pulling a mock-up of the label from my pocket. "Ever seen this in the consignments you've seized from raiders or smugglers?"

He held it close to his face then shook his head. "No. It doesn't even look vaguely like any I've come across." He gave me a macho grin. "And I've come across more illicit whisky labels than you've had hot dicks."

His crewmen let out another roar.

"Any of you maniacs seen this?" Harry shouted, waving the label at them.

The roaring gradually died away.

"I'll take that as a no then, shall I?" I asked, retrieving the mock-up.

Now for the difficult bit. The Fisheries Guard commander had a shortage of hair and a reputation as one of the most violent men in the city. He also came across plenty of previously unknown whisky on the vessels he boarded. Could he be the mystery man that Frankie Thomson's neighbour saw and heard? Several things counted against that already, things I'd pushed to the back of my mind till I saw him in the flesh again. For a start, unlike the man in Bell Place, Dirty Harry was built like a Sewage Department outside lavvy. Also, his voice was as deep as a bull elephant's, baritone in triplicate. And the clincher was that, like all his crewmen, he had a thick beard.

I had to be sure. "Were you guys on patrol last night?" I asked, trying hard to make the question sound innocent. I failed.

Silence fell over the mess like a sodden blanket. All eyes were fixed on me, including Davie's. He was staring in disbelief, his lower jaw loose. The crewmen's faces were set hard, but Harry grinned and came over to me. Close up, I registered that his left eye was glassy and immobile and remembered that the first time I met him he was wearing an eye patch. Apparently the Medical Directorate had found a false eye that fitted the cavity left by some no doubt long-dead assailant. Unfortunately it was green and the big man's other eye was brown.

"Is that an official question, citizen?" Dirty Harry asked, pronouncing my rank like it was a disease of the bowel. "Or are you just being sociable?"

"Sociable?" I laughed nervously and glanced at Davie. He was shaking his head hopelessly. "Just answer the question, Harry," I said, hardening my tone.

The big man stared down at me, the vein pulsing hard in his

skull. He raised his hands and flexed the fingers in front of my face. The skin was deeply stained by oil and the fingernails were full of some dark-coloured earthy muck. For several very long moments I thought I was dead meat. Then he laughed loudly.

"Aye, citizen, we were on patrol." His good eye didn't shift off me. "All of us. Got the logs to prove it if you want."

I held his gaze then nodded. "I'll take your word for it." The tension in the room began to slacken as soon as I said that. I felt an even greater stickiness in my armpits than normal during the Big Heat. "Time to go, Davie," I said, making for the door.

Dirty Harry suddenly appeared in front of me, moving much faster than I imagined he could.

"No, citizen. Time to drink." He gave me a leer to tell me that refusing the invitation would be an even worse decision than checking his movements. "We auxiliaries may not be allowed to do the lottery like ordinary citizens but we still get our hands on better booze than the winners are given. And since our masters and mistresses decided to cut back on patrol time to save fuel costs last spring, we're on for a heavy session more nights than not, aren't we, boys?"

The piratical mob yelled and whistled its agreement. I wasn't aware that the Fisheries Guard's activities had been curtailed. The Council had probably run short of ammunition to supply them with. After the land-based drugs gangs were driven out of the city years ago, Harry's guys were the only auxiliary unit authorised to carry firearms apart from the guards on the city line and border posts.

He led me back to the table.

"Right then, how many have we got?" He started counting the different brands in front of him. One of them was Braes of Oblivion so it was pretty clear who'd brought that into the city. "You're in luck, citizen. Only seventeen." He grinned. "That'll mean doubles."

I looked at the bottles. At least six of them were unopened. It was going to be a worrying night whether or not there was any nicotine around. Either way, oblivion was definitely on the cards.

I woke up on the floor of the mess hall, my mouth open and a pool of dribble next to it on the threadbare carpet. I thought I'd pulled off the great escape till I moved my head.

"Look at it this way, Quint. At least you're alive." Davie was sitting on one of the ruptured sofas, the skin above his beard pale but his voice jaunty. His capacity for drink never failed to amaze me.

I had my hand over my eyes as the sun was streaming in the unshuttered windows. "Where is everyone?"

"Don't ask me. They were gone when I woke up. Playing with their toy boats probably."

I staggered out of the building and took refuge from the sun in the Land-Rover. On the way out of the port area we saw no sign of the crews, though their boats were tied up in the Enlightenment Dock.

"Where to?" Davie asked as he waited for the gate to be opened.

"Pull up outside while I make some calls."

I spoke to Hamilton, who wanted to know why the hell I hadn't been answering my mobile. Not that he had anything spectacular to report. There had been no other bottles of the ultimate magic found, no traces of nicotine in the whiskies tested and nobody admitted to the infirmary with symptoms that could have resulted from poisoning. I told him no news was good news and signed off. Then I tried to get hold of Sophia. An auxiliary told me she was resting so I didn't disturb her – just wondered for a few moments if she'd been looking for me. And if she'd missed me like I would have missed her if I hadn't been forced to get shit-faced.

Davie was peering at me. "Where to then, Quint? I want my breakfast."

I examined my watch. It was smeared with something that

looked like it had come from deep inside my body. Eight o'clock. My old man's retirement home in Trinity wasn't far away. I told Davie to head there and got a sour look.

"The food's terrible in that place."

"Oh, you've eaten there before, have you, guardsman?"

"I have to do something during your regular bloody visits to Hector." He drove off through central Leith. Unlucky citizens with the Sunday morning shift were on their way to work, faces grim and clothes already soaked with sweat. At least for one morning in their lives they weren't being subjected to trial by headache. Unlike me.

"Hello, failure," my father said, glancing up at me from the book of Latin poetry he'd propped up on the table in the communal dining room. "God almighty, lad, what's happened to you?"

"Essential Council business," Davie said, pulling up a chair and helping himself to charred toast. "Whisky testing."

"Weren't you keeping an eye on him, guardsman?" Hector demanded, the twitch at the corners of his mouth showing how serious the question was.

"He had to try every single one for himself."

"All right, you two, that's enough," I said, pouring out the stewed tea from the bottom of the pot. Eating was not a viable proposition. "Let's get out of here," I said to the old man. The noise of his twenty-nine housemates clattering their false teeth and bickering over what the cook thought was porridge had got to me. I led him to a shaded part of the garden where there were a couple of tattered deck chairs.

"You should take better care of yourself, Quintilian. Excessive drinking destroys brain cells."

"Spare me the lecture, old man. You're not in the university now. Anyway, we really have been testing the city's whisky stocks. Didn't you notice that your dram wasn't distributed yesterday?"

Hector finally finished lowering his tall frame into the chair.

"Dram? We're lucky to see that more than twice a week. That bloody nurse . . ."

"Have you seen her this morning?" I asked, suddenly realising that I hadn't noticed the auxiliary who was in charge of the home.

"Aye, she's around." My father looked at me. "What's going on with the city's whisky, lad?"

I told him about the dead man and the Ultimate Usquebaugh.

He rubbed the stubble on his shrunken cheeks. "Sounds like you might be up against some real wise guys." He grinned. "Isn't that what they call them in those appalling American crime novels you used to read when you were young?"

"How would you know?" I often suspected that Hector raided my bookshelves when I lived at home before the Enlightenment, but he'd never admit to it. "You don't remember any cases of poisoning when you were in the Council, do you?"

I wasn't sure why I was asking him. Hamilton had been a guardian from the beginning and he would have told me of any case dating from before I was in the directorate. But I'd got used to sharing my problems with my father and, for all his physical decrepitude, he could still get to the essence of things.

He was shaking his head. "No. In those days the drugs gangs were more inclined to use automatic weapons and high explosives than Agatha Christie's methods."

I nodded then squeezed my eyes hard as the headache kicked in again. Time to hit Sophia for some pills.

"Look after yourself, old man," I said, getting up painfully. "And don't drink any spirits till I give you the all clear."

What must have been a seriously large bullfrog made its presence known from the trickle of the burn at the bottom of the garden.

"Brekekek-koax-koax," my father said. "Excellent symbolism, don't you think?"

I looked at him unenthusiastically. "This isn't the time for a lesson in ancient Athenian satire."

"At least you recognised my allusion to Aristophanes, laddie." It seemed I'd made Hector's day. "*The Frogs*, of course. And where does most of the action of that play take place?"

I racked my brains, coming up with more pain but no answer.

"In the underworld," Hector said, looking inordinately pleased with himself. "As I say, the symbolism really is excellent. For what is this city nowadays but hell on earth?"

I wished him joy of that observation and headed for the Land-Rover. As I got there, it struck me that what I told him about the poisoning had immediately made him think of the drugs gangs. It hadn't occurred to me to link poisoned whisky to the drug traffickers who would give an arm and a leg, if not a burned-out oesophagus, for access to the city. But my head was too dealt with to take that idea any further for the time being.

Before we got into the guard vehicle I put in a call to Hamilton and asked him to send an inspection team round to the Smoke on the Water club. The forensics squad hadn't reported any sign of grass or any other controlled drugs in Frankie Thomson's flat but maybe there was more going on at his place of work than met the eye.

"Where to?" Davie asked when I finished.

"I need the infirmary," I mumbled, cradling my head. "The brain surgery unit and make it snappy."

Sophia handed me a bottle of aspirins with a severely disapproving look. "I told you to cut down on that poison." She shook her head in annoyance when she realised what she'd said.

I slumped against the wall, too knackered to argue.

"Oh, for goodness sake." She glared at Davie as if it were his fault and raised her eyes at her assistant, who smirked at me. Then she led me into her private office and closed the door. "Was it necessary for you to carry out your own form of whisky testing? Didn't you consider the risks?"

At first I thought she was giving me an official reprimand,

something that guardians normally form a queue to do. Then I noticed that her eyes were wide open and moist at the corners.

"Hey," I said, going round unsteadily to her side of the desk, "I'll be okay." I touched her shoulders. "At least we know the Fisheries Guard haven't come across the Ultimate Usquebaugh."

Sophia shook my hands off. "You could just have asked them, Quint. You didn't have to show off like a wee boy."

I couldn't think of much to say in response to that, so I swallowed the pills and washed them down with water from the bottle she gave me. A heap of folders marked "Senior Guardian's Eyes Only" was piled up in front of her.

"Are you coping all right?" I asked, putting a hand on the back of her neck. This time she let it stay.

"I can manage," she said, looking up at me. "We have seminars to prepare us for the month as senior guardian." Her light blue eyes were circled with black rings.

"Oh, seminars." I risked a grin, which didn't do my head much good. "You'll be all right then." I leaned over her and put my cheek against hers. "Didn't you sleep last night?"

She shook her head, looking embarrassed. "Not much. I went to your place when I finished at around one. When I couldn't raise you on your mobile, I went back to Moray Place. I . . ." She pushed her chair back into me and got up, then went over to a filing cabinet and pretended to be looking for something.

"You . . . ?" I said, following her over.

She slammed the drawer shut and turned into my arms. "Oh, stop it, Quint. I was worried about you." She looked down. "I missed you, all right?"

I kissed her on the lips. "It's all right. I missed you too."

Sophia's cheeks reddened. "I don't know what I think I'm playing at."

"What do you mean?"

She glanced away awkwardly. "Oh, chasing you like a love-struck teenager." Her eyes came back towards me and flashed angrily. "You think I'm naive, don't you, Quint? I was celibate for years and now I'm like a nymphomaniac who throws herself at the first man she finds."

"Thanks very much," I said. I put my hand on her shoulder. It stayed there a couple of seconds before she shook it off. "I don't think you're naive, Sophia. There's very little evidence to support that conclusion."

She let out an angry sob. "There's . . . there's a lot going on at the moment, Quint," she said, swallowing hard. "I just . . . I just need some support."

I held her tight, ignoring the heat that our bodies generated in close contact.

"It's okay, Sophia. There's nothing wrong with needing support. What the Council used to preach about self-reliance is bullshit."

She rested her head against my shoulder for a few moments then pushed me away gently. "Come on, we have to work." She went back to her desk and picked up a notebook. "So where have you got to?"

"Utopia."

"What?"

"It means 'nowhere' in Greek."

"Indeed." Her eyes flashed angrily. "Be more precise if you can, citizen." She had suddenly turned back into the senior guardian.

The aspirins seemed to be having some effect. I sat down and looked at my own notes. "Right. I spoke to the guard command centre and the chief toxicologist on my way up here. No more bottles of poisoned whisky have been found. Checks are continuing in the bars and stores, and the chemists are still making tests."

"Tests that will take days to cover all the city's whisky," Sophia said, shaking her head. "We can't rely on random samples. Just because one batch of Spirit o' the Nor' Loch is clean doesn't mean that bottles from other batches haven't been poisoned. And whoever was behind the Ultimate Usquebaugh is probably capable of slipping bottles into the distribution chain even after testing."

I nodded. "You want to maintain the ban on supplies to citizens and tourists, don't you?"

"As a health professional, what else can I do? Even one more death would be a terrible responsibility."

"On the other hand, citizens might riot outside Supply Directorate stores and end up dead if the supplies aren't restored." I caught her eyes. "Remember what happened during the drugs wars."

Sophia bit her lower lip so hard that I thought blood would appear. Then she let it go and breathed in deeply. "Do you really think the citizen body will take to the streets over whisky?"

"What else have they got to look forward to after a day sweating their guts out at work? An hour standing in line outside the swimming-baths, a few pints of watery beer, an evening class on Plato's philosophy of education? Whisky's all that keeps a lot of them going, Sophia."

Her back stiffened and her gaze became truly glacial. Now she was the Ice Queen again, Big Heat or no Big Heat. "I cannot accept that analysis of Edinburgh society," she said. Not even my mother in her most reginal manifestation as senior guardian managed such a tone. "The Council has provided many benefits for citizens – housing, health, full employment, lifelong learning . . ."

"No cars, no television, no cigarettes," I continued. "No drugs, no music that the Council hasn't approved, no travel outside the city borders, no free will, not even the option of suicide . . ."

Sophia banged her hands down on the files in front of her. "Enough, Quint," she shouted. "Are you seriously telling me that applying sanctions against the families of people who attempt suicide is a bad thing?"

I gave up. Either you get the point about personal freedoms or you don't. Guardians have always subjugated the individual to the collective whole.

"Forget it, Sophia, okay? Just keep the chemists testing round the clock and then release stocks that have been fully tested. I reckon you've got another day before the pressure really starts building up."

She looked at me with an expression that suggested she might possibly follow my advice – if the Council went along with it, of course. "What about you, Quint? What are you going to do now?"

I emptied her waterbottle. "I'm going to interview the dead man's neighbours again. In the castle dungeons. Some of them may be holding out on us. If I find out anything I'll pass it on to Hamilton. He can brief the Council at the meeting."

Sophia looked up from her papers after I emptied the bottle. "And later?" she said in a small, shy voice.

"And later, senior guardian, I shall see you at my place. Eleven p.m.?"

She gave a nod so rapid that I almost missed it, then looked down again.

"Quint?" she said as I reached the door.

"Dearest?"

She went into freezer mode again. "If you turn your mobile off again during this investigation, I'll personally implant it in your alimentary canal."

I blew her a kiss and departed at speed.

Davie was getting on very well with the female auxiliary in the outer office. He was pissed off that we had to leave but brightened up when I told him we had a day of heavy-duty interrogation ahead. Unfortunately things went downhill from then on. Although some of the residents of Bell Place were definitely not keen on the Council and its works, they opened up when Davie and his pals gave them what the guard call "anti-citizen verbals". The problem was it really did seem that none of them had seen or heard anything around the time of Frankie Thomson's death. Even the storeman Drem stuck to his story.

So Frankie T.'s neighbour Mary McMurray, who I didn't send to the dungeons, was the only one who'd caught a glimpse of the man outside his flat. After a long hot afternoon in the cells we turned the rest of them loose. Another seventeen citizens who would happily spit on the Council's mass grave — and mine.

We ate some revolting stew in the castle mess, checked on the progress of the whisky tests — still no more poisoned bottles — and pulled in the staff from the Smoke on the Water club. The inspection I'd asked for had come up with no drugs in excess of those legitimately in stock. The auxiliaries who worked there were all clean as well, even the Prostitution Services Department lapdancers. In fact, they were cleaner than anyone else since they have rigorous monthly health checks. We reported to the public order guardian and wandered down the corridor from his office.

"What now?" Davie asked, yawning immensely. "It's half ten and I want my bed."

I'd just finished making a list of the accommodation occupied by all the Smoke on the Water people. I'd been considering asking Hamilton to put tails on them, but the idea of surveillance on auxiliaries wouldn't exactly have made him jump for joy. I reckoned I'd leave that for the time being. There was also the question of Napier Barracks personnel who knew Frankie Thomson before his demotion. Also postponed. My body and brain revolted at the idea of more work.

"Okay, you fader," I said. "Give us a lift home."

"Don't you know that walking is good for—"

The raised stump of my forefinger put paid to that question before he managed to complete it.

I opened my door and stopped dead. The light was on in my living room.

Sophia's head appeared from behind the sofa. "I finished a bit earlier than I thought," she said. "Unlike you, it seems."

"You know how it is." I closed the door. "An investigator's work is never done and . . ." I broke off as it became clear to me that the city's senior official was wearing nothing more than a black lace bra and knickers that were definitely not standard issue, even for her rank.

"It's so hot," she said, stretching her arms.

"It is indeed so hot," I agreed, rapidly pulling my T-shirt over my head. "You look pretty hot yourself." Believe it or not, the Recreation Directorate has noticed a correlation between high ambient temperatures and the demand for condoms.

She sat up straight and gave me a smile that started off shy but quickly became surprisingly lewd. "Come over here, you."

I complied, picking up a waterbottle that she'd put on the table. I cupped my hand and poured water into it.

"Quint . . ." Sophia's tone was a mixture of admonition and interest.

I dipped a fingertip in the water then ran it down the damp skin between her throat and her chest.

"Quint . . ." Interest was overtaking admonition.

I wet my finger again and ran it under the fabric of her bra. The nipple was already hard when I got to it.

"Qui . . ." Sophia's voice gave out.

"Hold on. I'm getting there."

She gave me a sharp look then pulled my hand forward so the remaining water tipped down the smooth skin of her stomach.

"Not quickly enough." She unfastened my trousers, put her fingers round my erect penis and pulled me towards her.

"What temperature do you think this organ is?" she asked.

"A little below melting point?" I hazarded.

"Could be," she said. She pulled the cup of her bra down and rubbed the tip of my cock against her left nipple.

"Approaching melting point," I gasped.

It was then that I noticed the door. In my excitement I'd forgotten to turn the key. It had swung open silently. I was confronted by a figure in dusty farm worker's overalls standing stock-still and staring straight at me.

"Have I come at a bad time, Quint?" The voice was deep and

hoarse. Despite the three years since I'd last heard it, recognition was immediate. "Or have you?"

Sophia had turned back into the Ice Queen and frozen solid. So much for reaching melting point.

"Katharine," I said, when I finally found my voice. "Ever heard of knocking?"

She laughed lightly and set down the backpack she was carrying. I heard the chink of bottles. Then she rapped her knuckles on the door.

"Knock, knock, who's there?" she said, then moved towards the sofa and took in my companion, a smile playing on her lips. The look she gave her wasn't humorous though.

I pulled up my zip and handed my T-shirt to Sophia, keeping my eyes on Katharine. There was something menacing about the way she was standing, as tense as a lioness about to attack. I wondered who she would go for first, Sophia or me.

I never was much of a fan of troilism.

Chapter Seven

———◦◦◦———

The three of us remained stationary for a few seconds, Katharine still leaning forward and gazing at Sophia with a faint smile on her lips, while I stood with my arms loose, wondering what the hell to do next. Then Sophia got to her feet, gathered up her outer garments in a single graceful movement and retired to the bedroom, the black underwear standing out against her pale skin. The door slammed behind her.

"Is that who I think it is?" Katharine asked, moving forward into the light.

"Who do you think it is?" I demanded. As she came closer, I got a better look at her. She was wearing a faded blue workshirt with the arms rolled above her elbows and matching trousers with the legs turned up over her calves. The visible parts of the limbs were tanned and muscular, her complexion weathered and healthy, though she was thinner than I remembered. Her hair, once auburn and short, was now straw-coloured and hanging down to her shoulders. Apparently investigators prefer blondes. But it wasn't only her hair and build that were different. The way her green eyes moved jerkily around the room as they fixed on objects made me uneasy. I wondered what she'd been through since I last saw her.

"She's the medical guardian, isn't she, Quint?" Katharine said. "I've seen her picture in the *Edinburgh Guardian*. We used to see the odd copy occasionally on the farm." She paused. "When there was a farm."

Her use of the past tense to describe where she'd been living sounded odd. She moved to the sofa and slumped down, then lunged towards the table and grabbed the waterbottle. She gulped thirstily from it.

"That's better," she said, wiping her mouth with the back of her hand. "I ran out of drinking-water this morning." She gave me a pleasant smile which I didn't buy for a second. "So you're screwing Council members these days, are you?"

Sophia chose that moment to reappear. She gave Katharine a crushing glare from the battery of offensive weapons that's issued to senior auxiliaries. "Who is this person, Quintilian?" she asked, favouring me with a look that was only marginally less devastating. Presumably she thought that using my full name would impress Katharine. She thought wrong.

"Quintilian?" Katharine repeated. "Only his father calls him Quintilian." She laughed in the throaty way that always used to weaken my knees. "What does that make you? His stepmother?"

Sophia drew herself back and tried to summon up a suitably glacial look. Her white blouse was buttoned to the throat and her guardian's tie knotted tightly, giving her the air of a headmistress about to lay down the law to a foul-mouthed kid.

Katharine ignored her and turned to me. "How is Hector, Quint?"

"He's okay," I replied. "Growing—"

"I asked for this person's identity," Sophia insisted, stepping forward and pulling her mobile from her pocket. "Kindly inform me or I will alert the guard."

I went over and eased the phone from her hand. "That won't be necessary," I said. "I can vouch for her."

Katharine's hand had also gone to her pocket. "You don't have to," she said, taking out a plastic-covered card. "I've got one of these, remember?"

Sophia looked in surprise at the "ask no questions", which is issued to undercover operatives by the Public Order Directorate. I got a hold of one for Katharine during the manhunt that was going on the last time I saw her.

"You work for the city?" Sophia asked disbelievingly.

"On and off," Katharine replied jauntily. Then she told the guardian her name. That went down like a bacon sandwich in Mecca.

"Katharine Kirkwood," Sophia repeated, her expression hardening even more. "I remember you from the murder investigation in '22. You are a demoted auxiliary and a deserter, are you not?"

"*Was* a deserter," I said, stepping between them before they put to use the unarmed combat skills they'd been taught on the auxiliary training programme. "The desertion charge was removed from Katharine's record." I ignored the look on Katharine's face that said "I can fight my own battles, sonny."

Sophia's body was still taut. "And what entitles you to burst in here without so much as a knock?" She hadn't got over being caught with her hand full.

Katharine laughed. "I can see Quint hasn't told you anything about me."

The guardian looked at me quickly, her eyes wide open.

"Em . . . Katharine and I used to have something going . . ." I said weakly.

"Meaning what, exactly?" Sophia's voice was suddenly tremulous.

"Meaning, among other things, that we did the kind of things you were indulging in when I arrived," Katharine said, her eyes flinty and unwavering despite the smile on her lips. "You know — frotting, sucking, fucking . . ."

Sophia's head jerked back like she'd been slapped. Then she walked purposefully towards the door, kicking aside the backpack Katharine had left in the way.

"Hey, watch that!" Katharine called. "It's fragile."

I stood and watched the door swinging on its hinges after

Sophia had gone. "Thanks a lot," I said. "You didn't have to be so graphic."

Katharine's laugh sounded almost manic.

"Nice lady, Quint," she said. I turned to discover her undoing the buttons on her shirt. "You do pick them."

I watched as she bared the firm breasts and dark brown nipples that I'd seen in my dreams for months after she left the city. Then the immediacy had faded and I'd been left on my own in the dark. Katharine frowned distractedly when she saw the direction of my gaze then went into the bedroom.

"Christ almighty," she shouted after a few seconds in the alcove that used to contain my shower. "Is there no water at all in this bloody city?" She reappeared with her shirt still off. "All I wanted was a wash."

"I thought you said you saw the paper from time to time. There's been water rationing for the last two summers. If you want a shower, you'll have to queue at the public facilities tomorrow morning."

Katharine poured the last of the bottled water on her hands and started rubbing them across her chest. I became aware that the melting point I'd been heading towards with Sophia was on its way to being achieved again in my trousers.

I managed to look away and went awkwardly over to what passes in the Supply Directorate for a kitchen table. It almost collapsed when I leaned on it. That reminded me of the missing lottery-winner. Fordyce Kennedy could have done wonders for citizen-issue furniture if they'd let him.

"What are you doing back in the perfect city, Katharine?" I asked, watching regretfully as she did her shirt back up again. "What's happening on the farm?" She'd been living with a group of collectivist dissidents twenty miles to the east the last time I saw her.

She came across, picking up the bottle of tested whisky I'd put on the coffee table and pulling the cork. "The farm?" She paused and drank deep, then passed me the bottle. "There's no farm,

Quint." Her eyes glinted and she gave another unbalanced laugh. "The farm's fucked."

"What do you mean?" I handed her back the bottle, having decided that whisky was surplus to my body's requirements for a day or two, and watched as she took another slug.

"What I mean is that we've given up." Suddenly her head dropped and she sat down limply at the table. "It's been hell these last couple of years, Quint. The high temperatures burned away most of our cereal crops in the summer and the endless rains in winter rotted the root crops before we could get most of them out of the ground." She raised her head and looked at me desperately. "Then there were the gangs. When the bloody Council decided to attack the ones who'd set up near the city border last autumn, they drove the psychos in our direction. We fought them off for months but we took too many casualties." She drank again and slammed the bottle down. "Eventually people just began to drift away. I was the last. The farm's a wasteland now." She stared across at me again, her eyes screwed up. "It isn't fair, Quint."

I moved my hand towards hers but she pulled back and stumbled over to the sofa. I heard a sob but I knew she wouldn't let me near her. At least that's what I told myself. So I took the easy way out and left her there. A few minutes later the lights flashed three times then were extinguished for the night. Lights out and curfew. I felt my way to the bed and crashed out, the whisky I'd downed last night at the Fisheries Guard base finally catching up with me. It had been a painful morning. The evening hadn't turned out much better.

Night was no improvement either. Images of Sophia kept flashing up at me, to be replaced by Katharine's bronzed face and worrying eyes. I thought I could hear Bob Campbell singing "Starvation Farm Blues" in the background.

I woke up and rolled around in the heat. Although the women had laid into each other like a pair of alley cats, there was something about Sophia's jealousy that didn't ring true. I knew Katharine of old. She said what she thought, which had been one reason for the problems she'd had as an auxiliary. But I wasn't so sure about Sophia. She used to be a guardian of the hardline-doesn't-even-begin-to-describe-me persuasion and she hadn't changed much, for all the new Council's softly softly approach. Why had she suddenly started spending time with a demoted auxiliary like me? And why had she, the city's senior medic, appeared when Frankie Thomson's body was found – before we knew anything about his DM record or the nicotine poisoning? Then there was the huge search of all the city's whisky – why had she forced that through? Had I been swallowing every hook Sophia had dangled in front of me? What if she was trying to ensure my involvement in something that would have a much more profound effect on the city than a guardian's unexpected sexual flowering?

I got up and stuck my head round the bedroom door. It was four a.m. and in the faint light from the windows I made out that Katharine was comatose, her arms flung wide and her forehead lined even in sleep. I looked around for something to drink but all I saw was whisky. That wasn't what I was after. I could have done with some water, but there wouldn't be any of that available until the drinking tank on the street corner was unlocked at six a.m. It struck me that I was also in need of what the bluesmen called "water of love". There was precious little of that in the city either.

After writhing around in my sweat-stained sheets, I finally dropped into a dreamless sleep so deep that a bathyscaph would have had trouble reaching me. Then I woke up with a jolt in bright sunlight. My watch told me it was after nine.

I stumbled into the living room and discovered an array of full waterbottles on the table. Beside them was a note imparting the complex message: "Back later, K." Katharine had obviously found a way of talking the waterman into letting her fill up without a local resident's card. She'd always been good at that kind of thing. I got dressed as quickly as I could after calling Davie to send down a vehicle. There were things I needed to check. On my way out I noticed Katharine had left her backpack inside the door. That definitely suggested she would return, something I found curiously comforting.

I went to Napier Barracks and tried to find out more about Frankie Thomson. I didn't get very far. There had been a change of commander since the dead man's demotion and the new guy and his team didn't know the former Napier 25 well. I found a couple of veteran auxiliaries who'd served with him but they didn't do much except confirm what I already knew. Frankie T. had kept himself to himself and in later years was hardly ever in barracks – he'd told one of them he was working double shifts at the Finance Directorate. One thing was interesting. Like me, both auxiliaries were puzzled about the demotion charge. As far as they were concerned, he'd never been much interested in sex. And even if he had harboured secret urges to stick his hands down women's tops, he could easily have satisfied those in the weekly sex session. Why do something as crazy as that in public and to an important foreign visitor's wife? Which begged another question – had he been set up in some way? They stared at me stonily when I asked that. Auxiliaries have never been much good at conspiracy theories.

I headed to the Finance Directorate. The great dome-topped block at the top of the Mound used to be the headquarters of one of Scotland's banks before the crash and its present occupants are no more forthcoming than their predecessors. The directorate archive is in the depths of the ornate structure and I was eventually allowed in to it after sticking my Council authorisation under a dozen auxiliaries' noses. Information was apparently subject to the same level of security as the city's foreign currency reserves. No one I asked admitted to any recollection of Napier 25. Even the deputy guardian, who headed the Strategic Planning Department where Frankie T. used to work, claimed not to know him. I wasn't buying it.

I had other ways to get what I wanted – one of which was checking files that the city's overworked bureaucrats produce then forget. In the former bank's musty basement I pulled the dead man's records and got down to some creative cross-referencing and indexing. Pretty soon I realised that someone had been there before me, though the consultation forms didn't contain any giveaway barracks numbers. Napier 25's existence in the directorate was documented as regards dates and worthless information like the rooms he'd worked in and the days he'd missed because of illness, but everything about what he'd actually done and which projects he'd worked on had been weeded – as with his file in the DM archive. What the hell was going on? The guy was just a heavy drinker who squeezed a tourist's tits and ended up as a bog cleaner, wasn't he? Why mess with his records? Then, when I was about to start banging my head on the desk, I found something that made me blink. His main service file was about as useful as a Supply Directorate sunshade, but in the directorate's staff transportation dockets I came across frequent references to a particular destination Frankie had been ferried to during the year before his demotion. And that was the Culture Directorate.

I went up the stairs to the opulent main hall scratching my head. Had the dead man been working on a project over there? There was no mention of that in any other folders I consulted. Then the timing locked in. Two years ago, when Frankie first started going regularly to the Culture Directorate, they'd been in the throes of Lewis Hamilton's favourite initiative, the one that now had hoardings all over the city, the one that fuelled ordinary citizens' desperate dreams and dressed up its winners as famous figures from history – the one called Edlott. I didn't know what to make of that.

"Nothing, Dalrymple." Hamilton's face was as grim as a martyr's when the fire began nibbling at his feet. "Nothing's been discovered by the search teams. No more poisoned whisky, no more Ultimate Usquebaugh labels, no more victims."

I nodded, blinking in the sunlight that was pouring through the windows of Lewis's office in the castle. I'd been having more worrying thoughts about Frankie Thomson's death. "We'll have to commence controlled whisky distribution if we don't find something soon."

"Surely you wouldn't go along with that?" he said, staring at me as if I'd just suggested that Council members should wear codpieces and carnival masks in the street.

"Obviously it's a risk," I said, looking across the table at Davie. He was trying not to get involved.

"Hume 253?" Hamilton wasn't letting him off the hook.

"Em, yes," Davie said, glancing at me. "As the citizen says, it's definitely a risk . . . a big risk . . ."

The public order guardian waited for him to go on then snorted when he realised Davie had nothing else to add. "What are we saying then?" Hamilton asked. "That the DM's death was a one-off? An accident?"

I shook my head. "Whatever way you look at it, someone put a lethal dose of nicotine in the whisky. The most pessimistic way of looking at it is that this is just the beginning. Whoever killed Frankie Thomson went to a hell of a lot of trouble, not just to organise his death but to leave the bottles of the Ultimate Usquebaugh in a very obvious place."

Hamilton had been scrutinising me as I spoke. "What do you mean, 'organise his death'? Isn't there still a chance that the citizen came across the bottles fortuitously?"

"I've been thinking about that. There are plenty of indications against it. For a start, as you've confirmed, no other bottles with that label or any other adulterated brands have been found."

"Which isn't to say that no others exist," Davie interjected. "We may just not have got to them yet."

"Possibly," I said, nodding. "But there's more to it than that. We've got a guy, the skinhead man, who was heard inside

Frankie's flat and seen outside it. Think about the set-up in the Colonies. The dead man's sprawled on the river bank – but where's the poisoned whisky?"

"On the kitchen table fifty yards away." The guardian's brow was furrowed. "And nicotine in that strength acts very quickly. So the victim was either rushed out of the house or . . ."

"Or he was given the whisky on the bank of the Water of Leith and the killer took the bottle back to the flat afterwards," I said.

"Why would he do that?" Davie asked.

"And why would he make so much noise in the flat and on the street?" I asked.

Hamilton looked at me. "They were singing drunken songs, weren't they?"

I nodded. "But why would the mystery man join in to the extent that the neighbour heard another voice? He could just have let Frankie get on with it and make us think no one else was there. The same thing with showing himself in the street. He could have done away with Frankie inside."

"What are you saying, Dalrymple?" the guardian asked slowly. "That the killer wanted to make it clear that someone else was present? Why would he do that? He made bloody sure he left no fingerprints."

"There's a difference between making an appearance and leaving traces that could lead to his identification," Davie pointed out.

"Correct, guardsman." I grinned at him then glanced back at Hamilton. He looked like a kid who'd just discovered that he's got ten pages of algebra problems for homework.

"You mean there's more to this than meets the eye," he said slowly.

"Could be," I replied. What my father said about drugs traffickers had come back to me. "Let's face it, you need reasonably sophisticated equipment to produce pure nicotine. Maybe we've got a drugs gang playing games with us."

The guardian's eyes widened. "Good God, man. That's a hell of a theory." He wiped his brow and thought about it. I could see he was keen. "I knew it, Dalrymple. We should never have relaxed the original Council's hard line on drugs and allowed the tourists marijuana and hashish. It's an open invitation for criminals across the border to get involved."

He might be right. I thought of Sophia. She shared Hamilton's views on the drugs policy. It might be in her interest to encourage a conspiracy like this to discredit that policy. Tightening up on drugs for tourists would inevitably lead to the repeal of those small citizen freedoms that had been approved recently. That would be a hell of an agenda. But I couldn't see how it tied in directly with Frankie Thomson's death.

The guardian's voice broke into my thoughts. "You are coming to the Council meeting, aren't you, citizen?" It sounded like Hamilton was living in hope rather than expectation. I took advantage of that.

"Davie can stand in for me," I said.

"But . . ." They both spoke at the same time.

"Very good," I said, giving them an encouraging smile. "With a little more rehearsing you'll be able to get the Public Order Directorate view across in perfect harmony."

"And where exactly are you going?" Hamilton shouted as I reached the door.

I'd suddenly thought of a very sensitive source of information. "I'll be sure to tell you if I find out anything useful," I replied.

That left me some room for manoeuvre. Because the person I was going to visit was as likely to headbutt me as he was to talk.

I got into a Land-Rover on the esplanade and asked the middle-aged guardswoman to take the road through the Enlightenment Park. In the old days it was Holyrood Park but the party was quick to change the name. The road circling the crags and the leonine mounds of Arthur's Seat used to be called the Queen's Drive until widespread disillusion with the monarchy made the pre-Enlightenment city council revamp that in the early years of the century. Now it's known as Citizens' Walk – appropriate enough in a city where private cars have been banned for decades. As we swung round the road's gentle bends, I looked out over the desiccated parkland. A cloud of dust was hanging over the slopes, churned up by the buses that take tourists up a dirt track to within a hundred yards of the summit on the other side. A few defeated-looking sheep were chewing what must have been meagre mouthfuls of grass, their spare flanks promising us locals thin soup and gristly stew. It was enough to make you turn vegetarian, except there was limited nutritional value in city farm cereals and root crops because of the Big Heat.

We negotiated the roundabouts and joined the road leading to Duddingston behind the city's biggest swimming-pool. It had been finished seventeen years before I was born in advance of the 1970 Commonwealth Games – when there was still such a thing as a Commonwealth and countries had funds to spare for sporting events. There would be a massive queue of citizens outside the pool on a day as hot as this, waiting for the quarter of an hour each individual is allotted in the eye-scorching, throat-burning water. Of course, the tourists don't have to stand in line. They have all sorts of aquatic delights in their hotels, from jacuzzis to showers with underdressed attendants for both sexes. I scratched an armpit, suddenly aware that I was in serious need of a wash. The way the driver moved her nose suggested she'd noticed too.

Crows rose up from the road ahead and we passed over the tangled remains of a lamb. Which, as the rooftops of the rehab centre came into sight, inevitably made me think of the man I was going to visit. Billy Geddes used to be my closest friend – my contemporary at school and university, fellow blues lover, the guy who joined the Enlightenment Party the same day as I did in the year before the last election and who went through auxiliary training with me. Then we'd gone in different directions. While my interest in crime led me to the Public Order Directorate, he was posted to the Finance Directorate and was soon the mover behind the city's most important deals. He reached as high as deputy guardian before he got his hands dirty and ended up in seriously deep shit five years ago. I had a hand in his downfall. I wondered if he'd remember Frankie Thomson – and, if he did, whether he'd tell me.

The Council turned the former Duddingston village into a centre for the rehabilitation of selected bent auxiliaries about a year ago. Until then even the idea that the rank between guardians and ordinary citizens might be susceptible to bribery, corruption, large-scale thieving and contact with criminal gangs beyond the border was totally unpalatable to the guardians. It was easier just to consign DMs like Frankie Thomson, Katharine and me to the rank of ordinary citizen. At least now they've admitted that bad boys and girls exist. Of course, they don't try to rehabilitate everyone – only those regarded as potentially useful to the Council.

Duddingston was the perfect place to put them. It's not too far from the city centre but remote enough to keep the inmates out of ordinary citizens' view. The fact that the village has high stone walls round most of its edges no doubt appealed as well. In pre-Enlightenment times there was a nature reserve and bird sanctuary by the small loch and the smart Victorian houses were priced beyond the range of even well-off professional types. These days the place is home to deviants instead of rare birds and what used to be a trendy pub houses the guard command post.

The driver pulled up at the barrier outside the village and I flashed my authorisation. To our right what remained of the loch, a small extent of swamp in the central depression, glowed dull brown in the sunlight. A couple of seagulls flipflopped across the mud looking for something to get their beaks round. The acrid smell of drying excrement hung over the place.

"Where to, citizen?" the guardswoman asked as the barrier was raised.

"Park outside the gate. I won't be long." I didn't want her to know which inmate I was visiting. It would get back to Hamilton sooner or later but I didn't see why I should make things easy for the old bugger. He wouldn't approve anyway.

I walked down Old Church Lane and passed a couple of guys who stared at my T-shirt and black trousers. The guardsman was satisfied after a glance at my card but the other one had no excuse for looking askance at my clothing. He was in the black and white striped overalls and yellow beret issued to inmates. They call the jokers "lollipops" in the guard but citizens don't have a nickname for them. Despite the Council's much-vaunted openness, only auxiliaries are allowed in to the rehab centre so ordinary locals never see the inmates' apparel.

I turned into what had been the churchyard and looked at the board on the wall. Inmates are given codenames – they have to earn back the right to their barracks numbers – and Billy was referred to as the Jackal. I suppose the Council thought that giving corrupt auxiliaries animal names is a neat way of emphasising their bestiality. The Jackal was still in residence in the old watchtower. Obviously his rehabilitation hadn't yet been completed.

I went in the door at the bottom of the building.

The white-bearded sentry made me sign in and then waved me up the narrow stairs. "The Jackal's right at the top," he called after me.

"I know," I said, feeling the muscles beginning to hurt already. The first time I visited Billy I wondered why he'd been stuck at the highest point in the rehab centre. The guy was in a wheelchair for life and he was hardly going to perform his own version of *Escape from Alcatraz*. Then I remembered that he had a track record of escaping official supervision.

I reached a heavy oak door and paused to catch my breath.

"Who's that?" The voice was more high-pitched and unsteady but I recognised it all the same. "Don't just hang around. Come in."

I decided knocking was unnecessary and pulled the door open. That was a mistake.

"What the—" The voice broke off as the wheelchair with its crazed, shrunken passenger cannoned into my legs and nearly sent me straight back down the stairs.

I got off my arse slowly. It had taken a heavy slam on to the flagstones.

"Nice driving, Billy," I said, pushing the wheelchair backwards.

"What the fuck do you want, you tosser?" Billy looked away from me and struggled to heave himself back into his room. "I thought you were my counsellor. I fucking hate him."

"Just as well I wasn't or you'd have been on punishment rations." I followed him into the square space at the top of the tower. It had tall, narrow windows on each side, the front one giving a view over the dried loch bed. Under this was a wide desk with a computer and screen. That was interesting.

"How did you get your hands on this?" I asked, moving over to the machine.

"That's typical of you, Quint." Billy banged into my legs again, making me turn aside before I got to the computer. "You arrive unannounced after months and don't even bother to say hello or ask me how I am. Always the fucking investigator." He shoved me further away from the desk, his arms much stronger than his withered frame suggested.

"Sorry," I said. I meant it. I still felt some responsibility for the events that put him in the chair. "So how are you doing, Billy?"

"Up yours, Quint," he said, his eyes flashing above the slack skin of his face. "What do you care?"

I put my hands on his shoulders and leaned over him. "I care, you self-pitying little shit. If only because there's still a tiny bit of the guy you used to be left under that jackal skin."

"Ha fucking ha." He looked away and I saw the flaky scalp under what remained of his hair. "You only visit me when you need something." Despite the heat in his room, Billy had his black and white shirt buttoned up to the collar and his sleeves down. He didn't like looking at his shrivelled limbs. I couldn't blame him.

I stood straight again then jinked round him to the computer. "Where did you get this, Billy?" The label on it said "Property of Culture Directorate". Well, well.

He spun his wheels and drove into me, smiling maliciously. "They gave it to me a few months back."

"They? The Culture Directorate?"

He nodded reluctantly.

"Why?"

He looked away, lips pressed tight.

"Why, Billy?" I persisted. "I can find out easily enough from the facility commander."

"What's it got to do with you?" he demanded angrily. "They wanted me to check the financial structure of the lottery."

This was getting more interesting by the minute but I didn't want to show my hand to Billy too soon.

"Is that right? They make use of your financial acumen even before you're fully rehabilitated? That sounds like the Council, all right." I glanced back at him. "I'm surprised you went for it. Unless you're using the computer for your own devious purposes as well."

"You'll never know, Quint." He let out a forced laugh that slowly faded away. "Don't worry, I'm not on line. They won't trust me with access to the directorate databank. I just sit here and massage their figures then play *Attila the Hun* 2015. It's the only computer game I could squeeze out of them."

I sat down on the bed and looked round the room. There were no chairs since Billy didn't need one and he didn't have many visitors. But all the walls were lined with bookshelves and I recognised some from Billy's collection of first editions. He'd started that when he was in the Finance Directorate and he obviously still had a good contact in the Library Department. He'd been allowed to keep his edition of Hume's *Treatise* as well as hardback novels by Waugh, Orwell and plenty of other big names. He even had a copy of *Red Harvest* that I'd coveted for years.

There was a rattle as the wheelchair moved across the bare floorboards of the tower room.

"What do you want to know, Quint?" Billy asked sardonically. "What can I possibly tell you that you can't find out for yourself using the methods you're famous for?"

I couldn't wait any longer. "Did you ever know an auxiliary numbered Napier 25?"

Billy kept perfectly still apart from a slight flicker of his eyelids. "Napier 25," he repeated, looking up at the ceiling. "Napier 25. Yeah, I remember him."

Halleluiah. "And?"

"He was with me in the Strategic Planning Department." He moved his eyes back to me. "Boring tosser. Pretty good at cost control and analysis though. I think he had a bit of a drink problem. What's your interest?"

I ignored his question. "Remember anything specific he worked on?"

Billy laughed. "Christ, Quint, it's five years since I was booted out of the directorate." His eyes flashed. "And since I got my head kicked in."

"I haven't forgotten," I said, holding his gaze. "Did you know he was demoted a year back?"

Billy shrugged. "How would I? He hasn't turned up here for rehab."

"No," I said, "and he isn't going to either. He died a couple of days ago."

"Lucky him." Billy looked down at his shrunken limbs.

"No, not lucky him. He drank poisoned whisky." I was taking a chance telling a DM about a classified case but I wanted to see his reaction. So far he'd been just a little too cool.

"You mean someone murdered him?" Billy asked with what seemed like no more than normal amounts of surprise and curiosity.

I nodded. "Ever heard of a whisky called the Ultimate Usquebaugh?"

Billy didn't take his eyes off me. "Sounds like quite a dram. They don't give us any booze in here, you know."

"Have you ever fucking heard of it?" I yelled.

He jerked back in his chair. The extent to which his body had been wrecked was suddenly very apparent. "No, I fucking haven't. Bastard."

I nodded. I was pretty sure he was telling the truth, at least about that. I went over to the window. The seagulls were still flapping around languidly, their shrieks cutting through the hot air. I was less convinced that Billy had been straight about Frankie Thomson. True enough, it was a long time since he'd been in the Finance Directorate.

"So you've been working on Edlott?" I said, trying to make my peace with him. "What do you think of it?"

"Fuck you," he said, turning away.

"Billy, I'm sorry. I needed to know if you'd heard of the whisky."

"Yeah, yeah," he said bitterly. "As if I'd know anything locked up in this school for unjustified sinners."

"Personally I think the lottery's a con," I said. The only way to get to him was by winding him up.

"You do, do you?" he said, swinging his wheels round. "The great financial expert Quintilian Dalrymple gives his opinion. Big fucking deal. Listen to someone who knows what he's talking about. Edlott's the ultimate success story. The citizens get a chance to improve the quality of their lives and the Council saves funds by deducting the cost of tickets from food and clothing vouchers. Everyone's happy." He grinned and displayed yellow teeth. Apparently the rehab centre didn't run to a dentist. "I'll tell you a secret for nothing. Soon the tourists will be able to play too."

I hadn't heard that before. "Whose bright idea was that, Billy?"

"Whose do you think, Quint?" He wriggled in an unsuccessful attempt at modesty. "See, I still have some uses."

"Good for you," I said, glad to hear that he was getting

something out of life. "Who should I talk to in the Culture Directorate if I want information?" I still needed to find out what Frankie Thomson had been doing on his frequent visits there.

Billy bit his lip. "Your best bet's the senior auxiliary in charge of operations. That's Nasmyth 05."

"Right, thanks." I remembered that was the barracks number I'd seen in Fordyce Kennedy's file. I wondered if there was any chance he'd heard about the missing lottery-winner. "Billy, there's something else. Do you know anything about—" My mobile rang and I broke off. I could see from the look on Billy's face that sentence interruptus was no more fun than the sexual variety.

"Dalrymple? Public order guardian here." Trust Hamilton to use his title on the phone.

"Yes, Lewis."

"Another body's been found."

"Shit. Whereabouts?"

"Baird Drive, to the west of the stadium at Murrayfield. There's a footbridge—"

"I'm on my way. Make sure no one touches anything. Out."

I gave Billy a brief wave on my way to the door. His response was pure abuse.

As I took the stairs three at a time on the way down the tower I continued the swearing Billy had started. I knew the footbridge Hamilton had mentioned.

It sounded like we had a second body by the Water of Leith.

Chapter Eight

———∞∞———

I pulled the road map out from underneath the driver's seat and
checked the access.

"You'll need to go past the stadium and turn left on to
Balgreen Road."

"I know where I'm going, citizen," the guardswoman said
sharply. She kept her eyes fixed on the road ahead, obviously one
of those who disapprove of DMs like me being involved with the
directorate. There's no shortage of them.

I let her get on with it and looked out at the giant cantilevered
construction around the former international rugby ground.
Now it's used for inter-barracks games, the vast stands echoing
the shouts of a few hundred supporters. Things were very
different at the sellout matches I went to in my teens, sixty-
five thousand souls going mental whenever a man in blue scored.
Scotland victories got fewer and fewer as opposition countries
ploughed ridiculous amounts of money into the game, but the
supporters still lived in hope. It gave the impression that some
sort of national consciousness existed. That was soon revealed to
be an illusion as the crime rate rocketed upwards and the drugs
gangs tore society apart. Then the politicians started taking the
easy option, preaching zero tolerance, isolationism and the like.
The riots weren't long in coming and then rugby was played in
the streets with people's heads for balls.

There was a blast from a horn behind us. I turned to see Davie roar past us in a Land-Rover, his arm jerking like a marionette's.

"I think he wants you to follow him," I said.

The guardswoman didn't even favour me with a glance. She floored the accelerator and took off after Davie like her tail was on fire. That shut me up.

We turned into a side street and slewed to a stop at the back of a long line of guard vehicles. Hamilton was surrounded by a group of his minions, some of them in white plastic overalls. He saw me and beckoned me over.

"At last, Dalrymple," he said, dismissing the auxiliaries with a single movement of his hand. "Where have you been?"

"Does it matter?" I asked, nodding to Davie as he joined us. "What's the story here?"

"Female citizen who works as a cleaner in the stadium spotted an arm under the bridge on her way home." Hamilton took us down the street towards the footbridge that led to an open expanse of grass between the houses and the rugby ground. As we got nearer, his pace slowed. "You go ahead," he said, his face pale. "I've seen all I want to." As usual, the public order guardian's interest in bodies had waned as soon as he got close to them.

Davie and I exchanged glances then crossed over the bridge to where a couple of scene-of-crime personnel were squatting. They pointed to the line of tape they'd set up around the area that would potentially reveal footprints. We scrambled down the bank further down and walked up the shallow stream to the shaded confines of the bridge. Our feet stirred up the bottom, making me think of the old blues motif – muddy water was a seriously bad omen. The curtain of blowflies under the struts didn't exactly bode well either.

"Bloody hell, Quint," Davie said in a low voice. "Déjà vu."

I stopped about five yards away from the body and let the water wash around my ankles. The dead man was certainly in a similar position to Frankie Thomson's. He was on his front, the left arm beside his torso but the right one extended at about ninety degrees, as seen by the female citizen. The legs were spread at a wide angle, but because of the proximity of the bridge supports the lower parts were bent backwards against the bank. As well as the head, the chest was in the water.

"What's that he's wearing?" Davie asked. "It's not exactly standard-citizen issue, is it?"

I moved closer and kneeled down in the water. It felt unnaturally warm, like a fluid that shouldn't have been released into the open air. Davie had a point. The dead man was dressed in a white shirt and black trousers but neither were of the basic style ordinary citizens get in exchange for their clothing vouchers. The trousers were more like knickerbockers, ending just below the knee, and the shirt had elaborate cuffs. I pulled on rubber gloves and picked up the right hand. Rigor mortis was not far advanced yet. There was a gold-coloured cufflink holding the material together. My bad feeling began to get worse. There are very few kinds of people kitted out with cufflinks in the city these days.

"Look at these boots, citizen," said one of the scene-of-crime auxiliaries.

I moved over and examined the footwear. They were high boots reaching up to the top of the dead man's calves, with a large number of eyes for the laces.

I stepped over the body and looked at the left hand. It was closed tightly around something that after inspection I saw to be white fabric.

"A handkerchief," I said, going towards the head. I put both my hands on it and moved it sideways gently. The rigor in the neck was tighter than in the arms but I managed to get a glimpse of something I'd been hoping I wouldn't see.

"What is that?" Davie asked. "What's caught beneath his collar?"

I beckoned to the directorate photographer to take a shot of what looked like a long, hairy caterpillar.

"It's a false moustache, my friend," I said slowly, my fears now confirmed. I'd seen enough of the features to recognise the dead man. "This is Fordyce Kennedy, the missing lottery-winner. They got him to dress up as Robert Louis Stevenson, remember?"

I sat back on my heels in the water as the realisation struck me. I was going to have to inform the two women we'd visited in the darkened flat in Morningside. That made my day.

Sophia arrived a few minutes after I'd sent Davie to liaise with the scene-of-crime personnel. She stood on the bank pulling on her protective overalls, an impassive look on her face. She didn't respond to my wave.

When she joined me under the footbridge, she started dictating detailed notes of the body's position to her assistant then kneeled down by the torso and continued talking. It was only after she'd finished her preliminary description that she acknowledged my existence by glancing up at me.

"There are broad similarities with the dead man in Bell Place," she said. "Taking the ambient temperature into account, I'd say he's been here for between eight and twelve hours."

I decided to play her game and pretend that Katharine's intrusion had never happened. "Cause of death?" I asked.

"No obvious signs of injury." She looked round and shook her head briefly at me. "We'll need to run tests on the internal organs."

I went up to her and led her a small distance away. "It's likely that we've got another case of poisoning, Sophia. You'll be testing for nicotine first, won't you?"

"We'll have to." Her expression was grim. "Have you found any whisky bottles in the vicinity?"

"Not yet. I've got Davie co-ordinating the search with the scene-of-crime squad."

Sophia turned away from the other auxiliaries under the bridge. Her face paled and for a few seconds she looked like a lost child. "What are we to do if it *is* nicotine again, Quint? There are already reports of citizen unrest in the suburbs because of the whisky ban." She looked at me anxiously. "I can't authorise resupply if there's even the slightest chance of lethal poisoning."

I took a chance and squeezed her arm in public. Bad move. She pulled it away instantly. "Look, it won't just be your decision. The Council takes collective responsibility, remember?"

"I'm aware of procedure," she snapped. "But I'm medical guardian as well as acting senior guardian. I've got nowhere to hide."

I nodded. "You never know," I said encouragingly. "Maybe this'll turn out not to be a case of poisoning."

She looked at me sceptically.

"All right," I admitted. "I'm not making that assumption." Then I told her the identity of the dead man.

"The missing Edlott-winner?" she said in puzzlement. "Is that significant?"

I shrugged. "Who knows? Maybe he didn't like being made to dress up as the creator of Long John Silver."

"Stevenson also created Dr Jekyll," Sophia said, grimacing. "I seem to remember that character created a dangerous potion."

I wasn't sure what to make of that. By the time I'd finished scratching my head, Sophia had gone to consult Hamilton.

A few moments later Davie came running down the river bank brandishing an object in a clear plastic bag. I recognised the Ultimate Usquebaugh label from some way off. Only a small amount of the dark amber liquid in the bottle was missing. Now I had no doubt there was a connection with the first death, but we still had to check the details.

At four o'clock we broke off to compare notes. Hamilton and Davie had debriefed the scene-of-crime squad while I was interviewing the woman who'd found the body and the citizens who lived in the street leading to the footbridge.

"Right," I said. "The medical guardian's taken the body to the morgue for post-mortem. I asked her to go ahead without me. The chief toxicologist is standing by so we should know soon if this is a case of nicotine poisoning. He's also got the bottle you found, Davie. What was the exact location?"

He pointed to a cross he'd made on the fine-detail City Guard map of the area. "It was protruding from a rabbit hole ninety-seven yards upstream on the east bank."

"The same bank as the body was lying on," the public order guardian said.

I nodded. "Any prints or traces on the ground around there?" Davie shook his head. "It's bone-hard."

"As it is everywhere in the city during the Big Heat," I said ruefully.

"And guess what," Davie said, looking at us and shaking his head. "I got a technician to dust the bottle. There were no fingerprints on it."

"It's clear enough that we're dealing with the same killer or killers," Hamilton said, jumping to conclusions with the certainty typical of the old school of guardians. This time he was probably right. "Like the other bottle, this one has only a small quantity taken from it. Enough for one lethal dram," he said, ramming the point home. "The relative distance of the bottle from the body is also a link to the previous murder."

I nodded and looked at my notebook.

"What have you discovered, Dalrymple?" the public order guardian asked.

"Not much. The female citizen who found the body didn't notice it on her way to the stadium for the morning shift. That figures because the arm is hardly visible from the west side of the bridge. She had a migraine and left work early so I suppose we were lucky. That bought us a few extra hours. She didn't see or hear anything overnight or in the early morning. The same goes for the other locals."

"Which puts paid to your theory about the killer deliberately showing himself at the Colonies, doesn't it?" Hamilton said.

I thought about that. "Not necessarily. Maybe the first death needed more stage-managing. Maybe that's why there were three bottles there as well."

The guardian stared at me, his brows knotting. "Stick to the basics, man. How the hell did the body get here? On a flying carpet?"

I took the map from Davie and opened it out. To the east of the bridge the open space of frazzled grass stretched all the way to the rugby ground three hundred yards away.

"They could have come across the playing fields, I suppose," I said.

"They?" Davie said.

"The killer or killers and the victim. It's not very likely that the dead man killed himself by drinking from the bottle, putting it in a rabbit hole then walking on till he keeled over. Someone took the trouble to leave the bottle in a place that wasn't too obvious, increasing the likelihood that *we* found it rather than some innocent passer-by. And the assumption has to be that they walked here." I gave Hamilton a grin. "Otherwise they have access to transport, which would suggest they're auxiliaries."

The guardian glared at me but managed to bite his tongue.

"That's very unlikely, of course," I said, twisting the knife.

"Quint," Davie growled.

I raised my hand. "Okay. I said we're assuming they walked."

"But the playing fields are fenced to the north and in the vicinity of the stadium," said Hamilton. "Plus there's a guard post over there."

I nodded and took a long pull from a bottle of water. We were standing in the burning heat in the middle of the road because I'd talked the guardian out of commandeering some innocent local's house for the duration.

"Right. And the residents to the west claim they heard nothing."

"What would there have been to hear if they were on foot?" Davie asked.

"They would probably have arrived after curfew so even footsteps would have been out of the ordinary. It's certainly odd that it doesn't seem to have been like Frankie Thomson's last minutes — no singing or sounds of carousing. But remember, the family told us that Fordyce Kennedy liked his whisky. I suppose he could have been completely out of the brain."

"Maybe he was killed somewhere else," Hamilton put in.

I nodded. "We can't rule out that possibility. Except in both those cases he would have been carried here, which would have made an obvious target for guard patrols." I looked back at the map. "I reckon they came from the south. After all, the bottle was left in that direction. And that way, beyond the old railway line, there's more open ground with houses backing on to it before you get to the Gorgie Road." I glanced at Davie. "You'd better get the scene-of-crime people to check for any prints or traces down there. And Lewis, can you put guard personnel on to taking statements from residents there?"

Hamilton gave me an ironic look. "I thought you'd want to do that yourself, Dalrymple. You're forever telling me that citizens would rather choke than open up to auxiliaries."

"True enough," I said, returning the look with interest. "It's just that I've got more pressing things to do. Like breaking the bad news to the dead man's next of kin." I moved away. "And getting them to identify the body."

I found Sophia and the chief toxicologist standing over Fordyce Kennedy. He had been opened up from throat to pubis and his organs removed. The green-coated figures looked up as the door banged behind me.

"Bad news, citizen," said Lister 25. "I've just completed testing for nicotine."

"And it was present in both the whisky and the dead man's stomach," I said.

He nodded at me dolefully.

"I can't say that comes as an overwhelming surprise." I turned to Sophia. "Any other signs of injury?"

She gave me a neutral look then shook her head. "Nothing at all. He doesn't appear to have been under duress."

"How about alcohol consumption?" I asked.

Again she shook her head. "Preliminary inspection of the stomach suggests that the only alcohol he consumed was the small quantity of poisoned whisky which killed him."

That was interesting. Fordyce Kennedy wasn't under the influence of alcohol when he went to the river bank during curfew – so why did he go there? Did someone talk him into it?

"If I could interject?" the chief toxicologist said, glancing at each of us in turn. "The amount of nicotine in the second bottle of the Ultimate Usquebaugh was considerably greater than in the first. The medical guardian and I are agreed that death would have been very rapid – probably a matter of seconds after the whisky was imbibed."

I looked at Fordyce Kennedy's remains and shook my head. Having your throat and gut burned out even for only a few seconds was still a horrific idea. I wondered what kind of bastard would inflict suffering of that degree on another human being. Or rather, other human beings, plural.

"Can you make him respectable?" I asked Sophia. "The relatives will need to see him."

"Of course," she said. "But only the face will be uncovered. And Quint? We won't be able to release the body for some time."

"I know."

Sophia came up to me. "You realise you can't tell his next of kin anything about the poisoning, of course. It's top secret until the Council decides otherwise."

I've never been a fan of the guardians' addiction to secrecy but there wasn't much I could do about it. "What are we going to tell them?"

"Heart attack. That's the most straightforward."

Straightforward for you maybe, I thought as I turned away. Telling lies to my fellow citizens is something I've never got used to. On the other hand, most murders take place within the immediate family circle, meaning that Hilda Kennedy and her children had to be treated as potential suspects. It might be in my interest to make them think they'd got away with it. Sometimes this job really makes me sick.

I called Davie from the guard vehicle that was taking me to the dead man's flat.

"No luck so far," he said. "Scene-of-crime are carrying out a detailed examination of the ground beyond where we found the whisky bottle but there are no obvious prints. I'm just going to start interviewing the locals in the nearest houses."

"Okay. Let me know if anything turns up."

"Where are you now?"

"Passing Napier Barracks on my way to notify the next of kin."

"Rather you than me, Quint."

"Thanks a lot, guardsman. Out."

I leaned back in my seat to avoid the glare of the sun from the west and wondered who had enticed Fordyce Kennedy to the killing ground at the Water of Leith. And why.

"Citizen Dalrymple," Agnes said, the languid look on her face quickly changing to one of alarm as she took in my expression. She was dressed in the same paint-spotted workclothes and scarf as she'd been wearing the last time I saw her. "Oh, my God. What's happened?"

"Is your mother in?" I asked in a low voice.

"Who is it, lassie?" Hilda Kennedy appeared at the far end of the hallway. She was knotting a scarf round her hair. It sounded like she was in one of her more lucid spells. When she saw me, she came forward quickly. "Don't tell me you've found my man? Have you found him?" Her voice got shriller as she registered the set of my face. I've never worked out a way of doing this that softens the blow. "Agnes, what's happened to him?"

"Can I come in?" I said as doors began to open in the stairwell.

Agnes took control and put her arm round her mother, who'd suddenly gone limp. "The sitting room," she said, nodding at me to go first.

I went into the room that was full of the dead man's handiwork. The curtains were drawn against the sunlight as before. This time the darkness was a relief. After a minute the two of them appeared. Hilda was clutching a handkerchief in one hand and I had a sudden flashback to her husband's tightly clenched fingers on the river bank. They'd have had difficulty prising them apart in the morgue to remove the square of cloth with the fake bloodstain that was meant to make people think of the tubercular writer.

"Just tell us, son," Agnes said dully. "Tell us what you've found."

I gave them the ID card that I'd taken from the dead man's trouser pocket.

"I'm afraid Citizen Kennedy has had a heart attack," I said, stepping closer to them.

Agnes's body stiffened like she'd been given an electric shock. She looked at her mother immediately. It was difficult to tell whether the older woman understood my words.

"Is he . . . ? Is he . . . ?" Agnes looked at me steadily but she didn't complete the question.

I nodded.

Hilda looked up and saw my confirmation. She shrank into her daughter's arms again and retreated into her own world. It seemed as private and impenetrable as a child's in the womb. Agnes let her down slowly on to the sofa and watched as her mother keeled over and wrapped her arms in their baggy sleeves around her thin body. Then she got up and led me to the far end of the room.

"Where did you find my father?" she asked in a controlled voice. Her brown eyes were moist but she wasn't allowing tears to form.

"Near Murrayfield stadium. Any idea why he'd have been in that area, Agnes?"

She shook her head. "We don't know anyone over there. Maybe it was something to do with Edlott."

"Maybe." That was a possibility but it wouldn't explain why he was out after curfew.

"My dad never had any problems with his heart," she said, holding her eyes on me. The challenge in them was inescapable.

I forced myself to meet her gaze, feeling like a reptile. I almost told her the truth about her father's death but breaking the Council security restriction on the killings would only have landed me in the castle dungeons. So I went on bullshitting her. "It sometimes happens that way," I concluded. After what seemed like an eternity she looked back to where her mother was, motionless on the sofa like a discarded doll.

"Agnes," I said in a low voice, going for broke in the bastard stakes. "According to City Regulations your mother will have to identify the body." I could have got an exemption for someone whose mental state was as unstable as Hilda's, but I wanted to see how she and her daughter reacted to the body.

Agnes wasn't disturbed. She leaned so close to me that I could feel the light spray of her saliva on my face. I caught the smell of paint in my nostrils again. "I know my mother will want to see him, citizen. So do I."

"Are you sure?" I asked disingenuously.

"I know my mother. I knew my father too," Agnes said. The challenge was in her eyes again. "He never died of a heart attack."

I shrugged then called Sophia to tell her we were on our way.

As we were leaving the flat, Hilda with a blank expression as she clutched her daughter's arm, I wondered about the surviving male member of the family.

"What about your brother?" I whispered to Agnes. "Shouldn't we try to let him know."

"Allie?" she said dully. "You'll have to find him first."

I stopped and turned to her. "He's not missing as well, is he?"

She shook her head. "Of course not. He was here at breakfast this morning, wasn't he, Mother?"

Hilda stared at her emptily, her mouth half open, then nodded. "Allie," she said, smiling. "He's a good lad, our Allie."

"Come on," Agnes said. She seemed to have developed an aversion to looking at me. I couldn't really blame her.

As they were getting into the guard vehicle, I called the command centre and got them to instigate an all-barracks search for Alexander Kennedy, known as Allie.

Sophia's people had done a good job. Fordyce Kennedy lay with his body covered and bandages wrapped around his head, the brain already removed. The dead man's face, despite the onset of rigor mortis, looked surprisingly calm. Hilda smiled as she touched her man's cheek. I wondered if she really understood what was going on. Agnes was holding her mother's arm, eyes fixed on her father's face. A nursing auxiliary gave them a pretty convincing story about what had supposedly happened and how little he'd suffered. It seemed to work because they left quietly enough after she'd patiently answered their questions. Hilda even mutely accepted the ruling that the body remain in the infirmary indefinitely.

As they were leaving I heard Agnes let out her first gasp of grief. I wanted to comfort her but I felt too guilty about the lies I'd told. After they left in a guard vehicle, I asked Sophia to assign a female nurse to look after them. That didn't make me feel any better. I wanted to be able to find out what went on in their flat in the immediate future. It had turned into a day that was heavy on deceit.

An emergency Council meeting was called for seven o'clock. I met Davie and Hamilton in the entrance hall of the former parliament building.

"Any joy?"

They both shook their heads.

"What, nothing at all?"

"No traces or prints, no witnesses to any sights or sounds overnight," Davie said, wiping the sweat from his face. His guard shirt was soaked.

Hamilton was standing by an ornate mirror tightening his Council tie. "How about you, Dalrymple? Any further on?"

Before I could reply the culture guardian came up, his expression as suave as usual. He had a fleshy auxiliary wearing a well-cut business suit in tow. That individual's cheeks were red and the waves in his fair hair looked unnatural. He also had a wide-eyed look that smacked of panic.

"Gentlemen," the guardian said, smiling with tight lips at Lewis and Davie. He ran a disapproving eye over my crumpled T-shirt and trousers. "Citizen Dalrymple. This is Nasmyth 05. He runs Edlott. I told him you might want to talk to him about the winner who has met with such an unfortunate end." He glared at me as if what had happened to Fordyce Kennedy was my fault then went into the chamber.

So this was the auxiliary who'd consulted the dead man's file and who Billy Geddes had mentioned. He pulled out a handkerchief and mopped his face. His demeanour was that of a man who wished he was in a faraway place.

"Guardian," he said, giving Lewis a respectful nod and completely ignoring Davie and me. "This is appalling news. How can it be that an Edlott-winner has been killed?"

I didn't think much of his manners. "Maybe you can tell us something about that, Nasmyth 05? Was there some part of his duties as an Edlott-winner that might explain why he first went missing and then got killed?"

He swelled up his chest and gave me a disdainful glance. "My department looks after the winners with the utmost care, citizen. I resent the suggestion that we bear any responsibility for what has happened." He looked at Hamilton for support. "Publicising this would be a disaster. People will stop buying lottery tickets if they think the winners are at risk." He shook his head frantically. "It's particularly bad timing given that we're about to extend operations to the tourist market."

"I'm sure Fordyce Kennedy thought it was bad timing as well," I said.

"What?" The fat man looked at me blankly. "Oh, I see."

The bell rang, announcing the start of the meeting.

"Go back to running the lottery," I said, walking past the auxiliary. "And expect me to come knocking on your door in the near future."

He didn't look too enamoured with that prospect.

The Council meeting was a fraught affair. Sophia had her hands full controlling a debate about restarting the supply of whisky. Despite the latest death, the Tourism Directorate was desperate that sales in the city-centre hotels and bars be authorised and the finance guardian was fearful about the loss of revenue. Even Hamilton argued for a partial resumption of supplies to citizens; he was worried about unrest spreading through the suburbs. After the chief toxicologist agreed to release stocks that had been tested, partial resupply to tourists was approved. Sophia looked uneasy but she bowed to her colleagues' arguments. They also voted to keep Fordyce Kennedy's death out of the *Edinburgh Guardian* and off the radio.

"Moving on to the details of the second poisoning case," she said. "I can confirm that nicotine has been found in the whisky and the victim's body. Time of death was between three and four a.m. this morning, and the strength of the dose of nicotine was such that the victim died on the spot. Analysis of the victim's body and clothes has revealed no fibres or traces of an assailant."

"Any sign of controlled drugs?" I asked.

Sophia seemed surprised by the question. "None. Why do you ask, citizen?"

I shrugged, not wanting to push the idea of drugs gang involvement yet.

The senior guardian's eyes bored into mine. "How do you propose to find the killer or killers, citizen?"

She had me there. I gave them a spiel about investigating the dead man's family and associates. I was also going to work on potential connections between the dead men. I didn't tell the Council about Frankie Thomson's visits to the Culture Directorate though. Could Edlott be the common ground between the murders? I was completely in the dark about that.

My flat was in the dark as well when I got back after curfew, along with the rest of the city outside the central zone. Davie and I had spent the evening following up the Kennedy family's records and checking out their relatives, friends and neighbours. None of them had the label "murderer" dangling round their necks. They all seemed to be normal hard-working citizens and there were no offence notifications of any significance against their names. The only dubious specimen was the son Allie. He still hadn't been found by the guard. There was nothing specific to link him to the poisonings so it was pretty hard to construct a case against him. Maybe he'd show up at the flat in Morningside after curfew – such things happen in the outer suburbs. I had a guard Land-Rover waiting at the end of the street in case he did.

I couldn't be bothered to light a candle when I got inside. I was so exhausted that I would be asleep as soon as my head hit the pillow. There was one thing I had to do before that happened. I pulled out my mobile and called Sophia.

"Senior guardian," she answered in clipped tones. It almost sounded like she got a kick out of using the title.

"It's me," I said.

"Me? Who's me?" Either she had incipient deafness or she was playing hard to get.

"Me, the person you've been having sex with recently." I was too tired for games. "Are you all right?"

"Why shouldn't I be?" she answered combatively. "Anything to report?"

"How romantic."

There was a pause. "Quint, I'm very busy. Please let me get on with my work."

"Oh for God's sake, Sophia. Katharine isn't around, if that's what you're worried about."

"What makes you think I'm worried about that individual? I'm not the one she's after."

"She isn't after me," I said, laughing weakly. "What gave you that idea?"

She paused again before replying. "I've been reading her file, Quint. She's a dangerous woman."

"Yeah, yeah. And I'm a pathetic tosser who can't look after himself."

"Your words, not mine." She cut the connection.

"Bollocks!" I shouted. A few seconds later there was a series of violent thumps from my neighbour upstairs.

I got to my bedroom by braille and sat down on the bed. A sudden movement from the other side made me freeze. I jumped back.

"Bollocks?" Katharine said sleepily. "How kind."

"Fuck!"

"It gets better and better."

"No, you gave me a hell of a shock. Where have you been? How did you unlock the front door?"

"Wouldn't you like to know?" She rolled over. "I think I'll pass on both your offers. Good night."

I nearly gave her a rendition of Mary Dixon's "You Can't Sleep In My Bed" but that would have made the neighbours put a contract out on me. Then I considered climbing in but the thought of Sophia discouraged me. She'd probably be round at the crack of dawn to carry out a dormitory inspection. So I went back to the living room and stretched out on my vertebra-wrenching sofa.

Where I sank into an exceedingly wet dream. Not one that had anything to do with Sophia or Katharine though. I found myself engulfed by water, tidal waves and floods of it. I was bobbing over a submerged Edinburgh in the midst of a crowd of motionless citizen bodies. In the background the Band were playing "Cripple Creek" con brio. I woke up in a sweat, gasping for breath and wondering why the two men who'd drunk the ultimate water of life had been found with their heads in the Water of Leith.

Then I had an idea that hit me like a truck. I didn't get much more sleep that night.

Chapter Nine

I woke up on the sofa with a serious crick in my neck and a thirst that Gunga Din would have had trouble assuaging. Fortunately Katharine had repeated her trick with the water-bottles. I thought she'd sneaked off again till I heard sounds in the bedroom. She appeared at the door, her hair ruffled and one of my T-shirts on the upper part of her body. It had lost a lot of colour in the wash house but the slogan was still visible: it read "Edlott – Ultimate Prizes, Ultimate Satisfaction". As long as you didn't win a stint in the Robert Louis Stevenson costume.

"When I got up you were sleeping the sleep of the just," Katharine said with a smile. "The just knackered. It was so sweet."

"Uh-huh. I'd have enjoyed it more if I'd been in my bed."

She raised her eyebrows. "No one stopped you getting in."

I staggered to the curtain and pulled it open. Then closed it rapidly. I was no match for the sunlight.

"I'll see you later," Katharine said.

By the time I turned round, she was at the door. "Hang on a minute. Where are you going?"

"I've got things to do," she said, bending over her bag and stuffing her dirty shirt into it.

"What things?" I went towards her, picking up a bottle of water on the way and gulping from it.

"Just things." She smiled at me again, this time a bit uncertainly.

"How the hell did you get in here last night?"

Her lips twitched. "You're the detective." She took hold of the door handle. "You work it out."

"You didn't," I said with a groan. "You didn't use that 'ask no questions' to get a key cut?"

"Very good, Quint. You haven't lost your touch." She pulled the door open. "Even if your taste in women has taken a nose dive."

"Here," I called, "when will you be back?"

The door had closed behind her before I finished the question.

I climbed the upper reaches of the Royal Mile, puffing and blowing like an unfit sea lion. It was sweltering in the confines of Castlehill and I stopped to get my breath. A crowd of Korean tourists in shorts and sunhats were gathered outside the Camera Obscura. I hoped they'd manage to see something of the city through the heat haze that builds up from daybreak during the Big Heat.

Then I caught sight of the solid walls of the reservoir that stands at the north-eastern corner of the esplanade. It holds a couple of million gallons of water and supplies much of central Edinburgh. What's called the Witches Well is on the top end of the reservoir building. Hundreds of unfortunate and no doubt innocent women were executed there, the last as late as the eighteenth century. My thoughts last night about the Ultimate Usquebaugh flooded back. Could there be a link with the city's water? If someone could put poison in whisky, why not in the water supply as well?

I wanted to talk to Lewis Hamilton but he wasn't in his office. His secretary told me that he and Davie had gone to interview a citizen in Murrayfield. I asked myself why they hadn't let me know about that, then realised that I'd managed to turn my mobile off accidentally. That would explain why I hadn't had an early-morning call from Sophia. I told the grey-haired female auxiliary that I'd wait for the public order guardian in his office. She wasn't keen but I waved my Council authorisation at her.

Lewis's office was as tidy as a junior guardsman's billet, the piles of folders on his large and spotless Victorian desk arranged in neat military lines. You'd hardly know there was a major enquiry under way. The table in the far corner with his computer terminal was a different story. A couple of manuals had been left open on top of the keyboard and bits of crumpled paper littered the surface. Obviously the guardian had been trying to track something down in the databank. He'd probably given up in disgust, too proud to ask for help. Even in a city where computers are restricted to senior auxiliaries who've always regarded them with extreme suspicion, Hamilton would walk away with the Technophobe of the Decade award. That was good news for me. It wouldn't be the first time I'd accessed the Council archives via his terminal. The fact that the guardian was so ill-disposed towards his machine meant that he never bothered to change his passwords as procedure requires. So I booted up, typed the word "Colonel" and got stuck in.

What I really wanted to do was sniff around the Edlott archive but I'd have to visit the Culture Directorate to do that. On the other hand, service records of all auxiliaries are kept in the Public Order Directorate's databank. Hamilton liked to have information on all the city's servants to hand – it was a way of making sure his colleagues in the Council didn't get above themselves. I was interested in Nasmyth 05, the senior auxiliary who had been dragged unwillingly to the Council building by his boss last night. And I also wanted to check out how much was on record about the black-market trade in marijuana and hash emanating from the tourist clubs. Maybe, in my dreams, I would even find some juicy connection – perhaps via Frankie Thomson – between the lottery and the drug trafficking that had got going since the current Council opened things up in the city.

Like I say, in my dreams. The lottery had been set up under the strict supervision of a committee of guardians and senior auxiliaries. If you excepted the basic policy of encouraging greed and personal profit in ordinary citizens (an exception the original Council would have gagged on in a couple of seconds), Edlott was fully compliant with normal control procedures. Nasmyth 05's record showed that he had followed instructions and treated the winners like some kind of minor royalty, earning himself a lot of approving reports from his superiors. His sexual orientation was noted as homo rather than hetero but the Council has no problem with that. He seemed to have a normal sex life with other such male auxiliaries in his barracks. And there had never been any reference to him having tried it on with the male lottery-winners – an activity that would have got him nailed as senior auxiliaries are strictly forbidden sexual relationships with ordinary citizens.

The trade in illicit drugs was more of a black hole. The guard had picked up twenty-seven citizens in possession of small quantities of grass and hash over the last six months. Twenty of those were underage specimens like the pair I'd run into in the Meadows. The Youth Development Department had taken them all under its wing, preventing the guard from carrying out its usual heavy-handed interrogations. The Public Order Directorate had so far not been able to identify any traffickers and the suspicion was that not much more than minor pilfering of the marijuana clubs' stock was going on.

I was printing out a list of the seven adult citizens caught in possession of soft drugs – none of them had prior Offence Notifications, suggesting they were hardly career criminals – when Hamilton and Davie came in.

"There you are, Dalrymple," the guardian said, looking unimpressed. "Where the bloody—"

"Sorry, Lewis," I interrupted, logging off. He didn't seem to care that I'd been playing with his computer. "Problem with my mobile."

"Problem with the 'on' switch?" Davie asked with a grin.

"Something like that, guardsman," I answered. Time to change the subject. "Any joy with the Murrayfield resident you've been questioning?"

"None," Hamilton said from the sink in the recess beyond his desk. He'd stuck his head under the tap to cool down. "He was just shooting a line about hearing a gang of dissidents outside his flat. His wife said it wasn't the first time he'd tried to make a name for himself."

Davie put down the waterbottle he'd drained. "I think it's fair to say it'll be the last time."

I nodded, wondering if the buzzing in the anonymous citizen's ears had started to fade yet.

"Just as well you're here actually, Dalrymple." The guardian gave me a smile I didn't like the look of. "The senior guardian tried to call you on numerous occasions earlier on. She's on her way to the castle right now. I think she's intending putting out an all-barracks search for you. She also made an uncharacter-istically crude comment about what she was going to do with your mobile."

Davie looked at me expectantly but I had no intention of explaining that to him.

Sophia arrived a few minutes later and went straight to the head of Hamilton's conference table, studiously avoiding my eyes. She was laden with folders and a leather satchel.

"Thank you, auxiliary, that will be all," she said to Davie after offloading a heap of files marked "Senior Guardian/Public Order Guardian Eyes Only".

"Hume 253 stays," I said, forcing her to look at me. It wasn't a pleasant experience. "He's been involved in the case from the outset." I had a feeling I was about to need all the support I could get.

Lewis Hamilton nodded reluctantly, unwilling to take on the senior guardian in public but equally unwilling to be left without backup from his directorate.

Sophia gave a sigh which suggested that men who needed their hands held shouldn't be involved in murder investigations. "Very well. We've wasted enough time this morning already. Give me an update please, guardian."

Hamilton reeled off a list of negatives — no witnesses in the vicinity of Fordyce Kennedy's body, no more bottles of poisoned whisky, no sightings of the dead man's son.

"Do we really think he's of interest?" Sophia asked.

"We don't really think anything about him," I said testily, pissed off that she'd addressed the question to Lewis rather than to me. "He's a bit of a mystery man, despite the fact that his mother and sister say he was at the family flat yesterday morning. That's why I want to talk to him."

Sophia looked at me dubiously. "Don't you have any other lines of enquiry?"

I leaned forward and filled a glass from the water jug on the table. I had the feeling she wasn't going to be overwhelmed by my ideas about Frankie Thomson, Edlott and the black-market trade in soft drugs but I tried them out all the same. Hers wasn't the only blank face when I finished.

"It's all very far-fetched, isn't it, Dalrymple?" Hamilton said, screwing his eyes up. I'd hoped he would be keen on nailing the lottery and drugs traffickers, given his intense dislike of both.

"Quite so," Sophia said. "Since you're here, Hume 253, what do you think?"

Davie looked at me apologetically then stuck the knife in. "There doesn't seem to be much evidence of any connection with the poisonings."

So much for creative investigation techniques. I should have stitched my lips together but I've never taken criticism well, especially not from guardians and auxiliaries. I couldn't resist the temptation to hit them with an even more far-fetched scenario.

"What's that?" I asked, pointing.

The three of them followed my outstretched arm past the missing joint of my forefinger to the jug I'd just poured from.

Hamilton and Davie glanced at each other nervously, wondering what idiocy I was up to now.

Sophia just opened a folder and ran her finger down a list of bullet points. "A water jug, citizen," she said without raising her eyes from the page. "Your point?"

So I was "citizen" again, was I? Time to play with a lead ball. "And how much are the contents worth?"

Despite the presence of two of his superiors, Davie had slumped down in his chair, a hand over his eyes. He'd never been able to cope with me baiting guardians.

"What are you talking about, man?" Lewis demanded, forgetting how often I'd hung him out to dry at this game.

"How much are the contents of the jug worth?" I repeated.

Sophia finally looked up. "How much is a pint or so of water worth? Next to nothing."

"You're wrong, senior guardian." If she wanted official titles, she could have them. "As wrong as it's possible to be in this city during the Big Heat."

Davie had removed his hand from his face. At least I was getting through to one of them.

"Would you mind telling us what you're implying, citizen?" There was plenty of irritation in Sophia's voice.

"Yes, stop playing around, Dalrymple," Hamilton said, his cheeks reddening.

Bingo. I had all three of them hooked. "The point is that maybe we aren't dealing with some crazy guys who are having a laugh by knocking off a whisky drinker here and there." I looked round the table. "Maybe we're dealing with people who are putting the squeeze on the city." One more glance round for dramatic effect. "If they can put poison in bottles of whisky, why shouldn't they have a go at the water supplies as well?"

All eyes were suddenly back on the water jug but no one made a move to refill their glass.

"That is pure supposition," Sophia said, looking at me like my marbles had been nicked in the playground and I hadn't noticed. "What possible grounds do you have for such . . ." she paused, searching for a suitably disparaging phrase ". . . such blatant scaremongering."

"Blatant scaremongering?" I said with heavy irony. This was turning out to be even harder to sell than I'd expected. "Have you forgotten where the bodies were located?"

"Of course not, man," Hamilton answered. "At the Colonies and near Murrayfield stadium."

"You're not being specific enough, Lewis."

"Next to the river," Davie put in, eyeing me uneasily.

"Getting warmer." I wasn't letting him off the hook either.

"With their heads in the river," Sophia said.

I nodded. "With their mouths in the Water of Leith." I looked round at all three of them again. "Am I getting through to you? With their mouths in the water."

Sophia returned my look thoughtfully. "That could just be coincidence."

"Coincidences only happen in crappy detective stories, senior guardian. I think the killer or killers are sending us a message."

Davie sat up straight. "Along the lines of 'I drank the water of life and look what happened to me'?"

"Something like that."

Hamilton wasn't completely lost in space. "Why didn't they put the nicotine in bottles of water then?"

He had a point. This was where my imagination slipped into overdrive. "Say these people are putting the squeeze on us. They're using nicotine because they've got some interest in the only people who are allowed to smoke in this city – the tourists.

They're putting it in bottles of whisky called the Ultimate Usquebaugh because . . . well, where is the word 'ultimate' used all the time in Edinburgh?"

"In lottery publicity," Sophia answered. She sounded seriously unconvinced.

"Correct. So maybe they're hinting that they could destabilise the city by messing up Edlott – whence the murder of a winner. And they're putting the bodies in the Water of Leith because they want us to understand what else they could do if they feel like it."

Silence cocooned the room like it does in winter when the heavy mist rolls in from the sea and smothers all the city's sounds. I glanced at my sweat-stained clothing to remind myself that it was still the hot season.

Then Sophia reached for the water jug, filled her glass and drank the contents down pointedly. "You can't seriously expect the Council to act on such a farrago of groundless suppositions, citizen. We've already expended a huge amount of auxiliary time checking the whisky stocks."

Hamilton wasn't buying it either. "Surely people who are intent on putting the squeeze on the Council would have sent us a list of demands by now, Dalrymple?"

I shrugged. "They might want to engineer a condition of panic first. Let's face it, citizen unrest at the temporary halt in whisky supplies has got you going, hasn't it?"

Sophia gave me a dismissive glance. "We're weathering that storm, as we'll weather any subsequent ones. Doubtless you have some suggestions as to how we should safeguard the city's water supplies." Now that she'd satisfied herself that I was barking mad, she'd reverted to formal language. It goes with her rank like bad taste in music goes with teenagers.

"Put a guard on every water tank, put a squad of guards on every reservoir and filter bed, put—"

"Thank you, citizen." The senior guardian was back with

her files. "I recommend that you refrain from favouring the Council with these wild ideas." She glanced up and raked me with frozen grapeshot. "I would further recommend that you open some new lines of enquiry immediately. If you wish to remain on the investigation." Apparently Hamilton's views on my suitability for the post of his directorate's chief investigator didn't interest her. Not that he looked exactly supportive.

I felt a kick on my calf. Davie inclined his head towards the door and stood up. I followed suit.

"One moment, citizen." Sophia raised her head again and put down her pencil. Her tone was even more biting. "There's something I want to bring to your attention." She leaned sideways and opened the satchel that she'd placed on the floor by her chair. Then she straightened up and put a bottle on the table. It was sheathed in a transparent plastic bag through which I could make out a familiar label. "You recognise this?"

"The Ultimate Usquebaugh?" I said. "Of course." I looked more closely and ascertained from the level in the bottleneck that a small amount of the amber liquid had been removed. I could also see traces of fingerprinting powder on the glass. "Is that bottle from Frankie Thomson or Fordyce Kennedy?"

"It has no connection with either of those citizens." Something about the sharp edge to Sophia's voice made my stomach somersault. "It came from your flat."

"What?" Davie, Hamilton and I blurted out the interrogative in unison.

"Or, to be more precise," Sophia continued, "it came from the backpack left there by your friend Katharine Kirkwood."

Now I was the one who was well and truly hooked.

Sophia let me wriggle for a bit. If I hadn't known that she was in full dictator mode, I'd have thought that she enjoyed seeing the shocked expressions on Davie's and Hamilton's faces. I suppose I should have told them about Katharine's reappearance.

They were never her greatest fans, but at least that way it wouldn't have looked like I was keeping her presence in the city to myself.

"Because I couldn't get through to you on your mobile, I went to your flat," Sophia said, fixing me with a look that would have withered cornfields if the Big Heat hadn't got there first. "You and the Kirkwood woman had left, but I found this bottle and another identical one in the pack I saw Kirkwood carrying when she arrived out of the blue." Her eyes didn't flicker when she mentioned that episode, nor did her cheeks redden. Behold the Ice Queen in full flight. "The chief toxicologist has tested for nicotine. He found it in both bottles."

I was finding it hard to make sense of this. Katharine had been involved with dissidents years ago and had served time in the prison on Cramond Island, but she'd also worked with me on two major cases. She certainly didn't think much of the Council and its activities, which was why she'd gone to live on the farm. That didn't make her a cold-blooded killer.

"A scene-of-crime auxiliary has dusted for prints," Sophia continued. "Apart from Kirkwood's, there is another set that is being checked against the archive." She gave me another glance. "You'll be relieved to hear they aren't yours, citizen." The hostility in her eyes suggested she still suspected I might have spent hours massaging the bottles with gloves on.

Hamilton's cheeks above his white beard had gone deep scarlet. "You've been using personnel from my directorate, senior guardian?" he said. "Why wasn't I informed?"

Trust Lewis to get involved in an argument about procedure rather than arrest me and get every auxiliary in the city looking for Katharine. On this occasion I wasn't complaining. Then again, Sophia had probably already given the latter of those orders. I wondered if she was about to transfer me to the dungeons.

"I am informing you now, guardian," Sophia said in a voice that brooked no argument. She turned back to me. "Citizen Dalrymple, can you cast any light on this development?"

"None at all." I returned her gaze stonily. "But I can tell you one thing for sure. Katharine's not a poisoner."

"How can you know that?" Sophia demanded. "She has a criminal record. She arrives in the city at the time the Ultimate Usquebaugh kills two citizens and she has bottles of it in her bag. At the very least she is a prime suspect."

I thought of the unbalanced look I'd seen in Katharine's eyes and the wild laughter she'd let slip. Could what had happened to the farm have driven her over the edge? And where the hell had she been spending her time since she came back to the city? I shook my head involuntarily. No way. I knew Katharine. I wasn't going to let myself be steamrollered by Sophia.

The senior guardian looked at me and moved her lips into an unlikely pout. "My first reaction was to have you taken off the investigation, citizen." I heard Lewis and Davie draw breath sharply. "However, I am prepared to accept your word that you know nothing of this matter."

That was easy enough to give.

"I also require your word that you will inform me immediately if Kirkwood makes contact with you in any way." She opened her eyes wide and waited for my answer.

"All right," I said after a short pause. Making promises to guardians that I don't keep is something I've got used to over the years.

Sophia nodded. "Very well. Get back to work. And try to work out some more constructive approaches."

She wasn't getting a response to that.

"Your flat is under surveillance by undercover operatives, by the way," she said as I got up.

"In that case you've got no chance of catching Katharine," I said with a bitter smile. "She can smell them a mile off. And don't forget, she's got an 'ask no questions'."

The two guardians gave me a look that even I could have lived without.

"Wanker." Davie stormed past me down the stone-flagged corridor towards the guard command centre.

"Hang on a minute," I said, catching him up. "You don't really think Katharine's involved with the murders, do you?"

He stopped and turned, letting me career off his solid chest. "We're supposed to be friends, aren't we, Quint? Why the fuck didn't you tell me that your old girlfriend had shown up again?"

I shrugged, avoiding his eyes. "It was a bit embarrassing, what with Sophia being involved."

"Embarrassing?" he roared, glaring at a timid-looking female auxiliary at the other end of the passage who almost dropped her files. "It's a fucking disaster area. You're bloody lucky you're not counting the cobwebs in the directorate's deepest dungeon."

"She isn't a poisoner, Davie," I insisted in a low voice. "You know she isn't."

"I bloody don't," he growled. His relationship with Katharine had been almost as stormy as the last king's with the people of Britain. "I saw her kill, remember?"

I nodded. "That was different, Davie. She saved my life then."

He stared at me then slowly lowered his eyes. "Yes, she did. That was a long time ago though. Who knows what might have happened to her since then?" He strode away.

"Davie, you will let me know if there are any sightings of her, won't you?"

He turned back to me. "All right. But next time tell me what the fuck's going on. Where are you going?"

"The central archive. I've got things to find out about Fordyce Kennedy's missing son. What about you?"

"We're still checking whisky stocks, remember?" he said

sardonically, heading away. "As well as looking for your fancy woman."

I walked down the Royal Mile to George IVth Bridge without losing more than a pint of sweat. After going into the archive in the former library, I drank noisily from the fountain in the entrance hall then stuck my head round my friend Ray's door. There was no sign of him. But his desk was something else. He usually kept it in the well-ordered fashion beloved of senior bureaucrats. Now it looked as if a paperchase involving a full squad of trainee auxiliaries had taken place across it. There were books strewn all over the floor as well, which struck me as curious behaviour for a bibliophile. Still, the room wasn't a bad metaphor for the current state of my investigation.

"Is Nasmyth 67 around?" I called to the sentry at the glass doors.

She looked at me snottily, as if to say "demoted auxiliaries can kiss my arse before I give them the time of day" and nodded once. That was all I got. It didn't seem worth asking for Ray's exact whereabouts so I went down to the document stacks. At least I wouldn't need to ask for help down there.

Before I pulled Allie Kennedy's file, I sat at a table and considered the question of Katharine. I'd have tried to get a message to her to warn her that she was a wanted woman, but I couldn't think of a way to do that. She didn't have a mobile. If she showed up at my place, she'd be grabbed before she could see any note I left. I'd just have to hope that her highly developed instinct for self-preservation would get her out of trouble. If anyone could stay free, she could. In the meantime it was up to me to prove that she wasn't involved in the killings. I'd been looking for something to fill my spare time.

I checked out the second victim's son with the thoroughness of a lice infestation controller in the city's primary schools. That involved a serious amount of cross-referencing. Although I'd cast an eye over Allie when I first investigated the missing lottery-winner, that gave me nothing more than a vague idea about him. Documentation on ordinary citizens collated by the various directorates is supposedly transferred on a weekly basis to the central archive. I spent an hour running between the stacks updated by the Education, Labour, Recreation and Welfare Directorates.

I didn't get much for my pains. Alexander Kennedy certainly wasn't one of the Enlightenment's success stories but neither was I. As I knew, he had a less-than-impressive school and work record, although the only formal notice of anything dubious apart from his spells in youth detention was a Public Order Directorate offence notification which hadn't been moved to his main folder. That referred to a case of gambling in a derelict house in south Morningside a year back. Nothing too worrying about that. There's no shortage of disaffected young people in the city who spend their evenings dodging the guard – who've got better things to do than chase them. The only other thing that I picked up was that Allie was registered as homosexual in his Sex Session Record. Before the current Council's opening up of the system, citizens had to attend a weekly sex session at their local recreation centre. Different partners were allocated every time in the original Council's drive to replace emotion with sexual variety – and to keep tabs on everyone. You had to declare yourself as either hetero or homo, bisexuality not being recognised by the Recreation Directorate who probably found it too untidy from a bureaucratic point of view. There was a long list of male citizens who Allie'd had sex with but none of the names meant anything to me. Frankie Thomson certainly wasn't on it.

I gathered my notes together and put back the files. I was going to have to check some of the details with the missing man's family. That idea didn't fill me with enthusiasm. On my way to the exit I looked into Ray's office again. This time he was in residence, bent over the chaos that was his desk.

"Hiya, Ray."

His head shot up, the eyes heavily ringed and the mouth slack.

He looked so bad that I almost expected him to croak "The horror, the horror."

"Jesus, what happened to you?" I asked.

"I . . ." He dropped his head again. "I . . ."

"You . . . you had a skinful last night?"

"No, I . . . I . . ."

"Don't worry, I'm not in a hurry."

Ray looked across at me and I realised that this wasn't just a case of the "Bootlegger's Blues". This was a guy who'd either had some very bad news or had just seen a ghost with its head in its hands.

"What's the matter, my friend?" I went round the desk towards him, but he dragged himself out of his chair quickly and stepped to the window. The sleeve of the pink shirt over his missing arm flapped like a dead flamingo's neck.

"Nothing . . . I . . . I just had a bad night." He stared at me dully. "Pain . . . pain in my arm. You know how it is."

After a fashion. I glanced down at the stump of my finger. It does sometimes give me a hard time. "Aye. Here, any news from that American dealer?"

His eyes sprang open. "Dealer?" he repeated. "What dealer?"

"You know the one. Chandler editions?"

"Oh." Ray's face slackened again. "Chandler. Yes. No. I mean, I haven't seen that dealer since you were last in." He turned away and peered out at the street beyond the heavy bars on his window.

"Ray?" I went up to him and saw him flinch. "Are you sure you're okay?"

He nodded impatiently as if he very much wanted me out.

"I can help, Ray," I said. "If you're in some sort of trouble . . ."

This time he faced me. He blinked uncontrollably then pushed me gently away. "Hit the road, Quint. You've got enough problems of your own."

He was right there even though he was only guessing. So I squeezed his shoulder and left him to his heaps of papers and scattered volumes.

It was only when I was out of the building that I remembered where I'd seen someone with a look of horror as deeply etched as the one on Ray's face. It was in Granton during the height of the drugs wars, after a City Guard unit had taken what then passed for the law into its own hands. A young guardsman was picking his way among the mutilated corpses with his eyelids stretched so far apart that for a second I thought his eyes would drop out. I was bloody glad I didn't get the kind of pain that had distorted Ray's features.

Chapter Ten

———>○○○<———

I called Davie. The barracks reports he'd been collating showed no sign of Allie Kennedy or — to my relief — of Katharine. The Ultimate Usquebaugh was keeping itself to itself as well. I asked him to assign me a vehicle, told him where I was headed and signed off.

When the clapped-out Land-Rover arrived, I sent the driver back to the castle on foot and set off towards Tollcross. The morning influx of citizen workers in buses was long over and the only vehicles on the road apart from guard vehicles like mine were tourist coaches and taxis. There were a few citizens on ramshackle bicycles held together with pieces of string heading towards the areas near the city line — houses damaged in the drugs wars years ago out there were finally being brought back into use. Soon I passed Napier Barracks and ran down the hill into Morningside. The Pentland Hills to the south shimmered light brown and dusty green, clouds of dust rising from the building sites as if sticks of bombs had just been dropped on them by one of the American air force's latest Skulk planes.

I turned into Millar Crescent and floored the brake pedal. The street was full of people clustered around the drinking-water tank. They were the unlucky ones who had the afternoon and night shifts — even though they weren't at work right now, they had to spend a large part of their so-called free time ensuring they had enough water to get through the day. I stepped out and looked over the lines of people in vests and T-shirts. Those who weren't queuing for drinking-water were waiting to use the communal bogs. I didn't see anyone from the Kennedy family, either male or female. A guard vehicle was parked further down. I'd already heard from Davie that the auxiliaries in it hadn't reported any individuals resembling Allie Kennedy.

I walked over to the drinking-water tank. It was at the end of the street beside the local bike shed. There was a heavy padlock on the inflow lid on top and I wondered how feasible it would be for someone bent on poisoning the supply to get it open. Very feasible indeed if you worked for the Water Department. I wondered what I had to do to get Sophia and Lewis Hamilton to protect what could be the poisoners' next target.

I climbed up to the Kennedy flat, breathing in the simmering, fetid smell of Edinburgh stairwells during the Big Heat. Agnes opened the door. A brief flash of surprise registered in her eyes when she saw me. There were dark rings around them. She was dressed in her usual paint-dotted clothes, the scarf round her neck tied in a double knot. Her raven-coloured hair was loose. It didn't look like she'd passed a restful night.

"Citizen . . ." she said, her voice fading away.

"You can call me Quint," I said.

"What . . . what is it?" she asked dully.

"Can I come in? I need to ask you some questions."

Agnes seemed reluctant to admit me. Finally she shrugged and opened the door wider.

"How's your mother?"

She had her arms crossed tightly over her chest. "Away in her own little world. I don't know if she really understands what's happened."

"Are you not working today?"

She raised her hand to her scarf. "My supervisor gave me the day off."

"Unusually decent supervisor," I said under my breath.

Bereaved citizens are entitled to take time off work only for the cremation service. In Fordyce Kennedy's case that wouldn't be happening for some time.

"That's the Council's new way, isn't it?" Agnes said. "Auxiliaries are required to be responsive to citizens' needs." I heard her snort derisively as I glanced into the rooms off the hall. The surviving man of the house wasn't around.

She led me into the sitting room. The curtains were drawn, allowing only a little of the burning sunlight in. Hilda Kennedy was on the sofa, keeled over against the arm. Her eyes were blank and a drop of saliva was at the edge of her gaping mouth. She looked like she wasn't just away with the fairies — she was dancing jigs with pixies, goblins, elves, sprites, the lot.

Then I realised that Allie wasn't the only person missing. "Agnes, where's the nursing auxiliary who was assigned to you yesterday?"

She looked up from wiping her mother's mouth with a handkerchief. "She went off in the middle of the evening."

"Went off?" I tried not to shout.

Agnes was helping her mother to sit up straight. "She got an urgent call. Around nine o'clock."

Hilda turned towards me, her face suddenly animated. "Allie's a good laddie," she said in a surprisingly strong voice. "A good laddie, our Allie." Then her eyes rolled and she slumped against the sofa arm again.

I finished swearing at the auxiliary's absence under my breath and watched as Agnes sat down next to Hilda on the sofa. The ornate furniture that Fordyce had made stood around us like a ring of memorial stones. I had a thought that didn't make me proud of myself.

"Agnes, is there any chance of a cup of tea?" I said quietly. "I was out of the house very early this morning."

She studied me for a few seconds then nodded. "Just let her be," she said, inclining her head towards her mother.

I watched her go then moved towards the older woman.

"Hilda?" I said in a loud whisper. "Hilda, can you hear me?"

Her eyes focused on me slowly.

"Hilda, where's Allie?" I said.

Nothing.

"Where's Allie?" I repeated. "Where's he been?"

A smile spread across her thin lips. "Allie's a good laddie. Aye, a good laddie." Then she lost contact and drifted back to the set of *A Midsummer Night's Dream*.

"Why didn't you ask me that question, citizen?"

I jerked back from Hilda.

Agnes was at the door, a cup in her hand. "I told you to let her be," she said. The look on her face was placid but there was an edge to her voice.

"Sorry, I was just wondering . . ."

"I'll answer all your questions, don't worry." She handed the cup to me.

I nodded, my mind suddenly elsewhere. The dark-stained wood around me had given me another idea. Maybe Fordyce Kennedy's cabinet-making skills had something to do with his death. I sat back in the unusually comfortable sofa and tried to make something of that. Illicit furniture smuggling? A black-market scam in fake antique escritoires? It didn't sound very likely.

"For your information, Allie was here last night," Agnes said.

"He slept here?"

"What do you think he did?" Her eyes flashed again.

"What time did he arrive?"

"Don't worry. It was before curfew."

I didn't expect anything other than that standard response. For all the Council's loosening up, citizens must be in their registered abode by curfew or face a month in the mines or on the Council farms. It wasn't likely that Agnes would shop her brother if he'd been somewhere else. Which is why I'd made sure the bloody nurse was posted inside the flat in addition to the guard vehicle on the street.

"Did you see him this morning?" I asked.

Agnes shook her head. "He was away early. I don't know where he's gone."

"How did he take your father's death?"

She looked at me like I'd deposited something nasty on the carpet. "How do you fucking think, citizen?"

I shrugged ineffectually. "Sorry. Can I see his room?"

"Can I stop you?" Agnes was keeping her eyes off me now.

I went into the second bedroom down the dingy hall. It was furnished with the usual Supply Directorate sticks and slats – there was nothing handmade by Fordyce in this room. But the bed had been slept in, the top sheet thrown back untidily and the poor-quality mattress and pillow indented. A few clothes had been tossed around the floor, none of them stained or marked in any obvious way. There weren't many others in the narrow deal wardrobe. I took a shirt and a pair of underpants for the forensics team to play around with just in case. Then I went over to the window. It was half open and gave a view to the backs of other flats across the overgrown strips of garden. I ran my hand above the frame and felt the rope that was the Fire Department's idea of an escape route in cases of emergency. It was coiled tightly and secured in its rack, which didn't necessarily preclude recent use. I wondered if that was how Allie had escaped the attention of the auxiliaries in the street. Despite the signs of overnight inhabitation, the room had the atmosphere of a pied-à-terre which was only occasionally occupied. There was dust on the bookcase and chest of drawers and nothing that suggested day-to-day occupancy – no crumpled bits of paper, no half-emptied cups, no hairs in the hairbrush under the small mirror. That made me think.

"Agnes?" She appeared at the door after a few moments. "How long is your brother's hair?"

She looked at me quizzically. "Why do you want to know that?"

I didn't answer.

"It's short, if you must know. Very short. He gets it clippered during the Big Heat."

"Clippered or shaved?"

"Number one clipper," she said, turning away.

That is, pretty much akin to baldness. Well, well. Had he been down to visit Frankie Thomson in the Colonies?

Before I left, I checked all the other rooms. Hilda's bedroom was neat, presumably looked after by Agnes, while the daughter's own room was much more homely. She'd painted the walls in pastel shades, hung curtains made from offcuts that she'd stitched together imaginatively and covered the bed in an attractive handmade bedspread. But none of that got me much further on. No Allie, no obvious bottles of the Ultimate Usquebaugh, no boogie.

I thanked Agnes for her help and left her to it. My departure didn't seem to make any impression on her at all.

Back at the Land-Rover, which was being studiously ignored by the locals in the water queue, I put in a call to Davie.

"Find the nursing auxiliary who was at the Kennedy flat last night and throw her in the dungeons till I'm ready for her. She buggered off after someone called her and I'm going to find out why. And another thing – replace the guard vehicle in Millar Crescent with an undercover surveillance team."

"Anything else?" he asked drily.

"You're going to love this. Find out from the Supply Directorate if there's a trade in furniture – fake antique or high-quality contemporary."

"Is that a priority, Quint? We haven't exactly got a plethora of personnel with time on their hands."

"A plethora?" I repeated. "Have you been reading Plato in the original Greek?"

"What do you think?"

"You'll find someone to run the check, Davie. If not, do it yourself."

I rang off after his first expletive.

I pulled up outside the Culture Directorate in Castle Terrace and flashed my authorisation at the guardswoman who'd raced towards me faster than the world's computing systems crashed at the millennium. As I got out, I took in the late-twentieth-century neoclassical pile in front of me. It was a huge block with tiers of windows, pavilions and domes on the top corners. In the past the Council handled culture from the old Royal Scottish Academy on Princes Street but since the beginning of the lottery they needed bigger premises. Culture in Edinburgh means Edlott these days. Half the auxiliary population seemed to be working on schemes to convince ordinary citizens that greed is good. I wanted very much to squeeze the man in charge of lottery operations to see what came out.

I went into the grand central entrance. The guardsman on sentry duty was dubious about my T-shirt and faded trousers but my authorisation did the trick again.

"Where will I find Nasmyth 05?" I asked.

"Rear atrium, second floor."

I moved into the open space inside the building. It was hotter than the Palm House in the Botanic Gardens. The architects who'd talked their clients out of a king's ransom put their trust in air-conditioning. There's no way the city's restricted power supplies could cope with that now, so the poor sods working in the Culture Directorate were even worse off than the rest of us during the Big Heat. I glanced at the intricate designs etched into the glass over the lifts. By contrast, stencilled "Out of Order" signs had been stuck on the doors since the Council deprioritised maintenance of non-essential machinery.

I looked up and caught a glimpse of Nasmyth 05. He was on the floor above me, moving his besuited bulk with surprising speed in the opposite direction from the staircase. The way his head was turned stiffly away gave me the impression that he'd spotted me and didn't want to hang around for a chat. I ran towards the stairs.

It was then that my mobile rang.

"Quint? Davie. Something's turned up."

I watched through the engraved-glass panels as the auxiliary in charge of Edlott disappeared from view on the far side of the atrium.

"Shit!" I yelled. "It had better be good, Davie."

"You decide. A guard patrol has found a seriously injured woman outside the city line in Colinton. Near the Water of Leith."

"Injured in what way?" I asked.

"Take your pick. Knife wounds, severe head wounds from a blunt instrument . . ."

"Any ID?"

"That's where it gets even more interesting. No card, no food or clothing vouchers, no Labour Directorate slip."

"Dissident? Deserter? Smuggler?"

"Could be, Quint. Or poisoner?"

I was already on my way down the stairs. The questions I had for Nasmyth 05 would have to wait. "Where is the woman now?"

"Approaching the infirmary."

"Meet me there. Out."

Then, as I was climbing into the Land-Rover, a heart-stopping thought struck me. Katharine didn't have any of the documentation Davie'd mentioned. Jesus, could it be her?

Things got even worse when I arrived at the infirmary. I'd been hoping the acting senior guardian might have had other business, but Sophia was already on the scene. The mystery woman had been taken to a secure room at the rear of the hospital. There were guard personnel all over the place. I detected the heavy hand of Lewis Hamilton.

The public order guardian was standing at the end of the

corridor talking to Davie. "Ah, Dalrymple. What do you think of this then?" He looked inordinately pleased with himself, which made me even more ill at ease. "We found Glaswegian cigarettes in the woman's pockets."

"Anything more exciting than that, Lewis?" I said, dropping into my normal role as ego-deflator. "Such as poisoned whisky?"

He shook his head mournfully. "Nothing else."

"So maybe she's just a tobacco smuggler then." The bravado in my voice was an attempt to conceal the panic that had gripped me. Was it Katharine who'd been beaten and stabbed? Had she been spending time beyond the city line? What could she have been doing out there?

The guard on the door admitted us. The ward was empty apart from the nearest bed. Sophia and a nursing auxiliary were bending over a figure, the torso of which was completely swathed in bandages. How bad was this about to get? If it was Katharine on the bed, Sophia would probably be grinning under her surgical mask. I almost rushed forward to push the medical guardian away. The strength of my feeling for Katharine startled me. I hadn't seen her for over three years and I was acting like a fifteen-year-old. What the hell was going on?

The patient wasn't moving. Over her face was an apparatus with pipes and leads running from it, making identification impossible. I felt my heart pounding as I stepped closer and took in the extent of the injuries.

"Quint." Sophia's voice was muffled by her mask but it sounded like she was pleased to see me. She'd even used my first name. That only made me more worried.

I bent over the top half of the woman's body, ignoring Sophia.

Then relief burst over me like the water from a broken dam. The left upper arm was unbound and I was looking at a bright yellow number four that had been tattooed on the skin. Looking and breathing in heavily. It wasn't Katharine. I'd seen her arms when she took off her shirt at my flat. There were no tattoos on them.

"Quint?" Sophia's voice was questioning now. "What is it?"

I got a grip and looked across at her. "I wonder if someone's been reading Sherlock Holmes novels."

She raised her eyes to the ceiling. Obviously she wasn't a fan of *The Sign of Four*. "Have you any more pertinent comments to make?"

"Not yet. Your patient seems to be in quite a state. What's the prognosis?" As the words left my mouth, it occurred to me that the medical guardian wouldn't normally take it on herself to treat every suspect the guard dragged in from across the city line. Why was she so interested in this one?

"I think she'll pull through but she'll be severely disfigured. The sight's gone in her right eye and she'll need major reconstructive work on her cheeks and nose."

"What happened to her?" I asked. As well as the extensive dressings on her head and abdomen, the figure's right hand was covered in bandages.

Sophia saw where I was looking. "She was worked over really badly. Those are defence wounds. The palm and fingers sustained deep knife cuts. She'll be lucky to keep all her fingers."

I looked at the stump of my own right forefinger. Compared with the wounds the woman had suffered, it was nothing. "What did the damage to her face?"

"Something like a pick-axe handle." Sophia shook her head and pulled down her mask. "I've rarely seen such injuries, Quint." She was pale even by Ice Queen standards. "Her face was struck repeatedly. With extreme force. It's almost as if someone were trying to injure her beyond recognition."

"What other wounds were there?"

"Six knife wounds to the abdomen. With those she was lucky, though it may not look like it. None of the major organs was pierced. She's lost a lot of blood but she should be out of danger now. More worrying is her head. She took at least four heavy blows to the rear of the cranium. I don't yet know the extent of damage to the brain."

I glanced over my shoulder at Hamilton and Davie. They were both keeping their distance from the mummy-like form on the bed. "When can I talk to her?" I asked, turning back to Sophia.

"It's impossible to say. Judging by the state of the wounds, I'd say she was attacked at least six hours ago. There's no way of telling how long she's been unconscious. She might come round at any time." She opened her eyes wide at me. "Or she might not come round at all."

I nodded then reached out and took her elbow to draw her away.

Sophia shook off my hand, looking briefly at a nurse, who immediately dropped her gaze, then staring at me. "What is it?"

"Any sign of nicotine poisoning?"

She shook her head. "She'd have died a long time ago if she'd swallowed adulterated whisky. You know how quickly nicotine works."

I nodded. "Something else. Did you authorise the nursing auxiliary to leave the Kennedy flat yesterday evening?"

"Certainly not."

"Would anyone else from your directorate have done so?"

"I'll check but it's extremely unlikely."

She seemed to be genuinely surprised so I let it pass.

"The Council meeting's in half an hour," Sophia said. "Are you coming?"

"No chance. Take Lewis with you. Davie and I have to check out where they found her."

"Quint?" Sophia said in a low voice. "The public order guardian told me there's still no sign of Katharine Kirkwood. I take it you haven't seen her?"

I nearly told her how relieved I'd been that Katharine wasn't the patient on the bed but I managed to swallow the words.

Davie had disappeared by the time Sophia confirmed there had been no order given to the absent nurse from anyone in the Medical Directorate. I knew where to find him. I went to the canteen and led him away from the remains of what seemed to have been a six-course lunch. In his Land-Rover I reached under the driver's seat for the detailed guard map of the city.

"Where exactly was the woman with the sign-of-four tattoo found?" I asked.

Davie turned left on to Lauriston Place and accelerated away. "By the river at Bogsmill Road. I told the patrol to wait for us there."

I looked up the street name in the index and found it on the map. "About half a mile outside the city line. Where the bad people hang out." Apart from those on escorted work details, Edinburgh citizens aren't allowed to cross into the suburbs outside the city line. The guard doesn't patrol the area in anything like as much strength as it does the residential zones, so dissidents and black marketeers play hide and seek with them all of the day and all of the night.

We hit the Slateford Road and I was struck by two thoughts. The first was that there used to be a hell of a good pub known as the Gravediggers near the junction. It had been turned into a citizen sex centre – maybe Freud was right and there is a link between Eros and Thanatos. I looked at the map again to confirm the second thing. As I thought, Bogsmill Road was only a mile and a half from the place where we found Fordyce Kennedy's body near the rugby stadium. I checked the scale. It was about the same distance from the Kennedy flat in Millar Crescent. The three places were within walking distance of each other. Then I shook my head, remembering that Frankie Thomson's body was found by the Water of Leith a lot further north. There was also the small matter of the fortified city line between Bogsmill Road and the other locations.

Davie had begun to slow down. A little beyond the city's slaughterhouses the road kinks and goes under an aqueduct carrying the few stagnant inches that remain of the former Union Canal, imaginatively renamed the Enlightenment Canal by the first Council. Then the road crosses the Water of Leith's trickling stream before bringing you up against the city line. During the drugs wars in the years after the Council took power, the Public Order Directorate erected huge concrete blocks at all the city's entry and exit roads. They're still standing, great monolithic memorial stones to the Council's policy of independence by exclusion. Except that now the paint's worn away from the maroon hearts and uplifting slogans, leaving dirty stains and patches of mould on the bullet-pocked surfaces. This is one of the few parts of the city where Edlott posters don't proliferate. Some crazy local had spraypainted "Southside Strollers Ru" near the gate. The guard had got him before he managed to complete the last word. He'd have rued the day he thought of that escapade all right.

The sentry on duty had an automatic machine pistol slung round his neck. The city line and outer border squads are the only guard units equipped with firearms, apart from the Fisheries Guard. When the fresh-faced guardsman spotted our vehicle he lost interest and opened the gate.

"Bogsmill Road's the next left," I said as we started off again. "Not far from the line, is it? How easy is it to cross the barrier these days, Davie?"

He shrugged. "There are eight feet of razor wire on the fences that run between each gatepost. The patrols check it regularly. If you've got the right gear you can cut your way through. People do it. There are reports of holes needing rewiring all the time. You know what the black market's like."

He turned off the main road at the junction where another Land-Rover was waiting for us. We followed it down to the road by the river and got out. The place was once a residential area but now it looked like it had been a dinosaurs' stomping ground. The walls of ruined houses were shattered, the roofs blown out by the anti-tank weapons the gangs liked so much. As for the doors and frames, they'd been wrenched away by citizens desperate for fuel during the freezing winters before the coal mines came back into operation.

"She was lying down there," said the patrol leader, a middle-aged guardswoman with multiple scars crisscrossing her face. She pointed to marker tape on the road near where it met a ramshackle bridge over the river bed. "Dissident bitch," she said, spitting into the dust. "Deserved all she got." She gave me a suspicious glance and put her hand on the grip of her truncheon. It wasn't hard to work out how she'd come by the injuries to her face. Plenty of older auxiliaries lost friends in the operations against the drugs gangs or got carved up in fights with dissidents and black marketeers. They tend to volunteer for permanent city line or border duty and they frequently don't take prisoners. We were lucky this one had played things by the regulations.

"Find out what the guard squad know, Davie," I said. "I'm going to scout around."

"Okay."

"Dry as a desert bone yard," I muttered, kicking the hard surface of the road. It had once been asphalt but twenty years of neglect had turned it into a dirt track with more pockmarks than an adolescent addicted to deep-fried chocolate bars. There were drops and spatters of blood on the dusty surface. Across the water the track turned into what I remember had been a nature trail when I was a kid. The trees along it were drooping skeletons, their branches and trunks casting faded leaves like flakes of desiccated skin. The place echoed with the dazed and confused songs of birds whose genes hadn't prepared them for life in the Big Heat. I found myself looking down at the meagre river and thinking of Frankie Thomson. It seemed like a long time since I'd kneeled by his body further down the same stream. I wondered if I was wasting my time. What could he have had to do with the woman who was nearly killed out here? What connection could Fordyce Kennedy have had with her? Christ, I hadn't even been able to work out a connection between Frankie and Fordyce yet. Maybe this was one of those cases that don't have connections. And yet – a homicidal attack so soon after the two poisonings in a city where murder is rarer than citizens who love the Council? A homicidal attack next to the Water of Leith. You had to wonder.

"No traces?" Davie called, finishing his conversation.

"Not that I can see. There's no way of telling which way she and her attackers came and went." I looked up and down the trail then moved back to the Water of Leith. "We'll need to get search teams out here."

"Why?" Davie asked doubtfully, flipping his notebook shut. "What do you expect to find?" I watched as Davie came across the bridge. He was shaking his head. "Nothing much from the guard patrol. They found the woman where the leader said and called in immediately. Apart from looking around the nearest buildings on the other side, they sat on their arses and waited for backup."

"You can hardly blame them in this temperature," I said. "To answer your question, what I expect to find is traces of the victim and her companions. If this has anything to do with the poisonings, we can probably forget finding anything that identifies her assailant."

"Companions?" Davie drank from his flask and offered it to me. "How do you know she wasn't on her own?"

"I don't," I said, handing back the flask. Even warm barracks water went down well in the burning sun. "But think about it. She had nothing on her apart from a few clothes. Dissidents usually come with the wherewithal to survive in the open for weeks."

"Maybe she was robbed," he suggested.

"Maybe. Or maybe she holed up somewhere nearby with her pals." I grinned at him. "Leaving us a large pile of helpful evidence, maybe including bottles of the Ultimate Usquebaugh. You remember the tattoo?"

He nodded.

"A yellow number four. I reckon there were three others in her little gang."

"Come into the shade, man," Davie said. "The sun's obviously getting to you."

"Ha. All the same, it's as good an idea as any you've come up with, pal. Call up a couple of squads to search the area. Till they get here, we'll do the job for them. You take the other bank. I'll stick to this one."

He looked about as enthusiastic as a kid in one of the city's primary schools on the morning of his quarterly political institutions test.

The trail on my side led away from the water and ended up at another heavily pot-holed road running alongside an expanse of overgrown fields. On the crest beyond them stood the ruins of what had once been Merchiston Castle School. It had been used by a particularly vicious drugs gang who called themselves the Boys in Blue. When the directorate finally caught up with them, the headbangers set fire to the former public school and turned themselves into the Boys in Red. I stopped and sniffed the hot air. Even this close to the city, you can smell the parched fields in the hinterland.

I moved on down the road, thinking of Katharine. She'd spent the last three years mucking out byres and picking potatoes. Had the end of the farm really turned her into a crazed killer? I didn't think so. She was passionate and strong-willed, as I knew to my cost. She walked out on me in 2022 because she thought I loved my job and myself so much that she didn't stand a chance. But I couldn't see her putting nicotine into whisky bottles. Then again, the way I panicked in the infirmary showed that my emotional involvement with her was still strong. How objective was I being?

The path led deeper into the woods. There was something about a spot where the road sloped back down towards the water that bothered me. I breathed in deeply. Dried leaves, earth, dust, a faint reek from the river bed – the same as everywhere else around there but not the same. Suddenly a raucous shriek came through the trees ahead, making me stop dead. The noise was repeated then another call at a slightly different pitch started up. I relaxed slightly. Crows. But it wasn't just the birds that had got to me. I stepped forward carefully, feeling that something was about to happen.

Then my mobile rang.

"Dalrymple? Public order guardian."

"What, Lewis?" I asked, still trying to put my finger on what was wrong about the glade around me.

"Get back to the city now." I realised that his voice was tense.

"What is it?"

"There's been a mass poisoning. There are two dead so far and over twenty more stricken and . . ." He broke off and the line went quiet.

"And?" I prompted.

"And . . . and it happened in your father's retirement home."

I froze, aware that an insect had flown into my open mouth but unable to move a muscle.

"Are you there, Dalrymple? Don't worry, Hector's not one of the dead. The senior guardian's supervising treatment of the survivors."

I felt the strength surge back into my body. I spat the fly out, turned on my heel and sprinted up the slope, only dimly aware that the crows had started to shriek again.

Chapter Eleven

"You're still alive, old man."

"So it would seem, failure." Hector looked up at me from his desk and his eyes creased. For a moment I thought he was going to break down. Fat chance. "Are you in charge of this poisoning investigation I've been hearing about?" he demanded. "If so, you're not doing a very good job."

Davie was over by the door of my father's room on the third floor of the retirement home. He wasn't doing a very good job of stifling his laughter.

"How come you didn't drink anything today?" I asked, moving over to the window. Down below, the street was jammed with ambulances and guard vehicles.

"Who said I didn't drink anything?" Hector was doing his old trick of standing up to adversity with extreme cantankerousness. He raised his hooded eyes to my face and was a bit taken aback by what he saw. "All right, all right, I'll tell you. I keep a stock of waterbottles in my wardrobe. Saves me going downstairs to get a drink all the time."

"When did you last fill them up?" I asked, pulling out my notebook.

"A couple of days ago, I think." He looked at the pile of Latin tomes in front of him. "Yes, it was Sunday. I'd just finished translating Martial's *Epigrams* i, xv. It's very fine, you know." He looked at us like a kid with a new toy. "Tomorrow is too late to live so get on with it today, that's the gist of it."

"Thanks for the advice," I said ironically. "Tell me, why didn't you go down to breakfast this morning?"

He spread his hands over his books. "Too busy with this lot. Anyway, you can have too much burned porridge, especially during the Big Heat. Wouldn't you agree, Davie?"

The guardsman shrugged noncommittally. The day Davie got too much porridge would be the day tourists lost interest in the Kilts Up Club in Rose Street.

"Can we get on?" I asked.

"Ask away, laddie."

"Did you see anything suspicious from up here? Anyone you haven't seen before?"

Hector gave a gruff laugh. "You mean a shifty-looking fellow carrying a big bottle with a skull and crossbones on it? Sorry to disappoint you, Quintilian."

"Any talk among the others?"

He shook his head. "They're all too busy with their illicit games of poker and their dirty magazines."

"Uh-huh." I inclined my head towards the door. "We'd better get going, Davie. The guardian will need help downstairs."

"If it's the water they're poisoning now, can I not drink the whisky?" Hector asked plaintively.

"No, you can't!" I shouted. When I saw the disappointment on his face, I relented. "Oh, all right. I'll send you down a bottle of malt that's been checked. For your personal use only."

"Don't worry, lad," he said, rubbing his wrinkled hands. "I won't be sharing it with anyone."

Guard and nursing personnel were moving to and fro in the wide Victorian hallway like well-choreographed dancers, though the nailed boots didn't quite fit in. Hamilton came out of the resident nursing auxiliary's office as we reached the bottom of the stairs.

"Hurry up, Dalrymple. The senior guardian's been asking for you."

"I'll bet she has," I said under my breath.

In contrast to the organised chaos I'd just passed through, the office was a pocket of remarkable calm. Sophia's team of medics had set up wallcharts and a field drug cabinet at one end and were working there with lowered voices. She herself was poring over the occupants' files at the desk.

"Your father's fine, isn't he, Quint?" she asked with a concerned look that surprised me. So did her use of my first name in public.

I nodded. "He had his own private water stock."

"I'll have the chemists check it all the same," she said, writing a note and handing it to one of her assistants.

Sophia stood up and moved to a corner, beckoning to me to join her. "It looks like you may have been right about the poisoners' strategy." She might have called me by my first name but she was finding it hard to look me in the eye. I didn't care about that. A frightening thought had just struck me. Did someone want my father dead?

Davie came in with a clipboard, looking sweaty and harassed. Hamilton just looked harassed — he recycled his sweat into vitriol for use on subordinates who stepped out of line. Lister 25 also joined us. His expression was that of a man who'd landed a starring role in his own worst nightmare.

"Very well," Sophia said. "Where do we stand?" That was apprently a rhetorical question because she didn't let anyone else speak. "The deceased residents have been removed for post-mortem and the twenty-one stricken men are being treated in a secure ward in the infirmary. Three of them are in a critical condition." She glanced over at Lister 25. "Chief toxicologist, do you have any news?"

The chemist nodded. "Preliminary tests on the tea drunk by the dead men at breakfast have shown that we are dealing with nicotine poisoning again."

The old man mustn't have drunk the tea, thank Christ. Sophia, Hamilton and Davie were looking outraged but I was more surprised by the small number of deaths and by the time between breakfast and the effect of the poison.

"What was the dosage?" I asked. "Shouldn't there have been more deaths?"

Lister 25 nodded. "Good point, citizen. The dosage was indeed much less strong than in the Ultimate Usquebaugh." He shook his head gravely. "It's pretty horrible stuff whatever the dosage. Especially for old people."

"We need to find the scumbag who put the nicotine in the tea." I looked at Davie. "Did anybody see an intruder?"

He flicked pages on his clipboard. "No. I've collated the statements taken from the residents who are conscious. None of them saw anyone or anything out of the ordinary."

"What about the water supply?"

"Drinking-water was delivered yesterday at ten thirty in the morning. I've relayed the driver and tractor numbers to the command centre. We'll track them down soon."

I looked round the room. "Where's the nursing auxiliary?"

"In shock," Sophia said, her stern tone expressing what she thought of that performance by one of her staff. "I'll be talking to her shortly."

I had no doubt of that. "I wonder where the nicotine was introduced into the tea chain, so to speak. The whole water delivery couldn't have been poisoned. Plenty of people must have drunk from it since yesterday morning."

Davie nodded in agreement. "Correct. Several of the residents have said that they drank water from the dispenser on the ground floor as early as yesterday midday."

"Right," I said. "So the nicotine must have been in the kettles or teapots. Or in the milk, I suppose."

"We're analysing all of those," said the chief toxicologist.

I shook my head slowly. "Not that the entry point of the poison will get us any further on if no one saw who put it there."

I leaned over the desk and grabbed the Visitor Log. According to what the nursing auxiliary had written there, the waterman and the postwoman were the only externals in the building yesterday. We'd be checking them out, but I had the feeling we were up against someone who knew how to work round the Council's bureaucracy.

"Quint?" Sophia said softly. "Have you considered why this particular location was targeted?"

"What do you think?" I asked, looking into her pale blue eyes. It wouldn't be the first time that Hector had unwittingly got himself involved in a murder case, but it would definitely be the first time a killer had tried to get at me by aiming at the old man. That made me more angry than I'd been for a long time. I managed to channel how I felt into thinking about the next stage of the investigation. Whoever was behind all this had just made a major mistake.

The rest of the meeting consisted of Sophia and Hamilton wrangling over how many of the city's auxiliaries should be committed to guarding the water supplies. He wanted every last one while she took a broader view – after all, the tourists still had to be looked after so that the city's income didn't dry up overnight. Apart from getting them to agree to post a guard unit at the retirement home, I didn't involve myself in the debate. I was too busy trying to work out who had both the desire and the means to have a go at me via Hector. Desire could cover any number of survivors with a grudge from the drugs gangs I'd broken up when I was in the directorate. Most of them were outside the city and impossible to lay a hand on. Not many people in Edinburgh would remember, let alone care, that my father had once been information guardian. It was years since he resigned from the rank so what could anyone have against him now? Except in my line of work you find out pretty soon that coincidences don't happen – meaning that the poisoning in the retirement home wasn't a random event. I reckoned I was being sent a message along the lines of "we know where your only relative lives". But who had the means to find out where Hector was? Retired citizen records are kept in the archive like all the rest of the city's documentation and the only people who have access are auxiliaries. There was already one of those at the top of my dubious specimens list.

"Where are you going?" Sophia asked as I moved towards the door.

Telling guardians you're off to put the boot into suspect auxiliaries is always risky. "I need to check something about the dead lottery-winner's family," I lied.

She looked at me for a moment, then nodded.

"Come on, Davie," I said.

"Oh no you don't," Hamilton growled. "I need Hume 253. In case you haven't noticed, we've got a crisis on our hands here."

I shrugged. I could handle Nasmyth 05 with both hands tied behind my back. As I passed him on my way to the door, Davie handed me a sheet of paper covered in the copperplate script required of auxiliaries. I hoped it wasn't a philosophy essay that he wanted me to look over.

In the street I flashed my authorisation and turfed a sour-looking guardsman out of the nearest directorate vehicle. It was a battered maroon pick-up. The last time I'd seen one of those had been at the Fisheries Guard base in Leith docks. As I started the engine, I wondered if Dirty Harry had sunk any raiders recently. I lost my grip on that thought as I struggled to engage first gear. Eventually I found it after provoking several guardsmen to ill-disguised mirth. I flicked them a V-sign with my mutilated right hand and pulled away, weaving through the crush of vehicles and personnel.

Heading for the city centre, I glanced at the screed Davie had written me. He'd somehow managed to find the time to look into what I'd dumped on him earlier. The Supply Directorate had advised that they knew nothing about any trade in fake antique furniture. That didn't necessarily mean there wasn't one but it left us with no leads.

"Great!" I shouted, pounding my thigh then swerving to avoid an elderly male citizen who'd obviously been sampling a secret stockpile of booze. As I passed, he made an impractical suggestion about what I could do with the pick-up.

"Ah-hah," I said, reading Davie's last line. "Now you're talking." The nursing auxiliary who should have stayed at the Kennedy flat last night had been located and taken to the castle dungeons. I decided to head there before going back to the Culture Directorate.

I pulled up on the esplanade, the sun beating down on the raised open space like it had been insulted by the asphalt and was now taking its revenge. On my way to what had once been the military prison, I wondered where Katharine was. I'd have heard if the guard had picked her up. What the hell had she been doing with two bottles of the Ultimate Usquebaugh in her bag? Surely she wasn't involved in the poisonings? Jesus. The thought ripped into me like a bayonet. She knew where my father lived. I stopped dead in the unshaded area between the command centre and the dungeons, my legs frozen despite the heat, and thought it through. No, I didn't believe it. Katharine knew Hector, she was fond of him. She wouldn't harm him. And besides, she didn't need to use the old man to get at me — she had direct access already. Or rather, she did have until the guard started watching my flat. I shook my head and walked on. No, Katharine wasn't behind the poisonings. I knew her better than that. Or did I?

I went down the steep steps to the additional dungeons Hamilton had prisoners excavate for themselves during the height of the drugs wars. They hadn't been much used in recent years except by rats but they were always good for scaring the shit out of people with guilty secrets. I showed ID to the overweight guardsman sitting at the end of the dimly lit passage. He'd spent so many years on duty down here that even the guardian didn't have the nerve to expose him to the outside world.

"Number thirteen," he said hoarsely. "Lucky for some." He started panting with excitement as I headed for the cell.

I struggled with the key and eventually swung the barred door open. The female auxiliary was cowering in the corner, her nurse's uniform stained by the filthy bedding and her white shoes badly scuffed. I brought my hand to my face when the stench from the waste bucket and the damp stone walls washed over me.

"Simpson 426?" I said, watching her as she drew herself up and wiped the sweat from her forehead.

The auxiliary eyed me nervously. She was young, only in her mid-twenties. Her light brown hair had once been in a tight plait but now it looked like a large bird had been trampling it into a nest. She looked even more worried when I showed her my authorisation.

"What's . . . what's this all about?" she asked in a faint voice. "The guardsmen who brought me here wouldn't say anything."

I sat down at the other end of the uneven mattress from her, keeping away from the wall of the narrow cell. Leaning against it was a bad idea unless you wanted your clothing to be impregnated by the rank liquid dribbling down from the roughly hewn roof.

"What's this all about?" I said, repeating her question with maximum incredulity. "How many derelictions of duty have you committed, auxiliary?"

"I . . ." She shook her head weakly. "None."

"None apart from this one?"

Her head made a couple of feeble movements sideways.

"This one being unauthorised absence from your post." I pulled out my notebook. "Now let me see. Who was it gave you the order to stay with the Kennedy family yesterday?" I looked down at her and smiled encouragingly. "Can't remember? It doesn't matter. I'm sure I've got it written down here."

I don't particularly like taunting people, especially young, frightened people. Unfortunately it's one of the few ways to handle auxiliaries, and even then their training often enables them to stand up to it.

"Ah, here it is," I said, pointing to the page and then looking more closely. "Fuck me, Simpson 426." Unexpected crudity is another handy weapon with the Council's servants. "You disobeyed an order from the medical guardian? The medical guardian who is currently senior guardian?" I inhaled the fetid air ostentatiously then wished I hadn't. "You must really love the smell of raw sewage in the morning." Disobedient auxiliaries are sometimes sent to the shit farm in Portobello.

"No, no, I . . ." The nurse broke off and shook her head, this time even more desperately.

I moved closer to her. She pulled her knees up to her chest and jammed herself as far as she could into the corner.

"There's some information I must have," I said quietly. "If you help me, I'll get you out of here."

The nurse's light brown eyelashes quivered. "I . . . I can't . . ."

"Yes you can," I insisted. "Alexander Kennedy, known as Allie. The son. Did he come to the flat when you were there?"

She stared at me, first with surprise then with relief. Maybe she thought she was in the clear. "Yes. He arrived in the middle of the evening."

"How did he come into the flat?"

She looked at me uncomprehendingly.

I spelled it out. "Did you see him come in the front door?"

She still found the question puzzling. "No," she answered after some thought. "No, I was making tea at the time. The daughter asked me to do that while she went out to tell the neighbours about her father's death."

"Describe the brother to me."

The young woman let go of her knees and leaned forward from the wall. "Medium height, pretty slim. Smooth complexion."

"What about his hair?"

"I didn't see it. He was wearing a sunhat pulled down low."

"What else was he wearing?"

"A really horrible string vest with big holes in it and a pair of standard citizen-issue shorts."

I scribbled notes. "What did he do?"

"He was closing the door of his mother's room when I came out of the kitchen. He stared at me." The nurse looked away, her lips quivering. "Then he asked me who the . . . who the fuck I was and what the fuck I was doing there."

She was a bit of a sensitive soul to be an auxiliary. I wondered how she coped with Sophia in full Ice Queen mode. "What did he do after that?" I asked.

"He said I should take the tea into the sitting room. And that his mother wouldn't be wanting any since she'd dropped off to sleep."

I nodded. "What happened after that?"

"I don't know." Simpson 426 pulled her knees close to her chest again. "I . . . I left."

I gave her a few seconds to squirm then brought my face close and locked my eyes on to hers. "You don't know because you left your post," I said in a steely voice. "Someone countermanded the medical guardian's order. Who was it?"

The nursing auxiliary slumped forward like a Homeric hero whose sinews had been terminally loosened by a sword stroke.

"Who was it?" I repeated.

The crumpled figure started jerking backwards and forwards. "I can't . . . I can't say," she sobbed.

"Yes, you can," I said, keeping my voice low. "Who told you to leave the flat? Who told you to keep the whole thing to yourself?"

No reply. She'd had her chance.

I moved closer to her and put an arm round her thin shoulders. "Come on," I said, less menacingly. "You've got to tell me." I put my fingers under her chin and slowly forced her head up. "Because if you don't, I'll order the animal at the end of the corridor to come in here and get the answer out of you any way he chooses."

She froze, her eyes springing open. "You can't do that," she gasped.

"Try me."

Simpson 426 summoned up the strength to push me away, a look of extreme disgust on her face. "It was Nasmyth 05," she said in a low, empty voice.

Bull's-eye. I kept quiet as the nurse continued, her head bowed.

"He arrived at the flat at nine o'clock and sent me back to barracks. He told me he'd have me demoted if I ever said anything to anyone." She buried her face in her hands.

I stepped back from her. "It was vital information," I said weakly. "I had to find a way of making you talk. I'm sorry."

She didn't move. For a moment I even thought she'd stopped breathing.

I'd reached the heavy steel door when the nursing auxiliary's voice stopped me.

"Citizen," she said, her voice close to a shout. "Fuck you."

That took the shine off having my suspicions about Nasmyth 05 confirmed.

It was only as I climbed out of the dungeons' Stygian darkness that the discrepancy struck me. Agnes Kennedy told me that the nursing auxiliary had received a call. She hadn't said anything about Nasmyth 05 actually being at her family's flat. Then I realised what that meant. If the nursing auxiliary was to be believed, Nasmyth 05 had been there at the same time as Allie Kennedy. I needed to question the Edlott controller even more than I'd previously thought.

I drove back to the Culture Directorate's headquarters at speed. Since my last visit a large stall had been erected outside the main entrance. It rather detracted from the building's grandiose façade as it consisted of a bright yellow tent and a series of full-length mirrors framed in imitation leopard skin. They matched the women in bikinis made of the same material who were handing out promotional material for the lottery. God knows where they came up with that marketing idea. Maybe the Prostitution Services Department lent them it.

The silver writing on a large black banner blinded me for a few seconds. I eventually managed to read "EDLOTT – THE FAIREST IN THE WORLD". Underneath it a girl a in a black Snow White wig stood pretending to eat an apple. The seven dwarves, a group of lucky boy winners, were clustered around her, peering at the ample breasts her cutaway bodice revealed. And I thought the Council disapproved of American cultural icons. The Culture Directorate might have been aiming at irony, though that's never been an Enlightenment strong point.

I remembered Nasmyth 05's lack of enthusiasm when I'd last been in the building and decided not to use the main entrance. Perhaps he'd told the sentries to advise him if I turned up. So I drove past the block and turned left at the service entrance, pulling on to the pavement near where an avant-garde theatre company had its base before independence. Now the place is given over to a floorshow featuring tourists who perform sex acts with their partners in public. It's known as "fucking karaoke".

I went towards a staircase that dropped at a steep angle into the building's foundations. Waste-disposal squads are notorious for leaving doors open and I reckoned this was my best way in. There was a sign reading "Refuse Only". I wasn't going to refuse an invitation like that but I had to take my handkerchief out and put it over my nose and mouth. Blocking the entrance was a vat of swill that no self-respecting pig would have had anything to do with. I pushed it back on its rollers and moved quickly through the cellar. Just as I reached the door at the far end, I spotted something I could use. My mother taught me that a small gift always makes a good impression.

I headed up the dim stairs, hearing the sounds of numerous pairs of auxiliary boots on the floor surfaces above. I wasn't too bothered about being clocked by the sentries now. As well as what I was carrying for Nasmyth 05, I'd taken a broom from the stores. I moved out into the open concourse. There were Culture Directorate staff all over the place but they paid no attention. If anything, they looked right through me. That's the way ordinary citizens are treated in places like this nowadays. Auxiliaries have to try so hard to be pleasant to us in public because of the user-friendly policies that they turn their noses up at us in restricted areas even more than before. Still, in my particular case that was understandable.

I made it past the defunct lift shafts with their elegant glass tracery without being questioned. I climbed the stairs and got the same lack of reaction from the auxiliaries I met on the first floor. By the time I reached the far end, I was lonelier than a 1990s American president in a ladies' seminary.

Then I bumped into the man I was looking for. Literally. He wasn't overjoyed to see me and he was even less impressed by what I was carrying.

"Oh, my God," he said, his voice shrill. "What is that?"

I looked down at the stripped calf's head I'd picked up in the basement. It was covered in a noxious slime.

"This is your lunch from last week, pal," I said, pushing it into his mock leopard-skin waistcoat and driving him into the office behind. "You forgot to eat the brains."

It wasn't long before Nasmyth 05 started to talk. The proximity of the calf's head to his face may have had something to do with that.

"Where was I last night?" he asked, wiping his forehead with his handkerchief, then remembering he'd already used it on his soiled waistcoat. "Oh, my God." He threw the stinking cloth down and rubbed his hands frantically over his face.

"Yes, Nasmyth 05, where were you last night?"

"Last night," he repeated. This was getting boring. "Last night?" he said, registering the look I gave him. "I was in barracks."

"Bollocks," I said.

"I beg your pardon?" He gave himself away by gulping like a dipsomaniac frog.

"I run two kinds of interrogation," I said. "One when I don't have a clue of the answer to my question and one when all I need is confirmation of something I already know." I let that sink in for a bit. "Guess what kind this is."

The corpulent auxiliary was suddenly sweating even more than the temperature in his office merited. The blinds had been partially closed and the spacious room was about as cool as it gets in the city at this time of year because the fat shite had equipped himself with one of the city's few fans. So why was he shaking so much that his waved hair had lost its carefully sculpted shape? I let him sweat some more. Eventually he summoned up enough courage to look at me.

"What is it you want confirmation of, citizen?" He glanced at the calf's head again. I knew he'd rather have mine on the desk in front of him.

"All right, here's how we'll do this," I said, smiling at him malevolently. "You tell me where you really were last night and I'll think about keeping the public order guardian off your back."

He swallowed again and looked hopelessly at the door. I'd secured it by jamming my broom through the handles. He was on his own.

"I told you." His voice was suddenly shrill. "I was in Nasmyth Barracks."

"No doubt you did get your bloated carcass over there at some stage," I said, moving closer to the reeking object on the desk. "But where else did you go?"

The auxiliary drew his upper body back as if he expected me to throw the calf's head at him. He was on the right lines.

"I . . . I went to offer my condolences to the bereaved family of the dead lottery-winner," he said, looking as relieved as a dying man who's been told he's on for reincarnation as Casanova.

"And I'm the love child of Margaret Thatcher and Frank Sinatra."

I thought that was pretty neat but Nasmyth 05 was looking at me in bewilderment. He was probably one of those auxiliaries who got good marks in the training programme by erasing all pre-Enlightenment data from their memory banks. Not a bad idea with the duo I'd mentioned.

"I look after my winners," he said in pompous tones. "And their families," he added rapidly.

"And why do you do that?"

"Because . . . because citizens invest all their hopes in Edlott."

A lot of them did, unfortunately. It showed how little they believed in the new Council's policies if all they could dream about was a cushy number dressed up in a spurious historical costume.

"Wonderful," I said, putting both hands on the sticky surface of the calf's head. "But there's a lot more to it than that, isn't there, Nasmyth 05?"

He stepped back and rested his heavy body against the windowledge. "No . . . no, there isn't."

"Why did you countermand the nursing auxiliary's order? You realise it came from the senior guardian herself?"

He went a paler shade of white. "No," he gasped, "no, I didn't. I . . . I didn't want the family's grief to be disturbed by one of us." He looked at my clothes. "I mean, by an auxiliary."

I believed that about as much as I believe in the divine right of kings. I wanted to ask what Nasmyth 05 had been doing in the flat with Allie Kennedy and I wanted even more to ask him if he'd told Allie Kennedy, or anyone else, where my father lived. But I reckoned I'd find out more by keeping tabs on him than I would by passing him to Davie. Besides, the fat man would be a lot harder to break than the nursing auxiliary. He was hiding something all right but even if he had been involved, I couldn't see him putting any more poison in the city's whisky and water now that he knew I was on his case. I needed to check a couple of other things though.

"Speaking of auxiliaries," I said, "or rather, of demoted auxiliaries . . ." I paused to watch his reactions. Nothing so far. "Did you ever have anything to do with a Finance Directorate operative whose barracks number was Napier 25?"

I reckoned his eyebrows moved more than he would have liked. "Napier 25?" he repeated. "I don't think so. Most of my dealings with that directorate have been at guardian and deputy guardian level."

Arrogant tosser. "He worked in the Strategic Planning Department and I think he was seconded here a couple of years ago."

"You *think* he was, citizen? Don't you know for sure?" Nasmyth 05 smiled mockingly then shrugged. "I have no recollection of him. You say he was demoted? What for?"

I didn't answer. I could have tried to strongarm him into letting me search the directorate records but I had the feeling that all traces of Napier 25 would have been removed, as in the other archives. Better to let the fat controller think I'd bought his story.

"Okay. There's just one more thing." I leaned forward before he could move and tugged his hair hard. Most of it stayed attached to his scalp.

"Ow!" he squealed. "What did you do that for?"

"None of your business," I replied. Now I knew he wasn't clippered underneath like the guy seen outside Frankie Thomson's flat. He was the wrong build anyway.

"Are you finished with me?" Nasmyth 05 asked, a tremor of hope in his voice.

"For the time being," I said. As I turned to go, I tossed the calf's head at his midriff. "Really, auxiliary. Your clothes are a disgrace."

Maybe the germs would extend his already liberal conception of "culture' even further.

"You didn't take him in?" Davie asked disbelievingly when I called from the ground level of the echoing atrium.

"No, I didn't. I'm going to get Hamilton to put an undercover team on him."

"Isn't that a hell of a risk if he's involved in the poisonings?"

"Maybe. We're getting to the stage of desperate measures. Anyway, I'm not convinced he's got anything to do with the murders. But he's got his fingers into something dirty, I'm pretty sure of that."

"Something to do with Edlott?"

"Maybe." I scratched my cheek. Could the lottery-winners be the answer? After all, they had more freedom of movement than ordinary citizens and Fordyce Kennedy had been found in an out-of-the-way spot. Was that the connection?

"Are you still there, Quint?"

I lost my train of thought. "Yeah."

"You will be discussing this with the Council, won't you?" Davie said sternly.

"Oh, aye," I said, signing off. I wasn't going to tie myself down to a time for that.

I went out of the front entrance to avoid the stinking basement. I was glad to see that Snow White had done one of her buttons up. There are some places you don't want to get sunburned during the Big Heat. A crowd of Edinburgh citizens had gathered round the stall, avidly listening to the spiel and exchanging salary vouchers for extra tickets. The scene struck me as very sad.

On the way to the Land-Rover a pair of crows swooped over me from the rocks under the castle. I remembered the harsh cawing I'd heard in the woods beyond the city line. I had unfinished business out there.

I called Hamilton and set up surveillance on the fat man,

telling him not to wait for Council clearance. Normally the public order guardian would have dragged my arse over a grill for suggesting that a senior auxiliary was up to no good, but the poisonings seemed finally to have got to him. Anyway, he'd have no compunction about nailing Edlott personnel.

"Where are you going now, Dalrymple?" he asked.

Before I crossed the city line again, I wanted to check someone else's story. "That would be telling, Lewis," I said secretively. "Out."

Chapter Twelve

———≫∘∘∘≪———

The building off Nicolson Street to the east of the university had once been a school. Despite the original Council's commitment to education, more recently some schools in the city centre have been converted to tourist accommodation – making money from visitors takes priority these days. The granite façade of the three-storey block had been cleaned, and it stood out from the soot-blackened buildings around it like a crown in an old man's mouth. The scaffolding had been removed and a sign declared "The St Leonard's Hostel Will Welcome Foreign Visitors in July 2025". There weren't many days of the month left for that to happen. Lines of hard-pressed citizens in workclothes were passing in and out of the main entrance rapidly, suggesting that final preparations were being made in an atmosphere of con-trolled panic. The facility was clearly aimed at the cheap end of the tourist market as it was outside the central zone, but the quality of workmanship was still a lot higher than the Housing Directorate's standards for ordinary citizens' homes.

I flashed my authorisation at the sentry on the door and pushed through the scrum of craftsmen and women in the hall. A guy putting a last coat of paint on the staircase's ornate iron railings watched me approach.

"Do you know where Agnes Kennedy's working?" I asked.

The decorator gave me the suspicious look ordinary citizens

reserve for members of their rank they suspect are actually undercover operatives.

"Who wants to know?" he demanded, licking his thin lips. The specks of paint on his face made him look like he was suffering from a terminal attack of blackheads.

"A friend," I replied.

He laughed humourlessly. "Our Agnes doesn't have many friends, pal." Then he gave me a smile I couldn't quite fathom. "Good luck to you. She's up there." He swung his arm up, flicking black dots on to my T-shirt.

I looked up to where he was pointing. "Bloody hell."

The citizen laughed. "Aye, you need guts to do her job."

I started to climb the stairs, craning up at the glass cupola three floors above. An elaborate system of ropes had been strung beneath it, from which a harness was hanging precariously. I felt my stomach somersault. I'd rather dig turnips for a month on a city farm than dangle from a contraption like that. Even when I got to the third floor Agnes was about fifteen feet above me, her body out in the middle of the stairwell. She was painting the convex frame of the cupola, her face set in an expression of complete concentration. She had on her usual workclothes, the mauve scarf tied round her neck and her head covered by a paint-spattered cap.

"Agnes," I called, not too loudly. I didn't want to provoke any sudden movements.

It seemed to take a few seconds for my voice to get through to her. Then she swivelled her head slowly and stared down at me. "Citizen Dalrymple," she said without emotion. "What a surprise."

"I told you before, call me Quint," I said. "Can you come down?"

She gave a hollow laugh. "You must be joking. Have you any idea how long it takes the gang to get me up here?"

"I need to talk to you. It's important."

"So talk." Agnes took her eyes off me and went back to her work.

I glanced round and saw a pair of male and female citizens fitting a door further down the corridor. They seemed to be the only others nearby. I showed them my authorisation and asked them to go downstairs for ten minutes. They looked pleased to get an unexpected break but pissed off that they'd miss my conversation with Agnes.

When they'd gone I went back to the stairwell and leaned towards her. Despite the heavy railing, my gut started to complain volubly.

"Agnes, what really happened last night?"

She stared at me, on her guard immediately. "What do you mean?"

"Don't mess about. I know who came to your place. I know who sent the nursing auxiliary away. Why did you tell me she got a call?"

Agnes took her gaze off me. She wiped her brush carefully on the rim of the paintpot and put it in her pocket. "Are you sure that's important, citizen?"

"Of course it's important," I shouted, annoyed by her reluctance to answer my question and by her refusal to use my name.

Her eyes met mine. "I'm sorry to disappoint you but there's no great mystery."

"How about letting me be the judge of that?" I said, making the mistake of looking down. What little was inside my stomach went trampolining.

"Allie asked me not to say that Nasmyth 05 had been there," she said with a shrug. "He said it wouldn't look good for a senior auxiliary to be seen in a citizen flat."

She was right there. Segregation rules bar auxiliaries of the fat man's seniority from visiting ordinary citizens' homes except on official business. I didn't buy what Nasmyth 05 said about taking care of lottery-winners. That didn't extend to taking care of lottery-winners' families after lottery-winners were dead.

"What did Nasmyth 05 want?" I demanded.

This time Agnes's eyes shifted away. "He's . . . he's got quite friendly with Allie."

I watched her as she took her paintbrush out again and examined the bristles closely. According to their files, Nasmyth 05 and Alexander Kennedy were both registered as homos. Was that what this was all about? The fat man having a bit of illicit sex?

"What went on when Nasmyth 05 was at your flat, Agnes?" I asked.

"I wasn't there all the time," she answered, sticking her brush in the paint again. That squared with what the nurse said about Agnes visiting the neighbours, but how long would that have lasted?

"What went on?" I repeated. There was no way I was letting her off the hook, even if her brother's activities embarrassed her.

She ran her brush along a casing then shot an annoyed glance down at me. "They were in Allie's room."

"When did the auxiliary leave?" I asked.

"I was in bed. I suppose it was about midnight."

There had been no report of the fat man leaving the tenement from the undercover operatives who were on the lookout for Allie. I'd have to check that.

"What's the problem?" Agnes said. "It's not Allie's fault that the auxiliary likes him."

That was true enough. Someone as senior as the Edlott controller could make life very difficult for an ordinary citizen who rejected him. Not that it sounded like Alexander Kennedy had done that. There was something dubious about their relationship, especially considering that his father, who was Nasmyth 05's original link with the family, had been poisoned to death.

"Can I get on with my work now, citizen?" Agnes asked in a long-suffering voice. "We're supposed to be out of here in two days."

"Thanks for your help, Agnes," I said. "Will you do something for me?"

She gave me a suspicious look.

"Will you let me know immediately if Nasmyth 05 shows up again? I'll leave my mobile number down here."

"All right. Goodbye." She dismissed me with a vacant look like a shop assistant in pre-Enlightenment times who'd just completed a sale.

I wrote my number on a scrap of paper and stuck it in the scroll of a railing. Then I returned to ground level, much to the approval of my internal organs.

I walked out into the blazing sunlight and immediately felt in need of water. Fortunately there was a mobile drinking station for the workers outside the building. I joined the queue but before I got to the front my mobile rang, provoking distrustful looks from the citizens around me.

"Is that you, Dalrymple?" Hamilton said, puzzled when I didn't answer with my name.

"It is. What's the problem?"

"I'm not broadcasting any details on air but you can take my word that 'problem' is an understatement. Try disaster."

"Great." I pulled out of the water queue.

"Where are you, man?"

I told him.

"Good, you're not far away. I'll be there in a couple of minutes."

I stood at the street corner, watching the lucky bastards who had the time and inclination to drink. I'd completely lost interest in wetting my throat. I was pretty sure Lewis's problem that was really a disaster had more than a passing connection with the fluid in the mobile drinking station.

The public order guardian's Jeep pulled up, brakes screeching. I jumped in.

"What's the story, Lewis?"

"An emergency Council meeting's been called. We've had a

communication from the lunatics behind the poisonings." Hamilton drove away from the kerb, took a right turn that sent me crashing into him then accelerated down the Pleasance.

"A communication?" I said as I struggled to put my seatbelt on.

"The buggers had the nerve to put a letter into the Direct Access box at the Council building."

I didn't manage to suppress a laugh. Someone knew exactly how to get to the guardians, both literally and metaphorically. The Direct Access box was set up by them a year back as a way for citizens to bring their problems to the Council's attention without involving the City Guard or any other layer of the bureaucracy. Confidentiality was guaranteed, although some of the guardians – including Hamilton, I heard – had wanted to put the box under permanent surveillance so they could identify the senders of anonymous messages. The new, user-friendly Council had voted against that and located the box round the corner from the entrance to the Council building. So whoever was behind the killings had found the perfect way to get in touch and the perfect way to shout "Can't catch me!"

"Shit," I said.

The guardian swerved on to Holyrood Road and headed towards the former parliament building. "What is it?" he demanded.

"I wish we'd put a surveillance camera on the box," I said. "It was the obvious way for the killers to get a message through without risk and with a guaranteed quick response." The Council had made a pledge to citizens that the DA box would be emptied every half-hour and urgent messages passed to the relevant guardian immediately.

"I'm amazed, Citizen Dalrymple," Hamilton said as he turned into the Council yard. "I thought you were in favour of increased citizen rights."

"Not for serial poisoners," I said, pushing the door open. "Anyway, what makes you think ordinary citizens are behind this? Personally I'm more inclined to suspect auxiliaries."

His reply was lost in the babble from a herd of nervous guardians on the steps outside the Council chamber. The upturned boat design of the building seemed very appropriate – as far as the investigation was going, we were flailing around in the water without the benefit of life jackets.

Sophia was already in the senior guardian's chair, her white blouse showing signs of wear and her hair untidy. She didn't favour me with an acknowledgement. She ran her eyes wearily round her colleagues then signalled to the doorman to shut us in. I wasn't surprised to note that the citizen members were again absent. They were no doubt being fobbed off with an extended stay in one of the city's top tourist hotels – full eating, drinking and screwing privileges thrown in to shut them up.

"This emergency meeting will come to order." The moment she started speaking, Sophia shrugged off every sign of tiredness and become the model leader. That's what power can do for you. "No doubt you are all aware why it has been called." In between her sentences there was total silence in the chamber. Despite – or perhaps because of – the senior guardian's authority, several of her colleagues looked out of their depth. They reminded me of auxiliary trainees after a showing of the documentary film *Mob Rule, London 2003*, which is used to weed out the faint-hearted.

"Public order guardian?" Sophia said icily.

Lewis Hamilton wasn't bewildered; he was in his element. He stood up and brandished a clear plastic folder containing a sheet of A4 paper. "This was found in the Direct Access box at two o'clock this afternoon. It was in an envelope bearing the words 'Council. Urgent'." He held up another plastic folder. From where I was sitting the contents looked like a standard-issue envelope made of greyish low-quality paper. "The writing is the copperplate taught in the city's schools, executed with a nib and the blue ink obtainable in any Supply Directorate outlet."

"What does it say, guardian?" I asked impatiently.

"I'm coming to that, Dalrymple." There was no hurrying Hamilton when he had the floor.

"Come to it now, please," Sophia said from her throne.

Red patches appeared on Lewis's cheeks. "Very well. The message reads:

> Council members, this is not a hoax. We are the purveyors of the Ultimate Usquebaugh. We are responsible for the deaths of Francis Dee Thomson at the Colonies and Fordyce Bulloch Kennedy at Murrayfield. We also put nicotine in three kettles in the retirement home at Trinity. You know what we can do. Imagine how easy it is for us to poison the water supply. We can kill hundreds of citizens. Hundreds of tourists. But we're not unreasonable. We're willing to do business. Fly the Enlightenment flag on the castle at half-mast at seven o'clock tonight to show you're ready to negotiate. This is your ultimate ultimatum."

Jesus, we were being terrorised by a bunch of comedians. At least I thought so. The Council members were sitting round the chamber with doleful expressions on their faces. Humour had never been their field of expertise.

"Citizen Dalrymple," Sophia said, "What do you make of this?"

I went over to Lewis Hamilton and took the plastic folders from him. "Any prints?"

He shook his head. What a surprise.

I scrutinised the writing. True enough, it was the standard copperplate that the original Council imposed on all the city's schools. It may have been good for social engineering but it was hopeless if you were trying to trace anyone. Still, it did suggest that the writer was a local, as did the use of Supply Directorate writing materials. The word "we" implied there was more than one of them. I made those points to the guardians.

"You mean we have spawned a group of mass poisoners in the city?" the culture guardian asked, a shocked look on his face.

"There's no shortage of dissidents who grew up in Edinburgh and took exception to the Council for one reason or another." I thought of Katharine as soon as the words left my mouth and twitched my head to expel the idea.

"Their background is hardly the point. How are we going to catch these madmen?" Hamilton said, managing to put his directorate's collective foot in a heap of elephant dung.

"Quite," Sophia said, zeroing in on him. "How are you going to catch them, guardian?"

I intervened before Lewis made a complete idiot of himself. "Let's concentrate on the message. What does it tell us? First, the writer and his or her associates have direct knowledge of the murders. None of the details given about the victims, locations and poison used have been made public. Second, they know enough about the set-up in Edinburgh to find a secure method of communicating with us. As the writing and the materials also suggest, at least one of them is a local. And third . . ." I ran my eyes round the guardians to get their full attention ". . . and third, they have an agenda."

Sophia nodded. "I agree. What do you think that agenda is, citizen?"

Time to liven things up. "That's obvious, I would have thought," I said with a tight smile. "To get as big a cut as they can of the city's tourist income."

There were sharp intakes of breath all round. As I expected, that hit them where it hurt. The tourism guardian exchanged anxious glances with his colleague in the Culture Directorate. After a few seconds the backlash began.

"That's pure supposition," the finance guardian said. He was young and keen, his downy facial hair and innocent expression contrasting with a rasping voice. "These people are just psychopaths with grudges against the city."

"They may be," I said, looking at him mildly before I struck back. "Though that also sounds like pure supposition."

The fresh-faced guardian's jaw dropped.

I didn't intend to give him the chance to get back into the debate. "The fact that they use words like 'do business' and 'negotiate' show that they're in this to make a profit."

The Council members started nodding like a bunch of puppets. It looked like I'd made my point.

"So what do we do?" Sophia asked, her air of authority beginning to dissipate.

"What we do is we play for time," I said. "They've already given us a bit of that. Make sure the flag on the castle is lowered this evening."

"Good God, man," Hamilton exploded. "That flag is the Enlightenment's main symbol of authority. If citizens see it at half-mast, they'll think the Council's losing its grip."

I grinned at him. "You mean it isn't?"

"Citizen," Sophia said sharply. "Bear in mind that your authorisation can be withdrawn at any time."

I thought about daring her to sideline me then went along with her. I didn't want any more innocent people to be poisoned and, besides, this case was far too interesting to miss.

There was a stony silence, which I broke. "Lower the flag this evening as they demand. You can do it for as short a period as five minutes since they don't specify how long. You can be sure they'll be on the lookout. If any citizen notices, you can pretend a guardsman tied a loose knot."

Hamilton wasn't keen but the other guardians agreed.

"Very well," Sophia said. "We'll buy you your time, citizen. How do you intend to use it?"

She had me there. I spun them a line about following up leads on Allie Kennedy and the still-comatose female with the sign-of-four tattoo. I didn't want to broadcast my suspicions about Nasmyth 05 yet.

Fortunately the public order guardian took over. He reported that search teams hadn't yet been sent to the area where the woman was found because of the need to mount guards all over the city's water supply network. It looked like that buck had stopped at me.

He also said that the waterman who delivered to my father's retirement home had been traced and interrogated. He'd been cleared as his tank showed no traces of nicotine, while three of the kettles in the home did. So some bugger had slipped in there without being spotted – presumably in daytime when the doors were all open and most of the old guys were out in the garden baking in the Big Heat. The postwoman had also been eliminated from the enquiry, meaning that she'd also been given the full treatment by the guard and stuck to her story. Finally, Lewis confirmed that no more bottles of the Ultimate Usquebaugh had turned up. Whoever was behind all this was running rings round us.

"No sign of the Kirkwood woman?" Sophia asked Hamilton. She gave me a sharp look.

"No, senior guardian," he replied. "But I'm still treating her as a suspect."

I'll bet he was. In his eyes Katharine's dissident record had always outweighed her subsequent rehabilitation.

"Anything else?" I asked, getting up to go. I was glad that Lewis had decided against mentioning – or had forgotten about – the surveillance we'd put on Nasmyth 05. I had a feeling the culture guardian wouldn't be too happy about that.

"Not for you," Sophia said dismissively. "My colleagues and I will discuss the threat to the water supply and its implications."

"You do that," I said, heading for the door.

"Citizen?" Sophia called. "Find these people. The Council is depending on you."

That made me feel really motivated.

Davie was waiting in the hall.

"What's going on?" he asked.

"We're drowning." I told him about the message.

"Jesus," he said when I finished. "What do we do now?"

"You tell me. We're running on empty as regards leads. The search squads I wanted to check out the area where the sign-of-four woman was found were never sent."

Davie nodded guiltily. "I know. The guardian made me rescind the order. I tried to talk him out of it but . . ." He shrugged helplessly.

"You can make up for that now by helping me do the search."

He nodded without enthusiasm. "I'm off duty now and I could do with some sleep."

"Tough, guardsman," I said with a grim smile.

We went out into the heat and got into his guard vehicle.

As we drove up the Royal Mile, I looked out at the tourists. They were strolling around with their usual mixture of shallow enthusiasm for the monuments and unwilling fascination for the bargains in the Supply Directorate's visitor-only stores. Prices were a lot lower than in their own countries and even if they wanted to, they couldn't buy tins of Air of Auld Reekie, waistcoats in Enlightenment tartan or guaranteed scrapie-free haggis anywhere else.

Davie took the corner at George IVth Bridge and accelerated past the central archive. I remembered how Ray had been the last time I was there and considered stopping to find out if he was any better. There had been something weird about his manner. I told myself to leave the poor sod alone. His arm was probably still giving him hell, thanks to the Medical Directorate's policy of prescribing nothing but the weakest painkilling drugs on grounds of cost.

We slowed at the junction with Forrest Road and I looked idly past Davie's head. A pick-up shot past in a blur of maroon, going in the direction we'd come from. I thought I caught a glimpse of Dirty Harry at the wheel, with some of his crewmen and a load of tools in the back. I wondered vaguely what a Fisheries Guard vehicle was doing in this part of town, then Davie rode the bend and the thought exited from my mind faster than an Edlott-winner's commitment to equality of property and opportunity.

Twenty minutes later we were standing on the bridge over the Water of Leith in Colinton, watching the narrow stream as it dribbled over the stones towards the centre. In the old days, with the mills and factories on its banks, it had been an artery running through the body of the city. These days during the Big Heat it was shrunken and sluggish – as good a symbol as any of contemporary Edinburgh's diminished potency. It seemed the poisoners were into semiotics as well as comedy. Or maybe they'd just been inspired by the blues song Ry Cooder and Taj Mahal recorded seventy years back – "If The River Was Whisky . . .".

"We'll have to split up, Davie," I said, looking at the guard map I'd taken from the Land-Rover.

"Is that a good idea?" he said. "You know the kind of people you can run into out here. Not that I'm bothered on my own account, of course."

"Of course not," I said. Davie wasn't in the habit of bothering about physical danger. "I'll just have to trust to fate. You take the west bank and I'll take the east."

"And I'll be in Currie afore ye?" he asked with a grin.

"Ha. We'll meet after the next bridge. At Redhall Mill."

He peered at the map then nodded. "Okay. Mind your back."

"Mind your own."

I watched his heavy frame shift away down the riverside, head moving from side to side as he immediately went into the search procedure he'd learned during auxiliary training. I headed off the bridge and followed the track I'd been down earlier. In the distance I could still hear the relentless cawing of crows but there wasn't much else going on in the parched undergrowth and woodland. I walked in a broad zigzag, hoping that I'd come across something I'd missed in the morning. I didn't.

Until a noise I couldn't place interrupted the drone of heat-dazed insects and chirrups from thirsty birds. At first I thought someone had punctured a bicycle tyre. I stopped and looked around. Nothing. I was about to move on when the hissing came again. This time unmistakably human. I reached for my mobile, suddenly aware that I had no means of defending myself. A vision of the dissident woman's battered face flashed before me.

"Leave the mobile." The order came from the trees on my left and was in quiet, controlled tones that made identification difficult.

I looked over but could see nothing. Slowly I put the mobile back in my pocket and raised my hands to the level of my chest without making any sudden movements. Plenty of the head-bangers who frequent the area outside the city line can put a knife through your chest from twenty yards.

"I'm on my own and unarmed," I said, standing very still and wishing I'd stuck with Davie.

There was a long silence, during which I reviewed my life and decided that there were still things I'd like to do — such as getting paralytic on several more birthdays and seeing the winter sun turn the castle walls the particular shade of reddish purple that no photograph can properly reproduce.

Then there was a quick movement to my left. I turned involuntarily, realising too late what a bad idea that was. Till I saw who it was.

"Katharine?" There was no mistaking the fair hair and bronzed features that had appeared from behind a tree trunk. Or the well-honed knife in her right hand. A wave of relief washed over me — she was alive, she was safe. Then I felt my heart still pounding in my chest. "Where the fuck have you been?"

"What's the matter, Quint?" she said, stepping out of the undergrowth warily. "I thought you'd be glad to see me."

The excitement became too much for me and I sank to my knees. I looked up as she approached. "Christ, I thought I'd had it there. Thanks a lot."

"Sorry." She kneeled down beside me. "I had to be sure you were on your own."

"I'm not," I said with a taut smile. I owed her a shock.

Katharine turned round rapidly, her body tense. "What do you mean?"

"Davie's with me." I touched her arm. The skin was surprisingly dry for all the sticky heat in the glade. "Don't panic. He's on the other side of the river."

She was up and away into the bushes before I could move a muscle. "Get off the path," she called over her shoulder. "There are some crazy people around."

"You're telling me," I said under my breath. I followed her into the undergrowth. "What the hell are you doing out here? There's an all-barracks search going on for you in the city."

She took a waterbottle from her belt and drank from it before handing it to me. The contents had a strange, inert taste but I was too thirsty to worry.

"I thought as much," she said, nodding. "I spotted what looked like surveillance people in your street and got a bad feeling. What do they think I've done?"

It was crunch time. Either I was right about Katharine or I was dead. "You had a couple of bottles of whisky in that backpack you left at my place," I said, watching her carefully. A cloud of insects had begun to form around us, sensing a pair of large meals. "Where did they come from?"

She returned my gaze steadily then laughed. "Are you telling me that the entire guard population of the city is looking for me because of a couple of bottles of contraband whisky?"

"Where did they come from, Katharine?" I repeated. "This is not a joke."

Her brow furrowed. "No, apparently it isn't. Well, if you must know, they came from here." She broke off and looked out from the cover of the bushes to check for unexpected visitors.

"What do you mean from here?" I demanded, glancing around at the undergrowth.

Katharine turned her head back towards me and gave me an indulgent smile. "Calm down, Quint. Not here as in this very spot." She squatted on the carpet of dried leaves. "I mean up the path about two hundred yards. There's a ruined mill house."

I wanted to tell her about the poison in the Ultimate

Usquebaugh but forced myself to get her story first like a good, impassionate investigator. "So how did you come across the bottles?"

She looked at me quizzically. "What is it about that whisky, Quint? You're not being straight with me."

"I will be. Just tell me how it came into your possession."

"If you insist." She folded her legs into a more comfortable position. "I was on my way into the city and I was looking for somewhere to lay up for the night." This wasn't exactly the most direct route from the farm to the city but I let that go. "Like I say, there's this old mill upstream. I heard voices when I got near it. Glaswegian accents, at least some of them. A couple of candles were burning inside but I couldn't see much through the window."

"You made sure you weren't spotted?"

Katharine wasn't impressed. "I know how to look after myself, Quint. You didn't think I was going to walk in the door and ask for a share of their dinner, did you?"

I shrugged. "How many people were there?"

"Four or five. I can't be certain. One of them was a woman."

Who was currently fighting for her life in the infirmary, I reckoned.

"They were arguing about something," Katharine continued. "I couldn't make out what. The woman was pissed off and the guys were laying into her. I didn't like the look of them. They were heavy types. Smugglers or worse. The kind we used to drive away from the farm. Pretty soon they put out the lights and turned in. Two of the men came out and one of them disappeared into the woods. The other sat down outside the door to keep watch. He lit a cigarette with a lighter that had a big flame." Katharine paused and looked at me, a strange smile on her lips. "That's when I recognised him."

I sat up straight. "What? You know him?"

Her smile got wider. "Oh yes. He was on the farm with me till about a year back. Peter's his name, Peter Bryson."

"What the hell was he doing here?"

Katharine raised her shoulders. "I didn't have time to ask him that. I got as close as I could to him and whispered his name. Fortunately he didn't raise the alarm." She looked down but I could see she was still smiling. "He was pleased to see me. Very pleased."

I felt a stab of jealousy. Christ, it was a long time since I'd experienced that emotion. "Oh, aye. When you say you knew him, what kind of knowledge do you mean?"

Her head jerked up and her eyes flashed. "You don't own me, Quint. You never did."

I dropped my gaze. "Sorry."

"You could have come to the farm with me the last time we were together," she said, leaning closer. "But you didn't have the nerve to leave your precious city and your bloody work. You didn't care about me that much."

She was right, though I kidded myself that things weren't quite as clear cut as she said. Time to get back to her story. "What happened with lover boy?"

Katharine glared at me. "Nothing to get worried about, dear," she said acidly. "Not this time anyway. I asked him what was going on. He told me he and his mates were out to make a killing in the city."

"Very funny."

Katharine looked at me uncomprehendingly. "Then one of the other men came out to join Peter. I made it back to the bushes before he saw me. Fortunately it was pitch dark."

"And then?"

"And then I waited till morning. I wanted to see if I could make contact with Peter again but they headed off towards the city line before dawn. I looked around the mill after they'd gone. There wasn't much there as they'd taken their packs with them and covered their traces to make it look like the place was deserted." She stopped and looked at me. "Then I found the whisky you're so interested in."

"Where was it? How many bottles?"

"There were three twelve-bottle cases, the top one five bottles short. They'd dug a hole in the corner and covered it pretty well. I noticed that the earth was a different colour there." She smiled bitterly. "Auxiliary training has its uses after all. Now will you tell me what's the big deal about the whisky?"

"In a minute. Finish your story first."

Katharine looked at me and shrugged. "I waited around to see if Peter would come back but he didn't. None of them did. So in the late afternoon I decided to move on to your place. I took a couple of the bottles for you." She stared at me sternly. "I decided against handing them over when I found you with your flies open and the medical guardian about to perform oral surgery."

I felt my cheeks redden. "Em, getting back to the people in the mill house. Can you describe any of them?"

"Not really," she said, shaking her head. "It was dark and I was peering through a dirty windowpane. I'd say they were all reasonably young. Peter's in his thirties, and he sounded the oldest. He's about five feet seven, thin, with very short black hair."

That made my ears prick up. Was he the one seen outside Frankie Thomson's place?

"And they were from Glasgow, you reckon?" I asked.

"Some of them certainly were. The woman and at least a couple of the guys. Not Peter. He's from Edinburgh like us. There may have been another guy with an Edinburgh accent but, like I told you, I'm not sure if there were three or four men."

"What were they talking about?"

"I don't know, Quint. They were trying to convince the woman to do something."

I remembered the injuries she'd suffered. "Did it sound like they might use force?"

"I don't think so. They were hard men but they weren't laying into her that badly."

I rocked back on my heels and thought about Katharine's story. Had she really come across the poisoned whisky by chance after an unplanned meeting with a friend? I couldn't see Sophia and Lewis Hamilton going for that. Something else occurred to me.

"Why are you back out here now?"

Katharine met my eyes and didn't look away. "I wanted to see Peter again."

I nodded slowly. "I thought as much. You were involved with him, weren't you?"

"Oh for God's sake, Quint, grow up," she said furiously. "Yes, I fucked him a few times. It was just the equivalent of a sex session on the farm, no emotions engaged. Satisfied?"

I turned away. I had no rights over her. Christ, I hadn't seen her for years. But what she'd told me still bothered me.

"I was worried about him," she went on. "He's smart but he's easily led. I think he might be taking too many chances."

"And you're going to look after him, are you?" I asked ironically. "Tell me, Katharine, why did you come to my place? You'd have saved us both a lot of trouble if you'd stayed out here."

She stared at me, then dropped her head. "You know what happened to the farm, Quint. I had nowhere else to go."

"So you decided to walk in on me three years after walking out on me. How kind."

"Stop it," she said angrily. "Stop it, Quint. I still care for you. I . . ." She crouched into herself and I realised how difficult it had been for her to say that. It was a lot more than I'd managed.

"Have you been back to the mill?" I asked in a softer voice.

She shook her head, still keeping it bent. "I was waiting till it got dark."

"Shall we go and check it out together?"

She looked up and gave me a surprisingly warm smile. "Yes. And then you'll tell me about the whisky, all right, Quint?"

I nodded then stood up, feeling the nerves in my legs tingling. It wasn't the right moment to let her know that Davie was due to meet me upstream. The crows that had been haunting the vicinity all day exchanged their harsh cries again. I wasn't sure whether they were mocking me for going along with Katharine's story or railing at me for setting her up.

Chapter Thirteen

———⋙◦◦◦⋘———

As we approached the mill house, I could see no sign of Davie. He was obviously being a lot more fastidious in his search than I was, though the fact that he hadn't contacted me on the mobile meant he'd drawn a blank. After meeting Katharine, I ignored everything else and headed straight for the semi-ruined building. It was two days since she'd been out here. I wondered if the stock of whisky was still buried in the mill. If we were lucky, we might even find its owners in residence. The prospect of catching Katharine's ex-boyfriend drove me forward.

The track veered towards the Water of Leith and I could hear its shallow stream trickling away behind a screen of dust-covered bushes to the right.

Katharine stopped and sniffed the air. The crows were having a momentary break from choir practice. "Do you smell what I smell?" she asked, giving me a dubious glance.

I breathed in and got a faint whiff of something sweet and sickly that immediately made the hairs on my neck rise. "Oh, oh." I watched as an inky-black bird lifted off from the crumbling wall in a clearing ahead of us. "Carrion."

She nodded. "Yes, but is it animal or human?"

I watched her as she started to move forward slowly. Was she spinning me a line? Did she already know what was in the mill? There was no way of telling. I was trusting her more than good sense advised and I should have got Davie over right away.

"Come on," she said, turning impatiently.

I caught up with her and ran my eye over the place. Ivy was growing over the high walls of the old building. Most of the windows had been pulled out but there was one on ground level that still retained its panes. That was probably Katharine's observation point. The ground in front of the mill house was overgrown apart from the pot-holed surface we were standing on. It looked like an idyllic scene from one of Walter Scott's medieval poems where the knight brings his lady for a bit of courtly lovemaking, no tongues allowed — apart from the smell, which got higher as we approached the shattered doorframe.

"See here," Katharine said, pointing at the faded grass to our left. A piece of wood about three feet long was lying there. One end was partially crushed where a metal head such as a pick-axe had been attached. There was a dull brown coating of dried blood on it, as well as small pieces of greyish tissue. The comatose woman's pounded face flew up before me again. She'd been found a quarter of a mile from here. It was beginning to look like she was the lucky one.

I put my hand on Katharine's arm. "I'll go in first."

"You think I can't take it," she said angrily, her eyes flashing.

"No, I know what you've seen in the past." I was pulling on rubber gloves. "I just don't want any potential evidence messed up. Stay here, okay?"

She nodded grudgingly.

I went in through the outer doorway and into a large open room — where I got, in quick succession, a couple of very nasty shocks. First, a gathering of black and dirt-grey crows flew up in a commotion of beating wings and alarmed shrieks, disappearing through a gaping hole in the roof high above. Then I saw what they'd been perching on and swallowed back what rose into my mouth. The birds hadn't left us much to go on.

"Jesus," Katharine said from the door, catching her breath. "Is Peter here?"

I motioned to her to stay where she was and kneeled down by the first body. The clothing had been torn apart by the crows' sharp beaks, as had the skin. All the soft tissue and organs accessible from above had been lacerated and pecked – eyes, lips, liver and so on. The only obvious way to identify the corpse's sex was by the stubble on what remained of the face. It was a man. I stepped over the reeking body to the next one. It was in a similar state, also lying on its back. Also male. And the same went for the third, although he was on his side, meaning that his left eye was still in situ. I turned the stiffened body round. Despite the post-mortem lividity, heavy bruising to the lower side of the face was visible. It was difficult to tell if there were stab wounds on the bodies as well as the marks of beating. I reckoned there were. Then I found something even more interesting. The man's shirtsleeve was ripped. Underneath was a yellow mark, a tattooed number four. I checked the first two bodies. The skin on their arms was torn, but I made out signs of four that matched the one on the woman in the infirmary.

"I'm coming in, Quint," Katharine said, moving forward before I could stop her. She bent down and studied the first body. "Oh no," she groaned, dropping to her knees. "Oh no." She put her hand out to the lacerated face.

"Don't touch him!" I shouted. "Sorry. Here, put these on." I handed her a pair of protective gloves. "Is it your . . . is it Peter Bryson?"

She nodded slowly.

I pointed to the yellow tattoo. "Have you ever noticed this before?"

"No," she said in a low voice.

"Are you sure?"

Katharine looked at me contemptuously. "Of course I'm sure. I saw him without his shirt often enough."

"Did you?" I said sharply. Her face tensed as she fought back tears. "Sorry."

"Who did this?" she whispered. Her face had lost its healthy hue and her voice was unsteady.

"I'd say there was more than one assailant. It looks like these guys were wiped out before they could fight back." There was no sign of defence wounds on their hands or arms so I reckoned they'd been taken by surprise and clubbed mercilessly. I looked at the earth-covered floor. There were no clear footprints. "It's almost like someone went over this surface with a branch to obscure any giveaway marks."

Katharine's head jerked up. "Why would a gang of violent killers bother with that?"

"Exactly." I didn't like the way this was going. But before I could take it any further, my mobile buzzed.

"Quint? Davie. I'm finished on this side. Nothing's turned up. How about you?"

I leaped to my feet, remembering that Katharine shouldn't be anywhere near a member of the guard. "No, nothing yet. Give me ten minutes."

"Right. Out."

I put my mobile back in my pocket and took Katharine's arm. "That was Davie. He'll be on this side of the river soon."

She slumped against me, her head on my shoulder. "I'd better go."

"Aye. It's probably not a good idea if he finds you at a multiple-murder scene."

She gave a bitter laugh. "No, the idiot would probably think I did it."

I raised her head. "He wouldn't be the only one. Katharine, I'm taking a big chance letting you walk."

She looked at me, her face hardening. "You don't think I had anything to do with the killings, Quint?" She sounded seriously aggrieved.

I examined the features that had appeared in my dreams so often in the past. Katharine's high cheekbones were more prominent now that her face had become thinner and the green eyes were as unfathomable as ever. I tried to imagine how Sophia and Hamilton would judge her. They wouldn't have bought her story about how she'd run into an old friend here and how she'd got the whisky. They'd assume she was in with the dead men or that she was involved in their deaths. Katharine had experienced all sorts of brutality as auxiliary, dissident, prisoner, Tourism Directorate prostitute and deserter; I'd seen her carry out a clinical killing myself. But she'd always been a victim reacting to violence rather than an instigator.

"Well, do you suspect me?" she demanded.

I shook my head. "No, Katharine. I trust you."

Her mouth slackened and she gave me a brief smile. "That's big of you."

"You're bloody right it is. I don't think even my powers of persuasion could convince the Council that you're in the clear. You were hanging around the murder scene on top of being in possession of poisoned whisky."

Her eyes opened wide. Shit, I'd forgotten she didn't know what was in the Ultimate Usquebaugh. Or if she did, she was doing a brilliant impersonation of a woman who'd sat on a live cable.

"What? There was poison in that whisky?" She turned towards the far corner. "It's been dug up, Quint."

We stepped round the bodies. Earth and stones had been piled up, and three spirits cartons with torn lids were protruding from a roughly excavated hole.

I looked round. "No bottles," I said.

"Quint?" Katharine said insistently. "Tell me about the whisky."

So I did. Her reactions were totally credible. She shook uncontrollably as she recounted how she'd almost opened a bottle to take a slug before she crossed the city line. Fortunately she'd decided she needed all her wits about her. That was a close one.

"Did you hear these guys mention the whisky when you were outside?" I asked.

"No. I told you, Quint. I couldn't make out what they were saying. But I did wonder afterwards what they were doing with it in this area. I mean, most smugglers use the coastline or hide the stuff in loads of incoming farm produce." She shook her head. "I was going to ask Peter about that." She glanced back at his remains and swallowed hard.

I put my arm round her. "Is there anything I should know about Peter Bryson, Katharine?"

"Such as what?" she demanded, shaking herself free. "How good he was in bed?"

"Calm down." I touched her hand. "Such as why he left the city?"

She looked at me less aggressively. "I don't know, Quint. Why does anyone leave the city?"

"Was he on the run? Did he have any criminal record or friends the guard knew about?"

"I told you, I don't know. He never spoke about the past." She shrugged. "None of us did. We weren't fans of the perfect city like you."

"Katharine, the whisky's been used to murder people. Was Peter Bryson a killer?"

"No!" she screamed. "No." Her voice lowered as she thought about it. "I saw him kill intruders on the farm." She raised her shoulders. "We all did. It was us or them."

That was a great help. "Davie'll be here in a minute. What are you going to do?"

She shrugged. "Go back into the city, I suppose."

"All right, but be careful." I scribbled my mobile number on a scrap of paper and handed it to her. "Ring me later. I'll let you know when you're in the clear. Don't go anywhere near my flat."

She nodded then leaned forward and kissed me hard on the lips. "Don't you go anywhere near that Ice Queen woman, Quint." She moved towards the bushes without looking back.

I rang Davie and told him where I was, then called the guard command centre. As I waited outside the ruined mill, I listened to the crows lamenting their lost meal from the branches of the surrounding trees.

The place rapidly turned from deserted sylvan glade to guard vehicle parking lot. Hamilton and Sophia arrived neck and neck, the senior guardian's Land-Rover just pipping Lewis's Jeep to the bridge. I could see how impressed he was by that. Then there was a lot of crawling around and watching Sophia work out a provisional time of death, which coincided with the attack on the female dissident last night. She also found stab wounds on all three victims. I left the guardians and the scene-of-crime squad to sift the details while I scouted around the building. A search team would be doing that soon – not before time – but I was worried about the fact that the crates Katharine had pilfered from in the mill were now completely empty. Had we found the poisoners but lost the poisoned whisky?

It didn't take me long to find at least a partial answer to that question. About fifty yards past the mill, the path swings even closer to the Water of Leith. At first I thought there were some unusually shiny stones in the flow. Then I realised that what had caught my eye were shards of glass. I called Davie then stepped gingerly into the shallow stream. The water was surprisingly cold despite its shallowness and the tropical ambient temperature. I lost my balance more than once on the moss-covered stones and in the patches of sticky reddish-brown mud. Then I reached the remains of the first bottle. The neck had been broken off but the label was clear enough. At least these bottles of the Ultimate Usquebaugh had been rendered harmless.

"What have you got?" Davie called from the bank.

I looked across at him, holding up some of the larger pieces of glass. "Last orders, gentlemen, please," I shouted. "This was the ultimate whisky and water."

An hour later we gathered outside the mill to compare notes. The chief toxicologist had arrived and taken possession of the

fragmentary bottles that had been fished from the river. A couple
had their lower parts intact and there were drops of amber liquid
in them so he'd be able to confirm what the labels already made
clear – that this was the poisoners' base camp.

Hamilton was wearing a self-satisfied smile. "A pretty good
afternoon's work, wouldn't you say?" he asked, looking round at
Sophia, Davie and me.

"It's far too early to jump to conclusions, guardian," Sophia
said, undoing her protective overalls and stepping nimbly out of
them. She turned to me and gave me a look that was marginally
less glacial than I'd been getting recently. Perhaps taking off her
outer garments in front of me had revived a happy memory.
"Citizen Dalrymple, what do you think?" she asked. We were
still on last-name terms though.

I rubbed the stubble on my chin, trying to get my story
organised. I had to be careful not to make any mention of
Katharine and what she'd told me. "Well, we're making progress.
The dead men were obviously involved in the poisonings. The
bottles of the Ultimate Usquebaugh in the river show that pretty
conclusively."

"And they were connected with the woman who's still in a
coma in the infirmary," Sophia put in. "The tattoos on their
arms confirm that."

I nodded.

"That's it then," Hamilton said, rubbing his hands. "Three
bodies here plus one in the infirmary equals four. The gang is
well and truly broken up."

"Hold on, Lewis," I said. I remembered Katharine's uncer-
tainty about whether there had been three or four men in the
mill. "It's not that simple." I paused as a young guardsman came
up and offered waterbottles. We all drank deeply. "As I was
saying, it's not that simple. For a start, who killed these guys?
The same people who threw the whisky into the river?"

The public order guardian was still smiling grimly. "I would
guess that another gang of dissidents or smugglers disposed of

them. Perhaps they strayed on to someone else's patch."

"But why would smugglers destroy the whisky?" Davie was taking his life, or at least his career, in his hands by going up against his boss. "Surely they'd be more likely to peddle it or drink it themselves."

"Exactly," I said, giving him some support. "And if they'd drunk it, we'd have found more bodies."

"Quite so." Sophia looked dismissively at Hamilton. "The fact is, we cannot be sure all the poisoned whisky has been destroyed. There's no way of telling how many bottles were in the cases to start with."

"And the scene-of-crime squad leader reckons that the glass in the river comes from seven or eight bottles," Davie said, flipping pages in his notebook.

"Right," I said. "So there could be twenty or more from this cache still at large. And who's to say there aren't other caches?"

Lewis was shaking his head but he didn't have the nerve to argue with Sophia in public.

"Anyway, there's something else." Three pairs of eyes focused on me. "The floor in the mill house has been swept. Even the earth around the hole in the corner has no clear prints. Probably branches were used. There are leaves all over the place."

"And what is the significance of that, Dalrymple?" Hamilton asked suspiciously.

"The significance is that the killers didn't want to leave any footprints we could trace."

Davie nodded. "They did a good job too. The squad haven't found a single decent footprint. They're still working on fingerprints but they haven't found any yet. The pick-axe handle is clean. Whoever used that was wearing gloves."

"Where is this leading, citizen?" Sophia looked at me with her trademark coldness.

"Well, dissidents and drugs gangs don't give a shit about prints." I glanced around them then went for the collective jugular. "But people wearing guard boots might."

For a few moments the only audible sounds were the hum of insects and the chatter of small birds. Presumably the crows had gone to find another source of nourishment.

Sophia turned to Davie. "Leave us please, Hume 253." She watched as he retreated to his vehicle then turned on me. "Be very careful, citizen," she said icily. "Do you have any hard evidence that auxiliaries carried out this crime?"

I shrugged. "You heard Davie. There are no clear prints." Hamilton snorted angrily. As far as he was concerned, I spent my life trying to implicate the rank below his in nefarious activities. The problem was, I'd sometimes been right. "Let's face it," I said. "Guard personnel wear nailed boots which leave distinctive marks. They're the only people in the city apart from miners who're issued with them. They're also trained in numerous forms of armed and unarmed combat, including how to use lengths of wood like pick-axe handles and knives. And don't forget – the message you got was written in copperplate."

"The word circumstantial is ringing in my ears, Dalrymple." Hamilton seemed to think that was a really smart comment so I ignored it.

"Also," I continued, "auxiliaries such as guard personnel have been made aware of the poisonings. Perhaps they beat the shit out of the perpetrators and smashed the whisky bottles out of a sense of duty."

That shut them up.

Sophia eventually gave up giving me the eye and looked at her notes. "As the guardian suggests, you have no direct evidence to make such an assertion, citizen. Besides, auxiliaries would have reported the incident."

The way she was avoiding looking at me suggested I'd at least given her something to worry about. Or let her know that I was on to her if she had planned the whole scam to show how dangerous the Council's liberal policies could be.

"What's important now is the flag," Sophia continued. "In

the light of this development, do we go ahead and lower it at seven o'clock?"

Hamilton said no and I said yes at the same moment. Sophia looked at us with a resigned expression on her face.

"You have to," I said emphatically. "There's someone else in on the poisonings, even if the lethal whisky has all been destroyed."

"How do you know that?" Hamilton demanded.

"It's obvious, Lewis. The ultimatum was posted in the Direct Access box this afternoon. These guys have all been dead for over twelve hours."

I had them there.

"You're quite right, citizen. I should have realised that," Sophia said, embarrassed at her oversight. "So the sign of four is really the sign of five, is it?"

"Who knows?" I said. "There might be a legion of them. Until we know different, we have to go on buying time."

Sophia nodded and looked at Lewis pointedly. "The decision taken by the Council stands." She turned towards her vehicle.

End of chat.

Davie and I collated the reports from the scene-of-crime squad and the other guard personnel around the mill house. No one came up with anything very exciting. Inside the building we found some personal possessions that probably belonged to the dead men as they came from outside the city. There were wrappers from chocolate bars that the Supply Directorate couldn't afford to buy from the multinationals, an empty packet of cigarettes called Sauchiehall No. 6 and some cans of an orange-coloured soft drink that claimed it could cure hangovers. There were also some clothes, mainly fatigues and other combat gear, as well as a few pairs of surprisingly good-quality male underwear. I was surprised that whoever had dealt with the guys hadn't walked off with that. There was no sign of any of the packs Katharine said the dead men had been carrying when they left at dawn two days ago. There could easily have been more bottles of the Ultimate Usquebaugh in them. Where were those packs now? The scene-of-crime people hadn't found them.

Hamilton came up. "We'd better get back to the city, Dalrymple," he said, looking at his watch. "It's not much more than half an hour before we have to lower the flag."

"All right," I said. "We'll meet you on the esplanade."

The public order guardian drew himself up and turned to Davie. "Take your vehicle back to the castle, Hume 253," he ordered. "Citizen Dalrymple is coming with me."

Shit. It looked like I was about to be read something a lot heavier than the riot act. I followed Hamilton to his Jeep, shrugging at Davie. He had a worried look on his face.

We took off and headed down the uneven surface at speed.

"You never learn, do you, Dalrymple?" The guardian glanced at me angrily then looked back at the road, swerving to miss a wide pot-hole.

"Steady, Lewis. You don't want to wreck your beautiful vehicle."

"Jesus Christ, man!" he shouted. "That's your problem, isn't it? You can never resist having a go. Did you have to suggest to the senior guardian that these killings might have been carried out by guard personnel?"

So that's what this was all about. "I have to act on what the crime scene suggests. There's no doubt that auxiliary involvement is a possibility."

Hamilton swerved round a tight corner and joined the road that led to the city line. As we approached the high walls of the gatepost, the ground on either side levelled out. It had been bulldozed to give the guard personnel an unimpeded view – and a clear field of fire.

"Exactly," the guardian said, shaking his head. "It's a possibility and nothing more. You're so obsessed by the idea of corruption in the system that you ignore other explanations. It's obvious that smugglers or drugs gangs are the most likely perpetrators." He slowed as he approached the steel barrier but not much. Fortunately the sentry saw the look on his superior's face. He swung the gate open in time. "Anyway, don't you think the senior guardian's got enough on her plate without you badgering her with crazy ideas?"

"She can handle them," I said, wondering if Lewis had any idea about my affair with Sophia. If he did, he wasn't showing it. Dissembling was never one of his strengths. I wanted to see if she would give any indication that she'd set the whole thing up as a means of increasing her power in the Council. It was a waste of time. She hadn't even blinked. I suppose Hamilton's hardline attitudes towards law and order should have made me suspect him too, but he was too straight to sign off on that kind of subtle conspiracy. I came back to the real world. "You agree now that it's a good idea to lower the flag?"

He nodded reluctantly. "I suppose so. You're right that someone else must have posted that ultimatum. It could just be a messenger who isn't in possession of any more bottles of poisoned whisky, of course."

"You hope." I looked out at the run-down suburbs around the slaughterhouses in Slateford. If the water supplies had to be restricted even more because of the threat of poisoning, it wouldn't be long before major unrest broke out. Citizens had already been deprived of whisky. You could hardly blame them if they rioted. Had that been part of the poisoners' plan?

Hamilton kept quiet as we headed towards the central zone, his mood no doubt improved by his rant at me. As we drove up George IVth Bridge towards the central archive, I thought of Ray and how jumpy he'd been the last time I saw him.

"Stop here!" I said.

Lewis jumped in his seat and braked hard. At least I was keeping him on his toes.

"What the bloody hell are you playing at?" he demanded.

"Something I need to check. I'll see you on the esplanade. Make sure your spotters are ready." I slammed the Jeep door. "Not that we've got more than a billion-to-one chance of nailing our man. He's hardly likely to stand on a street corner proclaiming, 'Oh, good, the nicotine poisonings have scared the Council into acceding to my demand,' is he?"

Hamilton grunted and drove on.

I went up to the fresh-faced sentry at the archive entrance and showed him my authorisation. "Is Nasmyth 67 in the building, guardsman?"

"As far as I know, citizen." He looked down at the log. "He hasn't signed out."

"Thanks." I headed into the relative cool of the former library.

Ray's door was half open. I tapped on it then stuck my head round. No sign of him but it looked like he'd been there very recently. There were files open on his desk and a cup of iced tea was on the blotter. I turned towards the window and looked out at the street. The spot at the kerb where Lewis had pulled up was right outside and Ray would have seen me getting out if he'd been sitting at his desk. I wondered if he was avoiding me. I couldn't think of a reason why.

"Oh. Excuse me." A middle-aged female archivist had appeared at the door. "I have a meeting with Nasmyth 67. Is he not here?"

I shook my head.

She looked at me dubiously through thick lenses in standard-issue Medical Directorate black frames. "I'll come back in a minute," she said.

I went over to Ray's desk and had a look at the folders. They seemed to be nothing more than a heap of records that he was checking. He'd started a list headed "Citizens Qualifying for Additional Library Cards" – if you take out more than a hundred Council-approved books a year, you get improved access to the stacks. I couldn't see anything suspicious in that. Then as I moved away I noticed that the floor in the corner behind the desk was covered in a thickish layer of dust. I moved the chair away and kneeled down. The dust was slightly gritty and had a musty smell that I didn't recognise. I've spent long enough in the archives to get acquainted with all the various odours; this one was new to me. What had Ray put there and where had it gone? I knew it must have been moved recently as the floors of senior auxiliaries' offices are cleaned every day.

"What are you doing, citizen?" The short-sighted woman was back at the door. "Who are you?"

I flashed my card at her then went for the exit. There wasn't time to look for Ray now but I was pretty sure he was up to something he didn't want me to know about.

"Did you find him?" the guardsman asked as I passed.

I shook my head.

"I'll tell him you were looking for him," he said, eager to please.

"No you won't. Unless you fancy a year digging coal."

The look on his face suggested that wasn't one of his fondest ambitions.

I found Hamilton and Davie at the northern wall of the esplanade. They were both scanning Princes Street and the gardens with binoculars.

"Any interesting sunbathers?" I asked.

The public order guardian lowered his bins and looked at me sternly. "What have you been doing, Dalrymple? It's nearly time."

I turned and gazed up at the black and white flag with the maroon heart that was moving sluggishly. Even at the top of the pole on the octagonal tower that's the castle's highest point there was hardly any wind. The sun was sinking gradually in the west but it was still hot enough to melt an ice floe. Which made me think of Sophia. I wondered where she was. Keeping up her close interest in the case by performing the post-mortems on the three dead men?

I looked down to the right. There was a lot of activity round the neoclassical temples that used to house Scotland's artistic treasures. These days the Culture Directorate uses the area around them to promote the lottery. Workmen were busy erecting mini-pavilions and stalls for the imminent official opening of Edlott to tourists that Billy Geddes had told me about. Advertisements for it had suddenly appeared on the hoardings. That would mean more foreign currency for the Council's coffers, though God knows what kind of prizes they were planning to attract their new well-heeled customers with. I had a feeling the lads and lassies in the Prostitution Services Department would soon be working double shifts.

"There it goes." Hamilton was staring up at the flag, shaking his head slowly. "Bloody disgrace."

"Calm down, Lewis," I said, watching the banner of the Enlightenment drop several feet. "No one except our friend will notice."

"Of course people will notice, man. Not everyone's as cynical as you."

Davie was shaking his head in resignation. I gave him an encouraging smile.

We stood around for five minutes like a bunch of prophets waiting for the end of the world. We were as disappointed as them when nothing happened. There was no sign of anyone in our view even realising that the flag had been lowered.

The guardian looked at his watch and pulled out his mobile. "Right, that's enough. Raise the standard again."

"How are you going to pull that off?" I said under my breath.

Hamilton missed that. He signed off and turned back to us. "What next?"

"We wait," I said, shrugging. "It's the other guy's move now."

"I've put a surveillance detail on the Direct Access box, Dalrymple."

"I hope they don't mind wasting their time," I said. "The chances of that channel of communication being used again are about as large as the chances of me winning the lottery."

"All citizens have the same chance," Hamilton said sarcastically, repeating one of Edlott's mantras. Even he didn't believe that the Culture Directorate went with whoever's ID number was tossed up by the draw. They only wanted worthy specimens like Fordyce Kennedy as winners.

"All citizens except troublemakers like me," I said.

Davie grinned derisively. "Don't flatter yourself, Quint."

An hour and a half went by and no contact was made. I went over to the infirmary to check on the post-mortems – nothing unexpected so far – then called up Peter Bryson's file in the directorate databank's Deserters Register. He was in it all right but there was nothing juicy to report. He'd been a cook in a school before he jumped the city line and there were no Offence Notifications against his name.

Davie and I took a break and went down to the castle canteen to refuel.

"What's on the cards then?" Davie asked after he'd disposed of what the serving woman described as a meat pie. She hadn't been too specific when I asked what kind of meat so I stuck with the cheese rolls.

"What's on the cards is I haven't a clue, my friend." I emptied my glass and refilled it with barracks beer. "Either the messenger gets in touch again – in which case he's probably a full-blown gang member with his hands on the poisoned whisky – or we're in the clear."

"What about the son of the second victim?"

"Allie Kennedy? Good question. I don't suppose there have been any sightings of him?"

Davie shook his head. "The command centre would have notified me."

I looked round the soulless basement room. There was no one near us. "How about the undercover people on Nasmyth 05?" I asked quietly.

"The Edlott auxiliary? He's been in the Culture Directorate all day. I told them to contact me when he leaves."

I nodded and drained my glass again.

"Quint?" Davie looked at me curiously. "You haven't asked about Katharine Kirkwood."

"Ah."

"What does 'ah' mean, arsehole?" Davie growled. "Have you been in touch with her?"

"Em, kind of. Keep that to yourself."

He glared at me then shook his head in disgust. He'd been doing a lot of that recently. "I hope you know what you're doing, pal. She's a suspect and—"

His mobile rang. Saved by the buzz.

"What?" Davie yelled. "You're in deep shit, son. Where are they now?" He listened. "Right. Hold on."

"What's going on?" I asked.

"It's the undercover man on Nasmyth 05. Apparently the auxiliary left his office twenty minutes ago. He walked to the Grassmarket and went into a citizens' bar."

I got up. "What are we waiting for?"

"There's more. He met up with someone. A young man with very short hair."

"Jesus. Tell the operative to wait for us there." I ran towards the door, knocking into a female auxiliary. "Why didn't the moron call us earlier?"

Davie caught up with me. "He said something about not wanting to bother us."

I came out into the crimson glare left by the setting sun. "Wanting to make a name for himself, more like. Well, he's done that all right. If we lose Allie Kennedy now, the jackass won't be undercover any more. He'll be under the bloody ground."

Chapter Fourteen

We screamed down the Royal Mile, went round the corner at the gallows on what seemed like two wheels and turned right on to Victoria Street. Tourists stood gawping as if we were part of the entertainment laid on for them.

"Which bar is it?" I asked Davie.

He leaned forward as he reached the bottom of the West Bow and weaved deftly through a detail of guardsmen dressed in seventeenth-century costume, their steel helmets and muskets attracting a bevy of Japanese with digital cameras. "Labourers" Bar Number 7," he said. "Shit!" he added in a shout as a small black tourist girl jumped forward, waving a plastic Enlightenment flag her doting parents had been conned into buying.

"Number 7?" I groaned. "That's all I need." When I was in the Parks Department after demotion, my squad of workers often used to go there for a couple of watery beers after our shift. Even five years on there was a good chance that some of the buggers would be there.

Davie stopped about thirty yards away from the bar. It was only two doors down from the Three Graces Club, one of the city's top nightclubs for loaded tourists, so the outside was well maintained. The black paint of the windowframes and the varnished wood panelling made the place look reasonably salubrious, but a gorilla in maroon dungarees was making sure no foreigners got further than the outer door.

"That's the undercover operative," Davie said quietly as we got out, inclining his head towards a nondescript young man in Cleaning Department overalls to our left. He was sweeping behind the replica of Canova's three divine naturists, his grey cap poking out behind one of the rounded buttocks. At least he had a job with a view.

"I'm Dalrymple," I said, leaning round the plaster statue's flank. "Is the target still inside?"

"First floor, second window from the right." The operative was having serious difficulty looking me in the eye – and not just because he didn't want to blow his cover.

I looked up at the first-floor window. Nasmyth 05 was clearly visible, his heavy torso resting against the fake Georgian frame. He was talking animatedly to someone I couldn't make out well. There was a blue workers' shirt and a pair of hands, but that was about all.

"Is it definitely a male he's with?" I asked, moving my head round the marbled thigh of one of the Graces.

The undercover man nodded. "He was waiting for the auxiliary outside. I saw them go in together. He's around five feet eight, pretty thin, with very short dark hair."

I pulled out my notebook and showed him a copy of Alexander Kennedy's file photo.

"Could be," he said, nodding. "Definitely could be. I didn't see his face very well though. He had it turned away from me."

"You know an all-barracks search is going on for this citizen, don't you?"

The bogus roadsweeper shrugged. "No. We often don't find out about that kind of thing till our weekly debrief."

So much for the Public Order Directorate's organisational skills. "Have you seen Nasmyth 05 with him before?"

He shook his head.

"All right." I gave him a heavy-duty stare. "If we nail the guy, you're in the clear. But the next time you fail to call in you'll be pulling that broom handle out of your upper intestine."

It looked like he got the message.

"Shall I call for back-up?" Davie asked when I returned to the Land-Rover.

I shook my head. "We can handle it. I know this place. The two of them are up top. The only way out is down the stairs. Let's hit them."

I didn't bother flashing my authorisation at the doorman. He'd already taken one look at Davie and decided he would step aside for a bit. I put my shoulder to the door and stepped into what was about as welcoming as the inside of the bothies that used to cater for generations of migrant workers, none of whom gave a shit about interior decoration. That mirrors the Recreation Directorate's attitude when it comes to fixing up ordinary citizens' drinking dens.

Silence fell before I'd got two paces into the throng. The drinkers in places like this can smell guard personnel before they see them. As far as these guys were concerned, Davie wasn't the only representative of the Public Order Directorate present.

"Hey, fellas, look who it is," came a booming voice from the far end of the bar. "Citizen Shitwit Dalrymple. What are you doing with the likes of us, Citizen Shitwit? After a bit of rough?"

I might have known Roddie the Ox would be here. When I was in the Parks Department with him, he used to supplement his beer supply by taking the other guys' alcohol vouchers in bent card games. It would be fair to say he wasn't happy when I clocked how he was cheating and put the word round.

"Come on," I said over my shoulder to Davie. I didn't want to give Nasmyth 05 and his companion any more advance warning than I had to.

"Come on," repeated the Ox in a falsetto voice. "Come on, big boy. The baddies are getting away." He moved his bulky frame into the centre of the room as the rest of the occupants broke into loud jeering.

"Oh for fuck's sake," I muttered, glancing at Davie.

"The two-step?" he asked, raising an eyebrow.

"Why not?" I moved towards the solid mass of flesh in front of me.

"Going somewhere, Citizen Shit——" Roddie didn't manage to finish the question because I took a measured stride and kicked him hard in the balls. As he jacked forward in agony, Davie came towards him. The Ox's face met Davie's raised knee at high velocity. I can't stand dancing but the two-step definitely has its uses.

We piled up the stairs, leaving the drinkers as motionless as a gallery of waxworks. I felt my heart pounding. It wasn't only because of the arsehole we'd left in a heap below. Was this the break I needed? Was the Edlott controller's companion the one who would tie everything together?

I burst into the first-floor room, motioning to Davie to stay at the doorway. Nasmyth 05 and his pal were the only ones there. The auxiliary had probably pulled strings to have the place to himself. He was already standing up by the time I got to him.

"What on earth's going on, citizen?" he demanded.

I wasn't paying attention to the fat man. I had the photo in my hand and was comparing the face of the young man with it. He had close-cut black hair, and he was the right height and build. Not only that but he looked vicious enough to have killed. But no way was he Alexander Kennedy. His face was disfigured by a harelip so severe that all the yellow teeth in the front part of his upper jaw were open to view. The Medical Directorate doesn't run to what it defines as non-essential corrective surgery.

"ID," I said, extending my hand.

The citizen looked at me with the sullen stare of someone whose expectations of life have never come close to great. Then he put his hand to the pocket of his workshirt and took out a dog-eared card. It told me that he was Euan Caborn, that he was twenty-one, that he lived in Granton and that he was a junior technician in the Culture Directorate.

"What are you doing here?" I asked him.

"What does it look like?" he said in a high voice, a spray of spittle flying from his impaired mouth. He glanced down at a half-emptied glass of heavy. "They haven't made drinking illegal now, have they?"

"Not that I know of," I said, turning to Nasmyth 05 and shaking my head. "Auxiliaries meeting citizens in citizen bars is contrary to the City Regulations though. What are you playing at?"

Nasmyth 05 looked at Euan Caborn, who returned his gaze steadily. Then he glanced at Davie. "Em, could we discuss this in private, Citizen Dalrymple?"

"Why not?" I gave him a smile. "The castle dungeons are very good for that kind of thing."

Caborn let out a squeal of laughter.

"Don't worry, son," said Davie, stepping forward. "You're coming too."

We took them off to the castle and gave them the hard man/soft man routine. It didn't get us very far. Nasmyth 05 was pretty unforthcoming. For all his effete appearance, he'd been through auxiliary training and he knew how to stonewall as well as the rest of us. Not that it mattered. Euan Caborn was very willing to talk, and he didn't seem to be bothered either by the cell's damp subterranean walls or by Davie's impression of a raging bull. I'd sent a guardswoman down to the archive to pull his file and everything he said was consistent with it.

"Right," I said after half an hour trying not to stare at his harelip. "Let's recap. You've been at the Culture Directorate for three months. Two weeks ago Nasmyth 05 started turning up unannounced at your workstation. He started giving you little presents – sandwiches from the auxiliaries' canteen, razor blades, books . . ."

"Mmm, very dirty books," Euan Caborn said with a salacious laugh. "From Denmark, he told me. *The Little Merman*, one of them was called. You should have seen the size of his flipper."

"You seen the size of my truncheon?" Davie said, moving his face close to the young man's. "So you started meeting the auxiliary after work, eh?"

"Aye," Caborn said, suddenly less defiant. "Just for a drink or two."

"Very likely," Davie shouted. "Are you telling me there was no messing about with each other's dicks?"

"Well, just a bit." The citizen raised his head again. "You can see from my file that I'm registered homo."

I touched Davie's shoulder. "It's all right, Euan," I said in soothing tones. "You're not at fault. There's something else I need to know."

He nodded slowly, eyes still on Davie.

I held the photo of Allie Kennedy out to him. "Have you ever seen this citizen in the directorate or in Nasmyth 05's company?"

He considered for a long time then shook his head. "No, I don't know him."

I reckoned he was telling the truth. There was no reference in his file to Kennedy being one of his associates. "One last thing. Has Nasmyth 05 ever asked you to do any special jobs for him?"

"Apart from sexual ones," Davie growled.

Euan Caborn gave a mocking laugh then shook his head again. "I don't think so. Like what kind of special jobs?"

I shrugged.

"Naw," Caborn said. "I'm a technician. I fix the machines when they break down. I never leave the directorate during working hours."

"And after working hours you go back to Granton and read your Plato, I suppose," Davie said with a sneer.

The young citizen's flawed mouth twisted into a smile. "Plato was homo too."

True enough. I tried another tack. "You ever smoked grass, Euan?"

"Me?" he answered in a shocked voice that wasn't too convincing. "I've got a clean record." That was true as well.

I remembered the scumbags I'd caught with grass in the Meadows. "Ever heard of the Southside Strollers?"

He looked at me blankly. Well, it was a long shot. He was from the north side.

I had the feeling Euan Caborn had nothing more to tell us so I decided to let him go. I got Davie to put a tail on him just to be sure. Then we went back into the Edlott auxiliary's cell.

The fat man was sitting on the rat-gnawed mattress. Despite the boiler-room temperature level, he was shivering. What had earlier been carefully arranged waves in his thick fair hair were now greasy strands. He looked up when we entered. The truncheon that Davie was slapping against the palm of his hand seemed to be a source of particular fascination.

"Right, Nasmyth 05, I'm prepared to cut you some slack."

There was a disbelieving grunt from Davie at the door.

"I might consider not reporting that you've had your hand in a young male citizen's underwear. Somehow I don't think you'd last long harvesting potatoes." He looked pathetically grateful. I took out the photo of Allie Kennedy again and threw it down in front of him. "You know we're interested in this specimen. I want you to tell me everything about your dealings with him." I gave him the eye. "And I mean everything."

The fat man drew his forearm across his forehead, making the auxiliary shirt even damper. Then he nodded slowly. "Very well." He glanced up at Davie timorously.

"Don't worry about Hume 253," I said. "He's very easy-going really." I put my hand on Davie's truncheon and stopped him smacking it against his palm.

Nasmyth 05 gave me a dubious look then started talking. "I visited the Kennedy family after the father won the lottery. I always do that. To show how seriously the directorate takes Edlott-winners."

I let him get away with that. The chances were that he and his mates in the Culture Directorate had carefully trawled the archive to find a respectable winner and put a false date on the consultation reference I saw in Fordyce Kennedy's file. Maybe he'd even looked for a winner with a son he fancied.

"I . . . I struck up a friendship with Alexander," the auxiliary said, his eyes down.

"You struck up an interest in his body, you mean," Davie said.

I twitched my head to restrain him. "And you started meeting Allie socially after that?"

He nodded. "I know it's contrary to regulations but I didn't mean any harm. I—"

"I don't care about the regulations, Nasmyth 05," I said. "I want to know everything you know about Allie Kennedy."

The fat man raised his eyes to mine and frowned. "But I don't know much about him. He'd never tell me what he spent his time doing. I knew he didn't work much because I checked his file and—"

"It never occurred to you that he might be up to no good?" Davie interrupted.

"Go and get us some water, will you, guardsman?" I said, motioning to the door. Sometimes Davie's hard man act is counterproductive. I waited till he went, giving me an unimpressed stare as he did so.

"All right," I continued, "Let's stop pissing about, auxiliary. We're both aware that Allie Kennedy is not one of the city's success stories. He might be into the black market or he might be into something a lot worse. All I want is to catch him. I don't give a shit what you've been up to with him." I bent over, put my hand under his heavy chin and lifted it so he had to look at me. "Unless you and he had anything to do with the poisonings." I hadn't forgotten the deaths at my old man's retirement home. "If you did, I'll use Hume 253's auxiliary knife on both of you."

Nasmyth 05 gulped. "I don't know what you're talking about, citizen. All I know about the poisonings is what I've read in guard bulletins."

"That had better be the truth, my friend." I let go of his chin. "So tell me about Allie Kennedy."

"He's . . . he's a sweet boy." The auxiliary's voice had suddenly become tender. "He never fitted into the system and now he feels lost. I . . . I've just been trying to help him sort his life out."

"No doubt. When did you last see him?"

The auxiliary seemed to be steeling himself to face me. "You know when. At the family flat the other night."

I remembered something that had been puzzling me about that. "How did you leave? The surveillance team didn't report you."

Nasmyth 05 gave me a shifty look. "Ah. Yes. I recognised one of them. I knew him on the auxiliary training programme. I asked him for a favour."

Brilliant. So much for the incorruptible nature of Hamilton's City Guard. "When are you going to see Allie Kennedy again?"

He shrugged. "We never arrange meetings. He calls me when he can get away."

Get away from what? I wondered. "Right, Nasmyth 05, here's the deal." I wasn't anything like sure that he was telling me the whole truth but I reckoned he was more use on the loose than in the dungeons. "The minute Allie calls, you call me." I scribbled my mobile number down. "Or the guard command centre. The same goes if he appears unexpectedly." I was going to keep the surveillance on him – using hand-picked operatives this time – but there was no harm in giving him the impression that he was free as a bird. "And Nasmyth 05?"

"Yes, citizen?" He eyed me nervously, registering the threat in my voice.

"I hope you've been straight with me. Remember the size of Hume 253's truncheon."

That sent him away without a spring in his step.

Davie was waiting for me at the end of the sweltering corridor. It looked like he'd been swapping torture stories with the cell-keeper. That lunatic's mouth was set in a slack grin.

"You let the bugger go." Davie said, shaking his head.

"Put your best people on him." I started up the worn steps. "I know it's a risk but I don't know how else we'll catch the mysterious Allie bloody Kennedy."

"What next?"

"We'd better check with the command centre."

There hadn't been any developments. No sign of Allie – surprise, surprise – no guard sightings of Katharine – thank God – and no further communications to the Council.

"Looks like we're in the clear for the evening," I said. "I'm going to use the public order guardian's personal shower then go home to crash. I'll see you tomorrow, Davie."

Hamilton waved me into the spartan shower room in his quarters without comment. He was bent over a heap of paperwork, his collar open and his white hair ruffled. I'd just come out from the blast of unusually cold water when my mobile rang.

"Citizen Dalrymple?" The female voice was clipped and officious. "The senior guardian requires your presence at her residence immediately. Out."

As I dried myself with a thin Supply Directorate towel, I realised how little I was looking forward to seeing Sophia. Something had gone seriously wrong between her and me and I had the feeling Katharine wasn't the sole cause.

I got a guard driver to take me down to Moray Place. As we joined the Mound, I looked out across the city centre. Darkness had fallen but there wasn't any great drop in the temperature. At least a light breeze was now ruffling the flags on Princes Street and making the tourists in the street cafés believe that Edinburgh in the Big Heat was worth it after all. A band in the gardens was playing Council-approved jazz – that is, distinctly trad, no dissonance allowed. People were walking about having animated conversations and laughing. Watching them, you could almost accept that the system was working. Till you remembered that the people having a good time were tourists and the only locals in the vicinity were the ones serving them. I glanced at the Edlott stalls round the galleries. They'd almost been completed and were already attracting the attention of visitors with money to burn on tickets. Was that what life in the city was all about nowadays? Winning free sex and whisky, or a soft job for life? Greed really was God in this supposedly atheist city. So much for the Enlightenment.

The Land-Rover set me down at the barrier in Darnaway Street. I didn't even have to show ID. The guardsman recognised me and let me through with a perfunctory nod.

I walked into the circular street where the guardians' accommodation has been since the Council came to power. The idea was that the city's leaders would cut themselves off from their families and live together in a kind of a bosses' ghetto. In the old days when there was a permanent senior guardian, a specific house was allocated to the holder of that rank. I had pretty unhappy memories of that edifice as my mother was senior guardian for years. The only time I saw her was when she wanted to drag me over the coals about some investigation that I wasn't handling to her satisfaction. I hadn't been back too often since she died in 2021. At least with the new rotation system of senior guardians, I didn't have to go to that house now. Even when they wear the badge of ultimate power for a month, guardians stay in their own residences.

The decorative lights in the gardens at the centre of Moray Place hadn't been turned on — I was glad to see the guardians weren't wasting the city's precious power reserves — so I followed the dim streetlamps round to the medical guardian's residence. The door opened as soon as I started up the steps.

"Good evening, citizen," a female auxiliary in a grey suit said brusquely, running a disapproving eye down my sweat-encrusted clothes. At least the body inside them was clean. "The senior guardian is waiting for you in her study. First floor."

As I climbed the curved Georgian staircase, it struck me that I'd never been inside Sophia's place before. She always came to my flat. She was probably worried that the woman on the door would have a nervous breakdown if she knew what her chief got up to with a demoted auxiliary. Not that her chief had got up to anything with me in the last couple of days.

A guardsman on the landing pointed to the far door then went back to his copy of the *Inter-barracks Sports Report*.

Since everyone seemed to know I was coming, I didn't bother to knock.

Sophia raised her head briefly from her antique desk. She didn't bother to speak or smile.

There was a bottle of water on the table in front of the fireplace so I went over to it and poured myself a glass. If she wanted silence, who was I to deny her? I sat down on one of the armchairs that guardians seem to choose especially for their lack of comfort and picked up a well-thumbed book. The senior guardian's current leisure reading was Patricia Cornwell's *The Body Farm*. In the past, Council members would have died rather than read pre-Enlightenment mass-market fiction. Now they're desperate to acquire the common touch. I hoped that volume didn't inspire her to rethink Agriculture Directorate policy. Or increase her interest in criminal conspiracies.

After five minutes Sophia closed the folder she'd been annotating and got up. She came towards me slowly, her bare calves below the grey skirt gleaming in the light from the ornate chandelier. She took some water then sat down opposite me.

"Well, citizen?" she said finally.

"Well, Sophia?"

She looked away in irritation, her ice-blonde hair flicking out of shape. "Don't make this any more difficult than it already is, please."

"What do you mean difficult?" I was puzzled. "You're the one who required my presence."

"Very well," she said, holding her back very straight. "Kindly give me an updated report."

So that's how she wanted to play it. No messing about, no

sweetness, no light. I reciprocated, telling her in unemotional tones about the current situation in the command centre – which she could have found out easily enough for herself. I decided to hit her with my thoughts about Nasmyth 05. That brought a hint of interest to her expression.

"Why wasn't the Council informed about the surveillance you had on the Edlott auxiliary?" she asked in full Ice Queen mode.

"If you and your colleagues were to be told about everyone being tailed by undercover operatives, you wouldn't have time to do anything else. Lewis Hamilton knew about it."

"Nasmyth 05 has a senior position in the Culture Directorate," she said angrily. "If you had the slightest suspicion, as senior guardian I should have been informed from the outset."

I looked at her, keeping my face blank. Was she just pissed off because I'd kept her in the dark or did she have some connection with the fat auxiliary she didn't want me to know about?

"Well?"

"Well what?"

"I'd like an explanation of why you didn't tell me, citizen."

"Oh for fuck's sake, Sophia," I shouted, jumping to my feet. "Stop all this 'citizen' bollocks, will you? We were sleeping together not long ago, remember?"

Spots of red appeared on her cheeks. "Yes, well, everybody makes mistakes." She gave me a piercing look. "As you of all people should know, Quint."

I attempted to step round the table and banged my knee on it. "What's that supposed to mean?"

She stood up and walked back to her desk, then stopped suddenly and faced me again. "You've seen her, haven't you? The Kirkwood woman."

I held her gaze but didn't answer.

"At least you aren't lying." She shook her head. "You're playing an extremely dangerous game. As far as I'm concerned, that woman is a prime suspect."

I took a deep breath before speaking. She was on to me, God

knows how. I thought I was the one who relied on hunches. "Be reasonable, Sophia. Katharine's not a cold-blooded killer."

"Katharine!" she shouted, losing her cool. "Katharine, as you call her, is indeed a killer. You know that very well. She's also a dissident and a deserter. Not to mention a former prostitute."

I gave her the eye. "Correct me if I'm wrong but wasn't the Prostitution Services Department set up by the Council? And Katharine was forced to work there after she came out of prison."

Sophia shrugged. "The details are irrelevant. I don't see any other suspect in this investigation with her record."

"Jealousy's a terrible thing, Sophia," I said, taking a pace towards her.

She went glacial again. "I can assure you that jealousy has nothing to do with my attitude to her, Quint. You'd better hope that there are no more ultimata and that you turn up something on Nasmyth 05 and the missing citizen soon." She turned away from me. "Otherwise the spotlight will move on to you as well as your girlfriend."

I wanted to give her a good shake but that would only have made her spit even more. Anyway, before I could make my mind up what to say, my mobile rang.

"Quint?" said a low, female voice that I recognised immediately. "Where are you?"

"At the senior guardian's residence, Davie," I said, enunciating like a ham actor.

"Ah," Katharine said. She gave a bitter laugh. "Don't even think about touching that woman. I'll call you later." The connection was cut.

I stuck the phone back in my pocket, hoping my face hadn't given me away.

"What was that about?" Sophia asked.

"It was just Hume 253 checking on my whereabouts."

"Why? Did he think you were in danger at my hands?" she said sarcastically. When guardians use sarcasm, you know they're out of their depth.

I shook my head. "Grow up, Sophia," I said, turning away and heading for the door. As I got there, I found myself wondering why she'd called me to her residence. I hadn't exactly told her much about the case. She didn't even give me the post-mortem results on the dead men from the mill. Presumably there was nothing unexpected to report. So why had she got me over? Surely, for all her display of indifference, it wasn't because she wanted to see me? I walked to the exit and let that thought float away into the open space of the stairwell.

Back in my flat I stripped off, took a slug of safe whisky and sat back in the uneven sofa as the rasping spirit slipped down my throat. I got a momentary rush but all the booze really did was make my internal organs burn as much as my skin was already doing in the cramped room. The windows were wide open but the place was still a sauna.

I went over and stood by the curtains, vainly hoping that the air outside was cooler. Sticking my head out, I looked down into the street. The undercover operative five doors to the right wasn't quick enough. I caught a glimpse of his dark shirt as he jerked back behind the stonework. Sophia was making sure that Katharine didn't slip up to me unnoticed. I went back to the sofa and took another pull at the whisky. I'd checked with the command centre on my way home – no further messages received and no more poisoned bottles discovered. Maybe the messenger was running scared and we were in the clear after all. I gave myself the luxury of ten seconds to wallow in that delusion.

As my eyes began to close, faces flashed up before me. First, Katharine. Where was she? If she didn't call again before curfew, she'd be out of touch until the morning – the limited number of public phones the Council has located around the city go dead overnight as part of the drive to keep citizens indoors. Well, she was capable of looking after herself. Then Nasmyth 05's bloated features appeared. The tail had reported that the senior auxiliary returned to his quarters in the Culture Directorate an hour ago.

The fat man was apparently so devoted to Edlott that he'd got himself a room above his office so he didn't have to go back to barracks to sleep. Which brought Ray's face up before me, the skin pale and lined as it had been the last time I'd seen him. As my brain sank into slumber, it struck me that he was a member of Nasmyth Barracks like the Edlott controller. Could there be some deeper connection between them? Could that have anything to do with the devastation on my friend's face and his erratic behaviour?

Ray disappeared into the void, to be replaced by a couple of faces I didn't immediately recognise. Young guys, one of them with red hair and the other with what he thought was the professional hard man's provocative stare. Then I remembered them. Colin and Tommy, the bagsnatchers in the Meadows. The Southside Strollers I'd asked Euan Caborn about. Allie Kennedy came from the south side of the city. Maybe those idiots knew him.

I made a feeble attempt to rouse myself, but before I could move I dropped into a black hole even sweatier than the dungeon I'd been in earlier. I thought I could hear the "Ventilator Blues" playing in the distance. Even in your dreams there's no escape from the Big Heat.

Chapter Fifteen

I woke up with a raging thirst, sunlight streaming past the curtains I'd forgotten to close. I hadn't had much time to queue for water recently and I could hear the racket from the large number of locals who'd already gathered in the street below. So I grabbed my mobile and took the easy way out.

"Davie, bring some water with you when you come to pick me up, will you?"

"Yes, sir," he replied sarcastically. "Anything else I can do for you, sir? How about some breakfast?"

"What a good idea. Out."

I found clean trousers and a Parks Department T-shirt that wasn't too stained. I was zipping myself up when my mobile buzzed.

"Quint? Can you talk?"

"Yes, Katharine. I'm on my own in my place." The Public Order Directorate doesn't run to surveillance equipment on mobiles, so as long as she'd picked a public phone that wasn't being randomly tapped we were okay. "Where are you?"

"Grange Cemetery. I spent the night behind a gravestone."

"You'd better spend the day there too." As the Council allows only cremation, the city's old burial grounds are dead quiet. "I'll try to meet you later on. Have you got a good book?"

"I can find ways to occupy myself."

I wondered about that. Did she have business in the city? I'd been convinced by the way she reacted to her friend's body at the mill, but could it have been an act? Did she know more about the Ultimate Usquebaugh than she'd let on? There wasn't time to take that any further. I heard Davie's heavy steps on the stair.

"Call me again in the afternoon," I said. "Keep your head down."

She laughed softly. "You know how good I am at that, Quint. Be good. And beware women in blouses and skirts."

"Out," I said as Davie came in.

"I only just got here," he said with a pained expression.

"Not you, idiot."

He came forward and tossed me a brown paper bag. "Who were you talking to?" he asked.

I pretended I hadn't heard and got stuck into the barracks wholemeal roll. I needed a whole bottle of water to wash it down.

"Wonderful morning, isn't it?" the public order guardian said, looking out over the sunlit panorama of buildings, firth and distant hills from his quarters in the castle.

"Maybe it is from up here," I replied testily. "Down in the streets where the citizens go, it's bloody sweaty."

"Oh come on, Dalrymple. Things are looking up. No more messages overnight, no sign of nicotine in whisky bottles or, thank God, in the water supply. What are you so gloomy about?"

"No sightings of Allie Kennedy, for one thing."

Hamilton sighed. "There's no firm evidence that the missing citizen's done anything, man."

"Why's he disappeared then?" I sat down at the conference table and pulled out my notebook. We were going nowhere fast in this case and I was pretty sure it wasn't over yet.

"Nasmyth 05 has been in the Culture Directorate since last night," Davie reported.

"Great," I grunted.

"There are still some leads we haven't followed up," Davie said, sitting down opposite me. He was trying to be helpful. Hamilton blithely continued his impression of a self-satisfied laird surveying his domain.

"Such as what?" I demanded.

"Such as the seven citizens who've been nailed for smuggling marijuana. I can find out if they've ever had anything to do with Allie Kennedy." Davie glanced over at his boss. "Or with the fat man," he added in a low voice.

I took the list he'd removed from a folder. Six of the grass traffickers had been down the mines for weeks, while the seventh was in a secure clinic. "It's a bit of a long shot," I said doubtfully.

"I thought you liked long shots," Davie said sardonically.

"All right, go and talk to them. Meet me outside the Council chamber at midday if you can."

He looked at his watch, raised an eyebrow and departed.

"You will be at the Council meeting, won't you, Dalrymple?" Hamilton said from the leaded windows.

"Yes, Lewis," I said, getting to my feet. "I can hardly wait."

"Where are you going now?" he asked.

"Not sure. I'll see you later."

I went down the corridor and out into the sun. If coins existed in Enlightenment Edinburgh, I'd have tossed one. As all citizen transactions are by voucher, I made do with going for the marginally shorter of the two long shots I had in mind. Davie would have let out a hollow laugh. It was either Ray, whose uncharacteristic behaviour was still puzzling me, or the two headbangers I decked in the Meadows. Since Ray didn't have any kind of criminal record or any connection with the suburbs on the south side, I went for Colin the carrot and his headbanger pal Tommy. I knew they'd be overjoyed to see me.

The Youth Development Department runs numerous residential centres for the city's problem kids. In the early days of independence, the Council favoured the minimalist approach to young recalcitrants – meaning the mines, the farms or an extended session with the inter-barracks boxing champion. Since the guardians (apart from the likes of Hamilton and Sophia) became user-friendly, naughty boys and girls get a much easier ride. They have their own rooms in rehabilitation centres, they're issued with clothes that are a cut better than the Supply Directorate gives the rest of us and they're allowed to listen to music that has only a passing relationship with melody, harmony or subtlety. But the inmates of the centres still get locked up overnight – and the poor darlings have to take part in endless counselling sessions and discussion groups.

I discovered from the command centre databank that Colin and Tommy had been assigned to a facility in Newington. The grey-bearded guardsman who drove me there was even more severe than most of his kind. His expression only lightened when we pulled up outside the neoclassical villa on the Dalkeith Road.

"Want a hand putting the squeeze on the wee shites in there, citizen?" he asked eagerly.

One of the old school of auxiliaries. I declined his offer and told him to wait for me. I climbed out and got an eyeful of Arthur's Seat and its scorched slopes. That made me think of Billy Geddes in the rehab centre over in Duddingston. He mentioned Nasmyth 05 to me what seemed like a very long time ago. It might be an idea to squeeze him for more on the Edlott controller.

After I got past the guardswoman at the gate – who was in plain clothes to give the impression that this wasn't a house of correction – I stopped and looked up at the extravagant building. It was a large rectangular block with tall windows to the left and right of the columns at the entrance. The Youth Development Department flag was hanging limply from a pole on the central tower's triangular gable. At least that meant the garish purple and yellow geometric design by a former inmate wasn't too visible. I went inside and asked for the two lads. While I waited, I took in the atmosphere. What was once an art gallery's spectacularly

opulent marble and glass hallway had been stripped and de-
graded into a typical Council institution with poor-quality wood
panelling and bare brickwork. Still, it was very clean. It wouldn't
do for the residents to live in squalor.

Obstreperous voices echoed down the hall. Obviously the
department hadn't worked its magic on Colin and Tommy
yet.

"Hey, Col, look who it is." The would-be tough guy nudged
his mate. "It's that investigator wanker. D'you reckon he'll have
us this time?"

"Naw," the carrot said. "We're ready for him, eh?" He didn't
sound too convinced.

I led them into a common room full of surprisingly comfor-
table-looking furniture where a couple of other inmates were
playing cards. I wasn't bothered if they heard what I was going to
ask.

"Getting on all right?" I asked the bagsnatchers.

"As if you care," Tommy said, staring at me dully.

"Oh, I care, son. Believe me, I care."

"Like fuck you do."

Colin let out a nervous titter.

I smiled at them. "I care so much that if you talk to me, I'll get
you out of here early."

That shut Tommy up. It also put a stop to the other guys'
game of cards.

"Eh, what d'you want tae talk about then?" Tommy asked,
getting as close to co-operative as he could manage.

"Allie Kennedy." I watched them closely as I said the name.
"Alexander Kennedy. Do you know him?"

There was a brief silence as all four of the common room's
occupants took up pretending I wasn't in the room. This was
getting interesting.

"I'll take that as a yes then, shall I?" I asked.

"Take it as anything you fuckin' like," Tommy said, his chin
jutting out aggressively.

I laughed then stopped abruptly. "Remember the guard commander you saw in the Meadows?"

Tommy glanced away but Colin nodded slowly, his mouth half open.

"He's an expert in the third degree." I smiled at them again. "In fact, he's developed something he calls the fourth degree." I paused for effect. "The Council doesn't let him use it very often. Something to do with the male victims having permanently high voices after it."

Colin's face blanched. Tommy and the other guys weren't looking too happy either.

"That auxiliary is just a call away," I said, hardening my tone. "So how about saving me some time and yourselves a lot of grief?" I looked round the room. "I'm talking to the four of you. I can see you all know Allie."

"Aw, come on," one of the card players whined. "This isnae anything to do wi' us."

"It is now, pal. Why don't you all have a chat about it?" I left them to huddle into a group and whisper acrimoniously for a minute.

"Awright," the putative hard man said, eyeing me as threateningly as he dared. "We know Allie Kennedy. But he's nothin' to do wi' the Southside Strollers. He's in a different league frae us."

"Fuckin' right," one of the card players put in. "He's a right fuckin' heidbanger."

I scanned their faces again. They showed a mixture of disgust and fear. "What kind of thing has he been involved in?"

"You name it, mister smart fuckin' investigator," Tommy said. "He moves grass, he pimps rough for tourists, he's intae the black market."

Pay dirt. It looked like my long shot had paid off. But the bad news was that Allie Kennedy was obviously a smart operator. He'd managed to avoid getting a Public Order Directorate record apart from that minor card-playing offence. And he'd managed to get himself a heavy reputation among the city's next generation of criminals. These guys were very reluctant to talk about him.

"Does he run with a gang?" I asked.

Four shaking heads.

"Naw," Colin said quietly. "He's a one-man show."

"There are stories about him dealing wi' people who get in his way," Tommy added. "Dealing wi' them so they don't bother anybody ever again. I reckon he's got contacts wi' the guard dogs."

This was getting better and worse by the minute. "I'll try not to tell Hume 253 you said that, Tom. So where does this criminal mastermind have his base?"

More shaking of heads, this time categorical.

"He's smart," Tommy said, a note of admiration in his voice. "He doesn't leave traces for you bastards to find." He grinned derisively at me.

I let that go. "When did any of you last see him?"

"I've never seen the cunt," Tommy said.

"Me neither," the carrot added.

The other guys were shrugging.

"What?" I yelled. "Allie Kennedy's got more of a reputation than the Scarlet Pimpernel in the shit-stained underworld you inhabit and none of you's even seen him?"

All four of them looked at me blankly like cows that have been standing in the rain for hours.

I turned to go.

"Here, what about gettin' us out early?" Colin called.

"Trust me," I said. "I'll fix it."

There were groans of disbelief from behind me.

"Here, citizen investigator," Tommy called.

I stopped and turned to face him.

He was grinning slackly. "Who the fuck's the Scarlet Pimpernel?"

Davie pulled into the yard outside the Council building a few minutes before the meeting was due to start.

"Good timing, big man," I said. "Get anything interesting out of the grass traffickers?"

He pulled his sleeve across his forehead and shook his head. "Nothing very hot. They all claimed they were solo operators. They pilfered from marijuana clubs and the Supply Directorate stores. None of them admitted any contact with auxiliaries, Nasmyth 05 included."

"Surprise, surprise. How did they react when you asked them about Allie Kennedy?"

"None of them knew him."

"That wasn't what I asked, Davie."

He looked at me with a puzzled expression. "What do you mean 'how did they react'?"

Hamilton's Jeep drew up. He got out and came over to us.

"Any sign of fear or trepidation?"

Davie scratched his beard. "Maybe, now you mention it. I wasn't really looking for that. They denied all knowledge of him pretty quickly, right enough."

I nodded. "You'll have to go back to them."

"What?"

I told him what I'd learned from the bagsnatchers.

"That's ridiculous, Dalrymple," the public order guardian interjected. "We'd have picked up rumours about this Allie Kennedy if he was that much of an operator."

"Would you? Maybe he's very good at covering his traces." Another thought struck me. "And maybe he hasn't been a big operator." I waved Davie away. "Until now." I turned and headed for the chamber.

Sophia brought the meeting to order without giving me more than a cursory glance. Yet again the citizen members were conspicuous by their absence.

"I was informed earlier that no further ultimatum has been received. I trust that is still the case?" she said, looking at us for confirmation.

Hamilton nodded.

"That is excellent news," the culture guardian said, a broad smile blooming on his face. "The Edlott tourist promotion will be able to commence as planned."

Sophia gave him an unfriendly glare. "It is less than twenty-four hours since the poisoners' initial communication was received, guardian. We are not in the clear yet." She looked down at her notes. "Besides, the city does not revolve around your directorate's promotions."

Hamilton nodded his head vigorously. The old hypocrite. For all his confidence that the threat was over, he'd have happily gone along with anything that messed up Edlott. Maybe that was Sophia's game too. I remembered my suspicions about her. Was I really serious about her having some involvement in the poisonings and the murders at the mill house?

"Post-mortems have been completed on the three men Citizen Dalrymple found in Colinton," Sophia said. "I am still waiting for various test results, but there is little doubt that they were killed in the same attack that left the woman with the matching tattoo in a coma. They have similar wounds from heavy, blunt instruments and from sharp, single-edged, non-serrated knife blades."

I nudged Hamilton. Sophia had just given a perfect description of the standard-issue auxiliary knife. The public order guardian stuck his chin forward resolutely but declined to look in my direction.

"Unfortunately," Sophia continued, "the female victim has not regained consciousness so interrogation is still impossible." She looked at me severely. "Citizen Dalrymple has some unsubstantiated ideas about the perpetrators of the attack. I suggest that we postpone discussion of those ideas until he succeeds in finding evidence to support them."

She probably thought that put me in my place.

"Surely only the four people with the tattoo were involved in the poisonings," the culture guardian said, standing up to Sophia with unexpected nerve. "Whoever sent that message was just a postman."

"Or woman," said the information guardian, promoting her gender and giving the senior guardian the perfect opportunity to nail me.

"Quite so. The Kirkwood woman is still at large," Sophia said, turning her icy gaze on me. "Citizen Dalrymple, have you made any progress at all in the investigation?"

Mention of Katharine made me wonder how she'd been spending her time this morning. I shook my head to dispel that thought and filled the guardians in about Allie Kennedy's reputation. None of them looked very impressed.

"Are you sure this is relevant to the poisonings, citizen?" the culture guardian asked.

I shrugged. "Have you got any better ideas?" That shut him up. The problem was that I ran out of things to say myself soon afterwards.

"Is that all, Citizen Dalrymple?" Sophia asked with a sceptical look. "Very well. I propose that we maintain the current high level of security on the city's alcohol and water supplies for another day. Public order guardian?"

Hamilton nodded. "My people can sustain that but I wouldn't want them to work continuous shifts for too much longer."

I had to pinch myself. Lewis Hamilton caring about his staff's welfare? What was going on?

"We'll review the situation at tomorrow's meeting," Sophia said. She glanced at me. "Thank you, citizen. I'm sure you must have some other leads to follow up." The implication being that the ones I'd been working on so far were worth as much as a citizen-issue wristwatch.

"Where to now, citizen?" the guard driver asked morosely. He'd written me off when I refused to let him loose on the bagsnatchers. Now I returned the compliment.

"Get out, guardsman," I said. "I'll drive myself."

He shot me a disgusted look then slid out of his seat. "Going anywhere near the castle?"

I was heading up the Royal Mile so I could have taken him most of the way, but he'd caught me at a bad moment. "Exercise is an essential part of the auxiliary's daily life," I said, quoting from Barracks Regulations as I slipped into first and pulled away.

That was my response to Sophia's high-handed treatment of how I was running the case. Pathetic, really.

I turned left and went slowly down George IVth Bridge, peering into the window of Ray's office at the central archive. He was bent over his desk with his head resting on his hand. I decided to catch up with him later. I wanted to know why the bugger had been avoiding me and to see if he could give me any dirt on his barracks colleague Nasmyth 05. But before that I had more pressing things to do.

The sentry on duty at the checkpoint by Napier Barracks knew me but she went through the motions of checking my ID and authorisation before she raised the barrier. The extra security measures seemed to be working, though the young guardswoman was handling the checkpoint on her own and she was sweat-stained and tired-looking. Most of her fellow auxiliaries would be guarding the alcohol stores, central reservoirs and water-tank depots. The question was, how long could they keep it up? A day or two more of this and the city would be watched over by thousands of exhausted zombies, giving miscreants a hell of a free run. Had Allie Kennedy or whoever else was behind the killings worked that out in advance?

I pulled into Millar Crescent and parked outside the Kennedy flat. Twenty yards further on a Roads Department squad had dug a deep and completely unnecessary hole in the street surface. This was the Public Order Directorate's idea of a subtle surveillance operation. I was bloody sure that Allie Kennedy would spot it as quickly as I had. I moved towards the door but saw Agnes coming from the water tank, weighed down by a couple of jerry cans. I went over and took one of them from her. She didn't resist.

"Citizen Dalrymple," she said, squinting into the sun. "What a surprise. More questions?"

"Just a couple of things." I put my shoulder to the street door and let her go past me. She was in her workclothes, the scarf round her neck drenched in sweat. Her hair was speckled and redolent of paint. I followed her up the stuffy stairwell, aware of the swing of her hips as she climbed quickly.

"Come in then," she said when we reached the third floor, her breath catching in her throat. "I'll just check on my mother."

She disappeared down the corridor into the far bedroom. I took the chance to have a look in her brother's room. It was exactly as it had been when I was last there, the loops of the fire rope above the window coiled as I remembered them.

"Citizen?" Agnes called. "You'll be more comfortable in here." She gave me a tight smile as I headed towards the sitting room. It was in its customary gloom, the curtains pulled almost to. At least the windows behind were fully open, although what passes for a breeze in Edinburgh during the Big Heat wasn't doing much to cool things down.

"Did you get off work early?" I asked.

She handed me a glass of water and nodded. "We're nearly finished in the tourist hostel. My mother's in a bit of a state and the supervisor let me come home."

"Do you need a nursing auxiliary?"

Agnes's eyes sprang open. Normally you have to be close to death before the Medical Directorate approves home care. "No, it's all right. She's quiet now. She just needs me to calm her down sometimes." She sat down on the sofa her father had made and beckoned to me to join her. "What is it you want to know, citizen?"

"Quint," I said. "Call me Quint."

"Okay." She looked at me steadily. "What do you want to know, Quint?"

"It's about Allie."

Her eyes stayed on me. "What about him? I haven't seen him."

I nodded. "That was one question. He hasn't been back?" I

wasn't being straight with her. I knew from the surveillance reports that he hadn't been spotted either by the operatives in the hole out front or by the ones who'd moved into a flat in the building at the rear.

She was shaking her head. "Not since he was here with the auxiliary."

"And you haven't heard from him in any way?"

"No." Her voice was suddenly shriller. "Why do you want him? He hasn't done anything."

I turned to her. Her head was still bent and she was knotting her fingers nervously. "Are you sure, Agnes?"

She glanced at me angrily, her eyes damp. "What do you mean?" she asked in a low voice.

"Your brother's got a bit of a reputation, hasn't he?" I said, studying her reactions closely.

She blinked then quickly wiped her hand over her eyes. "Reputation for what?"

"I was hoping you could help me with that."

Agnes got up quickly and went towards the door, then stopped and turned back to me. A great tremor shook her frame and she let out a sob. I went over and tried to put an arm round her but she shook me off and moved away again, this time to the window. She stood in the shade of the curtains and pulled a handkerchief from the pocket of her work trousers.

"I need your help, Agnes," I said, keeping my distance. "It's very important that I find your brother. Can you help?"

Her body quivered again. "No . . . no, I don't want—" She broke off as another sob racked her. "I can't. He'll . . . he'll hurt me."

Now I realised why she was so distraught. It wasn't because she was worried about her brother and was trying to protect him. It was because she was terrified of him.

"Has he hurt you before, Agnes?"

She looked at me with her eyes wide open then nodded slowly. "He's . . . he's always hurt me. Ever since we were kids. He . . . he likes hurting people."

I went over to her and led her back to the sofa. She let me take her by the elbow. Her limbs were slack now and she sat listlessly, the handkerchief twisted in her hands. I glanced over at the photos on the dresser. Allie looked more than sullen to me now. He looked positively malevolent.

"I've heard that he's involved in the black market and other illicit activities."

She kept still, only her fingers moving.

"Agnes?"

"I don't know what he does. He never tells me anything." She looked at me weakly. "Except to keep my mouth shut."

"You should have told me about him."

She shrugged. "Told you what?"

"Who he has dealings with, where he goes, that kind of thing."

"But I don't know any of that," she said, her voice rising. "I don't know anything about what he does." Her head dropped again. "Dad did though. He had a big row with Allie not long before he went missing." The words came out in a staccato fashion, as if their significance had only just struck her. "Oh my God." She looked at me desperately. "Oh my God."

I lifted my hand to calm her but, before I could, the door banged open.

"Allie? Is that you, Allie?" Hilda Kennedy stumbled forward, a heavy nightdress hanging loosely over her thin body.

"It's me, Mother. It's Agnes." She got off the sofa and caught her mother before she fell. "It's all right. I'm here." She put her face against the older woman's and lifted her upright. "Allie'll be back later, okay?"

Hilda's eyes were puffy. She looked at me blankly as if she didn't see me, never mind know who I was. Then she seemed to faint, her eyes rolling upwards and her body going limp.

"Here," I said, "I'll help you."

"No," Agnes said sharply. "No, Quint. I can manage." Her voice lost its edge. "She's used to me." She half pulled, half carried her mother out of the sitting room.

"You'll have to go," she said when I followed them out. "She needs me to be with her now."

I nodded. "You're sure there's nothing you can tell me about Allie's whereabouts?"

She shook her head slowly, her mouth caught up in her mother's long, tangled grey hair.

"All right. You will call me if you see him anywhere?"

"Yes," she whispered. "Now go. Please."

I went, trying to reassure myself that Agnes was safe enough with the surveillance squads around the flat. And went down to the Land-Rover to seek out another member of the female sex.

Davie came on my mobile about the drugs traffickers as I was driving up Morningside Road.

"You were right, Quint. These guys are seriously reluctant to talk about Alexander Kennedy. I threatened one of them with the fourth degree and he told me Allie took over his dealing patch. Listen to this. When a heavy went to lay into him, Allie threw acid in the guy's face."

"Acid? Jesus. Another version of the water of life."

"What? Oh, I see. The heavy's blind now."

"When was this?"

"A couple of months back. The traffickers reckon Allie put the guard on to them as well."

"Very interesting. Okay, see if they've got anything else on Allie. Like premises he uses, bars where he hangs out. I'll meet you at the castle later."

"What are you doing?"

He was better off not knowing that. "You're breaking up, Davie," I said. "Out."

"Over here, Quint."

I looked to my left and saw Katharine's fair hair appear at the side of a moss-covered gravestone. There was no shade in the

Grange Cemetery and I'd been wandering around getting roasted for ten minutes.

"At last," I said. "Didn't you see me arrive?"

"I had to be sure you weren't a guardsman," she said, keeping close to the ground.

I got down beside her in the knee-high grass. "Do I look like a guardsman?" I demanded, opening my waterbottle and handing it to her.

She drank thirstily. "No," she said, wiping her mouth. "You look more like a mobile scarecrow."

"Thanks a lot. You seem to have done a pretty good job of keeping the carrion birds away yourself."

"There are only old bodies here, Quint," she said. "So what's happening?"

I told her there had been no further ultimatum.

"That's good. That means I'm in the clear."

I looked at her. "How do you work that out?"

"If I was a poisoner, surely I'd have struck again by now." She smiled at me innocently.

"It's not quite as simple as that. The senior guardian—"

"Your girlfriend, you mean."

"My ex-girlfriend, Katharine. She seems to have lost all interest in my body."

She laughed. "How sad."

"The senior guardian still regards you as a prime suspect. You'd better keep out of the way till things develop further. Here, I got you this." I handed her a bag full of waterbottles and food I'd got at Napier Barracks on the way.

"Thank you, kind sir." Her voice was ironic.

"Katharine," I said, catching her eye. "What exactly have you been doing all day?"

She pulled a book out of her pocket. "As it happens, I've got a good read." She held up my copy of the collected Sherlock Holmes. "I borrowed this from your flat the last time I was there. You don't mind, do you?"

"As long as I get it back. You mean you haven't left the cemetery?"

She shook her head. "Where would I go? Half the bloody city's looking for me." I believed her, but I had a track record of believing what Katharine told me.

"Are you all right?" I laid my hand on her forearm. "I mean, it was a hell of a shock you got at the mill."

She looked at me then nodded slowly. The skin round her eyes creased only very slightly. "I'm used to shocks, Quint. What else is there to life?"

I couldn't think of a reply to that. She'd been through much more than I had in the past. It had hardened her but not to the extent other people thought.

Katharine touched my hand with hers briefly. "I wasn't that close to Peter," she said, pursing her lips. "Not that it's any business of yours."

I stayed a bit longer. We didn't talk much, just sat in the heat and listened to the faint noise of the city's limited number of vehicles in the distance. It was good to be with her.

"Keep in touch," I said as I got up to go.

"I might do," she said, looking up and smiling enigmatically. "And then again I might not."

I hate it when women play hard to get.

I passed the early evening in the command centre with Davie. For all his interrogation skills, he hadn't managed to get much else out of the drugs prisoners. They were shit-scared of Allie Kennedy but they didn't know anything about who he worked with or where he operated from. I tried to make sense of where that led us. We'd established a sexual connection between Allie and the Edlott controller. Allie apparently had his finger in the grass trade. Did that mean the fat auxiliary was into illicit drugs too? Somewhere in the distance I thought I could hear Victoria Spivey singing the "Dope Head Blues".

"What about the surveillance on Nasmyth 05?" I asked as we headed to Hamilton's quarters to report.

"Bugger all," Davie replied. "He's suddenly turned into a model auxiliary. All day and all evening at the Culture Directorate. No unusual contacts."

"Great. This is turning into a regular bloody ghost hunt."

"The public order guardian won't mind. He reckons the threat's passed."

There was a clatter of boots at the far end of the corridor. Lewis Hamilton appeared, his face red and contorted above the white of his beard.

"Are you sure about that, Davie?" I asked.

The guardian reached us and tried without success to catch his breath. "Death," he gasped eventually. "Suspicious death. In Buccleuch Place."

"Another one?" I groaned.

Then I felt my stomach turn over. There was a Nasmyth Barracks annexe in Buccleuch Place, and one of its residents was the man I'd seen in the afternoon with his head resting on his single hand – my friend Ray.

Chapter Sixteen

The twilight was well advanced as we ran out on to the esplanade, the western sky glowing soft and red. From the gardens below came the discordant sounds of competing bands interspersed with the screams of winners and losers in the tourist gaming tents.

"Why aren't they giving us an ID?" I demanded as we piled into Hamilton's Jeep.

Davie had his mobile to his ear and was straining to hear what was being said. He shook his head. "It's chaos over there. Everyone seems to have lost it completely."

"Oh for Christ's sake." I crashed into the guardian's side as he wrenched the wheel hard to the right and accelerated away.

"Auxiliaries have feelings too, Dalrymple," Hamilton said brusquely. "Or have you forgotten?"

I sat in silence, my heart pounding and my breathing quick. As we drove past the central archive I thought again of Ray. The lights in his office were on, thank Christ. There was a chance that he was working late. Then I remembered the dust in the corner behind his desk. What the hell was that from? Could it have something to do with the strange way Ray had been behaving? Why had he been avoiding me?

We reached what used to be the university area. I tried to distract myself by looking out at the buildings. The student union was turned into a tourist facility years ago and the great D-shaped hall where degrees were conferred is now a debating chamber devoted to Platonic philosophy. The Enlightenment's view of education never involved lectures and seminars – too much danger of freethinking there. The city's children have the basics drilled into them at school and those of them who are compliant enough undergo the auxiliary training programme. I was one of the last to go to the university and I only managed one year before the ultimate election and Edinburgh's declaration of independence.

The guardian slowed down behind a Water Department tractor, no doubt worried about scratching his pride and joy.

"Come on, Lewis, get past him," I said desperately.

The guardian hit the siren and swerved past the slow-moving vehicle, managing to acknowledge the salute from the guardsman who was riding shotgun on the water tank. "Calm down, man," he said. "We're almost there."

We turned into Buccleuch Place and drove down the cobbles to number 14. In the old days the street had been filled with university departments. I could remember coming to some interesting sessions on the social anthropology of the criminal here. Now it was in a state of advanced disrepair, a lot of the four-storey buildings boarded up. Nasmyth Barracks extension took up three houses halfway down. They had a delightful north-facing view over the blown-out remains of the David Hume Tower and other architectural monstrosities of the 1960s which had been devastated during the drugs wars. There were no funds for rebuilding – the Council's priorities lie elsewhere.

Outside number 14 a collection of guard vehicles was arrayed unevenly along the kerb. A crowd of unusually grey-faced auxiliaries had gathered outside the pilastered doorway.

"What is this?" I demanded. "Street theatre? Get rid of them, Davie. Apart from any witnesses."

He nodded and jumped down. Lewis and I followed him. It was remarkable how quickly the auxiliaries got a grip on themselves when they saw the guardian. The noise of agitated voices faded and a gap immediately opened up in the mass of bodies. Council members have some uses after all.

"Where's the deceased?" I asked a middle-aged guardsman who seemed to be in the know.

"Out the back. He took a dive from an upper-storey window."

My gut twisted. So it was a male. That wasn't all. I'd been in Ray's room a couple of times. It was on the third floor. I went down the corridor, past barracks notices and what the Interior Decoration Department imagines is inspiring artwork. The heavy door into the rear garden was open, not that you could call what was out back a garden during the Big Heat. It looked more like a patch of uneven brown concrete. A pair of auxiliaries stepped aside and I was confronted with the body.

At first it was impossible even to make out that it was a man, let alone one that I could recognise. The head was severely damaged, a wide pool of blood around it. The victim had apparently hit the ground face first, the rest of the body crumpling into the hard surface with enough force to break the spine and leave the lower part of the trunk pointing upwards in a parody of a Moslem at prayer. The legs were bent at the knees and partially splayed. I had difficulty finding the arms. The corpse was wearing a long-sleeved white shirt that was now soaked in blood. The upper limbs had been crushed beneath the chest.

I kneeled down by the body and looked up at Davie and Lewis. "Here goes," I said, biting my lip. I slid my hand slowly under the right side and felt for the arm. It didn't take long to ascertain that it was only a stump.

"Shit," I said, pulling away. "Fucking shit. It's Ray all right."

We followed standard suspicious-death procedures – cordoning off the garden, Ray's room and the stairwell; taking statements from witnesses; photographing the body and getting a preliminary report from the scene-of-crime team. Sophia arrived not long after we did and oversaw the medical side.

"Is there any doubt about the cause of death?" Hamilton asked as she was preparing to leave for the infirmary with the body. "It looks pretty obvious to me."

"I would remind you that four citizens have died of nicotine poisoning, guardian," Sophia said, giving him an icy glance. "Besides, nothing is ever obvious with suspicious deaths. That's why they're called suspicious."

She was right there, even though Lewis had a point in this particular case. At this stage, what bothered me more than the cause of death was whether my friend jumped or was pushed.

"I'll perform the p-m immediately," Sophia said, turning her eyes to me. "Are you going to attend, citizen?"

So I was still "citizen", was I? "Lewis can send one of his people to observe, guardian," I said, giving her a humourless smile. "I trust you."

Hamilton took a deep breath but Sophia just pretended I'd become invisible – which was probably the case as regards my status in her affections.

"What are you playing at, Dalrymple?" Hamilton hissed after she'd gone, his eyes bulging. "You can't talk to the senior guardian like that."

"Can't I?" I brushed past him and headed up the worn wooden staircase.

We spent the next hour examining Ray's room. He was unusual among auxiliaries in having private quarters. No formal reason was ever given, but I remembered Ray telling me that he thought the barracks commander didn't want his mutilated arm on display in a dormitory. Bad for morale or some such bollocks. That was probably why he'd been packed off to the barracks extension. Still, Ray hadn't complained. He got a pleasant room with a bay window that looked out over the Meadows. There were bookshelves all round the walls – it had probably been a departmental library back when the building was part of the university – and Ray had filled them with the volumes he'd collected over the years. Books, as long as they're not on the banned list, are one of the few things that the Council allows people to accumulate. The founders of the Enlightenment were rabidly opposed to personal property, seeing it as one of the main factors in the self-obsession that led to the break-up of the old United Kingdom. With Edlott, the current Council has actively encouraged citizens to be acquisitive. There's progress for you.

I spent some time crawling round the bare floorboards with magnifying glass and evidence bags but found very little to go on. The room was extremely tidy, as in all auxiliary barracks, bed covers folded perfectly and papers aligned carefully on the desk.

However, there were two things that made me stop and think. The first was under the bed, near the wall in the far left corner. It was an area of floorboards covered with a pale, gritty dust. I was pretty sure it was the same dust I'd seen in the corner of Ray's office. It looked like he'd moved something from his room to his place of work or vice versa. Maybe it was just a heap of files or books but I was still dubious. That dust wasn't like any I'd ever seen in the archives or in any bookstore. So where did it come from?

The other thing that caught my eye was also on the floor, near the open window that Ray had gone through. His books were arranged in alphabetical order, as you'd expect with an archivist. In that corner were those written by authors whose surnames began with the letters "L" to "O". And here was the striking point. There was a heap of what I counted to be fifteen volumes on the floor. They'd been pulled from the shelves in what looked very like a rushed and careless fashion, but that wasn't the strangest thing. They were all copies of poetry by, and studies of, one "Owen, Wilfred E. S." – as the shelf label written in Ray's delicate hand proclaimed. I squatted on the boards by the pile of books and tried to work out if there was any significance to that. Without success.

Eventually Hamilton called Davie and me into an adjoining room. The building was quiet now, the various investigating teams beginning to stand down.

"What have we got then?" I asked.

Davie looked at his boss, unwilling to speak first even though the public order guardian had been wandering around ineffectually for some time.

"Well, get on with it, Hume 253," Hamilton said impatiently.

"Yes, guardian." Davie flipped the pages of his notebook. "What I've got isn't much. There was hardly anyone else around earlier in the evening. Most of them were out on watch." He shrugged. "The continuous shifts."

I nodded. "Which Ray's seniority would have excused him from. He wasn't on his own in the building, was he?"

"Just about. The only others were a female auxiliary who was washing her clothes in the basement and a guardsman who came in to change his uniform a few minutes after eight. He went back on patrol almost immediately."

"And neither of them saw or heard anything out of the ordinary," I said, realising from his expression that we were out of luck.

He nodded. " 'Fraid not."

"Who found the body?"

"A trainee auxiliary on barracks immersion. She came back from duty at . . ." he checked his notes ". . . at eight fifty and happened to glance out of her dorm window. She isn't taking it too well."

"She'll have to get used to that kind of thing," Hamilton said.

"Thank you for that compassionate observation, Lewis," I said. "She didn't see him fall?"

Davie shook his head. "I noticed the dead man's watch was smashed. It shows eight forty-three."

"Very good, guardsman. Have you been reading Agatha Christie?" Both of them scowled at me. "Sorry. So we're tending towards suicide, are we?"

"Certainly seems that way to me, Dalrymple," the guardian said. He gave me a suspicious look as if he already knew I was going to disagree.

"And to me," Davie said, earning himself an approving nod from his chief. "The scene-of-crime people didn't find any prints apart from Ray's and those of other barracks residents who weren't around this evening."

I went over to the window and thought about Ray's room next door, visualising the Owen books scattered on the floor. Something about that corner was nagging me and it wasn't just the uncharacteristic lack of order. I let the line of thought go reluctantly and turned back to the others. "You're ignoring something," I said.

A wry look appeared on the guardian's bearded face. "Of course we are, Dalrymple. We're just a pair of clodhopping auxiliaries."

"Your words, not mine." I flashed him a smile. "What you're ignoring is the question why."

"Why the auxiliary would commit suicide, you mean?" Davie asked.

"Exactly."

"I would have thought that's clear enough, Dalrymple," Hamilton said. "He was burdened by the loss of his arm."

"Lewis," I demanded, "have you forgotten that suicide's illegal in this city? In particular for serving auxiliaries. You'd need to have a bloody good reason to allow your name and number to be expunged from the records and sanctions to be taken against your next of kin." The Council has always taken an adamantine stand against self-murderers, regarding them as arch-betrayers of the Enlightenment. I shook my head at them. "And that's not all. I know . . . knew Ray. I knew him well. He wasn't suicidal."

Hamilton hadn't given up. "Are you sure, Dalrymple? He could have been hiding it, especially from his friends."

I thought about how weirdly Ray had been behaving in the last couple of days — slumped at his desk with his head in his hand, keeping away from me. Then the look of abject horror I'd seen on his face came up before me again. Something had definitely been hurting him badly. But could that have made him throw himself out of the window? Christ, I'd offered to help. He turned me down, but I could have pressed him harder.

"Ray was a fighter!" I shouted, guilt eating into me. "You shouldn't be accusing him, Lewis. You should be proud that someone who sustained a major injury in the guard still managed to be a productive auxiliary."

The guardian took a step back. "All right, Dalrymple. Calm down."

I eventually got a grip, feeling Davie's eyes on me. I lost so many friends in the early years of the Enlightenment, I lost the woman I loved ten years ago. I suppose I should have got used to it by now, but it gets worse. You'd think as you grow older that absences would be easier to handle. They aren't. I still find myself fighting for the people who've disappeared, the people who can't fight for themselves any more – like Ray.

"Come on," I said to Davie. "We're done here."

"What next, Quint?" he asked, watching the guardian's back as it disappeared out of the door ahead of us.

"You tell me. I need a drink. If we can find one that won't poison us in this bastard city."

He opened his mouth to speak but my mobile went off first.

"Medical . . . senior guardian here."

"Get it right, Sophia."

"You'd better come over to the morgue." Her voice was sharp. "Immediately."

"What have you found?"

"Not on an open line. Out."

I was pretty sure my opposition to the suicide theory was about to be vindicated. That didn't make me feel any better.

Ray had been straightened out on the mortuary table, rigor mortis not having reached even the preliminary stages. Naked, he was a sad sight. His shattered, blood-drenched head was propped up by the wooden neck support and the stump of his arm was half raised like the barrier at a guard checkpoint. I heard Davie and Hamilton take deep breaths when they saw him. The large V-shaped incision had been made at the sides of the neck to enable removal of the larynx. Below, a single cut ran down to the pubis and the major organs had been taken out of the abdominal cavity. Two medical auxiliaries were bent over the body.

Sophia looked up from a bank of instruments against the far wall. Her face above the green surgical gown was very white.

"Let's have it then," I said.

"Leave us," she ordered her staff, turning her head towards Davie to exclude him too.

"My assistant stays," I said.

"Very well." Sophia sighed. "Much joy may it bring him."

I went over to her and grabbed her arms. "What have you found? I need to know."

She pulled her arms away. "Don't worry, Quint. I won't be keeping what the senior toxicologist advised to myself."

"What?" Hamilton stepped forward, his eyes wide. "How did the auxiliary die?"

"It was nicotine poisoning, guardian," Sophia said, dropping her gaze to the worn mortuary floor. "There are traces of whisky in the oesophagus. The Ultimate Usquebaugh again." She looked up at me quickly. "If it's any comfort, your friend was dead before he hit the ground."

I forced my eyes back to the body that had been split open on the slab. The poor bastard. Ray had been through enough; he didn't deserve any of this. Rage coursed through me. "No, senior guardian," I said viciously, "it isn't any comfort to know that he spent the last seconds of his life in agony with his mouth and throat burning up. It isn't any fucking comfort at all."

Sophia looked at me as if I'd just spat in her face. I felt Davie's bulk at my side.

"Cool it, Quint," he said in a low voice. "It's not the senior guardian's fault."

"Cool it?" I let out a strangled laugh. "How can anyone cool it in this place during the Big Heat?" I went over to a sink and splashed tepid water over my head. Eventually I managed to get my breathing under control.

Sophia had gone back to her slides and test tubes.

"Sorry," I said quietly. "Like you said, Ray was my friend." I glanced back at his remains, this time more dispassionately. If I was going to catch the bastard who killed him, I had to do as Davie said.

Sophia nodded curtly and picked up a clipboard. "The dose has been estimated at slightly over one and a half grains. Higher than the earlier cases."

"How did you get on to it?" I asked.

"I'd have checked for nicotine anyway but I realised very quickly that there was vomit in his mouth and throat. That's not exactly standard with people who fall to their deaths."

"I don't understand this, Dalrymple." Hamilton was shaking his head. "I don't understand it at all. There was no sign of any whisky bottle. That's not like the first two victims." He stared at me woodenly. "And there's been no further communication from the lunatics behind this."

"Not yet there hasn't," I said. "That could change at any time."

"There was no bottle left at the retirement home either," Davie said.

I nodded. "True enough. But you're right, Lewis. This latest killing is different. Whoever carried it out took a hell of a risk going into a barracks building and . . ." I broke off. Could there have been some pressing reason for Ray to be murdered? One that overrode the dangers of the killer being seen? I tried to imagine what that reason might be.

"And?" Sophia asked, impatient for me to complete my sentence.

Davie came to my rescue. "At least there's no question of it being suicide now."

"No," I said, still picturing Ray's room in my mind. "Not only was there no bottle but there were no drinking vessels. Someone brought the poisoned whisky into the room and took it away again after Ray drank some." I turned to Sophia. "Any bruises or scratches, that kind of thing, on the body?"

She shook her head. "Nothing that isn't consistent with the impact."

I scratched the stubble on my chin. "So it could be that Ray took the whisky willingly. And that he jumped rather than was pushed."

"Why would he have done either of those things?" Hamilton demanded.

I shrugged. "Maybe he thought the whisky was all right. And as for jumping, the window was probably already open. And he was in agony, his throat on fire. He was in desperate need of air." Then I remembered the pile of books by the window. What had Ray done in the last seconds of his life? When he realised he'd been poisoned, could he have tried to leave some kind of message?

"Maybe he wanted to land the killer in the shit . . ." Davie paused. "Excuse me, guardians. Maybe he wanted to attract attention."

Hamilton nodded. "Except nobody else noticed."

"No, but he probably panicked the killer," I said. "Whence, no whisky bottle left behind. He just headed for the exit at terminal velocity."

"He?" Sophia said, her eyes narrowing. "What makes you think the killer was a male? Your friend Katharine Kirkwood is still on the run. Maybe the bottles of whisky we found in her backpack weren't the only ones she had."

Davie and Hamilton looked at me expectantly, as if the senior guardian had spoken words of indisputable wisdom. Christ, maybe she had. Katharine's activities over the last couple of days

were as unfathomable to me as a Finance Directorate policy
paper. I didn't know whether I was coming or going with her. So
I went, passing Ray's remains and shaking my head. His killer
was going to pay a heavy price, no matter who he or she was.

"Where are you going?" Davie asked as he caught me up at the
infirmary exit.

"To check something out." I stuck my hand out. "Keys."

"I'll come with you."

"That isn't a good idea." I stopped by his Land-Rover, hand
still extended.

"At least tell me where you're going, Quint," he said
desperately, giving me the keys.

"To the houses of the dead," I said.

That gave him something to chew on.

"Katharine?" I spoke her name in a loud whisper for about the
twentieth time then walked into a gravestone the thin beam of
my torch had missed. "Fuck."

"Over here. And stop sweet-talking me."

I swung the beam round and caught a glimpse of her face a
couple of rows further on. "You've moved campsite," I said
accusingly.

"Got to keep you guessing, haven't I?"

I went over and sat down on the base of an unusually large and
imposing stone cross. It probably marked the grave of a Member
of the Scottish Parliament from the time before the country
began to break up – after 2002, most politicians ended up on
funeral pyres built by the outraged voters they'd ripped off.

"What are you doing here in the middle of the night?"
Katharine asked. "Did you bring any water?"

"Sorry." I extinguished the torch. The last thing I wanted now
was a guard patrol to pick us up. "I had other things on my mind."

"Like what?" She leaned towards me and I felt her breath on
my cheek.

I leaned back. "Like where were you earlier tonight?"

"What do you mean?" Her voice was immediately less warm.

"It's a simple question, Katharine. Where were you during the evening? In fact, where have you been and what have you been doing since you came back to the city? I need straight answers right now."

She was still close, her breath making my face tingle. "I haven't been anywhere tonight," she said quietly. "I've been here since you left."

I switched the torch back on and grabbed her jacket. There was nothing akin to a bottle or container that could have held whisky. The waterbottles I'd brought her were in a bag, empty. I took the tops off all of them and sniffed. No odour of spirits.

"What's going on?" she asked.

"I need to search you, Katharine. Hold still." I ran my hands down her upper body, feeling nothing in her shirt pocket. There was an interesting convexity underneath it.

"Are you having fun?" Katharine asked.

"Just a minute." I ran my hands over her trousers, finding nothing incriminating.

"Don't forget this," she said, reaching her arm round her back in a sudden movement.

The point of her knife was against my belly. I felt my armpits get sodden in a second.

"Oh, sorry. I'm holding it the wrong way. How careless of me." She flipped her hand over and pressed the haft of the knife against my stomach. "Take it if you want."

I shook my head. She nudged me then laughed and put the weapon back in its sheath in the small of her back.

"I haven't been anywhere today, Quint," she said, leaning her head against my shoulder. "Yesterday, apart from when I was out at the mill house, I lay low wherever I could. Waiting for you to get the guard off my back."

I breathed in deeply then decided to follow my instincts. I still reckoned Sophia was wrong about Katharine being involved in the poisonings. What possible reason could she have for killing

Ray? And she was in the clear as regards possession of the poisoned whisky – unless she'd stashed it somewhere else. But why should she? She wasn't expecting me to arrive in the middle of the night.

"All right," I said. "I'm sorry. Things have got nasty." I told her about Ray.

"God, how terrible," she said, squeezing my hand. She'd taken hold of it while I was speaking. "The poor man. Why should he have been murdered?"

I shrugged. "I wish I knew. But I'll find out, you can be sure of that."

She came closer and I felt her head on my chest.

"You didn't really think I had anything to do with it, did you, Quint?"

I shook my head slowly. "No, I—"

She put her finger against my lips, then replaced it with her mouth. It was a long kiss, the first good kiss I'd had for a long time. I suddenly realised that I'd never let Sophia get to me in the ways Katharine did.

"Quint?" she said when she finally removed her lips from mine. "Can I ask you something?"

The tone of her voice, questioning but tender, made my spine tingle.

"Go on," I said breathlessly.

"Do you think . . ." She stopped then turned away and laughed quietly. "No, I'm making a fool of myself."

I moved her face back towards me. "You're not."

"I am." She leaned her forehead against mine. "All right. If I stayed in the city, do you think we could make it together?"

The blood rushed to my cheeks. Fortunately she couldn't see them in the dark. "Make it together?" I repeated lamely. "You mean live together?" The words sounded distant, like someone else had spoken them. I was seriously shaken up. Katharine and I had spent only short periods of time together and I'd convinced myself that she didn't really care that much about me. There was a burning in my body that had nothing to do with the Big Heat.

"Is that such a horrible idea?" she asked.

"Em, no," I said. "No. But there are a lot of auxiliaries looking for you."

"We don't have to talk about it any more now, Quint. There'll be time for talk later." She kissed me again, then manoeuvred me to my feet and led me to a large flat stone. "I noticed this earlier and wondered if I'd manage to get you on to it."

I was pushed back gently but firmly on to some unknown rich man's memorial. Katharine pulled my trousers down. The dried moss on the stone stuck to my backside and for a split second I considered giving her a blast of Blind Lemon Jefferson's "See That My Grave Is Kept Clean". Katharine took her own clothes off rapidly then straddled me, reminding me of the first time we'd made love. That had been in the armchair in my flat, but al fresco was even more exciting. I ran my hand up the well-toned flesh and rubbed her nipples with my thumbs. They were hard and long, the flesh beneath them supple. She moaned as I crushed it softly.

"Do you think the old guy underneath minds?" she asked hoarsely.

"Christ no," I gasped. "Probably enjoying the view."

She lowered herself carefully on to my erect organ and then sat down in a controlled movement. I exhaled slowly as I was enveloped in her moistness. She started lifting herself up and down, leaning back and guiding my finger to her sensitive spot. I suddenly saw Sophia's face flash before me, her eyes cold and unwavering. I flinched.

"What's the matter?" Katharine asked, slowing her action.

I shook my head. "Nothing. Don't stop."

She leaned forward, her hair brushing my face. "I knew you before her, Quint." Then she pushed down on my midriff again. "You're mine."

I wasn't going to argue about that. I arched my back

upwards and reached a level the Climax Blues Band never even got close to.

I came to with a dull ache in my back and a warm body on top of me. It was dark in the cemetery but nothing like as dark as the satiated slumber I was blearily emerging from. Katharine was asleep, her breasts compressed against my chest and her face over my shoulder. She was breathing gently into my left ear. The dawn was breaking and the granite houses around the perimeter wall were beginning to take on their daytime grey-black hue. I wasn't too comfortable but I didn't want to wake Katharine. So I lay still and thought about things.

Things first of all being her. Did she really mean what she'd said about us making it together? Even if I managed to get Sophia and Hamilton off her back, I wasn't sure if I was up to sharing my space with someone else. Then again, ever since Katharine appeared at the door when Sophia had undone me, I'd been aware that I had strong feelings for her. But could I trust her? She was still a suspect as far as everyone else in the investigation was concerned. I wasn't sure she'd told me everything about Peter Bryson and what she saw at the mill house. I twitched my head to dispel the image of her friend's smashed face and torn body.

Then I started thinking about Ray. Ray on the ground in the barracks extension yard, Ray on the mortuary table; Ray's room with the open window, Ray's office — and the dust on the floor in those two places. What object or objects had left the dust, and where the hell did it come from? I thought about the books on the floor by the window in Buccleuch Place again. Ray must have pulled them off the shelves as he was fighting for air with his throat on fire. They were all Wilfred Owen books. Jesus. The recollection hit me like a sniper's bullet. He had a volume of Wilfred Owen poems in his office too. Wilfred Owen. What did it mean? What did the long-dead First World War poet have to do with . . . ?

I sat up with a start, grabbing Katharine's arms to stop her falling off.

"What is it?" she said, instantly awake and looking round for her knife.

I was shaking my head slowly. "Surely not," I muttered.

"Surely not what?" Katharine stood up and started locating her clothes.

"What?"

"Surely not what, Quint?" She gave me a push. "Has your brain gone into hibernation?

"In this temperature? Hardly," I said, snapping out of my reverie. "I've got to check something outside the city line. Do you want to come with me?" I pulled on my trousers and reached over for my shirt.

"What's going on?" she asked, staring at me doubtfully.

"I've just come up with a long shot that even I'm surprised by."

She stared at me. "Any chance of telling me what it is?"

"Let's go and see first. I don't want you to think I've lost all my marbles."

She picked up the last of her gear and gave me an ironic look. "What possible grounds could I have to think that?"

The guards at the gate were surprised by my appearance at six a.m. but they couldn't say no to my authorisation. Katharine was on the floor in the back of the Land-Rover with a tarpaulin over her. I didn't fancy Lewis Hamilton finding out that I was consorting with her. After we'd traversed the cleared ground beyond the city line, I saw her sit up in the mirror.

"Where are we going, Quint? We're pretty near the mill in Colinton, aren't we?"

I nodded. "That's the connection, I'm sure of it," I said under my breath.

"What?"

"Just hold on. We'll be there in a minute."

Katharine gave me an irritated look but kept quiet.

It didn't take long. The building I was heading for was only about half a mile from the city line. The Land-Rover ground up the hill, leaving a cloud of purple exhaust fumes in the still morning air. The houses on both sides of the road were in a terrible state, the windows and doors pulled out and the roofs denuded of slates. This area had been badly hit in the drugs wars and by looting from the south side before the line went up. Then, through the sickly trees, the great mass of stone with its tower and pavilions came into view.

"Is that where we're going?" Katharine asked, her voice betraying interest. "It used to be part of one of the universities, didn't it?"

"Before a drugs gang took over the labs and the guard went in with everything it had." The assault had happened before I had enough influence in the Public Order Directorate to change tactics and work on driving the scumbags out of Edinburgh without destroying all the city's buildings. "That's not all it used to be."

Katharine leaned over the seat and looked at me. "No? What else was it then?"

"During the First World War it was Craiglockhart War Hospital."

"Really." The interest faded from her voice.

"Yup. There were some famous people here. Siegfried Sassoon springs to mind." I glanced at her. "As does Wilfred Owen."

"I remember them," Katharine said, sitting back. "At school the boys loved all that pity of war stuff." She shook her head dismissively. "I preferred Sylvia Plath myself."

"Uh-huh." I pulled up by a tree trunk that was lying across the drive of the former hospital. "Let's go and take a look."

"Why?" she demanded, clambering out of the vehicle. "What do you expect to find here?"

"Who knows? It's a voyage of discovery." I went up to the tree trunk. The pot-holed asphalt beneath it had a layer of brownish dust that looked like it hadn't been there for long. I wondered if the guard checked the place out regularly. "Come on." I stepped over the trunk, feeling it move underneath me. It wasn't a particularly large tree.

"I'm right behind you," Katharine said.

I stepped away up the slope, my heart beginning to beat fast. I had the feeling I wasn't the first person to come here recently. It was only a few hundred yards from the spot where the comatose female was found – and a few hundred more from the mill house where her three companions, including Peter Bryson, were beaten to death. I was getting close to something but I still didn't have much idea of what it was.

"Nice place." Katharine was at my shoulder, pointing to the shattered windows and crumbling stonework. The pockmarks in the walls showed that the guard had still had plenty of heavy machine-gun ammunition to burn when they attacked.

The main entrance was completely blocked by a pile of collapsed masonry. Pigeons were cooing inside in a drowsy manner that suggested they weren't bothered by human company. Citizens have been known to cross the line armed with catapults to supplement their meat ration.

"Come on, we can't get in here. There must be another entrance."

She gave me a doubtful look then let me pass. I followed the building round to the left and met a wall of branches that didn't look natural. There were far too many of them and, as I kneeled down to look through them, I noticed a mass of unclear footprints in the dust covering the uneven flagstones.

"Hey, look at this," I said, starting to turn towards Katharine.

Then my head exploded and I plunged over a drop sheer enough to wrench my stomach out of my abdomen. I watched as it flapped sluggishly away from my clutching hands. There was a shrieking in my ears which gradually lowered in pitch, ending up as the mournful howl of a subterranean demon so desperate for soul food that even an atheist's like mine would do.

Hell's teeth, I thought. Then I was swallowed up in the abyss.

Chapter Seventeen

I seemed to be floating in the dark, my body chewed up by the ravenous being who'd been waiting for me to land in his vacant underground halls. Robert Johnson was down there with me, and "Me and the Devil Blues" was the song the old maestro had chosen. The universe, space and time, the big wide world had all been reduced to this inky blackness. It was a curiously restful state to be in — no past I could remember, no present to give me pain and definitely no future to look forward to. But then things went into reverse. The moaning noise started again, so low in tone at first that I could hardly pick it up, then inexorably rising till it turned into a long-drawn-out shriek that almost burst my eardrums. I opened my eyes warily but still couldn't see anything. I gradually became aware of a hard stone floor beneath me and of musty air cut with the bittersweet tang of rodent piss. I've never been good at waking up.

I brought a hand to my face and felt something sticky on the side of my head. Then I made the mistake of moving. A wave of pain coursed through my body and vomit surged up my throat. I managed to turn to one side so it didn't go all over my clothes. I lay perfectly still, trying to summon up the courage to move again, and pieced together what had happened. Christ, I hadn't been on my own.

"Katharine?" The pain flooded through me again, not quite as ruinously as before. "Katharine?"

There was no reply. No sound at all. Then came a distant noise I couldn't immediately place. It was regular and sibilant, softly insistent. Pigeons. There had been pigeons in the upper storeys of the old war hospital. I reckoned I was still somewhere in the depths of the building. But where was Katharine?

I had no idea how long it took me to drag myself into a sitting position – citizen-issue watches don't run to luminous hands. My head tolled like one of Hemingway's bells every time I moved. My throat was dry and painful and I could have used a gallon or two of water. Then I found something that made me whoop with joy till I realised that whooping wasn't good for my head – my torch was still in my shirt pocket. I couldn't lay hands on my mobile phone but you can't win them all.

I shone the torch round the room I was in. "Room" turned out not to be the correct term. It was more like a cavern, a hole in the ground, the entrance to a mine. There were piles of wooden props and heaps of earth by the walls. I had difficulty making sense of it because I could only see a few feet at a time in the restricted beam. It was like trying to do a jigsaw with only a box of matches for light. There was no sign of anyone else in the vicinity, no sign of Katharine. Then I flicked the beam further into the depths and got a couple of nasty surprises.

The first one paralysed me with fear. A snarling, bestial face leaped out at me from the surrounding gloom, eyes shining bright and murderous. I dropped the torch on to my legs and waited to be savaged. Nothing happened. I scrabbled for the light and gingerly shone it back in that direction. The face sprang forward again but I held the torch firm. Hell's teeth, all right. A statue of a dog with lips curled back and long pointed teeth was up against the far wall. It had been carved from some dark-coloured stone, only the eyes and dentalwork picked out in white and faded red. Good boy. Heel. Sit. Don't bloody move.

I crawled slowly over to the other surprise, a mound of objects covered in dusty plastic sheeting, the edges held down by lumps of stone. In the dim light I couldn't be sure but it looked like someone's private library that had been preserved for posterity. I made it over there without retching more than three times and rolled away the stones. Then I stuck my hand in and pulled out a heavy tome, carefully unwrapping the protective sheathing to reveal a soft leather binding. I opened the book, shining my light on the title page. And hit what for a book collector was the mother lode — a first edition of Samuel Johnson's *Dictionary of the English Language*, dated 1755, with the stamp of the British Library on its inside front cover. I let out an oath. Only one of the words appears in the great work.

Time passed — I didn't know how long — until there was a noise like thunder over to my right.

"Quint?" came a muffled shout. "Are you in there, Quint?"

"Davie? Is that you, Davie?" I headed for the door which I'd earlier tried and failed to open.

"Hold on."

I heard him giving orders, then there was a series of shattering blows to the heavy panels. Daylight streamed in through a cloud of dust. A few more applications of the sledgehammer and they were in. Very shortly afterwards I was out, breathing in what passes for fresh air during the Big Heat.

"Christ, it's good to see you, man," I said, holding on to Davie's arm. "Give me your waterbottle." I emptied it quickly and took the replacement offered by a muscular guardswoman.

"Better?" Davie asked when I'd finished the second pint. "What happened to you? You should get that wound seen to."

I shook my head and instantly regretted it. "No time," I gasped. A squad of guard personnel had gathered around us like a flock of curious sheep. I took Davie aside. "Look, keep this to yourself. I was with Katharine before I was belted."

His eyes shot wide open but he didn't say anything.

"There's no sign of her now. So whoever decked me and shut me in down there must have taken her away."

Now Davie was shaking his head. "Arsehole. She's a wanted person, Quint. Hasn't it occurred to you that she might be involved with the person who hit you? Christ, she might have hit you herself."

I stood in the sunlight outside the cellar entrance and thought about it. He could be right. I didn't see who knocked me out and Katharine had been behind me. Then I remembered the wall of branches and the footprints. I walked round the corner of the building and crossed the woodland to the place where I was attacked. There were more scuffmarks than before but none of them revealed any clear prints. On the other hand, there was no sign of a body – my body – being dragged through the undergrowth to the cellar. I didn't think Katharine could have got me there without leaving traces. If she did hit me, she must have had help.

I squatted down on the ground, my head in my hands. No, I couldn't go along with it. Katharine hadn't tried to stop me checking out the former hospital and she hadn't seemed particularly interested in it. There wasn't any way that she could have warned her associates either. Besides, we'd been together last night – we'd made love. I hadn't expected her to suggest that we try living together but I'd taken it at face value. Maybe I was just gullible. I had a flash of Peter Bryson's corpse. Had she been straight with me about him and the events at the mill?

"Are you all right, Quint?" Davie dropped down beside me.

"Yeah." I looked round at him. "How did you find me out here?"

"The command centre received an anonymous call. The voice was disguised. Something held over the mouthpiece. A guy said you were up here."

"A man?"

"Aye. I heard the tape. It definitely sounded like a male voice."

"Not Katharine then," I said triumphantly.

He pursed his lips. "That proves nothing and you know it,

Quint. She could have got a sidekick to make the call."

"Did you trace it?"

He nodded. "Public phone near the Easter Road greyhound track."

"Any witnesses?"

"Christ, no. You know what that place is like when the tourists are swarming."

"And no ordinary citizens are allowed anywhere near it when there's a meet."

"That's right." Davie glanced at me suspiciously. "What are you getting at?"

I shrugged and decided to keep my ideas about auxiliary involvement to myself for the time being. An auxiliary could easily have got through the barriers around the former football stadium and made a call. Sophia's face floated up before me, her eyes cold and her mouth set firm. Then I twitched my head. I was clutching at straws again. Davie was right. Katharine was a much more likely suspect. But still . . .

"What's down that hole in the basement anyway?" Davie asked.

I stood up unsteadily. "A regular treasure-trove, my friend. A collection of books and Egyptian objets d'art that must be worth a fortune on the global market. Jesus, there are dozens of first editions, most of them looted from the British Library. Walter Scott, Henry James, MacDiarmid, George Mackay Brown. Not to mention Raymond Chandler and Dashiell Hammett. Oh, and Wilfred Owen. That's how I got on to this place."

Davie raised an eyebrow.

"Remember the books Ray pulled out of his shelves? I reckon he was trying to direct us to the cellar. Wilfred Owen recuperated here when it was a hospital."

"Has this got anything to do with the poisonings, Quint?"

"Not sure yet. There's some connection between what was going on here and the poisonings. I think Ray may have seen something at the mill that got him killed."

Davie was shaking his head. "This is all pretty far-fetched."

"This isn't." I said, pointing to the side of my head where the blood had caked. "And the contents of the cellar aren't." I caught sight of my hands. The fingernails were encrusted with reddish-brown earth and gritty dust. I was pretty sure the latter would match the traces I saw in Ray's office and barracks room. I'd seen the red stuff under his nails too, but that wasn't the only place. I tried to remember where else and only succeeded in making my headache worse. "The anonymous call you got isn't a product of my imagination either, is it?" I added, forcing myself to concentrate.

Davie ran his fingers through the tangles of his beard. "Aye, right enough. What does it all mean?"

"Let's see if we can work that out, shall we, guardsman? Give me your mobile."

He handed it over. I called the culture guardian and asked him to organise a team of experts to catalogue what I'd found. I also told him to make sure that the Edlott controller Nasmyth 05 was kept in the dark about those arrangements. I wanted to ask him if he knew anything about what his barracks colleague Ray had been up to in the basement at Craiglockhart. Time for the fourth degree.

The Land-Rover I drove to the former hospital had disappeared, so I went back into the city with Davie. We put an all-barracks search out for the missing vehicle but it hadn't been logged through any of the checkpoints. What interested me more was my mobile. I took Davie's again and called my own number. It started to ring and my heart pounded as I waited for someone – Katharine? – to answer. But nobody did.

"Shit." I called the communications centre and got them to patch calls to my number through to Davie's, which I intended to keep. That meant whoever had my mobile could make outgoing calls – I wanted Katharine to have the ability to ask for help – but they wouldn't receive any.

"You can draw a new mobile when you get back to the command centre, Davie," I said. "In the meantime, let's see where the fat man is."

The duty undercover supervisor advised that Nasmyth 05 had just left the Culture Directorate in an official vehicle and was being followed. His current location was Nicolson Street, heading south. I relayed Davie's mobile number to the tail.

"I wonder where he's going," I said after we turned eastwards in Morningside. Then I had a thought that made me sit up straight. I should have examined the connection earlier. "Bloody hell, I might have known the cunning bastard would have his finger in this."

"Who?" Davie demanded. "What are you on about?"

"The Jackal," I replied, shaking my head. "Billy sodding Geddes. He's been doing freelance work for the Culture Directorate and he knows our man. Head for the auxiliary rehab centre at Duddingston. I'll bet you any number of bottles of barracks whisky you like that Nasmyth 05's going there."

"Not accepted," Davie said morosely. He'd lost too often to risk wagers with me any more.

We rolled into the car park outside the rehabilitation centre after Nasmyth 05 had cleared the checkpoint. A figure dressed as an electrician got out of a van and followed him in.

"I'll give the undercover guy a minute or two to confirm where the fat man's gone," I said, looking round at the desiccated lake bed and the tan sides of Arthur's Seat. The place still smelled of untreated sewage and the midday sun was beating down on us mercilessly. I took another gulp of water and wondered where Katharine was. There was nothing I could do for her now – just hope that she was managing to look after herself. She had a good record at that.

The mobile buzzed.

"Subject's entered the quarters of the inmate called—"

"—the Jackal," I said, completing the tail's sentence for him.

"Okay. We'll take it from here. Stand by in your vehicle. Out."

We went to the checkpoint and flashed ID. Whoever hit me and took my mobile hadn't taken my Council authorisation.

I stopped Davie outside the old church tower. "The usual, all right?"

"Me hard, you soft," he said, looking keen.

I nodded. "And don't worry if you can't follow what I'm saying. I'm going to have to make some of this up as I go along."

"That'll make a change, won't it?" he said with a broad grin.

I raised my middle finger and led him up the stairs. I'd hoped for a stealthy approach but you can forget that when you're accompanied by guard personnel wearing tackety boots. We piled into Billy's room without bothering to knock.

He and Nasmyth 05 hardly seemed to notice us.

"The computer, Davie!" I shouted, realising what they were doing.

He ran across the wooden floor and pushed the pair of them aside.

"Hit 'Escape'," I said desperately.

Davie punched keys then shook his head. "Too late."

I went over to the screen and watched as the words "File Deletion Completed" flashed up.

"Too late was the cry," Billy said with a malevolent grin. "Too fucking late." He let out a high-pitched laugh. "As usual, Quint."

I resisted the temptation to throttle him and shoved his wheelchair away from the computer. Davie grabbed Nasmyth 05 by the collar of his smart suit.

"Right, you two," I said. "It's time to have a wee chat."

The fat man glanced at Billy, his brow covered in a sheen of sweat.

"Don't worry, the disk's clean," my former friend said. "They've got no evidence." He gave me a sulphuric smile.

"Evidence?" I asked calmly. "That's a pretty elastic term in Enlightenment Edinburgh, Billy. You know that." I moved my eyes on to the Edlott controller to include him in the conversation.

"Let's face it, if the Council takes a dislike to you, your life's worth about as much as a bucketful of shite. Citizen shite, that is, rather than the sweeter-smelling auxiliary version."

Davie looked at me as if to say "I thought I was the hard man". I nodded at him.

"Anyway, I think Hume 253 wants to have a private conversation with you, Nasmyth 05. I'll leave you to him."

The Edlott controller gulped. His face went the colour of aged tripe and he let out a whimper. Davie hauled him away to the other end of the room and slammed him down on the bed.

"Don't say a word!" Billy shouted. "They're only guessing."

I grabbed the handles of his wheelchair and shoved him over to the window. "What the fuck have you been up to, you crazy bastard?" I hissed. "I thought you were being rehabilitated."

"I am." He gave me a brief, bitter smile. "What are you complaining about, Quint? I played fair. The last time you came here I put you on to Nasmyth 05, didn't I?"

"Bollocks to that, Billy. You didn't tell me anything I couldn't have found out for myself and you wanted the fat man to get an idea of the angles I was working." I glared at his misshapen face. "You always were a big fan of the double bluff."

"Did we have you thinking there was something rotten about the lottery?" He laughed manically. "We've been otherwise engaged, so to speak."

There was a squeal from the other end of the room. It sounded like Davie was making more progress than I was.

Billy looked round me. "Keep your mouth shut, Nicky!" he yelled. "Shut!"

"Nicky? On first-name terms, are you?"

"Why not?" Billy said, smiling loosely.

"This is your last chance," I said, leaning back over him. "Come clean or Davie'll squeeze it out of your pal."

"Fuck you, Quint," he said, spitting the words from twisted lips and spinning the wheelchair round in a surprisingly quick movement. "Don't tell them anything!"

"Right, that's it." I pulled out my handkerchief, which wasn't exactly freshly laundered, and tied it tightly round his mouth. Then I tipped the chair on to its back and left him upended on the floor. "Look at the ceiling for a bit." I checked he was breathing okay through his nose and went over to the others.

"I think Nasmyth 05's ready to co-operate," Davie said, straightening up.

The auxiliary was curled up in a ball on Billy's bed, his face soaked with sweat but untouched by Davie's hands. It didn't look like degrees three or four had been necessary.

"I ran through the programme of events and he decided against buying a ticket." Davie looked disappointed.

"You see? The threat is mightier than the cattle prod." I sat down beside Nasmyth 05. "Let's have it then. If you're a good boy, I might even put in a word for you in my report, Nicky."

It was strange to address the Edlott controller by name rather than barracks number but it seemed to make him relax a bit. He uncurled himself, keeping his eyes off Davie and glancing nervously at Billy, who was still ranting despite the gag.

"Never mind about Citizen Geddes," I said. "You, Billy and Ray have been doing some illicit trading, haven't you? In books and antiquities from Craiglockhart."

Nasmyth 05 looked at me in amazement. "How did you find out about that?"

"I'm an investigator," I said testily. "It's what I'm good at. What was Ray's involvement?"

"He tracked the collection down in the archives and priced the books," the auxiliary said in a frightened voice. No doubt he was remembering what had recently happened to his barracks colleague. "Some rich bibliophile got his hands on British Library stock after the London mob wrecked the place in 2003. There were pieces from the British Museum too."

"And they were stashed in the cellar at Craiglockhart in the early years of the Enlightenment?"

Nasmyth 05 nodded. "I think the collector had something to

do with the university that used the building. He was killed by the drugs gangs before he could move the stuff and they never found it. Access to the cellar was blocked by rubble."

I nodded slowly. It was beginning to make sense. Ray had worked out the location of the books and he'd traded them with foreign dealers, probably ones known to Billy from his Finance Directorate days. I remembered the American he'd mentioned when I asked for *The Lady in the Lake*. The books accounted for the gritty dust I couldn't identify in his office and in his barracks room. But a one-armed man wouldn't have been much good at clearing rubble.

"Who did the labouring work?" I asked.

The noise from Billy had turned into what sounded like choked laughter.

"Check that he can breathe," I said to Davie. "Well?" I turned back to the fat man. "Who dug the cellar out?"

"I . . . I don't know." He looked shifty.

"Davie?" I called. "Nasmyth o5's gone unco-operative again."

"No, really, I don't know," the auxiliary said quickly, cowering into the corner as Davie came back. "They were contacts of Ray's. I never went to Craiglockhart myself and I didn't meet them."

"Contacts?" I asked suspiciously. They would have needed transport. "Auxiliaries?"

He shrugged. "Perhaps."

"Are you absolutely sure you don't know their identities?" Davie asked, leaning over the cowering, timorous fat man.

"Yes, yes, I'm sure," he whimpered.

I reckoned he was telling the truth. There were other things I needed to know. "Alexander Kennedy." I watched as Nasmyth o5 twitched. "Was he involved in this?"

Billy went quiet.

"Allie?" The Edlott controller looked surprised. "No, of course not. Allie's just a friend."

"Oh, aye," Davie said.

I put my hand on his arm. "What about the foreign currency you made from flogging the books and so on? Where have you stashed it?"

Billy started laughing again under his gag.

"I . . . I don't know," the auxiliary said, suddenly looking like a man who's been comprehensively cleaned out. "He was in charge of that."

He being Billy Geddes, the Jackal, ex-deputy finance guardian and once my closest friend. I went back to him and lifted the chair upright, then undid his gag and wheeled him over to the fat man.

"The Council is going to string you two up," I said. "Your only chance is to come clean."

They stared at me, the fat man with wet eyes. Billy had a mocking smile on his twisted lips.

"No?" I asked. "All right, let's take it from the top. A demoted auxiliary who has some carefully obscured connection with the Culture Directorate is poisoned. Then an Edlott-winner goes the same way. Why does your directorate keep cropping up, Nicky?" I gave Nasmyth 05 an iron glare. "And then Nasmyth 67, a barracks colleague of yours, drinks the Ultimate Usquebaugh too. He found a stash of valuable books and antiquities in a building less than half a mile from the mill where the supposed poisoners are slaughtered. Now what the fuck's going on?"

Nasmyth 05 was quivering like a bludgeoned seal. "I . . . I don't know," he stammered.

"It's only a bit of business," Billy said in a low voice. "We're making some currency on the side. We don't know anything about the poisoned whisky."

"People are dying all over the city, Billy. Don't you care about that?"

"Piss off, Quint. They're not dying because of the deal we set up."

"No, not because of the deal. But there's a connection, I'm

sure of that." I looked into his rheumy grey eyes and tried
another pitch. "Do you know Allie Kennedy, Billy?"

He held my gaze. Then he glanced at the fat man and shook
his head dismissively. "Never even heard of him."

I almost believed my former friend. I probably would have if it
hadn't been for that brief look he gave Nasmyth 05. I knew Billy's
mannerisms. The little bastard thought he'd got round me.
There was no point in trying to squeeze him any more. He'd
rather swallow his tongue than open up to me. He still held me
responsible for his injuries. I'd have to look elsewhere for the
investigation's big break.

"What next?" Davie asked.

We were sitting in the Land-Rover outside the rehab centre
watching the heat haze rise over the dried lake bed. Nasmyth 05
had just driven off with a look of immense relief on his face. I
reckoned it was still worth setting him loose in case Allie
Kennedy made contact with him. I hoped the fat man was so
happy that he wouldn't notice the operative on his tail.

"What next indeed?" I replied. My methods had become
about as random as Edlott was supposed to be.

"I don't see where this is leading us, Quint," Davie said,
gulping from a waterbottle and handing it to me. "Billy Geddes,
Ray and the fat man were involved in illicit book trading. What's
that got to do with the people who sent the ultimatum?"

"Ray was poisoned for a reason, I'm certain of that."

"The Dalrymple hunch?" Davie asked sardonically.

The mobile I'd taken from him buzzed before I could reply.

"Where the hell are you, Dalrymple?"

"Lewis. I was just going to call you."

"Don't bugger me about, man." The public order guardian
sounded like he'd had a wisdom tooth removed without anaes-
thetic. "I've just covered for you in the Council meeting, God
knows why. The senior guardian has been asking for you
repeatedly."

"All right, Lewis, calm down. You told her I was coshed, I presume?" I hadn't fancied talking to Sophia for several reasons – most of them connected with Katharine.

"I did. Are you all right?" he asked, relenting slightly.

"I feel like shit but don't let that worry you."

"Very well, I won't. Where are you, Dalrymple? Have you discovered who was looting the cellar in Craiglockhart yet?"

I'd reported the treasure-trove earlier but said nothing about Nasmyth 05 or Billy. I didn't want the Council to haul them in and risk losing my only leads.

"Never mind about the cellar now. I'm with Hume 253 in Newington," I said, being deliberately inaccurate about our location. "There haven't been any more messages from the poisoners, have there?"

"Nothing. Which makes your friend the archivist's death even more puzzling, don't you think?"

"Mmm."

"By the way, you might be interested to know that the Land-Rover you drove to Craiglockhart has turned up."

"Bloody right I might be interested, Lewis. Where?"

"In a back yard in Liberton. Outside the city line."

"Okay, I'm sending Davie there immediately. Get a scene-of-crime squad on to it too."

"They're on their way. Where are you going?"

"There are things I need to check in the archive. Out."

Davie looked at me as he started the Land-Rover. "Any chance of you telling me what you're going to check?"

"No," I said, glowering at him. "The Dalrymple hunch is no laughing matter, pal."

"Am I laughing?"

I hadn't lied to Hamilton when I said I was going to check the archive – I just hadn't specified which archive. Nasmyth Barracks used to be the university veterinary college, which traded under the unfortunate moniker of the Dick Vet. Nowadays there are no vets in residence here, only a large number of dickhead auxiliaries. I got access to the barracks archive by waving my authorisation at the commander. She didn't like it. She was even more pissed off when I told her to keep my visit to herself.

I sat sweating in the poorly lit basement and went through Ray's personal file. Auxiliaries' documentation, apart from that relating to senior personnel like Nasmyth 05, is held in their barracks until they die, when it's supposed to be transferred to a central databank separate from the archive dealing with ordinary citizens. It was too soon after Ray's death for that to have happened to his file yet. I went through the pile of papers in the thick maroon folder quickly, disregarding the Personal Evaluations, Service Records and appraisals. What I wanted were the Close Colleague Lists. Every auxiliary's relationships are noted so that they can be controlled and curtailed if necessary. The Council's never been keen on auxiliaries getting too close to each other — you never know, they might start behaving like normal human beings. And even though citizens are treated more openly these days, the Council's servants are still governed by strict regulations.

I went back to the beginning of Ray's career as an auxiliary. He was three years younger than me and had completed the training programme in 2012. Then he'd done the usual tours of duty on the border before working his way up the guard hierarchy. I stopped and looked at the Close Colleague Lists for those years. There weren't that many barracks numbers on them. It seemed he'd always been a reserved type, happier with his nose in a book than down the barracks bar with the lads and lassies. I started writing the numbers in my notebook. I soon realised that even though there wasn't a multitude, there were still enough to keep me checking other auxiliaries' records for days.

Then I reached the last year Ray spent in the guard before he lost his arm and got a jolt that made my knees smash up against the underside of the desk. Christ, that was it. I remembered the pick-up truck I'd seen near the central archive. And fingernails discoloured by reddish-brown earth.

The Dalrymple hunch had paid off.

"Quint?" Davie had obviously got himself a new mobile. "We've found plenty of good prints on the Land-Rover's door and steering wheel."

"Have you now?" I was in an ancient transit van that I'd commandeered from the Nasmyth Barracks vehicle pool. "Some of them will be mine and Katharine's. I want you to check the others against the guard register in the castle."

"You think that guard personnel are involved?" Davie said. His voice was a mixture of surprise and extreme scepticism.

"I know that guard personnel are involved, my friend." I gave him the barracks number I'd found in Ray's file.

"What?" Now he was in shock. "You're kidding."

"No I'm not. Run the check."

"Where are you, Quint?" he asked. "Do I hear an engine?"

"Yup." I swerved to avoid a tourist bus at the East End of Princes Street.

"Where are you heading?"

"Let me know the result of the fingerprint check as soon as you can."

"Quint, you're not going to the—"

"Out."

I took the bend at an angle that made the clapped-out van's suspension creak horrendously then headed down Leith Walk at speed.

I stopped beside the Water of Leith thirty yards from the port and peered through the pockmarked windscreen. The barrier was down and I could see the sentry's beret-topped head in the booth. Beyond the fence there didn't seem to be much going on. The warehouses obscured the docks and it was impossible to tell how many boats were alongside.

I sat back and considered my options. Number one – call up Hamilton and send in the heavy squad. That would lead to plenty of casualties, given the high number of automatic weapons around the port area. It wouldn't do Katharine much good if she was down here either. I was pretty sure she was. Number two – call Davie and ask him to give me some personalised backup. Tempting, but I didn't want to get him shot to pieces. Number three – go in on my own. Even less tempting, but at least I might be able to reason with the man I was after from what would obviously be a position of extreme weakness. That might stop him shooting me for a few seconds. It looked like number three was the one.

My mobile went off in my pocket.

"Quint? Davie. You were right, you smartarse. The prints were so complete that they matched them almost immediately."

"Right." I felt my heart begin to dance a hornpipe.

"Are you by any chance down at the port, Quint?"

"Well spotted, guardsman."

"Wait for me. Don't go in on your own. You know what those guys are like."

"Come down on your own. I don't want Hamilton to turn this place into an Edinburgh version of Windsor the day the mob caught up with the royal family."

"Okay." He sounded very dubious. "But wait for me outside, all right?"

"Okay. Outside. Out."

But I was already thinking about Katharine again. For her, every second might count. At least Davie knew where I was now. That would have to do.

I looked ahead at the guard post. There was no way the sentry would let me in, even if I asked nicely, but a fuel truck had just pulled up at the gate. It was too good an opportunity to miss. I floored the accelerator and drove the Nasmyth Barracks van straight at the gap between the barrier and the truck. To my amazement there was enough space for me to get through, though I left a lot of rubber on the asphalt. I thought I'd made it into the compound without damage, but I was wrong. The tanker jerked forward as I passed him and caught my rear bumper. That sent me swerving all over the place. For an uncomfortably long moment I thought I was going to end up in the Water of Leith at the point where it runs into the Enlightenment Dock. I managed to straighten up in time.

Looking ahead, I saw the battered hulk that was the pride of the Fisheries Guard. It was in the process of casting off, its shoreside deck lined with crew members holding automatic weapons. In the shed-like construction that was the vessel's wheelhouse I saw two figures that I recognised immediately. One was Katharine, her eyes fixed on my vehicle as it careered towards the dock. The other was the man who'd left his prints on the Land-Rover: Jamieson 369, also known as Dirty Harry — the admiral of the bloody fleet.

I held the horn down to make them stop then slammed the brake pedal to the floor. Nothing much happened. Now I realised what the Nasmyth auxiliary had been trying to tell me when I took the van — the brakes were buggered. The Fisheries Guard vessel loomed nearer, the ropes now free of the bollards and being pulled on board by crewmen with curious looks on their faces. This time I had only two choices — hit the harbour wall or take a dive into the oil-topped, filth-ridden outflow from Edinburgh's river. The steering wheel jerked left and made the decision for me. It looked like I was destined for the Enlightenment Dock after all.

The van took off gracelessly into the exhaust-filled air astern of the boat then dropped like a cow doing a belly flop.

Into the Water of Leith. Or death.

Chapter Eighteen

I was in luck. The heavily scratched windscreen flew out in one piece the second the van hit the water. I was winded by the impact but I managed to scramble out of the gap before the vehicle started to sink. I found myself crouching on the foundering bonnet, looking up at the row of gun-toting headbangers along the boat's rail. The words "frying pan" and "fire" sprang to mind.

"You'd better throw the wanker a line." I couldn't see Dirty Harry but his rough tones were easy enough to recognise.

The Fisheries Guard vessel's engines were gunned as the skipper held its position in the middle of the narrow dock. I choked in the acrid fumes as I grabbed the rope and was dragged through the scummy water. That was all the help they gave me. I had to heave myself up to the rail and collapse over it under my own steam. Then the muzzle of a well-oiled Uzi was jammed into my neck.

"On your feet, knobsucker. The chief wants to talk to you."

It seemed like a good idea to comply with the hard-bitten crewman's order. I was shoved up to the wheelhouse, my wet boots skidding on the steps.

Katharine moved back from the door. "Are you all right, Quint?" she asked. There was concern in her voice but she avoided looking at me. She didn't seem to have been harmed.

Doubt suddenly laid into me like a pre-Enlightenment mugger. Surely she wasn't part of Dirty Harry's operation?

That fear didn't last long.

"Shut it, woman," the big man snarled, turning his good eye on her. Katharine stared back at him with undisguised loathing. "The two of you are seconds away from a watery grave."

"Christ, Harry, make up your mind," I said. "You just saved me from one of those."

He ignored that as he concentrated on spinning the wheel and ratcheting up the engine revs. The boat moved forward surprisingly smoothly. Despite looking like a wreck that had just been dredged from the sea bottom, it had been well maintained. Shouts came from the quayside and I looked out of the wheelhouse. A line of crewmen and dock workers were waving their arms slowly, their faces sombre. I remembered scenes in old war films showing U-boats being cheered out of port.

"Do they always look this joyful when you go on patrol?" I asked the captain.

Dirty Harry glanced at me then let out a string of sardonic laughs. "We're not going on patrol, citizen smart fucker," he said, his face hardening. "We're heading for the other side of the North Sea." He eased the engine controls higher. "And we're not coming back."

I watched as the buildings of Leith began to shrink in the distance. Harry steered east after we cleared the rocks round the harbour entrance. The juddering all over the boat suggested that maximum safe speed had been reached. I tried to talk to Katharine a couple of times but the skipper made it clear that was contrary to the ship's code of conduct by putting his hand on the haft of his auxiliary knife. So I was forced to suffer in silence as Arthur's Seat and the Castle Rock came into perspective in the Big Heat's hazy air and then began to fade away. Shit, this was not going the way I expected.

"Look, Harry," I said, going up to the piratical figure at the wheel. "I don't think this is a very good idea."

"Is that right, you fucking scumbag?" he roared. Getting up Dirty Harry's nose wasn't a very good idea either. "You fucked up our fucking treasure-trove, you forced us to desert and you came close to putting a van through my hull. I don't think you're an expert on good fucking ideas, pal."

I shrugged. "Personally, I think you're in the clear." I looked at him steadily, making him shoot an inquisitive glance at me. "Okay, so going along with Ray when he asked you to dig out the cellar in Craiglockhart was against regulations, but it's not necessarily a demotion offence."

I kept my eyes off Katharine. I was going to have to try a high-risk strategy to get us off the boat. If I wasn't careful, I would end up with her knife in my chest.

"I mean, disposing of those headbangers in the mill was a major service to the city," I said.

I felt Katharine go tense at my side. As I thought, she wanted more than a pound of flesh from the killer of her friend Peter Bryson. Fortunately she didn't act hastily.

Harry nodded slowly. "I might have fucking known. The genius has worked it out." Then he looked at me fiercely. "Have you found out who killed Ray? I want that fucker's heart."

Jesus, I was surrounded by avenging angels. I shook my head. "Not yet I haven't. But if you let me off this rustbucket I'll find the bastard."

His expression loosened slightly. "Aye, you were a mate of his too, weren't you?"

"I was. So how about it? Will you let Katharine and me go?"

He stared ahead. "Convince me it's worth my while, citizen."

I shivered and wrapped my arms round my upper body. It was cool out on the estuary and my sodden clothes had dripped what looked like gallons on to the wooden deck. I made the depressing discovery that my mobile had not come with me out of the van. Katharine was standing as still as a statue, her eyes locked on

Harry. I needed to use my rhetorical skills to get us off the Fisheries Guard's version of the *Titanic* before she leaped at the big man and tore his remaining eye out.

"Like I say, Harry, the Council will look favourably on the fact that you dealt with the people responsible for the poisonings. What happened? Did you come across them by accident?"

He looked at me suspiciously, letting me know he'd spotted that I was pumping him. Then he nodded. "Aye. A pair of my lads saw one of them near Craiglockhart and followed him back to the old mill."

"You went back there later, didn't you? And when you discovered the bottles of the Ultimate Usquebaugh you beat the hell out of them."

"Aye. They were headcases. We heard them talking about how they were going to put poison in drinking-water tanks. They didn't care how many people died until the Council gave them a cut of the tourist revenues." He grinned humourlessly. "Killing them was a pleasure."

"Killing you will be a pleasure," Katharine said, stepping towards Harry. "I knew one of those guys."

The big man didn't care. "They were all shites," he said emphatically. "All of them except the woman. She was well out of her depth. I heard the three men laughing about how the guardians would crap themselves when citizens and tourists started dying."

Katharine took a step back. It looked like her feelings for Peter Bryson were in the process of changing.

"Lucky for you that the woman who survived went into a coma," I said. "She could have identified you as auxiliaries."

He snorted. "You think we went about dressed in guard uniforms when we were out there? We changed back into them when we crossed the city line."

"Which you did when there were guard personnel on duty who knew you and turned a blind eye," I said, thinking on the hoof. "You still wore auxiliary boots in the mill house though.

That made me wonder. What about Ray? Was he with you on the attack?"

"Aye, the stupid bugger. He insisted on coming along. I don't know what he thought he could do with one arm. He'd have been better off sticking with his books."

"Did he see someone else there?" I'd remembered that Katharine wasn't sure if there were three or four men.

Harry turned to me. "How the fuck do you know that?"

"I'm a class act," I said, laughing till I saw the way he was looking at me. "This could be important, Harry. What did Ray see?"

"*Said* he saw," he corrected. "He said he saw another guy peering in the window when we hit the fuckers."

"Did he say what he looked like, this guy?"

The skipper raised his shoulders. "Said he was youngish, thin build, with very short hair. And a manic look in his eyes. He was only there for a few seconds but he spooked Ray completely. We had a scout around outside for him but there was no sign. Jesus." He turned to me, his face racked with unlikely anguish. "Do you think he was the fucker who killed Ray?"

"I think so. Have you ever heard of a citizen called Alexander Kennedy?"

He nodded. "The name rings a bell. Wasn't there an all-barracks out for him?"

"Yeah. But you haven't heard of him apart from that?"

"No. Was he in with those arseholes?"

"I think so." I stared at him again. "He's still on the loose, Harry. And I think he's got more of the poisoned whisky. You have to take me back. I can catch the bastard. He probably killed Ray, for Christ's sake. And he might kill dozens of other innocent people."

He glanced at me, squinting through his good eye then slowly nodding his head. "All right. But we're still getting out of this cesspit of a city. That's what Ray and I agreed with the arse-bandit in the Culture Directorate and that's what I'm going to do with my boys." He cut the revs. "There's something you'd better have a look at before you go, citizen smartarse."

That sounded interesting.

Harry pushed the wheelhouse window open. "Andy," he shouted, "bring one of those packs up here."

Christ, the packs that Katharine saw Bryson and his mates carrying. I'd forgotten all about them.

A seaman in an oil-drenched shirt came up the steps and dumped a good-quality backpack down. I hadn't seen one like that since I went hillwalking when I was a kid. It was definitely not the kind of article provided by the Supply Directorate.

"Take the wheel, Andy." Dirty Harry strode over and thrust a hand into the pack. "This'll get us started up over the water." He pulled out a transparent plastic bag stuffed with dry, greenish-brown shredded leaves. "This stuff is dynamite and there's plenty of it."

"Been sampling it, have you?"

"Going to shop me to the Council, citizen?" Harry laughed. "You tell them what you like, son. I'll be far away. This is a serious bit of gear. I heard the fuckers call it 'Ibrox Gold'. The gang bosses over in Glasgow must have been cultivating some new, extra-knockout varieties."

I leaned back against the bulkhead. How did the grass fit in with the rest of the case? The poisoners must have been intending to move it into the city and it was a reasonable assumption that Allie Kennedy was their contact. But did the deal start and end with him, or was Nasmyth 05 in on it? Was Billy in on it? And if they were, did that mean they knew about the Ultimate Usquebaugh?

Harry took the wheel back from his man. "We've got a load of old books and statues from Craiglockhart down below as well. Now all we've got to do is get as far away from Auld fucking Reekie as we can. After we've dropped you two."

I nodded, looking at Katharine. She was standing against the wheelhouse wall, her face blank. Harry was talking about

Edinburgh the way she'd often done in the past. Was she really serious about coming back to live in the city with me?

The big man spun the wheel and the boat came round, carving a frothing furrow in the sparkling waters of the firth. The crewmen at the rails looked up impassively, none of them questioning their chief's change of course. Even rebels are obedient in Enlightenment Edinburgh.

"Time you got your clothes wet again, citizen six brains," Dirty Harry said, peering through his binoculars. "The port's full of my former colleagues in the guard."

I stared at the crowd on the quay in the sunlight. I could make out Davie's large frame.

"Can you swim, woman?" the skipper demanded of Katharine.

"Even if I couldn't, I'd still jump to get off this rat-shit hulk," she said, her eyes flashing.

"Given up the idea of killing me then?" Harry roared. "I like your spirit, woman. You should stay with us. I'd make it worth your while."

"You'd wake up with your dick behind your ear if you tried."

He was still laughing as he cut the revs completely. The boat bobbed on the water about a hundred yards away from the outermost sea wall.

"Think you can make it?" Harry asked. "Not that I care. This is as close as I'm going."

"Come on, Quint." Katharine went down the companionway.

"I can fix it for you, Harry," I said. "The books and the antiquities are no big deal."

"Jump, you fucker," he said, a scowl spreading across his scarred face. "Jump. I've had my fill of this pit. Just crucify whoever killed Ray. And say goodbye to Davie for me."

"All right, big man." I went down to the deck and stood next to Katharine, then looked back up at him. Time to fly a kite. "What did you do with the bottles of the Ultimate Usquebaugh you kept, Harry?"

He shook his head. "Christ, you don't miss a thing, do you?

Don't worry, we smashed them up. Down in the port. I had this idea of using them to settle some old scores in the Council." He laughed bitterly. "Not even guardians deserve to die like that."

"How many bottles were there?"

He shrugged. "Can't remember exactly. Around twenty."

I nodded. So Allie Kennedy or whoever else sent the ultimatum didn't have much nicotine-tainted stock left — unless there was another cache.

"Jump!" Dirty Harry yelled. "Or shall I get the boys to toss you over?"

I looked at Katharine. "Ready?"

"Aye, ready," she said.

So we jumped.

The water in the estuary was much colder than it was in the dock. I forced myself to move my arms and legs regularly, trying not to lose my breath. Katharine forged ahead in a smooth breaststroke, her hair darker now it was wet.

"You didn't get hit at Craiglockhart?" I asked, getting a mouthful of very salty water.

"No. I'd have cut some of them but I looked round to see what they were doing to you and they managed to get my knife off me. Bastards. Is your head okay? I heard they locked you in the cellar."

"I wasn't there too long. Harry called Davie and told him where I was."

She looked round at me. "I suppose I'm going to be grabbed by the guard now."

"No chance. You're in the clear as far as I'm concerned." I heaved for breath, glad that the harbour wall was getting close.

"Do you think you can convince your girlfriend of that?" Katharine asked.

I let that go unanswered, and not just because I was short of breath. I remembered the doubts about Katharine that had gripped me more than once, the last time as recently as on the boat. I decided not to say anything about those.

We got to the outer mole. Fortunately there was a steel ladder on the steep sea wall. I let Katharine go first. Water cascaded from her clothes, which then stuck to her limbs and torso. If I hadn't been so knackered, I might have got excited. As it was, I wallowed in the shallows till she reached the top then hauled myself out with difficulty. That was enough bathing for one day.

As I pulled myself over the parapet at the top, I was met by Davie's face. He was not amused.

"Why the fuck did you enter the port on your own, you lunatic?" He looked out to sea. "Where's Harry going?"

"On a world tour." I collapsed over the wall and sat gasping. "He said goodbye." Katharine was sitting breathing easily and running her hands through her hair. "It's all right. I got some hot information from him."

"Just as well," Davie said, eyeing Katharine suspiciously. "There's been another message to the Council."

Davie pulled away from the port area, glancing in his mirror at Katharine and me in the back of the Land-Rover as we changed into the dry clothes that a Fisheries Guard auxiliary had given us. Hamilton had called and told us to get to the castle pronto for a meeting with him and the senior guardian.

"We should have sent the other boats to bring Harry back, Quint," he said, shaking his head. "The public order guardian's going to be very unhappy."

"Tough," I said, sticking my head through a T-shirt with a harpoon logo. Davie's jaw had dropped when I'd told him the big man's crew were the ones who killed the people in the mill house. "Even if the other crews agreed, Harry's guys wouldn't let themselves be taken alive. Anyway, the guardian's got other things to worry about."

"Like rioting all over the city if the drinking-water's poisoned," Katharine said. Her hair was tousled, the lighter colour returning now that it was drying.

"What are we going to do with her?" Davie said, glancing over his shoulder. "If we're taking her with us, she'll have to be cuffed."

"For fuck's sake, Davie, she's clean." I looked at Katharine. "Aren't you?"

She raised her middle finger and bent over to tie the laces of a battered pair of auxiliary boots.

"Uh-huh," Davie muttered. "You'd better be right, Quint. By the way, what happened to that van you took from Nasmyth Barracks?"

"Ah." I busied myself with the buttons on my fly. "It's in the car wash."

"What?"

"They should be able to pull it out of the dock. The brakes need an overhaul."

Davie let out a long sigh. He'd never thought much of my abilities behind the wheel. I was glad I hadn't disappointed him.

You could tell someone had hit the Council's spot. The esplanade was like a dodgems ring on a Saturday night in the time before the Enlightenment deemed fairgrounds trivial – which contemporary citizen diversions like Edlott aren't, of course. Davie managed to get up to the castle gate without being shunted.

"What about me?" Katharine asked. "Am I supposed to sit here and sweat to death?"

I shook my head. "No. You're coming with us." I was almost convinced that Sophia hadn't known anything about Nasmyth 05's scam with Billy and Ray – let alone anything about Harry's bloodbath – but I wanted to make absolutely sure. Parading Katharine in front of the senior guardian would definitely bring out the worst in her and, if jealousy was all it was about, I could live with that.

We passed between the statues of Wallace and Bruce. There had been a move by the original Council to take them down on the grounds that an independent Edinburgh had no need of Scottish heroes. They decided against it eventually, as the old warriors had been stuffed down the populace's throat so much in the years of pretend devolution that no one gave a shit any more. Besides, they're pretty neat sculptures.

I shook my head and brought myself back to the present. The case was heading to a climax and there didn't seem to be too many imponderables left. In my experience, that's when complacency sets in. If you reckon you're home and dry, prepare to be surprised. I wondered if there were any surprises left in this twisted tale. It seemed a lot more than five days since it started with Frankie Thomson's body lying by the Water of Leith and the bullfrogs barking their blues in the background.

We were waved through Hamilton's outer office by a female auxiliary who turned her nose up at Katharine and me. Davie knocked on the heavy door to the main office and opened it.

"At last. What have you been doing, Dalrymple?" Hamilton said, looking up from the conference table where he was sitting next to Sophia. He dried up when he saw Katharine.

"Catching wanted deserters apparently," the senior guardian said, giving Katharine an icy stare. "Have this woman placed in the cells, guardian."

"Not if you want me to catch the person who's threatening the Council," I said.

Sophia's face was even paler than usual. She was reacting as I'd hoped. It was hard to read her emotions, but the way she was holding her eyes on Katharine suggested she was extremely needled by her presence. That didn't exactly square with my idea that the senior guardian had been plotting to undo the Council's user-friendly policies. Sometimes I overdo the creative element during investigations.

"You think it's appropriate to issue more threats, do you, citizen?" Even when she was speaking to me, Sophia held her gaze on Katharine.

"That wasn't a threat, senior guardian," I said, noticing the minuscule flicker of her eyelashes as I used her official title. "It's the way it's going to be. Katharine wasn't involved in the

poisonings. Take my word for it or finish the case without me."
There wasn't time now to go over how Katharine had come by
the bottles of poisoned whisky.

Hamilton and Davie both found this exchange embarrassing.
They were looking at the floor, their cheeks red. On the other
hand, Katharine was having a great time. She was smiling at
Sophia, returning her stare without difficulty.

There was an extended silence then Sophia finally cracked. "I
think you owe us an explanation, Citizen Dalrymple," she said,
returning the favour with my own official title. "What have you
uncovered?"

I told them about Nasmyth 05 and Ray, excluding Billy
Geddes from the equation at this stage. Mentioning him would
just have driven Hamilton to apoplexy – he would have happily
exiled my former friend years ago. Then I filled them in about
Dirty Harry and the Fisheries Guard's role in the cellar at
Craiglockhart. That caused the public order guardian's face and
fists to clench and his breathing to quicken. I decided against
mentioning the Ibrox Gold at this stage in case he had a stroke.

"And you let Jamieson 369 sail away unhindered?" he demanded, glaring at both Davie and me.

"That is not our primary concern, guardian," Sophia said. It
looked like she'd followed the drift of my narrative. "I take it you
assume the short-haired male that the dead archivist saw at the
mill was the missing citizen Alexander Kennedy."

I nodded. "Who subsequently killed Ray. The overwhelming
likelihood is that he has at least a small amount of poisoned
whisky still in his possession." I looked at Sophia and Lewis. "So
tell us about the latest message you've received."

Hamilton glanced at Sophia for approval. She nodded
reluctantly, taking her eyes off Katharine.

"It was on a public phone this time," the public order
guardian said. "The caller rang the guard command centre at
two thirteen and asked for me."

"You spoke to him yourself?" I asked.

The guardian nodded. "I couldn't make out what was being said very easily. He was holding something over the mouthpiece."

"You recorded it, of course," I said.

Hamilton nodded and stretched over to the cassette recorder by his desk phone.

We all craned forward as the tape began to roll.

"Public order guardian." Lewis's voice was clear enough.

"I know you're recording this. Don't interrupt." The voice was slow and muffled, with an unnaturally deep quality. "We deal in nicotine death. We deal in the Ultimate Usquebaugh. Francis Thomson and Fordyce Kennedy drank it down. So did the old men in Trinity. We made you lower the flag on the castle. We killed the auxiliary in Buccleuch Place with the whisky too. You know what we think? Screw negotiations. We're going to do some tourists next."

Hamilton hit the stop button.

"Is that it?" I asked.

He nodded. "We traced the call to a phone in Marchmont – on Thirlestane Road near the swimming-pool. The doors had just been opened for the next session and none of the citizens in the queue could give a description of any callers."

"All desperate for their session in the water," Davie said.

"Confine yourself to the matter in hand, Hume 253," Sophia said sharply. "Well?" she said, turning to me. "What do you think?"

"I think this is the real thing, all right. The caller knew about the previous killings and the lowering of the flag. Not even auxiliaries knew about the flag." I gave them a humourless smile as their eyebrows jumped. It's always good to cast doubt on the rank that keeps control for the Council. "I can see why you're worried. If he has a go at the tourists, the city will be bankrupt before my next turn in the wash house."

Sophia's lips were dry. "Why isn't he negotiating? Wouldn't a criminal like this Kennedy want a cut of the action?"

I couldn't restrain a laugh. "A cut of the action? You've been reading too many American crime novels."

"Watch it, Dalrymple," Hamilton growled.

"All right," I said. "Yes, it's a fair point. Maybe Allie Kennedy's just a psycho who fancies messing up the city and the Council as much as he can. The grass traffickers said he was vicious." I ran my hand over the stubble on my cheek. The fact that the Ibrox Gold was no longer around might also fit with that theory. Allie and the deceased poisoners had apparently been going to get stuck into the drugs trade. Without the supergrass to sell, maybe Allie reckoned civil disorder was the best way to increase his profile.

"Are you still with us, citizen?" Sophia asked irritably. "What do you suggest we do?"

"Judging by the number of guard vehicles on the esplanade, you're already taking steps to build up the auxiliary presence in tourist facilities."

"The central tourist zone isn't exactly underpoliced as it is," the public order guardian said. "But we've increased the guard and the chief toxicologist's team is running as many checks as it can on whisky and other drinks consumed by tourists."

I shook my head slowly. "There are thousands of visitors in the city. All it takes is a few drops to be slipped into some unsuspecting boozer's glass in a bar and – bang! – 'Tourist Poisoned, Edinburgh Unsafe' is news all round the world."

"What do you advise then, citizen?" Sophia demanded, keeping up the level of formality in front of Katharine.

"I advise catching Alexander Kennedy as soon as possible."

"And how exactly do you intend to do that?" she asked acidly. "We've been looking for him for days without success."

"I'll get him, don't worry," I said, trying to encourage myself as much as anyone else. I turned and headed for the door, taking Davie and Katharine with me. I stopped when I got there. "By the way, you haven't forgotten that tomorrow's the official opening of the international festival of greed, have you?"

Sophia looked at me in full Ice Queen mode. "If by that you

mean the Edlott tourist initiative at the bottom of the Mound then, no, we haven't forgotten."

"Extra personnel have already been placed at the foot of the Mound," Hamilton said. "The drinks stalls nearby are being resupplied with stock that has been fully checked." The public order guardian's hesitant manner showed how confident he was about those measures deterring the killer.

"The matter will be discussed further at an emergency Council meeting at seven this evening," Sophia said. "I expect you to be there, citizen." She opened her eyes wide at Katharine. "Don't bother to bring your female friend."

"What makes you think I'd go anywhere near the place?" Katharine said, dropping to Sophia's level.

I opened the door and walked away. Despite what I'd said, I didn't feel very sanguine about laying hands on Allie Kennedy. But I had the distinct feeling that someone in the city would soon be drinking at the Ultimate Chance saloon.

"And now?" Katharine asked as we tramped down the echoing corridor.

"And now you go back to my place and listen to the blues."

"No chance." She grabbed my arm and held me back. "I want to be in on this, Quint."

I could hear Davie breathing impatiently behind us.

"This is a murder case, not a picnic," I said. "What's your problem? I'll be there as soon as I can."

"My problem?" she replied, flicking an angry glance at Davie, who suddenly started examining the flagstones. "My problem is that I want to come with you, not sit waiting in your slum."

Davie raised his wrist and looked at his watch pointedly.

"Oh, all right." I started walking again. "And not a word from you, guardsman." I glanced over my shoulder. "What's Nasmyth 05 up to?"

Davie made a call to the surveillance unit. "He's in the Culture Directorate. Has been all day."

"Okay." I stopped to let a guardswoman laden with files pass.

"So where are we going?" Katharine asked.

"The Kennedy family home."

"You reckon our suspect has popped back for a cup of tea, do you?" Davie asked ironically.

"Probably not," I said, as we walked into the blinding sunlight. "Have you got any better ideas?"

Apparently not.

We drove past the water tank at the end of Millar Crescent and stopped outside number 14. Further down the street, a gang of teenagers in tattered vests and shorts were knocking a football around near the hole being dug by the undercover operatives. I'd already checked with them on the Land-Rover's phone. Agnes Kennedy had come back from work about an hour earlier. Her mother had been inside all day apart from stints in the queues for the toilets and the water tank. Surprise, surprise – there had been no sign of any young men with very short haircuts. But I was surprised when I glanced up at the flat and saw that the curtains on the sitting room window were open. That made a change.

"Are all three of us going up?" Davie asked dubiously.

"I suppose so," I replied. "Unless you want to stay down here and referee the football match."

Davie looked through the dusty windscreen at the damage the players were visiting on each other's shins. "No thanks."

We traipsed up the stairs, breathing in the odour of over-heated citizens. I knocked on the door.

No answer. I tried again, this time harder.

"Who . . . who is it?" Agnes asked after a long silence. Her voice was low and unsteady.

"Quint," I said. "Quint Dalrymple." The door stayed closed. "Can we come in?"

There was no reply. I felt my heart miss a beat, wondering what had made her sound so frightened. The only time she'd been like this before was when she'd talked about her brother.

"Agnes, are you all right?"

"Em . . . yes. Look, just wait a minute, will you?" Her voice was still unsteady. "My . . . my mother's calling me."

"Open the door, Agnes," I called, rattling the handle.

"What do you reckon?" Davie asked. "Shall I put my shoulder to it?"

"What's going on?" Katharine demanded. "Didn't you hear the woman? Her mother's calling."

I remembered the rope in Allie Kennedy's bedroom and grabbed Davie's mobile. The number I punched out rang and rang, but there was no answer.

"What's happened to the surveillance guys at the back of the building?" I asked.

Davie raised his shoulders in a shrug.

Then I got through.

"Covert operations," came an officious female voice.

"What?" I shouted. "What the fuck's going on?"

"Who is this?" the woman countered frostily.

"Dalrymple, special investigator. What happened to the undercover operatives at the rear of Millar Crescent?"

"One moment, citizen." There was the sound of paper being rustled. "They were withdrawn this afternoon in response to the general alarm in the central tourist zone."

"Shit!" I yelled. Some bureaucratic tosser had obviously taken the decision to halve the surveillance. "Break it down, Davie!"

Katharine and I stood back as Davie hurled himself across the narrow landing and smashed his shoulder into the door bearing the surname that the murdered occupant had carved so carefully. The locks gave way at the second charge. I rushed in after him, wondering if anyone was in there apart from Agnes and Hilda. And how many bodies we were about to find.

Chapter Nineteen

"What the hell are you doing?" Agnes was standing at the far end of the corridor with her hands on her hips. She didn't sound frightened any more – just furious.

"Are you all right?" I said, slamming into Davie, who'd stopped abruptly. "I thought—"

"What did you think, Citizen Dalrymple?" she demanded, glancing into the sitting room. "That my vicious brother had come back to terrorise us?"

"Something like that," I said lamely.

"I hope you're going to replace the door," she said, looking beyond us to the pieces of firewood dangling from the frame. "Who's this?"

"I'm Katharine. Sorry about these idiots."

"I'll bet." Agnes said scathingly. "You're just another one of them."

"No I'm not." Katharine pushed past me and Davie. "Don't worry, I'll keep this pair under control."

The hostility left Agnes's face. She wiped her hands on her paint-spattered shirt and extended one to Katharine. "Sounds like we can do business," she said, leading her into the sitting room.

That gave me the opportunity to check out her brother's bedroom. It was in the state it had been on my last visit, the bed apparently untouched and the fire rope above the window coiled in the same way. There were no telltale scrapes or marks on the windowledge either. Before I joined the women, I put my head round the doors of the other rooms. No sign of the errant male sibling anywhere.

"Oh christ," I said to Davie, glancing back at the front door.

"Carpenter?" he asked.

I nodded and left him to make the call.

The main room was in its usual gloom. Agnes must have drawn the curtains before we got up the stairs. She and Katharine were talking to each other on the sofa while Hilda sat propped up against the arm of the matching chair, her head drooping forward.

"Is she okay?" I asked.

Agnes put her hand to the scarf round her throat when she caught my eye. "My mother? The same. She comes and goes." She glanced at her. "She was crying out for my father when you started banging on the door."

"Sorry about that. We're arranging for it to be fixed."

She nodded slowly. "What was it you wanted?"

I went over to the sofa and looked down at her. "Have you seen Allie, Agnes?"

She shook her head but didn't speak.

"Are you sure?"

She looked up at me. "Of course I'm sure. He hasn't been back since the night the senior auxiliary was here." She pursed her lips. "Like I already told you."

"And he hasn't made contact in any other way?"

Again she shook her head.

"Say it, Agnes," I insisted.

"No, he hasn't!" she said, the sudden increase in decibels making her mother jerk back in the armchair and look around vaguely.

"What is it?" Hilda asked. "Is that Allie?" Her grey hair was lank and tangled. The heavy nightdress she habitually wore was causing beads of sweat to form on her forehead.

Agnes went over to her and settled her down again. "Not yet.

He'll be back soon." She glared at me as she came back to the sofa. "She keeps asking for my father and for Allie." She let out a sob. "It's driving me crazy."

Katharine took her hand and gave me a fierce look. "Leave her alone, Quint," she hissed.

I nodded. I reckoned Agnes was being straight with me. "I told you before, I can arrange for a nurse to help with your mother if it's getting too much for you."

She shook her head emphatically, the ponytail that she'd gathered her dark hair into swinging from side to side. "No, she doesn't like it when there are strangers around." She gave me a meaningful look.

"Okay," I said, accepting defeat. "We're going. Sorry about the—"

"Leave us alone, citizen," Agnes said, her eyes wide open and moist. "Please."

Katharine squeezed her hand and got up. "Move, Quint, you sensitive soul."

"The man will be here for the door in half an hour," Davie said in the corridor, loudly enough for Agnes to hear.

I headed out.

"Do you think they'll be all right?" Davie asked on the stair.

"I think so. Allie Kennedy's too smart to risk coming here." I looked round at him. "But we'll put the surveillance team on the back of the building again just to be sure."

"Haven't you got anything better for them to do?" Katharine demanded.

I shrugged. If she didn't like what I was doing now, she'd hate what I was planning for later.

It was almost time for the emergency Council meeting. We dropped Katharine off at my place. It wasn't worth going into battle with the guardians over allowing her to attend and, besides, I didn't particularly want her to hear what I was going to propose.

Sophia walked up to the senior guardian's throne and the whispering that had been going on among her colleagues stopped immediately. They looked as nervous as a group of auxiliary trainees before their first delousing.

"This emergency meeting is in session." Sophia's voice had a hoarseness to it that I used to find alluring. Now it made me realise how much pressure she was under. I wondered if she would have been coping any better if Katharine hadn't appeared on the scene.

"The public order guardian has informed you of the message received from the poisoners," she continued, running her eyes round her colleagues. "It is essential that we do not allow ourselves to be diverted by threats. Do you agree?"

There was only muted support from most of the guardians. The tourism chief made his approval clear but he would – he had a lot to lose if services to the city's visitors were affected.

"Very well," Sophia said. "All directorates will take measures to function as normal and extra events will go ahead as planned. Reports, please." She turned to Hamilton, who gave a detailed list of the City Guard's updated deployment. Then she called on the culture guardian.

"Tomorrow's inauguration of the Edlott tourist facility is fully prepared," he said, rising to his feet. "Extra guard personnel in plain clothes have been drafted in, as my colleague noted, and all stocks of food and drink will have been vetted by midnight." The guardian was trying to sound confident but he wouldn't have won any prizes for amateur dramatics. His face was pasty and his hands seemed to have acquired their very own version of the shakes. "Senior guardian, are you still planning to make the draw?"

"Certainly," Sophia said. "I will be there at midday. Chief toxicologist?"

The pachydermic scientist got up and ran through a long list of checks on the whisky and the water that were now complete, and others that would be by tomorrow. He glanced at me as he drew to a close and raised his shoulders. His blank look suggested that the secret blues lover had been listening to Tommy McClennan's "Whiskey Head Man" more often than he should have recently.

"Can you guarantee that no tourist will consume a poisoned drink, Lister 25?" the tourism guardian demanded. He never showed much interest in anything outside his own directorate's remit.

The chemist's jowls flapped as he shook his head vigorously. "No such guarantee is possible, guardian." He glanced up at Sophia for support.

"Quite so," she said. Scientists sticking together is such an inspiring sight, especially when they've got about as much grip on things as a tourist in a city-centre gaming tent has on his wallet.

"I don't suppose there's any chance of postponing Edlott's greed initiative?" I asked in a quiet voice. I knew there wasn't but I wanted to soften them up.

They must have been practising the simultaneous heavy intake of breath.

"The initiative is worth a huge amount of foreign exchange to the city," the tourism guardian said firmly. "We've been planning it for months."

"And have you planned what you'll do if some poor sod clutches his throat and dies in agony in the middle of Princes Street?" I asked.

"That will do, citizen." Sophia's tone was dictatorial. "The decision to proceed is irrevocable." She gave me a hard stare. "Do you have any practical suggestions to minimise the risk?"

"I do." I smiled as I looked round the circle of apprehensive faces. "We need to find Alexander Kennedy, the prime suspect."

Silence. Stating the obvious often has that effect.

The culture guardian's hands were still shaking. "And how do you propose to catch that individual?"

I was tempted to tell him that his senior auxiliary Nasmyth 05 might be involved, but I wanted the fat man to be left alone in case Allie got in touch. Besides, I'd suddenly realised that all the Council members were staring at me expectantly. Now I knew how it feels to be the saviour – seriously shitty. I'm not cut out for it temperamentally. But I could still give them a push on the road to enlightenment.

"By using his mother and sister as bait," I said.

That got them going. The whispering started up again and I was treated to a series of filthy looks.

"How exactly would you use them?" Sophia asked.

"By putting them up on the platform with you and the rest of the VIPs and surrounding them with guards. I think Allie Kennedy will get the message."

"Which is?" the culture guardian asked.

"Which is – if anyone is poisoned, Agnes and Hilda will pay the price."

The whispering turned to scandalised babbling.

"You can't treat citizens like that!" shouted the welfare guardian. The bulky middle-aged woman had been behind many of the Council's more liberal projects. "We have a responsibility to protect them."

"I didn't say anything about actually harming the female citizens. But Allie Kennedy is probably the kind of screwed-up individual whose mind will work that way."

"Rubbish," the welfare guardian said dismissively. "How can you possibly know how his mind works? He may not even *be* the poisoner."

"He's the poisoner, all right," I said. "I'm sure of it."

"Are there no other ways of dealing with him?" Sophia asked. I suspected that she wasn't too concerned about using the women in the way I'd suggested, but she had to appear sympathetic to the less hardline guardians' views.

"Not that I can think of in the small amount of time we have," I said, flipping the pages of my notebook to give the impression I had dozens of other options that I'd weighed up carefully and rejected. "The all-barracks search for Allie Kennedy is still in force but he's managed to evade us so far. We have to assume that he'll carry on doing so. We're maintaining full surveillance on his home in case he shows up there."

"Also unlikely," Hamilton put in.

I shrugged. "All we can do is keep up the toxicological checks and hope some eagle-eyed guard spots the bugger." It was a mark of how worried the guardians were that none of them raised an eyebrow at my use of a proscribed word in the Council chamber. "And tomorrow we have to hope that the sight of his mother and sister puts him off whatever horrors he's got in store for your precious tourists."

There was silence again. It looked like I'd helped them to see the light. It's amazing how quickly the Council's moral precepts about citizen welfare are subordinated to the city's main source of income. Or rather, it's not amazing at all.

"One question, citizen," the tourism guardian said. "How do we know the poisoner's target will be the Edlott ceremony?"

I gave him a loose smile. "We don't."

The meeting ended shortly afterwards.

I went back to the castle with Hamilton to check his directorate's preparations.

"Are you sure you know what you're doing, Dalrymple?" he asked as he drove the Jeep to the far side of the esplanade. "It all seems a bit random."

"Look, Lewis, you know about needles and haystacks," I said, opening the door. "Trying to find a few drops of nicotine is God knows how many times worse, even in a city that rations water and booze. If the chief toxicologist doesn't turn anything up in the tourist whisky and water supplies by tomorrow morning, what else can we do? At least the sight of his mother and sister might make the lunatic think twice."

"What if he's already put the poison somewhere he can't get back to in time?"

I closed the door and looked at him over the bonnet. "Then we're fucked, Lewis. Or rather, the poor bastard who drinks the stuff is." I stamped off up the narrow causeway to the gatehouse.

Davie appeared in the public order guardian's quarters soon after. "Barracks" and chemists' reports," he said, laying a pile of folders on the conference table. "No sign of any contaminated liquid." He shook his head dispiritedly. "And no sign of the suspect."

I shuffled through the papers. The guard and toxicologist squads were spreading out in an expanding radius from the middle of the tourist zone but they'd never manage to check every bar, hotel, nightclub, whorehouse and snack trolley by the next day. I'd been trying to think of other locations that Allie Kennedy might target. The marijuana clubs were a possibility but all of them had already been scrutinised. It was equally possible that he'd aim at somewhere with a lower profile. In this tourist mecca there were hundreds of target zones.

"What about Nasmyth 05?" I asked.

"Still in the Culture Directorate," Davie replied. "No suspicious contacts or calls."

"Christ, he must be breaking all records for devotion to duty," I said. "Maybe that's what Edlott does to you."

Hamilton stirred behind his desk. "Shouldn't we bring him in and interrogate him again?"

I shook my head. "He's more use on the street. If he ever gets to it."

We sat and tossed more ideas round, put some of them into action and drove the command centre mad with orders and countermands. It was about as much fun as playing poker at a chimpanzees' tea party. I gave up at around nine o'clock and got Davie to run me back to my place.

"See you in the morning, guardsman," I said, yawning. "Six o'clock, okay?"

"Will you have finished with the Kirkwood woman by then?" he asked ironically.

"The Kirkwood woman? What kind of bollocks is that? You sound like the senior guardian."

He shook his head. "I hope you know what you're doing, Quint. Hell hath no fury like—"

"Oh for fuck's sake. Good night." I slammed the Land-Rover door behind me.

I climbed the stairs in the dim light, my interest in seeing Katharine not completely blown away by Davie's worrying mutation into Sophia. I opened my door and stood in the darkness for a few seconds. Then I turned on the light and took in the living room. No one there. I found that the bedroom was also unoccupied and felt my heart begin to pound in my chest. Where the hell had she got to? A vision of a short-haired guy with staring eyes flew up before me.

I pulled out the mobile I'd drawn earlier in the castle and got Davie to turn back. Maybe I wasn't the only smartarse who'd come up with the idea of using people as bait.

"What's going on?" Davie shouted as he skidded to a halt in Gilmore Place.

"Katharine's gone." I pulled open the passenger door and piled in. "Get moving."

"Where to?"

"The Kennedy place. I think Allie might have got her."

Davie turned the Land-Rover round, sticking his hand out of the side window to stop a tractor towing a water tank on the other side of the road. "Allie Kennedy?" he said dubiously. "Why would he have gone to your flat, Quint? Even if he did, he's hardly likely to have taken Katharine back to Millar Crescent."

"I haven't got any better ideas, pal." I grabbed the vehicle's phone, my gut writhing under a major acid attack. "Allie Kennedy might have been there since we last were."

I called the undercover team. "Shit. Something's not right in Morningside. The surveillance guys in front of the tenement aren't answering."

Davie had his foot to the floor as we ground up Bruntsfield Place past the citizen pitch-and-putt facility. "Have you tried the team at the rear?" he asked.

I punched the buttons. This time there was a response. "Unit 35."

"This is Dalrymple. What the fuck's happening up there?"

"What do you mean, citizen?" The voice was male, young and surprised. "We've seen no movement on this side of the target area for over an hour."

"When did you last talk to your mates at the front?"

"Em . . . about forty-five minutes ago."

"Jesus. All right, maintain your position. And don't take your eyes off those windows for a second. Out."

Davie leaned over and took the phone from me. He called ahead to Napier Barracks and got the barriers raised. We steamed through them like an All Black on the way to the try line in the days before sheep racing became the number-one sport in New Zealand. A couple of guard vehicles moved off and followed us down the hill to Morningside.

Davie heaved the wheel round. He entered Millar Crescent at speed and a crazy angle.

"Christ, where is everybody?" he gasped.

The place was completely deserted, the underpowered streetlights casting patches of yellow over the pitted asphalt. Normally during the Big Heat, evening is the best time of the day. People enjoy it like the Mediterraneans used to before the sea covered their coastal cities. The temperature drops to a more or less tolerable level and citizens congregate in the streets until curfew. I glanced at the water tank and felt a cold fist clench the base of my spine.

"Oh my God."

Davie finished standing on the brakes and followed the direction of my gaze. "You don't think the bastard's poisoned the whole street?"

"You do get that impression, don't you?"

A guard Land-Rover passed us and pulled up at the hole in the ground that was the surveillance team's cover. I watched as a bear-like guardsman went behind the maroon and white striped screen that had been erected. A couple of seconds later he reappeared, waving his arm frantically.

"What next?" I muttered, pushing the door open and running after Davie.

The undercover operatives had done a good job of establishing their credentials as road diggers. There was a large mound of shattered asphalt and earth in front of the screen. I noticed that there were a lot a recent footprints on it. There was also a partially deflated football at the kerb.

"They've taken a hell of a beating," Davie said, looking up at me from the trench in which two men lay motionless. They were covered in blood and dirt and, when I got nearer, I saw that they had been bound and gagged. Their mobiles had been stomped into small pieces.

"They're alive," Davie added, struggling to undo the lengths of cloth that had been tied round their mouths. Their heads lolled, making them look like throttled chickens.

"Leave them to the others," I said to Davie. "We've got to check out the Kennedy place." I turned to the guardsman. "Get a medical squad down here and tell the command centre what's happened."

He nodded and pulled out his phone.

As Davie and I walked towards number 14, I noticed citizens silhouetted against the windows all around. They were standing motionless, staring out at us.

"Panic partly over," I said. "It looks like people are alive and well."

"What do you think happened to the operatives?"

"Your colleagues will squeeze it out of the locals eventually. I would guess that our man got the yobs who were playing footie to beat the shit out of the auxiliaries. You know how popular snoops are with citizens."

I pushed open the street door and started to climb the stairs.

"Why would Allie Kennedy have done that?" Davie asked, his boots ringing on the worn stone.

"Let's leave the explanations for later," I said, struggling to keep my breathing under control. Where the hell was Katharine? Were we about to find her in the same condition as the guys in the trench or had she suffered something even worse? The Ultimate Usquebaugh bottle flashed up in front of me like an unholy grail in the gloomy stairwell.

We slowed as we approached the third floor. Davie moved ahead of me, his auxiliary knife drawn. Then he nodded to me to follow.

"The door's open an inch or two," he whispered as I got to the landing.

At least we didn't have to break it down again. The carpenter had replaced the shattered panels with unpainted slats. The combination of colours made the door look like it was the camouflaged entrance to a lair.

Davie looked at me and pulled out his truncheon. I gave him the nod and he made his move, using the City Guard's standard method – head down, weapons forward, bloodcurdling shout. It's always made me uncomfortable, despite the fact that I recommended it in the *Public Order in Practice* manual. I went after him, checking each room as we went. No sign of anybody or of any disruption. Then we got to the sitting room. It was pitch dark, the curtains fully drawn. I reached for the lightswitch then pressed it down.

And got a knife point against my jugular.

"Quint? You almost scared me to death."

"Katharine?" I heard my voice come out like a frightened child's. The pain in my neck disappeared but my heart was still halfway through a sprint. "What the fuck . . . ?" I leaned over and took a deep breath. As I straightened up, I saw Hilda Kennedy sitting in the armchair. She was staring at me like I was a ghost.

"Fool," Katharine said to Davie. "Why did you charge in like a jackass in a china shop?"

"Why were you sitting in the dark?" he countered angrily.

"Because I thought we were about to be assaulted by a psycho wearing heavy boots." She laughed humourlessly. "I wasn't far wrong, was I?"

I pushed them apart. "That'll do, children." I gave them a frosty glare that wasn't anything like as good as one of Sophia's. "What the hell are you doing here, Katharine? I've been shitting myself about you."

"What do you mean?" she asked. "I left a note under your door."

"What? I didn't see it."

"Sorry," she said with a shrug. "I did try. I sat around for hours. When you didn't come back, I thought I'd come and see if you were here. I used my 'ask no questions' to get a lift in a guard vehicle." She laughed softly. "The guardswoman was kind enough to replace the knife Dirty Harry took."

"So where's Agnes?" I asked.

"Search me. I got here about half an hour ago. The carpenter was just finishing and the mother was on her own. I've been trying to keep her happy."

Davie and I exchanged glances. "You didn't notice anything strange going on in the street?"

"Strange?" Katharine looked at me quizzically. "I suppose it was a bit quiet."

I told her what had happened to the surveillance team.

"That must have happened before I got here. I didn't see any movement from behind the screen."

"No, you wouldn't have." I walked round the room. It was the same as it had been when we were there earlier.

Hilda Kennedy watched me as I circled the furniture. Her eyes were restless and damp, her body loose. She was now wearing crumpled citizen-issue blouse and trousers that looked several sizes too big for her. When I stopped and returned her gaze, she suddenly smiled.

"Good lad, Allie. You came back to your mother."

I went over and sat down next to her. "I'm not Allie, Hilda," I said quietly. "Do you know where he is?"

"Good lad, Allie," she repeated, clutching my arm.

I pulled it away gently. "Where's Agnes, Hilda?"

She looked at me then smiled again. "Good lad, Allie," she said, this time more in hope than certainty. Her head dropped and she started to weep.

"Well done, Quint," Katharine said, giving me a fierce look as she came over to comfort the woman.

Davie and I went out into the corridor.

"What do you reckon, Quint?"

"Allie Kennedy's several steps ahead of us," I said, shaking my head. "I reckon he came back to get his sister out. And to demonstrate that he's got us wrapped round his little finger."

"He left his mother behind. We can still use her to distract him."

I nodded slowly. "We can. But remember what happened to his father. I don't think he's too bothered about his parents."

"You could be right. What do we do now?"

I went into Agnes's room and sat down on the bed. It had been made up neatly, the pastel-coloured covers carefully arranged. I ran my eye round the different fabrics she'd hung on the walls and at the scanty collection of Supply Directorate cosmetics that female citizens get on the chest of drawers. Agnes and Allie. Christ, had she been pulling the wool over my eyes from the beginning? She'd given the impression that she was a dutiful daughter and that she grieved for her father but maybe the person she was really closest to was her brother. What if she'd only been pretending that he hurt her? What if she was a lot smarter than I'd given her credit for? Maybe Allie hadn't come back for her; maybe she'd gone to meet him somewhere. I remembered how much she'd been in control of herself after her father's body was found. She managed to keep going to her job after that shock. Her job. Jesus. Her job was at a tourist hostel that was about to open its doors for business.

I leaped to my feet and ran into the sitting room. Katharine looked up in alarm from the sofa, where she had her arm round Hilda's shoulders. "Davie and I have got to go. Stay here with her. I'll send a nursing auxiliary."

Katharine stood up. "Where are you going?"

"I'll tell you later. Get yourself back to my place. And don't disappear again!"

She opened her mouth to speak but I turned away and sprinted down the corridor, Davie at my heels.

"What is it?" he shouted.

"I think I know where they are," I said over my shoulder. "But I don't know if we're going to get there in time."

It seemed to take an age to drive across the south side to the tourist hostel off Nicolson Street. We got stuck behind a sewage tank in the Grange's narrow backstreets and had to take a long way round. I called the Medical Directorate during that time and asked for an auxiliary to be sent down to Hilda. Davie was driving like a madman, the tight smile on his lips suggesting that he was having an unusually good time. I tried to find out from the Tourism Directorate if the hostel had been opened yet but the switchboard was permanently engaged. No doubt all personnel were concentrating on the Edlott inauguration.

"Call for backup," Davie said as we careered on to Newington Road.

I shook my head. "We can do that when we get there. I don't want your boss sending the whole of the guard down. If the hostel's in operation, there'll be plenty of tourists who can be turned into instant hostages."

"So how are we going to play it?" he asked, giving me the exasperated look I always get when I bend guard procedures.

"By ear, my friend. Like all the best bluesmen."

"Ha." He floored the accelerator and swerved past a delivery van.

As we went past, the shocked driver mouthed the words "Fucking guard arseholes".

"Okay, it's down the next street to the right. Pull up on the main road."

We jumped down, leaving the doors open. Nicolson Street was quiet, the citizen curfew only minutes away. Tourists in the central zone are allowed out all night these days. I just hoped that if the new hostel had any guests, they'd been packed off on a group outing to the Haggis Sucker Club or some such place. I held Davie back from the corner then I stuck my head round gingerly. I was confronted by a façade with very few windows lit up and the large banner advertising its imminent opening still draped above the door.

"We're in luck," I said, pulling my head back. "The hostel isn't open yet."

Davie took a look. "According to the sign, it's going to be opened tomorrow." He stared at me. "Bloody hell. It's a perfect target."

I nodded. "And I bet we find that the booze in the bar and the water supply have already been checked by the toxicologists."

"Christ, the bastards could kill dozens of people if they tamper with things now."

"Exactly." I started round the corner.

"What are you doing, Quint?" Davie caught up with me. "We can call for backup now. There's no danger of tourists being taken hostage."

I kept moving. "Call for it. I'm going in before brother and sister nicotine do a runner." I heard him start talking into his mobile.

A middle-aged guardswoman appeared at the top of the steps as I approached.

I flashed my authorisation at her. "Anyone inside?"

"No, citizen," she said. "The last cleaners left an hour ago."

"Have you checked all the doors?"

She nodded.

I stepped back and looked up at the building. The only lights were in the upper stairwell. I remembered speaking to Agnes there when she was dangling from the roof in her harness. There was a good chance she'd have worked out a way to get into the building, probably using the fire escape at the rear.

"When your lot come, send some of them round the back to cut off their escape route," I said when Davie caught up again. "Then bring the rest upstairs."

"Wait, you mad bastard," Davie called.

"Neither mad nor a bastard," I said with a nervous laugh. Then I took the guardswoman's key and let myself in.

I checked the ground floor quickly, turning on as few lights as I could. The bar looked pristine, the seals intact on the bottles of whisky to the rear. The place was as quiet as a mausoleum and I found myself being drawn upwards, peering at the cupola that Agnes had been painting. I started running up the stairs, feeling the muscles in my legs tighten.

I got there with the breath rasping in my throat. I tried to avoid looking down into the cavernous gloom in the depths of the stairwell and wondered where the hell the Kennedy offspring were. The hostel's water tanks would be between the ceiling and roof. Maybe they were crawling around up there pouring nicotine into the supply. I dismissed the idea. You'd need a lot of poison to have an effect in such a large volume of water and I was pretty sure Allie didn't have that much left.

I went from room to room, checking under the newly made-up beds and behind the cheap wooden clothes cabinets. No sign of anyone. The sound of guard vehicles drifted up from the street in the hot night air. Allie and his sister were going to have to make their move soon if they wanted to get away. I squatted down in the hallway near the cupola and slapped my hand on the floor. It was beginning to look like I'd been wrong about the hostel after all.

Then I was caught in a web that a black widow would have killed for. I jerked round and only succeeded in tying myself up more securely. My arms were pinned against my torso and my legs, still bent at the knee, were knotted tightly together. I felt a blow against my side and toppled over on to the pungent pile of the recently laid carpet.

"Citizen Dalrymple," my assailant said in a calm, deep voice. "You've got yourself in quite a bind."

"It's over, Agnes," I said, craning round to look up at her. "The place is surrounded. Where's your brother?"

She laughed. "Closer than you think." Then she bent over me and brought her face down to mine. I was surprised to find that her breath was rank. "Allie's going to get you."

She stood up and grabbed the straps of the painting harness she'd tied round my chest. Then she began to drag me bodily towards the railing around the stairwell. My stomach liquefied.

"No, Agnes, no!" I forced myself to stop squealing and tried to distract her by talking. "Your brother got you into this, didn't he? I can help you, Agnes."

She let out a hollow laugh, panting from the exertion of dragging me.

"The Council will be lenient if you help me catch Allie," I gasped, trying to wedge my feet against the skirting boards. My boots made a loud scraping noise as they ran along wood that Agnes had probably painted.

"You haven't got a clue, have you, citizen?" she said, smiling at me malevolently as she rammed me up against the railing.

I was vaguely aware of shouting from the ground floor and the thunder of auxiliary boots in the entrance hall. Then the noise faded altogether as my blood started rushing about my veins. Fuck, I'd been so blind. I'd been sold a gigantic dummy and bought it without a thought. Agnes was wearing the same clothes that she always wore — the work shirt and trousers dotted with paint, and the scarf. But I'd never seen her neck bare, never seen her in a skirt, never wondered about her unusually deep voice or the hair that she often touched like she was checking it was still in position. Jesus Christ, how cretinous can you get?

"Don't!" I screamed as I was manoeuvred up the railing, the heart designs on the steel supports gouging my face and scalp. "Please, Allie! Don't!"

There was a pause in the movements and then a dark laugh. "Too late," came a hoarse whisper. "It's all too late, citizen."

I wriggled frantically as I was moved on to the banister and managed to grab a stanchion with my left hand. I heard Davie shouting my name from lower down and felt a crushing blow on my fingers. But I didn't let go.

"Don't!" Davie's voice was near now. "Don't do it!"

Then the weight of the body that had been on top of mine was suddenly gone. There was silence for a few moments, followed by a sickening crack. Heavy hands took hold of me and swung me back over the railing. I didn't let go of the ironwork for a long time.

Davie cut the harness from my limbs and torso then helped me to stand up straight. I looked down into what was now a blaze of light in the stairwell and took a deep breath. The body of my assailant lay spread-eagled on the tiles of the entrance hall, the pool of blood around the shattered head glistening like an obscene halo.

"Jesus," Davie said, shaking his head. "She just jumped headfirst. No warning. I didn't have a chance to stop her."

"Him, not her," I said, kicking the remains of the harness away and thinking of Ray. There was some ironic justice in the way his killer had fallen to his death.

"What?" Davie was staring at me in amazement.

"That was Allie Kennedy," I said, walking to the stairs unsteadily.

"Disguised as his sister?" Davie said, his voice faint. "Never."

"A case of barracks malt on it, my friend."

He looked at me doubtfully then nodded. "You're on, Quint. That blow on the head you got this morning must have been worse than I thought. Are you seriously telling me that Allie dressed up as his sister and took the piss out of us for the whole investigation?" He shook his head emphatically. "No way. I know a woman when I see one."

"Not this time you didn't." I pushed through the crowd of auxiliaries on the ground floor. They'd gathered in a ring around the body.

"What's going on here, Dalrymple?" Hamilton demanded, breaking through from the other side.

"Wait and see," I said, kneeling down by the corpse's midriff. I took in the circle of faces then turned to what was on the ground. I was about to transgress scene-of-crime procedures but I didn't care. I rolled the limp body on to its back carefully, hearing gasps of astonishment from the guard personnel who'd dutifully read my manual. Then I heard them breathe in even more rapidly as I undid the trousers and pulled them down. Underneath were standard female citizen off-white knickers. Allie Kennedy had taken his cross-dressing seriously. I grasped them at the sides and jerked them down.

And got a surprise that knocked the confidence, stuffing, bravado and anything else you care to mention right out of me. There was no sign at all of male genitalia. No penis, no scrotum, no nothing. Just a V-shaped tangle of black pubic hair. I felt like a necrophiliac caught in the act.

The worst was yet to come.

"What do you think you're doing, citizen?" Sophia asked, her voice low but sharp as a dagger of ice. "Leave that woman alone and come to my vehicle. Immediately."

I followed her through the gap opened up by the appalled auxiliaries, my cheeks on fire. Lewis Hamilton's were pretty scarlet too.

Even Davie looked horrified. Despite the fact that he'd just won a bet with me for the first time in his life.

Chapter Twenty

I didn't have a good time in Sophia's Land-Rover but I eventually managed to explain what I'd been doing.

"Why did Agnes Kennedy kill herself?" Sophia asked.

"Christ knows," I replied. My hands were still shaking and the raw patches on my arms and scalp were stinging. "She saw she was cornered. I suppose she couldn't face a lifetime down the mines."

"It's a great pity we didn't have the chance to interrogate her," Sophia said, shaking her head in frustration. "Her brother is at large and we don't know what he's planning. I take it he's still the prime suspect?"

I nodded. "Oh yes. I'm not sure exactly how involved Agnes Kennedy was with the poisonings. She was at work here or with her mother in the flat for a lot of the investigation. She was obviously up to no good in the hostel tonight. Her brother's the guy we really want though."

Sophia put her hand on the door then stopped. "Quint," she said, turning towards me and moderating her chilly aloofness slightly. "We may as well face it. We're finished, aren't we?"

"Um . . ." I looked ahead and saw Hamilton standing on the steps with an impatient look on his face. "This isn't a good time to talk, Sophia."

"It's all right," she said, freezing up again. "It was a rhetorical question." She engaged the door handle and stepped down. She strode purposefully towards the public order guardian but I was pretty sure she was hurting inside. The question was, would she find some way to take it out on Katharine?

I got out and went over to them.

"The chief toxicologist is en route," Hamilton said. "Obviously his people are going to have to check every bottle in the place."

"Obviously," I said, trying and failing to catch Sophia's eye. She must have suspected that she and I were history ever since Katharine came back, but the way she was taking it made me feel uneasy.

"The tourism guardian's on his way," Lewis added, looking at us uncomfortably. Even he had spotted that something was going on. "He wants to know if he can go ahead with the opening of the hostel tomorrow."

"Fucking hell," I said, trying to shock Sophia into showing some emotion. "The building may contain the water of death and your colleague is dreaming of additional tourist income."

That didn't even raise a blink from Sophia. "It will clearly be impractical to proceed with the inauguration of this facility," she said in guardianspeak. "You are to maintain the search for citizen Alexander Kennedy. The Edlott inauguration will go ahead tomorrow."

"I would recommend postponing the latter until the former is successful," I said, dropping into her patois. "If Allie Kennedy finds out his sister's dead, who knows what might happen?"

"How do you imagine he will become party to that information?" Sophia asked.

That was enough linguistic torture. "Don't ask me," I said, giving the pair of them a sardonic stare. "Maybe he's got friends in the guard."

Hamilton's chest puffed out as he prepared to lay into me but Sophia saw what I was doing and put her hand on his arm.

"Meaning that you're guessing, citizen," she said.

"Correct," I muttered, heading towards Davie's vehicle.

"Citizen Dalrymple," she called imperiously. "I was informed that you requested a nursing auxiliary to attend the suspect's mother. Under the circumstances I felt it advisable that the woman should spend the night under guard in the infirmary. You still intend to make use of her tomorrow, I hope."

"I suppose so," I replied, without much enthusiasm.

"I have also been told that your friend Kirkwood insisted on accompanying the woman," Sophia said, her eyes flashing cold fire. "Kindly ensure that she leaves my directorate premises immediately."

I raised my eyes to the warm blackness of the Edinburgh night sky. It was clear that Allie Kennedy didn't have a monopoly on poison.

I found Katharine and Hilda in a secure room in the depths of the infirmary, a guardsman outside the door. I flashed my authorisation. Before he let me in, I got him to call the nursing supervisor.

"Hello, Quint," Katharine said in a low voice. She was sitting in a chair next to the bed. Hilda was lying on her side, fully dressed, her arms wrapped round her body. She looked shrunken and weak. When I approached them, Hilda began to whimper. She put out an unsteady hand and took hold of Katharine's arm.

"What's she saying?" I asked, unable to make out the older woman's babbled words.

"She keeps talking about Allie and Agnes," Katharine replied. "What good children they are and how they're going to look after her." She looked up at me helplessly. "She won't let me leave. They tried to throw me out when we arrived but she wouldn't let go of me."

There was a knock on the door.

"Hold on," I said. "I'll talk to the supervisor."

The balding man outside had a clipboard in his hand. He kept his eyes on it as he addressed me impatiently. "Citizen Hilda Kennedy. Refuses to be examined, no apparent signs of physical injury, mental condition unstable, presence· in infirmary authorised by medical guardian. What more do you need to know, Citizen Dalrymple?" He glanced up briefly then turned to go.

I grabbed the back of his green tunic collar. "Just a minute, pal." I heard the guardsman swallow a snigger. "You're supposed to co-operate, not read me a fucking lecture."

The auxiliary shook my hand off but the fight had already gone out of him. "I'm very busy, citizen," he mumbled. "How can I help you?"

"Thank you," I said, taking in his barracks number. "Simpson 177, why has Katharine Kirkwood been locked in with the patient?" I gave him a look which made it clear that bullshit was not a valid currency.

He went into reverse. "I . . . I had no choice. Citizen Kennedy became uncontrollable when we tried to remove the other woman. I wanted to avoid any unnecessary injury to either of them."

"All right." I wondered what Sophia would say if she found out that Katharine was still in the infirmary. "Have you thought about sedating Hilda Kennedy?"

"We can try," he said doubtfully.

"Do that." I didn't want Katharine stuck in the hospital overnight.

When a nursing auxiliary arrived with a plastic cup containing some pills, I followed her in. Hilda took one look at us and started screeching like a terrified monkey. Then she pulled Katharine in front of her with surprising strength.

"Forget it!" Katharine said after a short bout of high-volume wrestling. "I don't mind staying with her. She doesn't have to take those pills if she doesn't want to."

The nurse backed off. I let her go.

"Are you sure?" I asked, as Katharine detached Hilda's hands and gently helped her off the floor. The older woman collapsed on the bed, her energy reserves used up.

"It's only one night, Quint," she said, breathing heavily. "I'll be fine." She stroked Hilda's sweat-soaked brow. "Did you find the others?" she asked.

I bent over. "Agnes is dead," I whispered. "Allie's still on the loose. I'll be back first thing in the morning. Will you be okay?"

Katharine nodded and smiled playfully. "You can pay me back tomorrow."

"I'll look forward to that," I said, laughing. As I got to the door, I heard Hilda's voice.

"Allie? Agnes?" she called. "Allie? Agnes? Where are you? Come to your mother. Allie! Agnes!" Then she started to weep wretchedly.

The idea of using her as bait was giving me serious grief.

I spent the night in the castle keeping an eye on developments. Such as they were. The toxicologists found traces of nicotine in several miniatures of whisky in the mini-bars in five of the hostel's rooms. I reckoned that Agnes would have poisoned a lot more bottles if I hadn't got to her when I did. The scene-of-crime squad found a bottle two-thirds full of the Ultimate Usquebaugh in one of the top-floor store cupboards. When the tourism guardian was advised that poisoned whisky had been located, he immediately tried to go ahead with the opening of the hostel. But Hamilton wasn't taking any chances. I smiled when I heard him tell his colleague what he could do with that idea.

Davie came up from the command centre at four a.m. and gave us the news that Allie Kennedy was keeping up his impression of a Platonic ideal form – all-present, all-defining, but impossible to put your finger on.

"No sightings of anyone answering the suspect's description by any of the barracks patrols," he said, tossing the latest logs in front of me. "Of course, he could be dressed as a woman." He gave me a derisive grin. "Then we'd never spot him."

I raised the middle fingers of both hands at him.

Hamilton looked at us disapprovingly over a barrage of files.

"It'll all come down to good old-fashioned Public Order Directorate security arrangements," he said. "We'll nail the madman before he can do any more harm."

I nodded my head slowly. If he believed that, he believed that organised conflict between rival tribes of football fans had nothing to do with the break-up of the United Kingdom in the early years of the century.

At seven the next morning, I turned down the corridor in the infirmary that led to the room containing Hilda and Katharine. In the dim overhead light I made out the sentry by the door and got a shock that made my heart go into overdrive. His back was propped against the wall and his legs were spread across the floor. I started to run towards him.

"Guardsman!" I shouted.

Nothing.

"Guardsman!"

This time I got a response. His body jerked into life and he swung his head towards me. When I skidded to a stop, he was on his feet and fumbling with his beret.

"You arsehole," I said. "I thought you'd been got at."

"Sorry, citizen," he said, avoiding my eyes. "I've been doing double shifts."

"Okay," I said, getting my breathing under control. "Forget it. Let me in."

He fumbled with the key and opened up.

"What's going on, Quint?" Katharine said, her face showing alarm.

"Nothing. I panicked."

"Allie?" Hilda said, sitting up and smiling expectantly. "Is that you, Allie?" She looked to both sides of me.

Katharine and I exchanged glances then she spoke to Hilda in a low voice.

"Don't worry. They'll be back soon. It's time to get up now."

Hilda stared at Katharine like she'd never seen her before.

"Allie? Agnes?" she called plaintively. "Don't leave me all on my own."

Watching the woman's desperation made me feel worse. Overnight I'd changed my mind about using Hilda at the inauguration. She was so fragile and unbalanced. I remembered the closed curtains and Agnes saying that her mother didn't like the sun. Besides, the sight of Hilda under guard might make Allie Kennedy even more determined to strike. But Sophia wouldn't listen. She insisted on sticking to the plan when I called her from the castle. She even said she wanted Hilda at the Edlott facility at the bottom of the Mound for the whole morning. There was nothing I could do to talk her out of it. I wasn't looking forward to telling Katharine.

I tried to separate the women but Hilda started wailing. I had to shout into Katharine's ear and hope that Hilda wouldn't get even more agitated. Fortunately she calmed down quickly.

"You bastard," Katharine said when I finished, her eyes narrowing. "You're going to use this poor woman as bait? That's disgusting."

"I tried to talk the senior guardian out of it—"

"The senior guardian? You mean your tight-arsed friend Sophia. I might have known that bitch was behind this." She gave me another fierce glare. "But it was your idea, wasn't it?"

Hilda was sitting on the bed, her grey hair hanging loosely over her face.

I raised my shoulders weakly. "It's about the only chance we've got of stopping him in his tracks."

"Bullshit, Quint. The Council's got ten thousand auxiliaries to do its dirty work and you want to use a woman who's half-demented by what's happened to her family? You make me sick."

I felt pretty sick myself. "There's a guard vehicle waiting," I said, looking at my watch.

Katharine shook her head then helped Hilda off the bed.

"Allie?" she asked hopefully, her shoulders drooping and her legs in the crumpled citizen-issue trousers unsteady. "Agnes?"

I smiled helplessly at her and headed for the door. If the day continued the way it had started, I'd have to think about finding a new line of work.

Princes Street during the Big Heat. Flags hanging limply in the still air, tourists taking refuge from the sun under the maroon and white canopies of the street cafés, music from the bands in the gardens drifting over the masses. And today, hundreds of extra guard personnel in uniform around the Edlott installation on the steps of the former Royal Scottish Academy – not to mention hundreds more in plain clothes all over the place. By eleven o'clock the crowds had already started to gather at the booths and tents that the Culture Directorate had set up in the paved area to the east of the neoclassical temple. Huge banners draped above the Doric columns proclaimed the virtues of Edlott in various languages. The lottery was "Best for Value, Best for Prizes, Best for Excitement" – probably right if you were a cheapskate tourist who fancied a free blow job at one of the city's knocking shops. The pairs of sphinxes at the front and rear of the grandiose building gazed into the distance with fully justified superciliousness. And all the time the tourists were pouring drinks of all kinds from the kiosks down their throats, I could hardly bring myself to look.

A rostrum had been erected halfway down the east side of the mock temple, and Hilda was put in a seat at the front of it from the start. Some of the tourists gave her curious glances, wondering about the badly dressed woman with the restless eyes and unwashed hair who was sitting centre stage. Maybe they thought she was part of some expressionist cabaret that the culture supremos had laid on, unaware that Edinburgh's version of theatre is unencumbered by creativity of any kind. Then again, the squad of armed guardsmen around her probably suggested she was our equivalent of royalty, with that institution's traditionally dire taste in clothes. Katharine was at the back of the dais, leaning against a column. From time to time Hilda would look round and smile weakly when she saw that Katharine was still nearby. I reckoned it wouldn't be long before she started calling her Agnes.

I kept my distance, not fancying any more blasts of Katharine's righteous anger. The Public Order Directorate's mobile operations unit – a nice title for the clapped-out caravan that was almost as old as Lewis Hamilton – had been parked at the end of the row of Edlott ticket booths against the Princes Street Gardens railing. Davie, Hamilton and I tried to co-ordinate the guard activities but there were so many personnel in the area that we had to leave most of them to their own devices. Time went by incredibly slowly and I found myself sticking my head out every few minutes to check that Hilda and Katharine were still in position. We had auxiliaries with binoculars all round the area but none of them reported any suspicious sightings.

Finally, there was a buzz on one of the caravan's phones.

"Senior guardian's vehicle approaching," a red-haired guards-woman announced.

We piled out of the door and moved through the crowd towards the rostrum. Loud music that was supposed to combine local folk rhythms and stately magnificence blared from the speakers hanging under the streetlights as Sophia arrived in an open carriage. Fortunately the horses weren't startled by the noise or the crowds. She stepped down gracefully in front of the dais, wearing a white blouse and a long Enlightenment tartan skirt that must have been horrendously hot. The culture guardian came over to greet her. The seats on the platform were now full, Hilda still to the forefront and Katharine next to her. I spotted Nasmyth 05 to the rear, a notebook in his hand and a lot of sweat on his brow. I'd been keeping track of him. He hadn't been anywhere apart from the Culture Directorate until he arrived here. He seemed to be taking his department's big day very seriously. To his left was a group of citizens sporting fake smiles and historical costumes. They were former winners of the lottery. At least Fordyce Kennedy had managed to avoid this parade.

There was more strident music, then the culture guardian stepped up to the microphone at the front of the rostrum and started blathering on about the wonders of Edinburgh and, in particular, Edlott. Maybe he was working to a subtle plan, because the tourists soon stopped paying attention to him and got stuck into buying more lottery tickets. Eventually his voice rose to a crescendo as he introduced the senior guardian. There was a round of applause which started off feebly but was quickly boosted by the large number of auxiliaries present. They should have been concentrating on spotting Allie Kennedy – all of them had been issued with a copy of his file photo.

As Sophia rose from her seat, Nasmyth 05 appeared in front of the platform. He ushered on a group of porters pushing a clear plastic, heart-shaped contraption. It looked as if it had been ripped out of a replica dinosaur's chest and the maroon streamers trailing from it were like severed arteries. Trust the Culture Directorate to consign Edlott's balls to the emblem of the city. By this time I'd pushed my way to the front of the crowd. I caught Katharine's eye. She smiled humourlessly and gave a quick shake of her head. Being forced to listen to Council bullshit was probably the worst torture she could imagine. I wasn't exactly enjoying myself either. At least Hilda had perked up. She seemed to be trying to follow events, her face more animated.

"Dear and honoured visitors," Sophia said, her voice ringing across the crowd from the speakers. "The independent state of Edinburgh is proud to welcome you to this inaugural international draw of the city lottery. We, the representatives of the citizen body on the Council of City Guardians, hope you will agree that Edlott is the ultimate lottery. The ultimate thrill." She looked round the gathered multitude and graced them with a smile warmer than any I'd ever received. "Have you all bought your tickets?"

There was a hiatus as tour guides translated the senior guardian's words and hustled the few remaining customers to the booths. Sophia watched as the activity gradually subsided and the ticket sellers began to pull down the shutters. Nasmyth 05 nodded to her when all the booths were closed.

"And now it's time to roll the balls!" she cried with remarkable zeal. Guardians will do anything for tourist money.

The former winners at the edge of the podium pulled flags from their pockets and started waving them frantically. The only thing that suggested Sophia might be uncomfortable with her involvement in this idiocy was the involuntary step to the rear that she took when the first ball was ceremonially dropped into the heart-shaped container by the culture guardian. She stayed away from the microphone as the preparations for the draw continued, beads of sweat glistening on her forehead.

Then, as the last ball went in, it happened. There was a sudden movement to Sophia's left. Arms were wrapped round her neck and chest and she was forced to bend backwards, her legs unable to open much in the tartan skirt. The crowd gave a collective gasp, then everything went quiet and the balls in the drum rolled slowly to a standstill. Katharine was motionless, leaning forward in her seat with her mouth open. As I looked closer, I saw the small bottle that had been jammed between Sophia's lips.

"Dalrymple! Tell the guard to stand back!" Hilda's harsh voice was picked up by the microphone and projected over the silent mass of people like feedback from a seriously spaced-out guitarist. Her eyes focused on me. "You know what's in the flask, don't you?"

I nodded. "No one's going to make a move on you, Hilda." I could see Hamilton to my left. I signalled to him to call off his people. God knows where Davie had got to. The guards responded to his command and space began to clear around Hilda and Sophia.

I stepped towards the rostrum. "What do we do now?" I shouted.

"What we do, citizen, is go for a wee talk," Hilda said, her voice shrill. She dragged Sophia to the left, heading off the platform. In front of them I saw Nasmyth 05 trying to get out of the way, his face as pale as suet.

"Get the front door open," Hilda yelled.

"Keep the crowd back," I said to Hamilton. Auxiliaries started doing that. I saw guardsmen at the north end of the mock temple moving tourists away from what had been the main entrance to the building when it was a gallery. Hamilton took charge of the microphone. He was always at his best telling large numbers of people what to do. He asked for calm and a restrained clearance of the area, pausing to allow the guides to translate. I followed Hilda and Sophia round the front corner. They were on the steps under the columns, frightened tourists spilling away from them on to Princes Street.

"What the hell's going on?" Davie said from behind me.

"Where have you been?" I demanded.

"Sorry. Caught short." He stared ahead. "Is that Hilda Kennedy with the senior guardian?"

I nodded. "Ready to give her a lethal dose of the Ultimate Usquebaugh."

"Bloody hell. What now?"

"She wants to talk. Keep close."

I waved the guard personnel on the pavement back and went up the steps. The heavy door was standing ajar, a guardsman looking sheepish beside it.

"What happened?" I asked.

"She took my knife," he said. "Told me she'd kill the senior guardian if I—"

"All right," I said, biting my lip and turning to Davie. "Stay here. I'll keep in touch by mobile. And tell Hamilton to watch his step. If Hilda Kennedy wants to be escorted out of the city, we'd better comply. Otherwise we'll be a senior guardian short."

Hilda's voice came ringing from the marble halls. "Dalrymple! Get in here on your own or the bitch dies."

"Jesus," Davie gasped. "Do you want my knife, Quint?"

I shook my head. "That'll just make things worse."

"Worse?" Davie said as I went in. "How could they possibly get worse?"

Chapter Twenty-One

Hilda Kennedy wasn't taking any chances. She dragged Sophia well inside the disused building and found a spot in a long room that offered no cover to anyone trying to sneak up behind her. I walked in slowly, my footsteps ringing in the empty hall. It had been the Culture Directorate's headquarters until a few years ago but now it was empty. There had been plans to turn it into a disco but the acoustics were too bad, even for music as dire as that.

"Stop there!" Hilda shouted when I was ten yards from them. "Empty your pockets and lift up your shirt. Slowly!"

All I had on me was my mobile, my Council authorisation and my notebook.

"Right," Hilda said when she saw I was clean. "Use that phone to get Nasmyth 05 in here." She gave me a sharp smile. "And I want that Katharine woman as well."

I felt my stomach flip then saw the flash in Sophia's eyes. She was still bent over, Hilda's arm round her neck. The flask had gone now, replaced by the auxiliary knife. The point was against her side.

"In the meantime, let's get comfortable," Hilda said. "You, senior fuckhead, get your blouse off." She loosened her grip and allowed Sophia to stand up, keeping the knifepoint close to her midriff.

Sophia pursed her lips then did as she was told. When she'd removed her blouse, Hilda made her turn round and examined her bust under the good-quality bra.

"Great tits, don't you think, Citizen Dalrymple?" she said. "Stand still now. Both of you." She put the knife between her teeth and quickly tied Sophia's arms behind her back with the arms of the blouse. The knot was so tight that Sophia's shoulders were forced back, making her chest jut out.

"Aye, very nice," Hilda said, the knife back in her hand and peering at Sophia again.

I was finding it difficult to look my ex-lover in the eye, or anywhere else for that matter, so I concentrated on her assailant.

"What are we going to talk about then, Allie?"

There was a laugh then suddenly Sophia was shoved to the ground. "Stay there, bitch." Alexander Kennedy turned to me, a loose smile on his face, and pulled the grey wig off. His own hair was as closely cut as the witness in the Colonies and the nursing auxiliary who saw him had reported. "When did you work that out, smart fuck?"

"Too late," I said, shaking my head. "Far too late. I should have put it all together sooner but your sister distracted me." I decided to play tough with him. "She killed herself, you know, Allie. Took a three-storey dive in the hostel and smashed her head open."

His face clenched in a spasm then the sick smile came back. "You were careless. I heard you whisper that Agnes was dead last night. You sure you didn't push her, Citizen Dalrymple?" He squatted down beside Sophia and ran the knifepoint down from her neck to the space between her breasts.

It looked like I'd goaded him far enough. "She tried to throw me over first."

He laughed harshly.

"But the guard interrupted her."

He breathed in hard. "Agnes," he said in a low voice, then leered up at me. "Agnes? Allie?" he said in the voice he'd affected as Hilda. "Allie! Agnes!" He laughed again. "Christ, you're so fucking thick."

I kneeled down as well, trying to think of a way to stop him doing damage with the knife. "You didn't answer my question, Allie. What are we going to talk about?" I looked round, hearing the sound of footsteps at the other end of the hall.

"Let's wait till our friends arrive, shall we?" he said, putting the knife blade against Sophia's throat.

I watched as Katharine and the Edlott controller approached, both of them staring at the tableau we formed.

"Here you are, Nicky," Allie said to Nasmyth 05. "I was sure you'd want to see me one last time."

The fat man's lips quivered. He drew the back of his hand across his forehead, keeping his eyes off me.

"And here you are, Katharine," Allie went on. "I was sure you'd like to see how Hilda ended up."

"To hell with you," Katharine said, eyes hard as stone. "You don't scare me."

Allie laughed. "No, I don't scare you. But I've made you and your boyfriend here look like class-one morons." Sophia quivered as he spoke and looked down. He gave her a quick glance. "Oh, aye. Have you got something going with Citizen Dalrymple too, beautiful?" He smiled at me mockingly. "Oh dear, how complicated. Maybe I can simplify things." He moved the knife down to her chest again.

"Allie, don't," Nasmyth 05 gasped. "Please don't. I can help you get out of here."

"Shut up, Nicky," the killer said. He turned his gaze back to me. "Don't you want to know the details of how I took the piss out of you, Dalrymple? I'll bet you do."

So that was it. He wanted to show off. Fair enough. The longer I kept him here, the more likely I'd be able to work out how to nail the bastard. Not that I had much of a track record of accomplishing that so far in the case. But I wasn't going to let him have it all his own way.

"Maybe you can just fill in the gaps, Allie," I said, giving him my version of a psychotic smile. "Let's see. You used to spend your time terrorising the other peabrains on the south side and doing shitty little smuggling deals outside the city line."

He looked at me without blinking.

"Then you met this sleazeball." I grabbed the Edlott controller's arm. "As well as playing with your dick, he put you to work." I was flying on empty now but I wanted to find out how involved the fat man was.

"Very good," Allie drawled. "And what kind of work was that, citizen?"

He wasn't giving me any free gifts. I took a guess, not a particularly wild one given Allie Kennedy's background. "Grass trafficking?"

"And this week's winner of the lottery is Quintilian Dalrymple," Allie announced with an ironic laugh. "Lottery's right, isn't it?" he said, his face hardening. "You're guessing. If you'd worked that out before, Nicky would have had his balls removed."

I shrugged. "You gave us other things to think about, Allie." I turned to the Edlott controller. "You should have talked when you had the chance. Now you're mine."

The auxiliary kept his eyes off me, his hands twisting convulsively.

"Leave Nicky alone," Allie Kennedy warned. "This is my show."

I hardly heard what he said. Things had finally fallen into place. "That's what this is all about, isn't it? Illicit drugs." I smacked the palm of my hand against my forehead. "I might have fucking known." I saw the fat man glance up at Allie. "You were forcing the lottery-winners to move dope around the city, weren't you, Nasmyth 05? They can get about much more freely than everyone else. And Frankie Thomson was in charge. He wasn't an old waster, he was running the grass trade on the ground."

Allie's slack smile was back. "Very good, citizen," he said, nodding.

More pennies dropped. "The grass trafficking was organised in advance," I said, grabbing the auxiliary again. "Frankie Thomson, Napier 25 as he used to be, gave financial input when you were planning Edlott. You set up the lottery with a built-in drugs scam."

"We never thought . . ." Nasmyth 05 stammered, ". . . we never thought it would end in murder."

Allie Kennedy laughed. "That wasn't all you never thought."

"Frankie Thomson deliberately got himself demoted by manhandling that tourist woman," I said, trying not to lose my line of thought. "And you weeded the files to cover his tracks." I let go of the Edlott controller's arm and pushed him away.

"All done?" Allie asked snidely. "Now you can get back to me."

I nodded slowly. "Right. One day – or more likely night – you came across four smugglers at Redhall Mill. They had the bright idea of putting nicotine, which they'd probably got hold of in Glasgow, into Edinburgh people's whisky. They wanted a way into the drugs trade and they wanted to cause a bit of chaos for the Council first. They'd gone to the lengths of printing labels for the Ultimate Usquebaugh. And they had full packs of heavy-duty grass known as Ibrox Gold which was bound to go down well with punters here."

"The ultimate water of life and the ultimate grass," Allie said, giving a bitter laugh. "What more could an Edinburgh citizen want? You're doing all right so far, smart fuck. The four smugglers wanted a piece of the marijuana clubs."

"Uh-huh. So you volunteered to be their local agent." I stared at him accusingly. "And you picked the victims. Including your own father."

Allie Kennedy shrugged. "They didn't care who I took out. They just wanted to get the guardians shitting in their pants."

I nodded. "But you had other ideas, didn't you? You saw the chance to shaft Nasmyth 05 and set yourself up as a major player."

"What?" Nasmyth 05 sounded more shocked than Caesar

when Brutus spiked him. "It's not true, Allie. You didn't have anything to do with the poisonings."

"Why do you think I asked you to find out where this fuck's father lived?" the poisoner said.

Nasmyth 05 went into a state of collapse. He staggered back then sat down on the marble with a heavy slap. "No, no," he moaned. "Not you, Allie, not you."

Allie Kennedy gave an empty laugh. "Yes, me, Nicky. The smugglers were very happy to take my advice. And I wanted to get rid of Frankie so I could run his network."

I nodded. "The smugglers wanted someone with a marijuana club connection. And they wanted the body to be left by the Water of Leith to hint that the water supply could be got at whenever they wanted."

"You're not so thick after all, are you?" Allie said with a hollow laugh. "So tell me why I did for my old man."

I glanced at Sophia. She was lying with her eyes half-closed, her face turned away from her assailant. "Take the knife off her," I said. "None of us is going to jump you."

"Keep talking, Dalrymple," he said threateningly. "I'll do what I like with the knife."

"All right, all right." I stood up and tried to shake the pins and needles out of my legs. I could feel Katharine's eyes on me but I kept mine away from her. I didn't want Allie to get any ideas about trussing her up like Sophia. Then I suddenly thought of his mother. What the hell had he done with her? "Where's Hilda, Allie?"

"Don't fuck with me!" he screamed, standing up and kicking Sophia hard in the stomach. "Tell me why I killed my father."

I had to take a chance. It looked like he'd done for Hilda too, and Agnes must have known about it. "I don't know, Allie. Had he been refusing to handle dope?"

"Aye." Allie Kennedy's expression became even deadlier. "That wasn't all the sick bastard did though."

I remembered his father's file and the fact that the grown-up children were still living in the family flat. I'd put it down to them being unusually close but maybe their ties were a lot less healthy than that. There was no point in being reticent when Allie was holding a knife to Sophia. "Did your parents abuse you?"

There was a long silence. He stared at me, biting his lip, then finally looked across at Nasmyth 05. "Is he right, Nicky? You know, don't you? It never got into any of our files but I told you about it."

The Edlott controller's breathing was shallow. "Yes, Allie, yes. Your father and mother made you and Agnes do terrible things."

"Terrible things?" Allie laughed. "They weren't much different from what you do to me, Nicky."

Nasmyth 05's head had dropped. "Yes, but you're an adult, you were willing . . ."

"Was I?" Allie asked, an empty smile spreading across his face. "Was I really? You'll never know."

"How long have you been cross-dressing?" I asked.

"It seems like a lifetime," Allie said lightly. "It was a way of escaping when I was a kid. I never had much in the way of a beard and I experimented with make-up for years. Not that the crap from the Supply Directorate deserves to be called make-up. I got good stuff on the black market. Depilatories that don't burn your skin off, for a start."

There was a movement on the floor. "He tried to kill your father in the retirement home, Quint," Sophia said, turning her head to glare at me. "He killed your friend Ray. Why are you even talking to him?"

Allie kicked her viciously again then crouched down beside her. "Shut up, bitch, or you get to die sooner than I planned."

"Take him, Quint!" Sophia screamed. "Don't worry about me."

I leaned forward on to the balls of my feet but then I saw Allie's dead eyes. They locked on to mine, issuing a clear challenge. My breath rasped in my throat and I felt the heat in the airless hall smother me. I couldn't do it.

"Sit down, citizen," he said with a hoarse laugh. "Sit down, both of you. We're not finished yet. And you," he said, punching Sophia twice in the mouth, "shut your face." Blood flowered on her lips.

Katharine sank down but only after she'd given Allie the eye again. She wasn't being a great help.

"Go on then," the poisoner said, looking at me. "Tell me what else I did."

"The senior guardian's right," I said. "You had a go at killing my father to distract me from your trail."

He nodded, grinning like a child who'd won a game.

"And this fat shite found out for you which retirement home he was in," I continued, glancing at the auxiliary. I would be dealing with him later – if there *was* any later for him and me. "How did you get past the nursing auxiliary?"

He laughed. "Simple. I used to be a postman. I put on my uniform and slipped in after the main delivery. No one noticed me."

"You were wasting your time," I said. "My old man's okay."

"It kept you off my back for a bit," Allie said, raising his shoulders. "What do you care? Your father was luckier than the others."

Bastard. He didn't care how many people he killed. "So were you. You weren't inside the millhouse when the smugglers were taken out by a Fisheries Guard unit."

"Fuck knows what those animals were doing at the mill," Allie said, anger finally reappearing on his face.

I wasn't going to tell him about the books and antiquities at Craiglockhart if Nasmyth 05 hadn't. But I did want to know what had happened to Ray. "You managed to stash some bottles of the Ultimate Usquebaugh before the attack. But you were spotted by one of the attackers—"

"That fucker with the one arm," Allie interrupted. "He wasn't so lucky. Agnes saw him in Buccleuch Place when she was on her way to work so I went to check if it was the same guy. When I

realised it was, I sorted him out. I needed another victim to keep
you wankers on your toes and killing him did that. As well as
making sure he couldn't identify me. Fuck knows why the tosser
jumped out the window. He gulped the whisky like he had a
death wish."

I heard the words ring in my head. Maybe Ray did want to
end it all. He'd been traumatised since he saw Dirty Harry's men
in action at the mill. But I still doubted he would have killed
himself if Allie Kennedy hadn't forced the Ultimate Usquebaugh
on him. I bit my tongue to stop myself asking Allie if he knew
why his sister had jumped. The little turd would probably
butcher Sophia.

"Go on, citizen," Allie said insistently.

I nodded slowly. "All right. After the smugglers were hit, you
decided to deliver the threat they'd planned for the Council."

"Why not?" he said. "Anything to fuck this place up. Besides,"
he added, laughing lightly, "I reckoned a bit of civil disorder
would be good for business."

I glanced at Katharine. She was staring at Allie relentlessly, her
body tense. Shit. I'd seen her concentrating like that before. It
meant that someone was about to receive the benefit of the
unarmed combat training she did as an auxiliary. Except that
getting to him from a seated position would be hopeless, even for
her.

"So that's it then," I said, feeling the sweat trickle down my
sides. "The life and times of Allie Kennedy. What now?"

"The life and times of Allie Kennedy," he repeated. His voice
was suddenly less intense and his body sagged, the knife loose
against Sophia's chest. It was almost as if he'd lost interest now
that his exploits had been recounted in public. Then he shook
himself hard and came back to life. He looked round at us and
clocked Katharine's intent expression.

"What now?" he asked, fumbling in his trouser pocket. "Time
for the end game." The small bottle was in his hand. He
unscrewed the cap and sniffed the dark brown liquid inside.

"Pure and deadly." He gave a high-pitched laugh. "Just like me."

Then he leaned towards Sophia and crushed the bottle's business end against her broken lips. "If you're interested," he said, "what's left of my mother is in a burned-out house in Greenbank." His body tensed as he prepared to force Sophia's head back. "This is for Agnes."

I looked at Katharine and opened my eyes wide.

Then we scrambled to our feet and leaped forward.

Chapter Twenty-Two

Sophia had managed to turn on to her front by the time we got to them but Allie grabbed her hair and twisted her head back round. A strangled gagging came from her mouth, dark liquid coursing over the uncongealed blood on her lips.

Then Katharine took Allie Kennedy out with a well-directed kick to the left shoulder. He spun back against the wall, the bottle still upright in his hand. I got hold of Sophia under the arms and dragged her backwards, booting the auxiliary knife away as I went.

"Move your arse!" I yelled at Nasmyth 05. "Get help."

He looked at me blankly for a moment then stumbled down the hall towards the main door.

"Quint," Katharine said, her voice sharp. "Look."

I raised my eyes from Sophia, who was on her side spitting for all she was worth. I was struggling to undo the knot in the arms of her blouse.

Allie Kennedy was sitting against the wall, tears running down his face. "Agnes," he moaned. "Agnes."

"Don't!" I shouted. "It's not worth it!"

He nodded his head weakly at me in contradiction then put the flask to his lips and gulped down the contents. The ultimate measure of the water of death. For a few seconds nothing happened. Then a great tremor racked his body and his head jerked forward. Frothy vomit gushed over his thighs and his head shot back, thudding hard against the wall. His torso slid slowly down to the floor and he lay still.

Davie came storming in not long afterwards, leading a squad of guards. They stood around in bewilderment as I helped Sophia to her feet and draped her torn blouse round her shoulders.

"You didn't swallow any, did you?" I asked, grabbing a guardswoman's waterbottle and handing it to her.

She shook her head as she rinsed her mouth out. "My mouth's burning but the infirmary should be able to handle it." She allowed herself to be moved towards the exit by a medical auxiliary then stopped and looked round. "Is he dead?"

I nodded.

"I have to thank you then, Quint," she said.

"Not me. Katharine got to him first."

Sophia looked behind me and nodded her head slowly. "Thank you, Katharine Kirkwood," she said. There might have been a smile on her battered lips.

Davie watched her go. "What happened?"

"Quite," said Hamilton, stepping forward. "Was that female citizen really a male?"

"She was," I said.

"Does that mean I'm not going to get my whisky after all?" Davie demanded.

I laughed. "No, my friend. I'll honour the bet."

The public order guardian stared at us.

"Did he swallow the poisoned whisky?" Davie asked.

"Yeah," I said. "He killed himself rather than end up in our hands."

"Like his sister."

"Like his sister." I was about as far from understanding how their minds worked as it was possible to be. I went over to Katharine. She'd moved away from Allie Kennedy's body and was propped against the wall, her head bowed. "Nice one," I said. "I can't say I thought you had it in you to save Sophia."

She looked up at me, running her hands through her hair. "Me neither. In the end I just forgot who she was. I didn't want that little shit to kill anyone else."

"Come on," I said, taking her arm. "I could do with some fresh air."

"Where are we going to find that in Edinburgh?"

She had a point. Outside it was sweatier than ever, the air thicker than a barracks canteen treacle pudding. We sat on the steps of the mock temple and gazed out over the empty space in front of the rostrum. The tourists had all been shepherded away and the heart-shaped drum stood deserted, the streamers lank and the lottery balls in a heap at the pointed bottom.

"So much for greed," I said as Hamilton and Davie joined us.

"Don't worry," Lewis said scathingly. "The culture guardian is no doubt already planning a relaunch for next week."

I nodded. Nothing would get in the way of the Council's drive for tourist income.

There was a dull rumbling in the distance behind Arthur's Seat.

"What was that?" the guardian asked, his face registering alarm.

"Dissident attack," I said. "Allie Kennedy told us it was planned."

They bought it for a couple of seconds then Davie's boot made contact with my backside.

"Very funny, Quint. The case is finished." He looked at me uncertainly. "Isn't it?"

Suddenly a blast of surprisingly cool wind hit us and the sun was obscured by quick-moving dark clouds.

"The case is finished all right, my friend," I said, standing up and walking out into the open. "And here comes the real water of life."

There was a long-drawn-out roll of thunder which climaxed in an ear-shattering boom. Lightning flashes strafed the city and blinded us momentarily. Katharine came out into the empty square to join me. We stood with our arms extended as the rain splashed across us in a great wave.

After the Big Heat, the deluge.

Over the next few days things calmed down in the city. The rain washed out the last of the high temperatures and Edinburgh became a sweet-smelling oasis. The city's reserves of water shot up and citizens were given permission for an additional two showers a week, which made them ridiculously happy. I took the time to listen to some blues – Muddy Waters seemed appropriate. I also drank a lot of poison-free whisky and caught up on the sleep I'd missed during the investigation. Well, not that much sleep. Katharine was staying at my place and we discovered that our bodies were the repositories of half-forgotten, seriously arousing secrets. There was no mention of Peter Bryson, her former friend turned dope trafficker and poisoner.

Eventually Davie got so pissed off by my repeated refusals to take the chair from behind my door that he tied a rope to the roof and abseiled down to the bedroom window. Apparently the Council were tired of waiting for me to give my final report.

So I went to the chamber and told them everything I knew. I couldn't understand why they needed to get it from me since Sophia had heard everything Allie Kennedy and I had said. She herself was playing the Ice Queen in hearts as well as spades, refusing to look even in my general direction. After I'd finished, she announced that the female dissident who was in a coma had died. The Water of Death Case was definitely closed.

I headed off rapidly when the meeting ended – I had unfinished business with Katharine at the flat.

Davie revved up the Land-Rover when I got in and backed out of the Council yard. "Get on all right?"

"Waste of time, pal," I said.

"Aye, you've got much better things to do with your time now that Katharine Kirkwood's an Edinburgh resident again."

"I'm just following my old man's advice. Remember the Latin poem he was translating? Tomorrow's too late to have a good time so I'm getting on with it now. You know Katharine's record. She's a serial vanisher. One morning I'll wake up and she'll be gone."

"Aw, come off it, you jackass. Anyone can see she's smitten with you." Davie laughed as he pulled away up the Royal Mile. "You're not exactly indifferent yourself."

"Thanks for your interest, guardsman," I said loftily. "This is a private relationship, not a production of *Romeo and Juliet*."

"Or *The Taming of the Shrew*."

"Very funny." I looked at his bearded face more seriously. "No word from the search squads on the south side?"

He shook his head. "Do you think Allie Kennedy was telling the truth about his mother's body being out there?"

"God knows. Probably. The bastard was very proud of all the mayhem he caused." I ran my fingers through my hair. It was longer than usual because Katharine had refused to let me have it trimmed. She told me I looked like an escaped convict. "My guess is that Allie experimented on Hilda to find out how much poisoned whisky was necessary to kill his victims."

"Jesus. Do you think he and his sister really were abused by their parents?"

I nodded. "Probably. There had to be some personal motivation for what happened with their father."

"Not just anti-Enlightenment angst?"

"You've been reading too many existentialist novels, guardsman."

"That'll be right." Suddenly he glanced over his shoulder. "What the . . ."

We jerked to a halt underneath the gallows at the Lawnmarket. I straightened up, rubbing my neck gingerly. A Land-Rover in much better nick than Davie's had forced us to the kerb. Sophia was at the wheel. She turned round, raised her forefinger and beckoned me towards her.

"Oh-oh," I said. "If I'm not home by midnight, put out an all-barracks search."

"No chance, Quint," Davie said, his face split by a grin. "This is one case you'll have to solve on your own."

Sophia kept her eyes off me as I climbed in then drove away, turning on to Johnston Terrace.

"What's going on?" I asked when she didn't speak.

"Nothing is going on, citizen," she said. Her lips were still swollen from Allie Kennedy's blows and from the whisky flask he'd rammed against them. "I'm taking you back to your flat."

"Any chance of you calling me Quint, Sophia?"

She glanced at me coolly. "None whatsoever, citizen."

I shook my head. So that was how she wanted to play it. I kept quiet as we headed down the rain-soaked asphalt, the castle rock looming up to our right. The scent of recently drenched vegetation came in through the open windows.

"Oh, very well," Sophia said in irritation. "I wanted . . . I wanted to thank you, Quint."

"For what? I told you it was Katharine—"

"For the successful conclusion to the investigation." She shot me a fierce look. "I've already thanked the Kirkwood . . . I mean Katharine Kirkwood for saving my life."

I shrugged my shoulders. "It was a seriously complicated case, Sophia. If I hadn't been so blind about Hilda, I could have saved you the hassle at the Edlott ceremony."

"You did more than could be expected." Then she glanced at me angrily. "Although, as usual, you treated the City Regulations with complete disregard. You were lucky the Council overlooked the fact that you allowed the Fisheries Guard personnel to desert."

"Do I have you to thank for that?"

"On the other hand," she said, ignoring my sarcasm, "you have enabled the Council to maintain a reasonable level of tourist income despite last week's fiasco."

"No doubt you'll make it all up this Saturday." I looked at

her. "I don't care about the tourist income, Sophia. Even though I hate Edlott and its culture of greed almost as much as I hate auxiliaries who put the boot into citizens for no reason. I suppose people do need something to dream about. What I care about is that citizens' lives aren't made any more difficult than they have to be. That means keeping the user-friendly policies that the current Council's instituted." I held my eyes on her as she accelerated past the Culture Directorate and its banners advertising the rescheduled inaugural ceremony. "Maybe if the welfare services had been better in the past, Allie and Agnes Kennedy wouldn't have ended up the way they did."

Sophia nodded. "I know what you're saying, Quint. I may not have been the greatest supporter of recent Council measures but I accept that citizens deserve more freedom than they had in the past." She looked at me and gave a brief smile. "Don't worry. We won't be going back to the bad old days." She frowned. "Although I still believe that liberalisation has been the cause of too many problems."

Trust Sophia not to give in without a fight. But I reckoned she was being straight with me so I returned her smile – and felt a stab of guilt that I ever suspected her of being involved in the killings.

As we went through Tollcross, Sophia turned to me again. "You may be interested to know that Nasmyth 05 has been demoted. He's in the rehabilitation centre at Duddingston."

I'd got over my urge to crucify the fat auxiliary for passing my father's address to Allie Kennedy. Sophia's words made me think of another resident of the rehab facility. "Don't you think it's time the Council used Billy Geddes's talents officially again? He could make the city a lot of money. As long as he's properly supervised, of course."

"I'll put it to the Council. We need all the help we can get."

I laughed. "Well said." To my surprise, Sophia laughed as well. We stopped outside my place.

"Go on then," Sophia said haltingly. "She's waiting for you, isn't she?"

I watched her face, which was half turned away from me. Her swollen lips gave her an uncharacteristically fragile look though her eyes were as unwavering as ever. "Are you okay about this, Sophia?" I asked in a low voice.

She sat motionless for a few seconds. Then she looked at me and smiled more warmly. "I'll survive, Quint. I know she has a prior claim." She faced the front again. "To be honest with you, the original Council's celibacy rules suit me better."

I didn't think she was being honest with me but I wasn't going to argue. I leaned towards her and kissed her on the cheek. "See you at the next murder."

"An appropriately unromantic way to say farewell," she said drily. "Now go. Before I change my mind and have Katharine Kirkwood expelled."

I didn't hang around to see if she was joking.

I raced up the stairs and put my key in the lock. "I'm home," I called, only realising after the words had escaped how odd they sounded. I hadn't used them since Caro died ten years ago.

No reply.

"Katharine?" I said, walking into the living room. "Katharine?" My stomach suddenly felt hollow. I ran to the bedroom. No sign of her there either. "Katharine?" I went to the sofa and sat down, my legs weak. Surely not. Surely she hadn't left the city again? There had been no sign that she was unhappy. Christ, she was the one who'd poleaxed me by suggesting we get back together.

I stood up and went over to the door. The carpet was unattached there and a couple of days earlier we'd found the note she'd left me when she went to the Kennedy flat – it was caught on the floorboards underneath. I stuck my fingers in and filled the ends of them with splinters. Nothing.

"Shit!" I shouted. I started sucking my nails. Then I remembered her backpack. If that was here, she would definitely be back. I ran to the bedroom again. It wasn't there.

"Shit!" This time my shout was so loud that my neighbour to the rear started pounding on the thin wall.

I stood in the middle of the room shaking my head. Then I realised there was only one thing to do. I went over to my cassette player and put on John Lee Hooker. The old genius was in the middle of "One Bourbon, One Scotch, One Beer". That was a hell of a good idea. I hadn't seen bourbon since I was eighteen but I had some barracks heavy that Davie'd given me, and a bottle of decent malt – no words beginning with "u" on its label. So I cranked up the decibels to drown out the neighbour's complaints and drank. It didn't make me feel much better.

The hand on my shoulder made me jump though. By the time I looked round Katharine had moved over to the cassette player and cut the volume.

"What are you doing?" she asked, looking at the booze.

"Where have you been?" I yelled, taking in the backpack on her shoulder.

"Shopping. There was a delivery of vegetables at the store," she said, screwing up her eyes. "What's the matter?"

"Jesus, Katharine. I thought you'd buggered off, that's the matter." I emptied my glass of whisky and washed it down with beer.

Katharine came over to me and took the bottle gently from my hand. "Quint," she said, a smile breaking across her tanned face. "That's very sweet." She kissed me on the lips then put her arms round me. "I didn't know you cared."

"Didn't you?" I said, nestling against her and breathing in the smell of newly washed hair. "Neither did I."